MY LITTLE ARMALITE

James Hawes is the author of five novels, including *A White Merc With Fins* and *Speak for England*. He is Senior Lecturer in Creative Writing at Oxford Brookes University and lives in Cardiff.

JAMES HAWES

My Little Armalite

VINTAGE BOOKS
London

Published by Vintage 2009

2 4 6 8 10 9 7 5 3 1

First published in Great Britain in 2008 by
Jonathan Cape

Vintage
Random House, 20 Vauxhall Bridge Road,
London SW1V 2SA

www.vintage-books.co.uk

Addresses for companies within The Random House Group Limited
can be found at: www.randomhouse.co.uk/offices.htm

The Random House Group Limited Reg. No. 954009

A CIP catalogue record for this book
is available from the British Library

ISBN 9780099513254

The Random House Group Limited supports The Forest
Stewardship Council (FSC), the leading international forest
certification organisation. All our titles that are printed on
Greenpeace approved FSC certified paper carry the FSC logo.
Our paper procurement policy can be found at:
www.rbooks.co.uk/environment

Printed and bound in Great Britain by
CPI Bookmarque, Croydon CR0 4TD

To Nerys Lloyd and our three sons

Prologue: The Primal Scream

Darling, it's three a.m. and I'm sitting here in my clever little study area under our stairs, just where I should be. But I'm afraid I'm not working on the Very Important Paper. Instead, I'm recording this prologue, headset in place and hands free for . . . well, listen.

Do you know that sound? Of course not. Let's hope you never will. But millions of living men know it just as our ancestors knew the knap of flint on flint, the screech of blade on whetstone, the drone of bombers overhead. The soft click of shells being thumbed home against the surprisingly gentle spring of a . . .

That noise again outside! Now, *that* one you know all too well. A carful of hooded little sods snarling and rapping past, rattling our Victorian sashes. At three a.m.! So much for *on the borders of the conservation area*. Yes, OK, cities have alway been noisy, but the Pooters only had trains to ignore, not deliberately unsilenced primate bloody braying. Even uPVC units would only dull it, but uPVC is obviously out of the question and we simply *can't afford* quality double-glazed hardwood sashes right now. Even if we wanted to invest even more in a depreciating bloody asset. So we say (especially to ourselves) that you get used to the noise, that we hardly notice it, that it's just part of life in this vibrant, diverse . . .

Fuck, ow! Sorry, darling, shit, *that* noise was me banging my head on the underneath of the staircase. Again! I know, I know there was nowhere else for my desk to go, even with no piano for you. I'm not saying there *was*, it's just that . . . *hardly notice*? It's three bloody a.m.! We've got a baby scarcely sleeping through, kids to get to school, careers to service. *Hardly notice?* Christ, when *we* were twenty (which isn't *that* long ago!) you had to shove a half-warmed kleftikon around a dirty plate if you wanted a drink after eleven. At midnight, London (where ordinary people could afford to buy in Zone 2) was settling to sleep. By four in the morning (which we hardly ever saw, even at twenty) the streets were patrolled only by defenceless milk bottles. And now? Now midnight is just the start for the uppers-raddled shits whose little brothers and half-brothers and step-brothers will make our darlings' schooldays hell if I don't do something fast. What was so bloody bad about grammar schools anyway? Oh, if those little *fuckers* . . . Sorry, darling, but, well, if they knew that I could walk out now and just put a whole clip right through their tinted bloody windows and into their stinking . . .

. . . sorry. Not very liberal. I admit that it's hard to restrain myself from employing my new skills. When you know that you *can* do something, morality easily follows suit. But my sights are set higher than tactical victories, however tasty. A prophet armed at last, I'm aiming for the only thing any of us can do, nowadays: I'm going to make *bloody* sure that our own darlings are ahead of the pack when the ice caps finally melt, the floodgates burst and the border guards tear off their uniforms, throw down their guns and run.

Of course, there's a chance it'll blow up in my face.

Not literally, I mean. But figuratively it's possible. My cover story of Muslim extremists is good and timely. In the present funding-friendly climate it's hard to see why any thinking copper would *want* to challenge it. But I still might get caught.

In which case you'll need financial support. Which is why I've recorded my story for you to sell. I don't believe my fate will be without some resonance. The world must be full of ex-lefties riddled with despair, bafflement and shame. If it isn't, it's full of cretins. This might tide you over until my pension kicks in. As far as I know they can't strip me of my superannuation rights for having stepped a wee bit beyond the liberal consensus! Knowing that you're financially catered for, I'll sit happily in my prison cell, vastly respected by my stupid and violent companions due to the *nature of my offences*, as smooth and smug as those men in every life-insurance junk-mail flyer: men who have *provided for their loved ones adequately* and *protected their mortgage*.

Christ, that bloody word again, that primal scream of our times!

What? Did we ask for the earth? For gravel drives, lofty gables, double fronts and all-round gardens? No. All we wanted was the sort of everyday thing navvies chucked up by the tens of thousands all over north London between Dickens and Hitler to house medium-grade clerks. Just the usual modest period semi, for God's sake, with a pair of tallish bays and four half-decent bedrooms, set ten feet or so back from the pavement of an averagely quiet residential street within realistic toddler-wheeling distance of a fair-sized park with the standard ducks and suchlike in any, repeat *any*, repeat *any*, *old* part of Zones 2 or 3 that lies a safe-ish height above sea level and diesel fumes, with ordinary human neighbours who sleep at night and reasonable schools where our children will not go in fear because they speak normal bloody English.

Well?

Sorry?

Was that really so much to ask in return for twenty years' unbroken CV in a highly respectable graduate career?

Ah.

I see.

Of course. Silly me. I was forgetting we've committed a mortal sin that will blight the rest of our lives and our children's too: *we didn't buy a house in London last millennium*. End of family story. Social mobility crash-stops. History swallows us up.

Oh, but I think not.

Do you hear this noise, darling?

Listen.

Cthlick!

I'm pressing the last round down. My clip is full.

So be it. The world has chosen to renege on the clear agreement I made with it back in nineteen eighty-four. All I am doing is setting things right. There is a fine Anglo-Saxon tradition which holds that crime is in fact not crime, riot not truly riot and even revolution not really revolution at all when it aims merely to restore good old normality.

Result? Happiness.

If all goes well tomorrow, if my gun doesn't jam and shoots straight, if I don't lose my nerve at the vital moment (which would be quite understandable), none of the friends who will, in the fine years to come, gather from the neighbouring streets to eat no doubt organic meat and drink good red wine around our big old table in our high-ceilinged home whilst we discuss the burning cultural and political issues of the day, guided, as we have ever been, by the wise and liberal comments in *The Paper* that morning, will ever suspect me. We'll simply have become what we always were, round pegs in round holes, with no gap for darkness to shine through. Even you'll never know.

I'll have come back from my war and I'll never speak of it.

We'll have not truth, but love.

And I'll remain for ever the boldly liberal man whose story I've set down over the last few long, lonesome evenings but who now, as I sit here under our stairs at three a.m., trembling somewhat, it is true, at what I am to do tomorrow, as well I might, but firm in my intentions, my little Armalite and I all ready at last (*at last!*) for manly action, seems so very far away from me that I find I can scarcely recall his name . . .

PART ONE

Summons

1: What I Knew About Guns

I, John Goode, was a normal, liberal man who, apart from stoning policemen during the Miners' Strike (as I frequently admitted at dinner parties), had honestly never even fantasised (as far as I could remember) about seeing anyone getting physically hurt (apart from Maggie and George W. Bush, obviously).

I'm sure I would have stayed that nice man my whole life long, but one November evening, while I was out planting some young plum trees in our small London garden, I found a machine gun buried under our little patch of lawn.

Actually it's an *assault rifle*.

But how was I to know the difference (if any)? What did I know about machine guns? Nothing. I wasn't American, so I'd never met otherwise-sane folk whose domestic equipment included machine guns. I wasn't European, west, east, north, south or middle, so I'd never been made to spend time in a barracks, learning about machine guns. And I wasn't from the Rest of the World (pretty well all of it, except for the bits that still have Elizabeth on their coins), so I hadn't been used from birth to seeing snappily dressed paramilitary policemen swanking around the place, slinging machine guns.

No, I was English, and though my militarily useful years (now gone) had coincided almost entirely with an era (now past) when her central foreign policy was readiness for a war (now unthinkable) in which national annihilation was the probable outcome, England had never remotely expected me to go soldiering. So like most normal Englishmen, I had never felt the slightest need to concern myself with developments in personal weaponry.

It's true that some three months before, while sitting in a taxi from Paddington to WC1, feeling important (because I hadn't been in a black cab for years, let alone when someone else was paying) and excited (because I knew I had a real chance of getting this job, which meant London was beckoning me home at last) and scared (because I might yet blow the interview, thus probably dooming myself and my beloved family to northern cities for ever), I had seen quite a few guns.

Amazed and affronted, I had seen English bobbies swanning toughly about with small machine guns and stylish earpieces as they patrolled the concrete-block ramparts of the American Embassy. The mere fact of cradling guns seemed to make them swagger heavily from overfed hips, in a deeply un-English fashion. Next thing, they would be wearing reflective bloody shades. Oh, some of them already were.

I laughed with outrage at this charade and asked my cab driver (until then we'd been happily chatting about the weather, as required by local custom) what the hell good were machine guns against suicide bombers, eh?

What, for God's sake (I demanded roundly), did the famously incompetent, historically corrupt and structurally racist Metropolitan Police intend precisely to do if somebody suddenly tugged sweatily at a suspicious belt amid those innocent visa-queues of people? Just open up, with no doubt inaccurate little machine guns, from every angle? In the middle of London? Ridiculous. Even if it really was a terrorist for once and not just some poor bloody Brazilian plumber with skin a shade too dark for his own good, adjusting his trousers at the wrong time and place! They would probably kill more people that way than would ever be hurt by a small bomb going off in an open space. You didn't have to know a thing about guns (and thank God we don't have to, here!) to see that the whole, well, yes, *charade* was complete nonsense. Just the government trying to make us feel under permanent threat, obviously. And how did we get into this mess in the first place, with terrorists in London? By kowtowing to the bloody Yanks and their insane neo-imperialist war of choice!

My arguments were so clearly sound that the cab driver contented himself with chewing his gum and looking in his rear-view mirror.

No, I knew nothing about guns and had no desire to know more. Naturally, I had been taken, as a boy, and had, just two weeks ago, taken our own children, now that we were living in London (*at last, at last! Daddy has delivered!*), to see the chocolate soldiers in Whitehall, horse and foot. But when I noticed that my sons were more interested in the flak-jacketed police standing nearby with their stupid bloody real little machine guns again, I hurried us on, with a stout huff of public annoyance, assuring little Mariana, for all around to hear, that we would come here again to see the funny soldiers and their nice horses, for longer, properly, once London *got back to normal*!

I was, in short, uninterested in guns. I recall, for example, one Sunday some few weeks ago, shortly after our arrival here, when I was out with one of my new colleagues, shopping for the lunchtime joint, and we popped in somewhere for a quick sneaky schoolboyish one on the way back, to chat about matters sporting and cultural, the way liberal Englishmen do. Guns did, in fact, enter the conversation, but only as follows:

—Hey, here's one. Before the Civil War, the American

one, I mean, not ours, what was the most popular sport in America?

—God knows. Shooting bison? Shooting Native Americans?

—Ha ha! No. Cricket!

—Cricket? In America? You sure, John?

—Well, it said so in *The Paper*.

—Oh. Oh, well then.

—But will you find that in any Hollywood costume drama? Not bloody likely.

—Yes, the Yanks don't give a damn about truth, do they? It's all myths with them. I mean, take those pistols, that kind Hollywood is obsessed with. What *are* they called? You know, John, those big black pistols that obviously make Tarantino's knickers catch fire?

—Magnums?

—No, that's that ice cream they market as if it were a blow job.

—Oh yes. Talk about the sexualisation of advertising! All those airbrushed models with fuck-me eyes and red lips, dribbling chocolate. Outrageous!

(Momentary contemplative silence, with beer.)

—Absolutely, John. Anyway, the thing is, I just don't believe that if you get shot with one of those pistols you *fly backwards*. It can't be possible.

—God knows.

—Well, it can't be. You know, Newton's first law, or whichever it is.

—Second, I think. But yes, it's all balls. Why we allow the Yanks to inflict their gun culture on us is beyond me. And the rest of their so-called culture! For God's sake, we had the Men of the West speech in *Lord of the Rings*, then *Troy*, then *300*, and now *Beowulf*. Aryan bloody myths, all of them, all stuff Hitler would have loved! What's Hollywood going to give us next, eh?

Russell Crowe as Siegfried, wiping out dark-skinned baddies from east of the Danube? The implications for our children's world scare me, they really do. Same again?

—Mmm, please, John.

—Two more, please. I mean, look at the French. They have masses of state support for their *own* culture, and it's *real* culture. We must all be mad, staying in this half-American dump when we could be living in bloody great farmhouses in France with no mortgages! Brownings?

That was how much I knew about guns.

And no doubt I would never have learned anything more about them if I hadn't found myself, at forty-five, not having been single since before the Berlin Wall came down, alone for a whole week, out all by myself in the cold and the wet and the big, dark south-London night.

2: The Very Important Paper

I was not supposed to be doing anything at all with plum trees, let alone at night. I was supposed to be working away, safe and warm, at my laptop, in my cleverly arranged little study area under the stairs.

Sarah, my beloved wife, had taken our ten-year-old twins, Will and Jack, and Mariana, our unplanned little late-come darling, away that very evening, for a whole week, after surprisingly little negotiation, so that I could finish and then give my Very Important Paper (as it had become known in the family) to the upcoming national peer-group conference. She had not done all this just so I could mess about, quite unnecessarily, with small fruit trees in the dark and the rain!

—*Bye, darlings!* I had called, reminding myself too late that I really must stop myself doing that ridiculous English thing of addressing my children as though they come from several decades ago and several notches up the social ladder. —*So sorry I can't come too, but well, you know, I've got to get the Very Important Paper done, to make things better for us all. Daddy's Work again, eh? Still, it's already got us to London, hasn't it? What's that, Jack? Well, no, that's true, we didn't actually ask you if you wanted to move to London, but sometimes there are things that adults just, anyway, look, hey you loved the Science Museum the other day, right? Sorry, darling, sorry, I was just trying to be, you know, anyway, hey, boys: a week off school! In Spain! Lu-cky! Now, you be good for Mum, right? And for Granny and Grandad. And don't poke those guns in people's faces, please. No, Mariana is a person as well. What? No, you*

can't be 'a people' Jack, it's 'a person'. Sorry? Well, yes, OK,
that's true, Will, very good, yes, 'a people' is grammatically
possible, you're right. No, Jack, Will's not being geeky, and
that's not a word we use in this family, he's just right, in
certain cases, yes, you can say 'a people', though I'm not
sure generalisations like that are usually very wise and . . .
yes, yes, of course, sorry, darling, I was just, look, Jack, Will,
just shut up for a minute, stop answering back and do what
you're told or Mum'll take those bloody stupid guns away
from you and chuck them in the bin! What? Well, sorry,
darling, but I thought you wanted me to, sorry, yes, of
course, I was just, oh, Mariana, don't cry, Daddy'll see you
soon, he'll be . . . Well I didn't know she'd dropped her toy,
did I? Right. Yes. Bye, darling, drive safely. This will be
worth it. I promise!

I waved a last goodbye, turned back to the house,
went in, shut the front door, knelt beside the little
antique table under the stairs, unfolded the small leaf
of the table, swung the miniature gateleg out beneath
it, patted the early nineteenth-century mahogany with
satisfaction, stood up carefully so as to avoid banging
my head on the underneath of the staircase, pulled my
laptop forward, opened it, turned it on, went the few
steps into the living room to draw over my rather nice
Edwardian captain's chair and sat down to work.

For several minutes, I stared at the Very Important
Paper.

My week had seemed barely enough to finish it, in
all honesty. Hardly adequate at all really, when you
thought about it. Negligible, to be brutally frank, when
compared to the vast swathes of outside-office work
time available to so many of my rivals in this vital
forty-something leg of the career marathon. Men
married to women who did not expect help with the
kids. Men unlikely ever to be encumbered with kids.

Men who could afford nannies. It was, well, yes, actually, there was no way round it, to be quite honest it was almost *unfair*, when you thought about it, to expect me to keep up with these so-called colleagues just by having one little week of pure work.

But now, those same seven, no eight nights suddenly felt like rather a long time.

—Ridiculous, I laughed aloud at myself. Of course a family home seems a little funny when there is no family there. To it, then, and no more nonsense.

The organisers had given the Very Important Paper one of the plenary sessions, no less. I had hardly believed it when I got the call. *Plenary!* The very word set off, as it always did, a cocktail of fear and ambition that started my guts bubbling softly. My field is pretty specialised, you see. It would only take a dozen of my rivals to drop dead for me to be a made man. And all of them would be sitting there, watching and listening: every hirer, firer and decider of lives. If I brought it off! The strong applause, the looks of approval from the frontmost rows, as mysterious but vital as in some meeting chaired by Stalin. In the coffee break one of the real Big Beasts awards you a whole minute of his full attention (your peers instinctively back off a scarcely measurable fraction, the bastards, making a tiny but unmistakable clearing for this drama of gracious condescension). Suddenly you're right in the mix, on everybody's longlist: *him*, you know, still young really, recently moved to London, you know, the one who gave *that* plenary paper at the conference? Oh yes, of course, *him* . . .

There was something missing from the VIP, though, and I knew it. What was it? Come on, this was a technical problem, no more. Exposition, presentation, communication. I scrolled up and down through the document. Now and then I felt I almost saw what needed fixing, a shadow between my lines, but it kept flitting away again, like a fish in dark water. I cleaned my new, frameless designer spectacles for a while (they had been expressly purchased for the giving of the VIP). Then I decided that before settling down properly, I might as well do a bit of admin and check my emails. I'd have to do it sometime this week, after all, so why not get it out of the way right now?

I logged on with the usual distant glisten of hope that today *the* email might be waiting for me. You know, *the* email, the one that somehow makes the offer out of the blue or opens the door at last after all your knocking.

For a fraction of a second my heart leapt as I saw that one message was from the assistant to the PA of the acting European editor of *The Paper*, in reply to my jolly invitation to come and hear the VIP. But it was only an automatic allegedly out-of-office reply, the stuck-up Islington shits.

I mean, for God's sake, I had appeared, and only back in 1990, for very nearly a whole minute of total screen time, on a BBC *Newsnight* special devoted to the reunification of Germany! What did I have to *do* for *The* bloody *Paper* to look twice at me?

The rest of my mail was largely from my third-year students, who had, it seemed, banded together to swamp my inbox with complaints that the books I had done for my A levels in 1981 were 'a bit heavy' for today's finalists. The faculty's Teaching Quality Assessment Guidelines obliged me to reply to each of these whingeing messages personally, in some way at least, within seventy-two hours. There were also three messages from the Teaching Enhancement Unit demanding to know why I had still not filed my own New Appointees' Mission Statement, my Annual

Personal Development Plan, my Course Aims for each module and a Personal Student Goals Statement for each of my students on each of these modules. Not now. Nor did I, naturally, bother answering yet another plea to sign an e-petition against (!) my own union's recently declared policy of boycotting all academic visits and exchanges with Israel.

I decided that I would go out into the garden and de-pot the three small plum trees we had bought two weeks before. Good idea, yes. A nice bit of light, future-oriented and family-centred exercise, then a clean start, clear up the pathetic admin and then straight into it at dawn tomorrow. Exactly. I had plenty of time, for God's sake, a whole seven days and nights. No, eight.

Outside, the rain had just stopped, the air was fresh and clean. Some unusual combination of the elements had allowed a real winter night sky to replace, for once, the muggy orange sodium-lamp haze that normally passes for darkness in London. Venus was already riding high and although the moon was still below the horizon, its light put silver tints into the ozone-eating vapour trails. Pretty nice. And what better picture of trust in the future than a man planting young plum trees for his children under this picture-book sky?

Soon I was working away, my spirits high and rising. In the limitless places behind my eyes, as I dug and planted and trod down, I was breasting a rainbow-crowned hill after a stiff climb, knowing that beyond it would lie, spread out beneath and before me, a wide-screen vision of glorious summer uplands. I hoofed the spade in yet again, and heard vast chords lurking at the edge of my mind, like pre-echos on old vinyl, ready to be unleashed in a triumphal soundtrack of spiritual homecoming:

London, at last!

3: London, at Last!

The only place to be in England, the natural capital of Northern Europe!

I had got us here, as I had always promised I would. True, it had taken a decade or so longer than I had expected, and had also required a stroke of luck (the first-choice candidate for my new job had dropped suddenly out). But after all, everyone needs a break and, one way or another, we were here at last.

And well, really, I ask you: what city can compare?

Where else for a career to burgeon, a family to thrive? Our twin boys would not grow up as beer-swilling teenage bumpkins hanging around the desolate malls of some godforsaken regional so-called centre till the last bus left for their muffled home in the arse-end of nowhere. No, no, not that, not for them! Jack and Will would be cool Young Londoners, travelcard-carrying junior-sophisticate citizens of a perfectly hyper-diverse, postmodern world. Our baby daughter would become no daydreaming backwoods hayseed, lined up for seduction by the first drawling, trust-funded bastard who coolly offered to show her the big world from Mummy's Spare Flat in London. No, no, not that, not she! Mariana would blossom into a laughing metropolitan princess of the *puh-lease* put-down, as blithely familiar with great museums and legendary stages as with multicultural street markets and colourful slang, a fine girl swimming free but unavailable in the infinite variety of London life.

And for Sarah and me, ourselves now in the perhaps

slightly tardy flower of our days? Oh, thank God, no more worthy little galleries laughably proud of their few second-division Impressionists! Never again some condescendingly stripped-back and down-casted travelling production of last year's alleged West End hit! From now on it would be the real things, the things we had always known were there to be ours. If not here, where? If not now, before we got really and truly middle-aged, when?

Stop now? Give up? Down tools? Not I!

In I struck with the spade again, panting lightly but positively basking in my manly aches. Beside me by now stood, stoutly pruned, straight and true, soundly trodden down, two new-planted plum trees, each some seven feet tall. The third young *Prunus nigra* was waiting, ready to complete the careful line across the lawn. A tree for each of my children. Soon, very soon, I would be quaffing that bottle of Olde English organic ale. And smoking a single cigarette from the new pack, which was meant to, and which certainly would, last me for the whole week. Around my canines my gums itched and watered, primed for the good old twentieth-century bite of bitter beer and smoke. I rammed my spade decisively, one-handed, down into the earth beside the hole. And that, said Jack, was that, surely?

I moved over to the last treelet, firmly placed my wellington-booted feet on either side of the black plastic tub, gripped it hard between my ankles, bent to grasp the slim trunk low down and heaved carefully upwards. My back gave polite though firm notice that it could no longer be taken for granted, but the mass of soil and roots, somewhat dried out and shrunken by neglect over the past few busy weeks, slid easily from its pot. I lowered the root ball carefully but confidently into the hole.

Shit.

Not quite deep enough. Another three or four inches. Fine. Christ, I was going to murder that beer. Then, for once, a really long bath and a great, early, baby-free night. Excellent. Up early tomorrow and straight down to work, work, uninterrupted, wonderful, career-cracking work at last!

Lay down the tree, then, gently does it. Boot the spade in again. Never mind the blisters. The cold, the wet, so what? Enough of my back, already. Next summer we would all have plums, from our own garden. Our *London* garden. Mariana would be almost three next summer; she would be charging around the lawn in little red shoes, talking gorgeous half-nonsense. Jack and Will would lift her up to pick her very first, very own plums with her little hands. Sarah would smile. I would have delivered happiness, at last.

Dig, dig, dig.

If the VIP went well, who knew? In a couple of years, I might be earning enough to service the mortgage by myself. Sarah would not have to work just to keep her career going and bring in the, to be honest, ridiculously small (yet, to be even more honest, very necessary) net difference between her taxed wage and the child-minding bills. She would not have to be exhausted or feel guilty about not seeing enough of Mariana. The plums would be sweet. We might even have enough money to move to *north* London . . .

—Ow, shit! I cried, for in the midst of this heady thought, my spade butted squarely on to something under the ground and jarred to a sudden, total halt.

I was caught flat, mid-rhythm. My ankle shot painfully outwards, twisting my knee and thigh after it. I pitched helplessly forward, let go of the spade with both hands and with a desperate lurch managed to get my digging foot freed up just in time to make earth-fall on the far side of the hole. My trailing left foot, though, caught the lip of the pit. This sneaky little trip-tackle took out my whole leg, and my momentum flung me bodily earthwards. I felt a whack and a burn as my right shin smacked into the iron blade, but before any actual pain could register my nervous system was swamped by a depth charge of agony as the stout spade handle flew upwards and walloped me full in the balls.

I had not been seriously thumped anywhere by anything for several decades, let alone by a solid lump of wood right in the testicles. Volts of icy heat flashed down the insides of my thighs, leaving me lying there, retching, fighting for breath and with a deeply unpleasant hallucination that I was back in the play-ground of my vicious seventies Devon comprehensive, rolling on the pitiless tarmac, clutching yet again my bruised *taters*.

—Christ, you fucking little bastard! I gasped, once the power of speech returned. Disentangling my legs, I scrambled growling to my feet, stuck my glasses back on my nose, swung the spade up high with my right hand alone, snatched the steel shaft neatly with my left hand, mid-air, as it fell back *(ha!)* and glared back down into the pit, ready to decapitate whatever had dared to cross me.

Empty, dark and dumb, the hole simply waited.

4: Into the Hole

—Oh for God's sake, I sighed.

Digging and filling and treading down the previous two holes had warmed me up, even before that smack in the balls sent blood flying around my system. Now the sweat was cooling my skin in the wintry night. My brow had the slabby sheen of cold wax. My specs slid on my nose. My chest seemed to have been rubbed with fridgy lard. My damp shirt back clung clammily on the hated pads of flab astride my kidneys.

At forty-five, I was by no means terminally unfit as such. I could still swim a twenty-five-metre length underwater, though these days I burst gasping to the surface, ripe with carbon dioxide, scrabbling for a hold on the slippery tiles, the blood thudding hard behind my eyes. But I had a sort of superstitious awe of cold, hard, dirty labour. I would never remotely have considered driving my kids on a motorway with wheels I had *bolted in place myself*. Married and a multiple father, at forty-five I watched young tattooed men blithely flipping cast-iron manhole covers to check my drains, or insouciantly manoeuvring washing-machines single-handedly for me, and felt as though I were paying not to have work done, but for the right to watch these circus feats of unthinking grace and strength.

I peered down, then made several vengeful prods into the soil at the bottom of the hole. Whatever the thing down there was, it was large, solid and curiously semi-hard. Not so much flexible as almost bouncy. Something man-made, for certain. A door off an old fridge, for example? An ancient tyre? Whatever, it was bloody certain to be large and heavy and hard and awkward and sharp and dirty and wet and cold and scrabbly. It would be very unpleasant, if not actually impossible, for me, alone and without even gloves, to lever and haul from the earth.

Asbestos sprung nastily to mind.

Well, hold on, just one minute, I was not wrestling in the dark with a bloody great lump of old and friable asbestos, not without proper gloves and a facemask at the very least, no thank you very much. True, I could recall my father happily blowing blue dust out of car brake drums (—*Want a go, John?*), but now even the toughest of migrant workmen knew better. If there was any chance it was asbestos there was absolutely no shame at all, none whatever, in going straight to the Yellow Pages and hiring men with tattoos.

But what if I did get men with tattoos and they found it was indeed asbestos? Well? What exactly happens if a large piece of old asbestos is found buried in your garden? Don't the men with tattoos have to call the council? Do they seal off the road? Strip the whole garden? What a disturbance to start my precious week of work!

Or a wartime bomb?

By no means impossible. Just twenty years before my birth, one set of Northern Europeans had been trying as hard as they could to kill as many as possible of another set of Northern Europeans, right here. A doodlebug. An unstoppable V-2 even, hull oxidising slowly, warhead sweating but still ticking away a foot from my foot . . .

Nonsense, all nonsense.

Was I a mere four-eyed pen-pusher to be scared off by the thought of a little hard lifting? By ridiculous

imaginings? Was I now going to scuttle back to my
laptop, leaving the job unfinished and still hanging
over me? This week of all weeks, my make-or-break
time?

No, no. I would be done with it this very night.

I stalked over to my garden shed and kicked about
in the dark, looking for a certain small metal crate. This
was my father's folding blue toolbox, which had been
formally presented to me on my last visit, my father
having decided that his days of using it were over. I
knew roughly where it was, even without a light,
because I had that very day taken from it his old Stanley
knife, to help the boys with a plastic model. After no
more than three or four trips and bouts of cursing, I
found the box.

I knelt down and pulled on the cold metal handles.
The halves of the lid, greased annually by my father
for fifty years, slid smoothly apart. For the second time
that day, smells from my childhood filled the shed. Oil
and sawdust: Daddy's toolbox. I scrabbled around in
it until I located his trowel. It had been drop-forged in
Birmingham, a seamless hunk of metal, back when all
that China made was tea: I had often watched my father
use it to chop bricks in two with a single blow. I walked
out of the shed again and tossed the old trowel on a
whim high in the air. It rose, tumbling upwards, above
the height of the garden wall. For an instant it caught
the light from the still-unseen moon. I held my right
hand out and to my amazement felt the whirling handle
slap flat back down into my grasp, as though drawn
home by unseen wires. If only our boys had been there
to see that! Daddy cool. Then I looked down into the
hole, knelt, took my weight on my left hand and
scraped.

My knees grew damp, the soil piled up around the

edges of the hole, the hidden outlines down inside it hardened, and in two minutes I found myself crouching about a foot above the flat top of a medium-sized suitcase.

5: The Armalite

I put down my trowel and used my soft, bare hand to rub the last thin crust of earth from the top of the suitcase.

It had obviously been sealed with great care. Layer upon layer of yellowed tape had been wound horizontally round the join of lid and body, like mummy cloth, then smothered in now-hardened, crumbling gunk.

What could be inside? What did people bury in carefully sealed suitcases?

Cautiously, I dug my right hand down and in beneath the corner of the case. The earth rammed up under my fingernails, wet and gritty. I tried to lift, but found that the thing was far, far heavier than I had guessed. From my kneeling position, I scarcely managed to raise it six inches out of the earth. It seemed almost impossible that anything this size could weigh so much. Childhood visions of buried treasure flashed back across my mind. Who knew?

I leaned my right ear close to the lid, closed my eyes to hear better, then whipped my fingers swiftly out so that the corner of the suitcase fell hard back down again. There was not the slightest sound of anything whatever shifting or jingling: but the impact sent an unmistakable whiff of hydrocarbons puffing out straight into my face.

I coughed, and blinked behind my glasses. I took my weight on my left hand again and began to probe the join of the suitcase with the point of my trowel. The putty or grout had aged badly, and came away in lumps.

The swathing bands of old tape beneath ripped and tore easily. Soon all that was holding the lid in place was a single modest lock, rusted almost to nothing. I stuck the point of my trowel in behind the lock and twisted gently. The rotted stumps of the rivets on the backplate creaked free of the plastic, and the whole lock came clean away with no more fuss than a child's milk tooth.

I now slowly inserted my trowel between the lid and the body of the suitcase. Boldly, I twisted and flicked. As I did so, I sat swiftly back a bit and turned my face away, just in case. The lid shot up, reached vertical, ran out of momentum, hung for a second, then fell slowly backwards on to the earth. The suitcase now lay there, broken-backed, wide open to the moon.

The reek of old, damp garages filled the night.

I leaned forward once again, to look. The suitcase was packed almost to the brim with some sort of yellow-grey grease. I caught a glimpse of bright white and saw that a large, tough, see-through plastic envelope had been carefully taped to the inner face of the lid, evidently to keep it free of the thick gunk. Inside was, clearly visible, a card with words written in black felt-tip pen:

MAY 1989

Also in this envelope, wrapped yet again in even more plastic, possibly vacuum-sealed by the look of it, was a wad of fifty-pound notes. The wad was very fat and tightly packed indeed.

I had seen impossible, absurd amounts on paper when house-buying, of course. But never this, in all my life, never such actual cash. For several heady seconds my heart leaped with breathtaking daydreams. A vast and shiny new Volkswagen MPV (—*What do you think of her, boys, the Mystery Machine or what, eh?*). A deliriously uncapped, full-month family holiday at last (—*How do you fancy the Peruvian Andes and the Inca Trail, boys?*). A serious chunk off the top of the bloody mortgage (—*Yes, that's right. I believe there are no penalties involved? Excellent*). Then I realised that although these notes seemed so familiar and real, having been used for many years of my very own adulthood, they were in fact as worthless now as a suitcase full of East German marks.

The full burden of my years and my repayments settled again on my shoulders. Absent-mindedly, I knelt closer once more. The knuckles of my left hand sank, cold and wet, into the soil. I leaned forward and slid the blade of the trowel carefully down into the petrochemical goo. I stirred. It was as thick as old, cold porridge. In the depths, the point of the trowel nudged a hidden lump.

An unseen something gave and the trowel slipped quickly another three inches down. I turned it this way and that, but could sense nothing more.

Up I pulled, and whatever it was came too. A shape broke the surface and the fat grease started to slide from it in a slow, thick waterfall, as if it were a damaged submarine rearing up into the night from deep down in some slimy sea.

Curiously, I lifted the trowel up to the pale light of the moon. The object was strangely lumped and deformed-looking, about two feet long and perhaps four or five pounds in weight. My trowel had evidently gone clean through the plastic wrapping at some point where there was a hole or gap inside, catching fast.

I turned and held it up against the moon, so that the

light could shine through the plastic. Yes, I had hooked on to some kind of handle on the top of a . . .

—Jesus Christ almighty, a fucking Armalite! I yelped. I threw the thing hastily back into the suitcase, stepped back, tripped over the spade and fell heavily on my back, my specs flying from my face. My eyes now blurred by astigmatism and short sight, I watched while the package sank away again in unnerving slow motion. As it disappeared, a stony shower passed across my cheeks and neck, a river of tiny, icy pebbles.

—Hey, what's up, mate? called a deep, male voice some six feet away in the darkness. —Oi, you deaf or what? Hell-o?

I froze.

6: Opening Up

The estate agent's cheaply photocopied brochure had not lied. Ours was indeed *a most secluded and private end-of-terrace garden*. Actually, *secluded* meant that it was small and overshadowed, and *end-of-terrace* meant that beyond it lay a ghastly alleyway, always half-blocked with burst-bellied plastic rubbish sacks heaped up like the uncollected dead of some merciless urban war.

How had we failed to notice all this when we were house-hunting? Because by then we knew, having slogged for weeks around low-ceilinged, Artex-ridden hovels with white plastic windows, that this little house, jerry-built for the nineteenth-century working classes, its smattering of garden completely sunless, was, incredible as it seemed, the only bloody period three-bed property we could afford in the so-called Clapham Borders that was in the catchment area of the supposedly sort-of-OK-ish school. We could believe the estate agent, or despair. So we believed.

But as I now lay here, flat on my back in the moonlight, three feet from a real live Armalite machine gun, with a voice in my head asking how the hell I knew it was an Armalite anyway and another questioning me loudly from the alleyway, the garden just seemed very, very lonely.

I stayed there and scanned the darkness, keeping absolutely quiet, trying to give no sonic clue away, whilst at the same time patting the grass for my specs. At last my hand fell on them. I hooked them behind my ears and pressed them silently back on to my nose.

—I said *you all right*, mate? shouted the voice from the alleyway again. —Oi, we know there's fucking someone in there. The words *behaviour* and *suspicious* spring to mind, mate.

I swallowed as softly as possible. As far as I knew, the alley was used exclusively by criminally inclined teenagers in hoods. But this was not a teenage voice. It was the voice of a fully grown, mature male. A man loud and confident in his pure and unmistakable local accent. A man happy to walk dark alleyways by night and confront total strangers on a whim.

A man, moreover, who had said *we*.

Who was *we*? Could it be the police? Surely, though, the police would have *said* they were the police? And not have said *fucking*? But if it was not the police, well, who else, what *we* else, would dare to address me in that tone, in my own garden, in England? The silence seemed to creak. A sweet tickling cloud of cigarette smoke drifted in from the alleyway.

—Oi, this is the Neighbourhood Watch here, mate. You going to answer? Last chance, or Uncle Joe's coming over that fucking wall!

—Neighbourhood Watch? I asked, and scrambled to my feet.

—Aha, there you are then. That *your* garden, mate?

—What? Mine? Well, yes, of course.

—Oh. So, you must be Doctor John Goode, neighbour?

—Um, yes, yes, that's right, that's me!

—We heard someone shouting and screaming and moaning, didn't we, Uncle Joe?

—Rrrrrrrr! said what had to be a large dog. I was not keen on large dogs, or on people that kept them. I considered that owning a large dog was a statistical indicator of fascistic tendencies.

32

—That's OK, that was just me! I called over the wall.

—The words *shagging* or *fighting* or *dying* sprang to mind, Doc.

—No, no, I just, I was just, oiling the mower, and I, um, hit my thumb, you see. And I must have shouted a bit. Sorry. Well, thanks for, um, for taking the trouble to ask. Goodnight!

—Oiling the mower, Doc? This time of night?

—Sorry? Um, well, yes, oiling it, for the winter, you see.

—Oh yes. Very sensible.

—Right, well . . .

—Well then, Doc, you going to open up?

—Open up?

—See you round the front, yeah?

—The front? I asked moronically, as though I had indeed heard this word used once, but not in my last several incarnations on earth.

—Come on, Uncle Joe, time to meet and greet the new man on the block.

7: Thank You, Sir, and Goodnight

I stood and listened to the merrily retreating steps of man and dog, my own feet rooted far more firmly than either of the little trees freshly planted beside me. Why the hell had I ever left my quiet little desk under the stairs?

Well, call the police, obviously.

What else can you do if you find an Armalite in your garden? Actually, it might be good to have the Neighbourhood Watch as a witness, to prove to the police beyond doubt that I had simply unearthed the gun right here and now.

Ridiculous. There would be no doubt anyway. I was a respectable lecturer, for God's sake . . .

Dang-Dong! went the front door bell.

I jumped, found I was still standing over the hole and suitcase like an idiot, hurried to my back doorstep, struggled to get off my muddy boots, fell over, banged my head on the door-jamb and swore. I raced through the kitchen, sliding sock-footed on the tiles, and hurriedly washed my hands as well as I could.

Dang-Dong!

—Yes, yes, coming!

I dried my hands, oh God, grease on the dishcloth, and grabbed for my week's packet of cigarettes. The Neighbourhood Watch had been smoking. So if I was smoking as well, that would make me seem, and therefore feel, tougher and more like him. And anyway I was suddenly dying for one. Christ, yes, I was going to give up, all right, —*Yes, yes, Daddy is going to stop*

34

completely very soon indeed, promise, but not on a day when I had just found a bloody Armalite under my lawn and the police were about to come charging round and . . .

Wait.

I stood stock-still. From here I could see, at the end of the short, narrow hallway, the figure standing as a shadow against the streetlight beyond the original Victorian stained-glass door about which the estate agent had made such a ridiculous (but successful) fuss.

Think.

I mean, this is serious.

What exactly do the police do if you call them and say you've just found an Armalite in your garden?

Christ, they turn up by the dozen, no doubt. If not the score. The hundred. Yes, with guns and dogs and flak jackets. All wired and cocked. Better make *bloody* sure they know that it was *you* who called them! Give them an exact description of yourself, stressing the middle-aged, the specs and especially the *white*.

And even assuming they do not just blow your head off by regrettable mistake, what do they do, once they have got the gun? Just say thank you sir and good-night?

As if!

They drive you away to some bombproof cell for questioning, then order half the street out of bed and take the house to bits looking for more Armalites, is what they do, of course. And what exactly happens if the police decide to take your house apart? Do they put it back how it was? Or just roughly? Or not at all? Do they pick up the bill? How long does it take? Does insurance cover it? Does the trashing of one's property by the anti-terror police count for insurance purposes as a side effect of terrorism? Or of war on terrorism?

And does a war on terrorism, having being called such by the Prime Minster of a country, count within that country, for insurance purposes, as a normal war, i.e. not count at all?

What would happen to my precious, unique, once-in-a-parenthood week of pure work? How would I ever get the Very Important Paper finished?

Dang-Dong!

—Rrrrrr!

—Yes, yes, coming!

Well, I had no choice.

Shit.

The police would question this maniac with the dog as well. Of course they would. Very carefully. I'd already behaved suspiciously. I hadn't told him straight away. I'd lied about a lawnmower. What would they make of that?

—*Now, sir, it seems that your first reaction was to lie to the Neighbourhood Watch, doesn't it? To try to cover up the fact that you'd just found an Armalite. That's rather strange isn't it, surely, sir? Can you perhaps explain?*

Oh my God.

The bloody anti-Iraq-War march last year!

8: Not in My Name

I slumped against the wall of our little hallway and my fresh-scrubbed palm went unbidden to my forehead.

The Iraq march.

Oh God.

All goes well until William needs a pee. The police are gazing very coldly on anyone who looks like trying to break ranks from the planned route. They seem in no mood to listen to hasty explanations, shouted desperately over the noise of those stupid bloody SWP chants and ridiculous whistles. We decide we must just stop, home-made banners and all, mid-march. It is only a child peeing, after all. A bit old to be doing this normally, true. Especially in his own eyes. We have to stand around to shield William from pre-teen embarrassment as, red-eyed with resentment, he pisses in the street. Our friends half-heartedly offer to stop along with us, but are more or less forced onwards. The small, still-childish trickle comes with maddening slowness as the great column of people shuffles unstoppably by (—*Sorry, sorry, William. For God's sake, darling, pee straight. No, no, not if straight means straight on people's shoes! Christ, sorry, er, mate. I mean, um, Imam. No offence intended, I didn't mean Christ as in, well, I mean, I know you, your religion respects Christ too. Anyway, I'm not a Christian as it happens. Not that I'm anti-religion as such, of course, it's just . . . anyway, sorry . . .*). William has finished at last and now Jack, quite predictably, quite understandably and yet very, very irritatingly, decides that he, being undeniably a twin and thus clearly entitled to fully equal rights of parental fussing on the basis of perceived rather than actual need, also needs to do a wee.

By the time the boys are both done, rezipped and once again holding up their touchingly miniature NOT IN MY NAME banner (on which we spent most of yesterday afternoon), we are hopelessly separated from the happy gang of like-minded old college pals with whom we were planning to spend the rest of the day marching and picnicking and finding child-friendly north-London pubs that serve real ales, and suchlike jollity. We try to call mobiles, try to make ourselves heard over the din, try to make back-up plans. Then we look around, our spirits in sudden free fall. We have been engulfed by wild-eyed SWP members, pale faces alight with the unholy glow of certainty. There is no escape. With Sarah heavily pregnant, we can hardly try to barge speedily forward through our fellow marchers. Nor do we feel like risking a confrontation with the brooding line of armoured policemen. Christ, in my days on the Miners' Strike they still just had ordinary helmets and coats and looked like humans! Hmm. Perhaps if we *hadn't* thrown bricks at them back then? Yes, well. There they are, anyway, looking as if they might quite like to make a fight of it, and here we are surrounded by loony Trots and the stream of protestors surges on about us, all shoulders and elbows, eventually forcing us to shuffle on regardless. We stall and slow as much as possible to let the screaming SWP overtake us. Perhaps we can find the Quakers? If we march with the Quakers for a bit, singing and smiling inanely, the police might see that we are essentially harmless and let us leave the march. But it is not the Quakers who now envelope us. It is, instead, the toughly silent, semi-masked Northern acolytes of some aged and bearded Muslim cleric. This ancient scholar-cum-tribal-chieftain smiles with Olympian, or at any rate Araratian, condescension at me and even absent-mindedly ruffles the hair of our sons (they smile nervously, sure of parental approval later), but he does not seem to even register Sarah's existence.

And it is just then that I notice the policeman, not twelve feet away, openly taking pictures with a very large camera. Pictures of us. Of me. With these people.

It was a legal march, for God's sake, what were we doing wrong? Nothing. Nothing at all. Merely exercising our democratic right to object peaceably, although perhaps in somewhat ill-chosen company, to a war for which we were paying in many different ways but about which we had not been consulted and with which we did not agree. Nothing wrong at all. And yet. What if those same marchers about me had, more recently, been CCTVed outside some mosque vowing publicly to ritually disembowel anyone insulting God and warning that the *real* Holocaust (as opposed, presumably, to the one that they claimed never happened) was yet to come?

What if, when I called the police about the Armalite, the police checked everything, *everything* that they could possibly have against my name? Which of course they would. It was an Armalite, for Christ's sake, and this was these days! The most plodding common sense might quite reasonably suggest a connection between my having an Armalite buried in my garden and my having recently been photographed marching in the proximity of associates of supporters of glorifiers of terrorism.

Would they hold me for a fortnight? Or a month? Or however long it was they could hold you without charge these days? That man who had worked on computers for the 7/7 bombers and had gone to the police was *questioned for two weeks*, it had said on the telly. And he had been a definite Good Guy! Questioned for two weeks! What would happen to my Very Important Paper if they even questioned me for a few days? And hence, my career? And hence, our children's futures? And hence . . .

Dang Dong!

—Open up then, Doc!

—Rrrrrrrr!

—Yes, sorry, of course, just washing my hands!

Christ, I just needed to think.

I needed peace, that was all, just for a moment, just so I could work this one out sensibly.

OK, right, just say hello, be civil and get rid of the idiot. Then decide, calmly and rationally, what exactly to say when I called the police as obviously I was going to . . . For example, I would certainly have to make sure I didn't say *Armalite* when I phoned them! I mean, I didn't want them asking how come I, an ordinary Englishman, had recognised this particular brand of machine gun, did I? Christ, no. I didn't even want to think about it myself . . .

I raced back to the garden, bootless, kicked the lid of the suitcase shut, ran back through the house to the front door, took a deep breath, stuffed a cigarette into the corner of my fixed smile, set myself in as bluff a shoulders-back blue-collar manner as I could strike without blatant absurdity and cried, —Aha, hi there! more loudly than I'd meant to, and flung open my house.

9: The Big Match

The Neighbourhood Watch was shaven-headed, ear-studded, and dressed in a leather blouson jacket over tight jeans rolled up to show the whole length of his Dr Martens boots. Around his rumpy neck hung triple ropes of gleamingly cheap but indubitable gold, so heavy that their major design influence seemed to be Bronze Age throat armour. He was carrying a mighty-looking, battle-scarred cricket bat over his right shoulder and was accompanied by a large black dog mutated by generations of carefully selective inbreeding until its barrel chest and stumpy legs had become little more than a chassis to carry a square, pig-eyed head, the salivating jaws hard-wired into a fiendish perma-grin.

So although he was a solitary man a whole head shorter than I and no younger, I was deeply unconfident about getting rid of him quickly. Many unpleasant playground experiences had taught me that whatever interesting anthropological theories sociolinguists may deduce from our use of terms like *highness* and *superiority* and *elevated status* and so on, in brute reality being noticeably taller than other males, when those males are white trash from violent and stupid backgrounds, simply means that nature has arranged things perfectly for them to leap suddenly up and head-butt you smack across the cheekbone and nose, often breaking your NHS specs.

I had always sworn that this would never happen to our lovely boys. I would do anything to stop that. I mean, anything short of giving up my career, obviously.

This was a case in point. You see, I recognised man and dog immediately. They lived diagonally across the road. The man was the father of three repulsive boys between the ages of about eight and eleven, fattened up (I assumed) by pizza and cable TV yet somehow still thumpingly sporty, who went to the same primary school as Will and Jack. I had noticed them, father, boys and dog, on the first day I walked our sweet sons schoolwards. The Neighbourhood Watch had been chatting away to a boiler-suited Afro-Caribbean fellow resident, and had casually swatted his eldest boy around the head for interrupting him. The blow had resounded up the street, but the meaty lad had scarcely winced: his two younger siblings had laughed delightedly at this little bit of slapstick and had continued hooting even as their elder brother kicked them both hard up their arses in displaced revenge. Then the muscular family had proceeded on towards the school with every appearance of high humour, pausing only for the dog to crap hugely in the middle of the pavement. I had secretly feared the worst for little William and Jack. What chance did our lovely boys have amongst young thugs raised to think of a full-blooded smack on the head as the first reaction to any daily provocation? I was pretty sure no actual violence had happened to them in school yet, though they had been quieter since the move and had hinted at being mocked for their posh non-London accents.

No, they would not suffer! Not if I could help it in any way. I mean, OK, obviously, I wasn't going to drag them to live in a seventies brick box with plastic windows on a suburban, Tory-voting estate in some place halfway to Brighton at the end of some overland line no one has ever even heard of, just because there is actually a quite decent local school there. I mean, you can't just give up *completely*, can you? But apart from that, I would do anything, *anything*, to stop them being bullied.

So I was certainly not going to risk alienating this no doubt opinion-forming alpha bloody neighbour (and thus his tough sons) by seeming anything other than perfectly normal for SE11.

—Ah, hello, I said, forcing my hand not to flutter up and needlessly press my glasses back higher on to my nose.

—Nice to meet ya, Doc. Phil George. A steak-like hand was held out. As I shook it, I did my best to make my own grip loose yet wiry.

—Hi, Phil! Hi. I'm John. John Goode. So, hey, you're the Neighbourhood Watch round here, eh? Thanks for keeping an eye on things. I must join. Once I get settled.

—You like a bit of a scrap, Doc John, ha ha? He mimed a thoroughly convincing burst of ringcraft, his fists pulling up barely short of my face at each move.

—Oh, hey, you know. So, do you have, um, scraps, in the Neighbourhood Watch?

—Not of our choosing, Doc, know what I mean. But, see, I got some old mates down the cop shop, haven't I, and like they said on the QT, who's to say a decent law-abiding council-tax-paying Englishman, out all on his own, hasn't just come back from knocking a cricket ball about the park, for the family dog to fetch? See? Here's the ball, right here. My kids' cricket ball. Catch, Doc John! Butter-fingers! Got Uncle Joe's fresh teeth-marks in it, see? And his fresh gob on it, as you can no doubt feel, ha ha ha! All kosher, just in case some clever fucking lawyer tries to catch me out. We all do it, see, Doc John. Always go out on our tod, always with a dog and a ball and a bat, always make sure we get seen up the park every time we go out on patrol. The Neighbourhood Watch thinks ahead! The words *prepared* and *be* spring to mind! You got a dog, Doc John?

—Um, no, actually.

—Well, you could always take Uncle Joe for a walk, eh? Who's to say a decent law-abiding English doctor can't help his neighbour out by taking his mutt for a stroll, eh? Have to get him used to you first, of course. Ain't that right, Uncle Joe? That's right.

—Rrrrr!

—Uncle Joe, eh?

—Yeah. In memory of my old man. First time I saw him down the dogs' home, killing a Dobermann, I knew that was the name for him. My old man always used to say it was Uncle Joe tore the guts out of the German army, see.

—As Churchill wrote, I added, significantly.

—Did he? Well there you go. Good dog now, mostly. Took a while to knock it into him, of course, but then it does, doesn't it? So there we are: I just happen to be out with the bat and the ball and the family pet, and if I see some little cunts up to no good, well, obviously, it wasn't me that kicked it off, was it? I'd back me and this old bat and Uncle Joe against any three little Albanian cunts, knives and all. What you reckon, eh, Doc John?

The massive cricket bat was swung in a jocular way so that it stopped a fraction of an inch from the side of my head.

—Right!

—Take that Merc of yours, Doc John. It is yours, the silver Merc? Thought so. Spotted it, new car on the block. The Neighbourhood Watch notices these things. The words *posh* and *bit for round here* sprang to mind.

44

Now, how long d'you reckon that Merc badge on your bonnet would last round here without the Neighbourhood Watch, eh? Not fucking long, is how long. Still, if you got it, flaunt it, eh? Ha ha!

I needed to get this ape away from my house, but I could not have him thinking me (and thus, our boys) posh and different, so I quickly replied.

—Flaunt it? I only paid five grand for it, er, Phil. In the free ads.

—Five grand in the free ads? Mmm. Sounds all right. What's she got on the clock?

—Ninety-five K, I replied, with practised ease. —Full history too.

—Here, you done well there, Doc John.

The basking sun of normality lit me from within. What higher praise can a blue-collar Englishman give to his new neighbour than to say that he got a good deal on his motor? I would make sure I got him to tell Sarah this, because she had still not quite accepted that when I had gone out two months before, empowered to buy a normal one-owner family car just out of warranty from a reputable dealer but had returned with a seven-year-old Mercedes with ninety-five K on the clock and three names before mine on the logbook from some bloke in the free ads, I had been acting rationally. Proud and happy, I chatted briefly to Phil about build quality, reliability and depreciation curves.

—Whatever you say, Doc John. Or should I say, Einstein! And of course, Mercs is Mercs.

—They are, I nodded sagely.

—Makes you feel like you made it, Mercs.

—Well, I suppose, sort of, in a way . . .

—Yeah, and with that star on the bonnet you can play Focke-Wulf pilots in the Blackwall Tunnel, eh?

Achtung! For you, Tommy, in your Mondeo, ze war is over, budabudabuda, boom! Ha ha ha! And the Neighbourhood Watch intends to keep that star right there, Doc John, on your bonnet, not round the neck of some little Albanian cunt, eh? And if you ever find yourself with nine points on your licence, like anyone can these days, just let Phil know, say no more, soon fix you up with a nice pair of new plates for the fucking cameras and no harm done to anyone, eh? We generally ask for a couple of quid a week contribution from our neighbours, Doc John. Just to defray expenses and show willing. Twenty a month do you? Less than having your windows cleaned every Friday, innit? Which I also arrange, round here. Sign you up for both while we're at it? Why not? What's a tenner a week to a medical man, eh?

—Right, I said, searching my pockets.

After all, I hastily lectured myself, I mean, yes, admittedly it does sound bizarre to us, at first, the notion of private security. Bloody American, it sounds. Because we are so used to the big State. But consider: to Marx and Engels, at any rate the early Engels, the very notion of the State serving the People would have been laughable. To them, the State meant Otto von Bismarck. And remember: whose side were the police on during the Miners' Strike, eh? Well, exactly! When you think about it, really, without being blinded by preconceptions, who would you rather have walking your streets, looking out for you? The paid hirelings of the State, always clamouring for new powers and more of your taxes, laughing at 'civilians' when the microphones are off? Or your own neighbours, actual real working-class people, who you know by name and who just ask, pretty reasonably it has to be said, for a little voluntary contribution to . . .

—Hey, Phil, sure, great, sign me up for both! There

you go. Um, the only thing is, look, Phil, about this *doctor* business . . .

—Gotcha, eh, Doc John? Big Brother is watching you. The Neighbourhood Watch sees all. Ha ha, don't look so worried, it was just the postie told me. Your secret is safe with me. I know you medical men like to keep mum about it.

—I'm not *that* kind of doctor, actually.

—What, you a vet?

—No, I teach at University College London.

—So, you're a teacher?

—No, no, a lecturer.

—What, like a professor?

—Sort of. Well, yes. But more junior.

—So, what, you just *call* yourself doctor, for a laugh?

—No, God, it's totally, er, kosher. I've got a doctorate. In fact, you can see it. It's there, hanging on the wall.

I stood aside and pointed to where my framed parchment hung in our little hallway. To my horror, Phil took this as an invitation to walk straight past me and into our house. Beyond which lay the garden. And the gun. I found myself standing helplessly there for a moment as the vile black dog bundled in between my legs.

—Um, Phil, if you don't mind, the dog . . .

—What, you don't like dogs, Prof John?

—No, no, love them, it's just, my wife, the carpets, the baby, hey, you know. I shrugged and rolled my eyes at the mysterious ways of women.

—Oh, well then. She who must be obeyed, eh? A whipped dog is a happy dog, eh? Ha ha! Uncle Joe, you sit outside. Sit. Stay. I said fucking stay or you'll get more of that! So, right you are, let's see this certificate. What, this it? What's that, Latin?

—Yes, actually.

I looked quickly up and down the street, as if the anti-terror police might already be watching the house, then I dived hastily after Phil, over my own threshold, and slammed the door.

10: Sash Windows

Phil stared at the framed mock-parchment doctorate certificate on the wall of our hallway. I stared at the gleaming back of Phil's head, and at the roll of fat or muscle that bulged above his collar. How was I going to get rid of him now?

—Very posh, said he.

—Well, I only put it there for when my mum came to visit, actually. I just forgot to take it down. You see? *Doctor John Goode*. Me, ha. I only really use it to please her. And sort of, impress my bank manager, ha. Not that it does, unfortunately.

—Mums is mums, Prof John.

—Well, exactly, Phil.

—What's it all about then, Prof John? Life, and that?

—Sorry?

—Well, it says here *Doctor of Philosophy*.

—No, no, I'm not in philosophy, it just always says that, you see. I teach, I mean, lecture, in German. And on Germany.

—Oh well, you'll know all about the Nazis and the occult then.

—Actually, that's not exactly my field.

—You ought to know. I'll lend you a book. Very interesting indeed.

—Mmm. Thanks, Phil. So, well, look, um, Phil, I'd invite, er, offer you a drink, but, well, the fact is, I was, um, actually, I was just going out myself. For a drink, you know.

—Off to catch our boys on the Big Screen, eh, Prof John?

—Our boys? Oh, I mean, yes, God, wouldn't want to miss, um, our boys in the, the Big Match!

—Me too, your alley was my final call tonight. Not the same, watching at home, is it? Got to be down the pub for the England match!

—Absolutely!

—Which boozer you going down then, Prof John?

—Hmm? Oh, I, we only just moved here, as you know, so, what with the baby, I haven't really had time to . . .

—You should come down your own bloody local, you silly sod. Tell you what, we can go down together. It ain't posh, the old Red Lion, but it is your local. Nice new Polish barmaid too, sweet as a nut.

Whatever, just get him out of the house. Yes, why not have a pint down the pub instead of that bottle of organic ale? No difference really. And then, think about it. Surely, this was a chance to help Jack and William out at the new school? Yes! What if they come back from their holiday to find that their very own dad is now a drinking mate of this bling-hung fascist maniac, the father of those three super-sized boys? Comprehensive London might yet be made safe for them. Daddy will deliver. Certainly worth a quick pint, to achieve that. In fact, not taking this chance, it having been offered, would in a very real way be neglecting the boys' best interests. Work, after all, for a family man, is not just about Very Important Papers!

—Well, great, yes, the Red Lion sounds . . . great.

—Neighbours, not strangers, that's us, Prof John! That's Phil's philosophy for you! Ha ha ha. So, this the family then?

—Sorry? Oh, look, I . . .

Phil had walked straight past me and on into the

living room, and was now standing crouched by the mantelpiece, squinting at our small collection of family pictures in their little frames. I sidled quietly crabwise behind him, in order to place myself casually on guard at the door to the kitchen.

Apart from the usual dusting of plastic crap (light-sabres, small foam rings from electric guns, game-machine cartridges), the room was dominated by the carefully laid-out parts and instructions for a large-scale Flying Fortress, which I'd been helping Jack and William with. And I was happy now to place my right foot beside Grandad's knife, my father's blue-grey metal-handled craft knife, which lay on the Flying Fortress's instruction sheet. The ground seemed suddenly firmer, as if my sons' undoubted maleness had added a few vital pounds to my own.

—Twin boys, eh, Prof John? Got her with both barrels, eh? Ha ha ha! Three boys, I got. We'll have to get the little sods all out down the park together for a kick-about, eh?

—Great, yeah, love to!

—And a baby girl, eh? Pret-ty. That's nice. But the words *ahead* and *trouble* spring to mind. Every little fucker in the street sniffing round. Now that's a nice house. That where you used to live, Prof John? Come down in the world a bit, haven't you, ha ha?

—No, it's Sarah's parents' house. Down Exeter way.

—Very nice. Don't suppose there's many of them, down Exeter way.

—Sorry?

—Well, whose fucking idea was it to let a million illiterate medieval cunts in who think we're all filthy fucking unbelievers and our girls are tarts because they don't wear fucking blankets over their heads? Exactly. No one's idea. No one wanted it. It was a fucking stupid cock-up, that's all it was, but no one's going to admit it because there's fuck-all anyone can do about it except send the cunts back to Allahu-fucking-Akbar-land and no one's going to do that, because they can't, so we all have to pretend it's fine. Exeter way, eh? How much'd a place like that set you back down Exeter way? I suppose you can pick that sort of thing up dirt cheap, all the way out there?

For a second or two we both looked at the picture of Sarah, the children and me standing in front of Sarah's parents' house. A perfectly normal, solid, three-storey Victorian semi with two bays and a real attic room above and sash windows, a proper little front garden with a child's swing and a genuine drive, more than enough to park a car on, leading up to a neat red wooden garage door. I had always wanted a house like that. I could still remember with complete clarity deliberately stopping the first time I walked up to that door, so that I could look in for a moment at Sarah all alone at the piano, in her own perfect world. Sarah's parents were only schoolteachers, for God's sake, whereas I was a fully fledged university lecturer . . .

—Cheap? Not any more, I said to Phil. —Not even in Exeter.

—Nice-looking bird, your missus, Prof John. Often thought so in the street. This your old man, then?

Phil pointed a sausage-like finger at the other large photograph over our fireplace. This showed me back in 1989 (the glorious summer I won my first job and Sarah). I was being held playfully in a necklock by a grinning, bearded man with extremely large and hairy forearms.

—My dad? God no, that's, it's . . .

I thought for a moment about trying to explain. But I decided that this was not the time.

—. . . oh, it's just a German friend of mine. A writer. And a sort of politician now.

But Phil was no longer listening. He motioned for me to be quiet, and his ears pricked visibly back on his bald head. I cocked my head as well. We could hear the yapping laughter and cheery joshing of a young male war band passing by in the street. Phil's ears relaxed.

—Na, that wasn't the Albanians.

—Oh, good.

—That was that little cunt Dave Phipps and his scummy brothers from three doors down.

—Oh.

—That's why the Neighbourhood Watch pays special attention to your end of the street, Prof John.

—Right.

—I mean, they say crime doesn't pay, right? Well they're almost right. It doesn't pay *very well*. You tell me, Prof John, how much d'you reckon those little cunts make, selling a bit of dope and coke and nicking phones and doing motors over?

—Is that what they do?

—Don't you worry, even those cunts have got enough brains not to shit in their own nest. Not when they know the Neighbourhood Watch is watching them! I'll tell you how much they fucking make. Not much, is how much. Not enough to fucking live. Except, guess what? You and me and everyone else pays those thieving cunts dole on top of it. Which makes it worth their fucking while to go out thieving! Now whose bright idea was that, you ask? No one's, is whose. It's just another fucking cock-up and no one's going to do anything about it, because there's nothing they can fucking do about it, except abolish the fucking dole full stop for every little cunt under twenty-one with no kids and no one's going to do that.

—Well, yes, Phil, I see your point. But isn't there something that can be done about them? I mean, like call the council? Or the housing association?

—Na. It's their own place.

—What?!

—Well, their dad bought it before they was born. Like mine, see. Lucky, I suppose. Not like the stupid sods who come along nowadays and tie their bollocks to a huge fucking mortgage for the rest of their lives just so they can pay silly fucking money for . . . no offence meant, Prof John. Present company excepted, eh? Ha ha! You put that study thing in, under the stairs, did you? Can you really work in there without banging your nut all the time?

—Oh, yes. Well, just about.

—I see. Course, they put an extension on for the kitchen. Always wondered. Units not bad. French windows, very nice. What you got outside in the garden, Prof John? All down to lawn, is it, what's left of it? What you been planting? Apple trees? Thought you said you was oiling the mower? Mind if I take a look? Think you'll get enough light for apples? Or are they plums?

—Plums, yes. But no, stop, Phil, wait!

My hand shot out of its own accord and grabbed at hairy muscle and bone. It felt as though I had taken hold of a horribly warmed-up leg of raw, bristly pork. I looked down. My grasp scarcely reached three-quarters of the way around Phil's big wrist.

—What? You OK, Prof John?

—Phil, listen, this is, aha, well, ha, sorry, love to show you the garden, but, but . . . but look at the time! I mean, hey, what about the England match?

—We still got half an hour, Prof John.

—Yes, that's true, but, Phil, what about the, *the*

54

warm-up! We can't miss the warm-up, down the pub, for an *England* match! Can we?

—Now that's what I call philosophy, Prof John! You are so right. What's the England match without a few pints in the warm-up first, eh? Yeah, the lads'll be there already. Here, if that's what you teach them at college, I'll send my boys after all, ha ha ha!

—Look, I'll just, I've just got to send a quick email. Why don't you go and get the first one in, get us good seats? Here, I'll give you the money.

—You're on, Prof John. What you drink? Nice cold lager?

—Um, yes, yeah, great.

—We'll save you the best seat in the house, Prof John. Meet the lads. Go on then, send your message, chop-chop, don't want to let your beer get warm and flat. You be there, or I'll come back looking for you, ha ha! Come on then, Uncle Joe, the words *beer* and *lots of* spring to mind, eh? Ha ha!

—Rrrrrr!

11: Einstein and Newton

In the garden, the moon was now high. I raced out from my back door, half-expecting to find that the Armalite had in the meantime escaped from the suitcase by itself. The suitcase was still closed, of course, just as I had left it, with the Armalite within.

Or at least I assumed it was, because nothing had moved. Even so, I found myself already about to lift the lid of the case, just to make sure.

I forced myself to stop. There was no rational way, no way at all, that anyone without superhuman powers could have sneaked over the wall and dug the gun from out of the grease whilst I was talking to Phil. It was impossible. Which meant that if I now really did allow myself to open the lid of the suitcase to make sure the gun was still there, this would cleary imply that I, (Dr) John Goode, had in fact accepted that the impossible was at least theoretically possible and that the laws of nature might in principle have been suspended tonight in SE11.

I refused to countenance this notion. According to the rules believed by Newton to be absolute at every time or place, the gun must still be there, *was* still there. Yes, of course, I knew that Einstein had shown (apparenty) that Newton's laws are subject to infinitely small (yet, in the infinite vastness of infinity, eventually infinitely significant) variations at vast speeds or tiny measurements (or whatever it was that Einstein said). But SE11 was a normal place. Well, comparatively.

Enough. I planted my feet and my mind firmly. The

world turned normally. Normally, for the world. Einstein might be fine for subatomic particles, but Newton still ruled in *my* garden. So I acted logically. I quickly spaded a thin covering of earth back over the suitcase and towed the unplanted tree across the dug patch. It lay there, now irretrievably unpotted. Pale fingers and hairs of root trailed feebly from the big lump of earth, undefended from the killing night and cold. In the wet darkness, it looked too much like something you might dig up in a nasty Bosnian forest. But I had no time to worry just now about the tree.

My course was rationally clear.

I was going to go the pub, come back, go out again, dig the garden again as if nothing had ever happened just to get some fresh earth on my hands and boots, then call the police as if I'd just found the gun.

Yes, my work time would be disturbed, but there was no helping that. What else could I do? I was a normal Englishman; I had found an Armalite; I would call the police. So long as there was no reason for them to be at all suspicious of my story, no complications about what I might or might not have said to Phil and why, they would have no reason to ever suspect me of anything, or check up on my past or . . .

Stoutly, I turned my back on the hole and marched back into the house to find clothes for the pub, suitable for watching England in

I opened my wardrobe and swiftly grabbed a pair at random from the monoculture pile of 34/30 Levis which were all I had bought in the way of jeans for the past twenty years. I struggled into them. Shit, come on. Must've shrunk in the bloody tumble dryer. I was not a 36 waist, I refused to be a 36 waist, I had always been a 34 waist and . . . aha! There. Fine, really.

I bounded down the stairs, got to the front door,

patting my pockets to make sure I had grabbed my keys and money.

But at the door I stopped dead.

Christ, I didn't even know what the hell *the England match* was!

How could I walk into a south-London pub not knowing that? I raced back down the hall, diving into my little study area to check on the web. In my hurry to reach my laptop, I thwacked my head solidly on the side of the staircase.

—Ahh! For Christ's sake, stupid fucking ridiculous little bloody . . . ! I roared, and sank to my knees, blinded with the pain.

When I looked up, I found that I must have managed to hit a key before being felled. The Very Important Paper had leapt out of hibernation and was standing there once more on the screen before my eyes, bright and mocking.

For a vertiginous second, as my brain settled back from the thump, I was absolutely convinced that my work had somehow converted itself into a bizarre and completely illegible font. Then I found that I could indeed read the letters but that the words now refused to combine into any meaning. I stared at my work and felt panic rise.

I shook my head, like a dog shaking off water. I had more important things to do. Survival things. I had to make sure that no one down the pub would realise that I knew absolutely nothing whatever about soccer.

12: The Last Person

My lack of devotion to football had been, of course, nothing unusual among the youthful intelligentsia of my college days. It was in fact highly fashionable. In 1980, sport was for rugger-bugger Tories and their lumpen lackeys. Sexy post-punks and their radical ilk smoked rolling tobacco, drank Guinness, talked revolution.

At some point in the late eighties or early nineties, this all died. Soccer mushroomed even in the liberal pages of *The Paper*. I, though, took no more part in this sea change than I had in the Summer of Love. I was rarely even aware of who was leading the Premiership, and for my national team, I felt emotions which only a good German or a decent Yank can possibly understand: mere relief whenever the gang of repulsive thugs allegedly representing *us* got kicked out of whatever, thus ending the revolting hysteria.

Ah yes, here it was. Sports News on Virgin Media. The Big Match.

—Oh no, for God's sake, I groaned. It was the worst possible result. England were playing France tonight.

I loved France dearly. France was the main surviving alternative model to free-market neo-con American ultra-liberal imperialism. France was cultured. France resisted Coca-Colonialism (as I intended boldly to call it in the VIP). France had workers' rights and a concern for social traditions. And splendid wine and attractive cafés and bold strikers and people who drove tractors through the walls of McD's. France had not invaded Iraq. It was true that most of these could be said of

Germany as well, but, like most people who study Germany, I did not really like the place very much. I found it fascinating but entirely unloveable. France, on the other hand, was very highly loveable. It was European. It *was* Europe. Yes, there was the odd glitch in liking France, such as Greenpeace boats being bombed and nuclear tests being continued, despite worldwide pleas, on the orders of Machiavellian Presidents who called themselves socialists but had collaborated with the Nazis. And the fact that France's multi-ethnicity seemed confined to the football team. But these were aberrations. Without France, and hence without the EU, where would we be? A mere client state of America! Had I found myself in a friend's or colleague's house with England vs France on the telly in the background, I would have openly applauded every French goal, as in all likelihood would the friend or colleague. But I could hardly do it in the local bloody pub, sitting next to Phil.

In any case, what was I thinking of? I couldn't stay and watch the match anyway. I had to escape from the pub soon and get back home to sort out the bloody gun.

But how could I leave an England match halfway through without making Phil and all Phil's mates think I was a weirdo who merited a nutting and whose sons deserved a good kicking? There was only one way: I had to get someone to call me away from the pub on some urgent pretext.

Who?

Sarah would still be on the plane. I could hardly leave a message asking her to call me as soon as she landed. Telling her that I had found a machine gun in our garden might well worry her somewhat, possibly even ruin the holiday. If I tried to tell her any other story she would know I was lying and suspect the worst. But I had to call someone, to get them to summon me from the pub.

There was only one person left.

13: Heiner Panke

As I waited for the phone to be answered, I drummed my fingers and looked absent-mindedly at the photo of the bearded man with his arm round my neck.

The man in the photo was, of course, Heiner Panke, the subject of my PhD thesis ('Heiner Panke's Stories: The Strategic Self as Literary Resistance in the GDR', Frankfurt, 1989). We had become good friends and in 1991 Panke had sworn to me personally, in writing (I still had the letter), that I need have no fear of the revelations flooding out of the old East Germany. *My little doctor, I can swear to you here and now that no one will* ever *find my name on a list of Stasi agents, those scum who betrayed their friends for peanuts.* Armed with this scriptural promise, I had continued to make sure that Panke's books stayed on the reading lists (we academics may be appallingly underpaid these days, but we are still the gatekeepers of literary immortality, backlist sales and British Council grants). In 2003, files from the former Soviet Union revealed that Panke had indeed never been a wretched little Stasi agent who spied on his friends for peanuts. No, he had been a fully paid major in the KGB from 1977 to 1989, spying on everyone, including the Stasi itself.

A blow, of course, but fortunately no humanities lecturer has ever been kicked out just for being utterly wrong. After all, not a single university expert on East Germany in the summer of 1989 had predicted the fall of the Berlin Wall at any time in the foreseeable future.

No one lost their job over that little matter, did they? Certainly not. And things blow over. Those were confusing times, after all. We all made mistakes, back then . . .

—Hello?

—Oh, hi, Mum, it's only me. Look, just a quick one to ask a favour.

—Of course, dear. How are the children?

—What? Oh, fine. Away, actually, with Sarah and her parents.

—With Sarah's parents? They could have come to *us*.

—Oh, I didn't want to bother you.

—It wouldn't have been any bother, dear. I would have liked the visit. Still, you know best. Have you got them started on the piano yet?

—Well, no, actually, you see, Mum, the house is a bit small and . . .

—Oh, you can always make room for a piano! Are you coming down then?

—No. I mean, not just yet.

—You used to come down so much more often.

—Mmm. Mum, look, it's just, I've been sort of, well, nabbed into going out and I'm trying to work.

—How *is* your work, dear?

—Fine, fine. I'm giving a paper at the Oxford conference. A plenary paper, actually.

—Are you still writing about that man of yours who was really a spy?

—Yes, actually. Look, Mum, could you call my mobile in about half an hour? I need an excuse to escape from these people so I can sort out the bloody machine . . . the washing machine. Which is broken.

—You're not going to try to mend it yourself, are you, John dear?

—Mm? Oh, no, just, well, you know, Mum, just take a look.

—You've got better things to do with your time than that!

—Of course, Mum.

—So, how is *London*? Have you been to any interesting lectures and concerts?

—Oh, well, you know, it's early days, Mum, and with the kids and work, and . . .

Cha-chonk!

—John? My father's voice came in on the line from his shed. I licked my lips and swallowed. I could picture my father out there at the end of the garden. He had been out at work or out in the shed all my life, content to spend his days with no distinction other than having been the only conscript in his platoon of the Gloucestershire Regiment to have come back entirely whole from Korea.

—Aha, hi, Dad, there you are. So, how are you?

—Middling. Have you tried looking in Kentish Town?

—Dad, it's too late, we're here now. Anyway, I told you, yes, we looked everywhere in north London.

—You should have asked your mother and I to come up and help you.

—Your father and I *did* live in London for many years, you know, dear.

—Mum, Dad, I know, I can even remember bits of it. But look, it wouldn't have done any good. We paid the going rate and that's all there is to it.

—Oh, but those ruddy estate agents can pull the wool over anyone's eyes, John. Bloody vultures. The lot of them deserve to be shot. They'll skin you alive unless *you know the area*, you see! Have you looked in Finsbury Park? Or Archway?

—Dad, we looked everywhere. There isn't anywhere people didn't find years ago. We even looked in Hackney, for God's sake, even though Christ knows what we'd do about schools there.

—Well, I don't understand it. Your mother and I are only ordinary working people . . .

—. . . workers of the brain, John, but workers!

—Yes, Mum.

—John, when you were born we almost bought a semi in Cricklewood. And we could have done it too, quite easily, you know. Have you looked in Cricklewood?

—Way out of our league, Dad.

—That was before we decided to move back to the West Country, for the air, dear, for your health. And your father's nerves, of course.

—Yes, Mum, I know all that.

—I suppose we were silly sods, looking back. I suppose we should have bought the bloody thing and kept it for ever. Bought in to capitalism.

—Mmmm, yeah, maybe, Dad.

—But you see, dear, we all thought that with the White Heat and everything, well, that was all going to change, wasn't it? It was going to be what you *did* that mattered, not what you *owned*.

—Yes, Mum, that would have been nice.

—John, look, I don't bloody well understand it. You're a *university lecturer*, for God's sake. Your grandmother in Cricklewood cleaned for several university lecturers and *they* all lived in St John's Wood and Hampstead. Or Swiss Cottage, at least. Have you tried Kilburn? It's full of Irish, of course, but it's not too far out, by tube. What did you say you were earning now, John? How much? Are you sure? Your cousin earns well over double that and he's only an accountant.

Christ, in my day accountants were just glorified bloody bookkeepers, that's all we thought of them and that's all they were paid . . .

—Dad, I'm fine, don't worry about me! We're very happy here. Look, Mum, Dad, I've got to go now. Will you call me in half an hour, Mum? We can have a proper chat then.

—That'll be nice. Don't worry about things, John dear.

—John, take my advice: if you just tighten your belts for a bit, you'll soon be able to pay off some of that bloody mortgage.

—Yes, Dad.

—Oh, and next time you come down, take the old A304. It's much shorter. You see, if you come off at . . .

Listening to my father's useless information, I suddenly realised that my utter ignorance of Wii games and the latest bands would soon become an inability to say anything meaningful to our sons about anything. I would be able to tell them about what had worked for me in the last quarter of the twentieth century, but that would be just as much history to them as my father's insights into how one got on in the world, or got from A to B, in the fifties and sixties.

—The A304. Right, Dad. Look, I've got to shoot. I mean, I've got to shoot off. Go back to work. Mum, call me later then?

—I will, dear. Don't worry, I'm sure something will come up.

—Oh yes, Mum, don't worry.

—Here, what about looking in West Hampstead, John? Or Queens Park?

—Bye-e!

I slotted the phone back into its wall-mounted recharger. It bleeped. I looked down at the toy-littered floor and wondered for a second where the hell I was.

66

Christ, what a time to find a bloody gun in the garden!
Just when I was . . .
Stop!
Suddenly I knew exactly what to do.

14: What We Do Not Know

Three minutes later I stepped back from treading down the earth in the refilled hole.

So simple! Sod the bloody police. This was my week of work to save my life. It was my last chance to make things right, to have my education pay off at last, restore justice to the world. The gun could wait there safely until I came back in triumph from Oxford.

There are many things hidden in the earth. Roman coins pour out on to the boots of men digging for gas mains. Cattle plod about upon the gold-stuffed ship graves of Saxon kings. Priceless chalices, buried in fear, their sole keepers hacked to death without talking, wait for millennia a mere foot too deep for the yearly plough. Things get forgotten. Whole valleys full of kings. The Warsaw Pact. The gun had lain quiet for twenty years: it could stay there for one more bloody week.

Yes, once the VIP was safely done and delivered, I would call the cops and they could hold me for as long as they liked! Of course, it would be pretty stressful for Sarah and the kids to find the house full of armed police and myself under arrest, but everything would soon be cleared up. Hmm. And actually, Sarah could hardly expect me to pay back all those nights and days of childcare if I was in a police cell, could she?

True, it might feel bizarre, this week, to look out at my garden and know there was an Armalite lying there. And obviously, I'd never be able to tell Sarah that I'd deliberately waited a week before calling the authorities. For the rest of our lives I would have a little, tiny, harmless secret from my darling wife.

Well, so what? I was man enough for that. It was a marriage, for God's sake, not a confessional. I mean, it would not be the first time I'd kept a meaningless little secret from Sarah.

Had I told her that the first-choice candidate for my new job had in fact dropped out because he had taken a serious look at house prices and decided to keep his family in their leafy, well-schooled suburb of Leeds? It had seemed unnecessary. Had I told her that among my many reasons for wanting to leave Sheffield had been the fear that a certain little affair with a postgraduate student (not strictly speaking one of my *own* students, of course!) was getting a wee bit out of hand? Why would I tell her that? I mean, for God's sake, I'm a *humanities lecturer*. What does anyone expect?

What we do not know . . .

That was OK then.

I walked out of the front door for the first time since Sarah and the kids had left. The small, quiet house leaped away from behind me and gave way to the big loud London night. Our Victorian ceilings, high perhaps by modern standards but still low by human standards, were replaced instantly by the vast and timeless sky. I looked up at the stars and breathed deeply: my troubles fled from me at the speed of light.

I headed for the pub.

15: An Englishman's Nightmare

My pubbing days lay deep in the last, lost century. Of course, as you age, pubs naturally turn from exciting places where you never know what is going to happen into boring places where the same old thing happens into gruesome places where nothing is ever going to happen again. But in my case this natural process of disillusion had been underlined by geography.

When entering upon my chosen career, you see, I reckoned without the plain statistical fact that most university lecturers in England end up working for most of their lives in (and hence dragging their wives around) cities in the North or the Midlands.

I did not like cities in the North and the Midlands. They made me feel foreign. The drinking folk in these places (from whom, as *the people*, I expected great things) read newspapers I despised, passionately followed entire sports of which I knew nothing whatever (rugby league, for God's sake) and, while being authentically pro-Trades Union and anti-Tory, happily voiced opinions on immigration, asylum and punishment, corporal or capital, which left me blinking into my beer with the effort to avoid fatal eye contact. So, what with my responsible career, beloved wife and young children, I had not spent much time in the saloons of Sheffield, Leeds and Birmingham over the past decades. I had not been into a pub of an evening since we moved.

But tonight I was going out in the night to a London pub for the first time since 1989, and so I strode up to the Red Lion with a certain long-forgotten excitement.

I may even have been softly whistling a jig or reel. I cannot swear against it.

Then I found myself in an over-heated miniature Sky-TV multiplex that happened to serve unbelievably expensive lager and amazingly cheap spirits. I stopped dead and gazed around me through my misting specs.

Apart from the Big Screen there were four high-mounted television sets of large domestic size, making sure that no corner of the pub could possibly escape the Big Match. The Big Screen itself, with its ceaseless, insane bombardment of pub-quiz information zipping below the pictures and scrolling to the right of them, was half-masked by the heads of standing male drinkers, of whom a statistically improbable proportion were shaven-headed, their ringed ears standing out in alarming silhouette against the bright plasma.

I had landed myself in every liberal and cultured Englishman's worst nightmare: I was alone and surrounded at night by illiberal and uncultured Englishmen of perfect head-butting age and size, in noisily festive and patriotic mood, wearing replica football shirts.

—Mind your back, mate, said a voice, as three pints of lager sailed choppily past my left ear and a large beer gut squelched across my back. I turned, trying to smile in a bluff way, making sure I did not look down my vulnerable nose from on high. I never actually got as far as the manful quip, because the England teamsheet went up on the Big Screen. Everyone cheered and looked round. An Englishman amidst Englishmen, I could hardly do otherwise.

Each of the England players now got a few manic seconds of dedicated screen time, a flick-cut montage of their palatial homes, all-blonde girlfriends and bizarre celebratory routines that their semi-human ancestors would no doubt have understood perfectly well. In order not to seem completely ignorant of the dramatis personae if forced to chat about them later, I hoovered up the information flashing madly over the screen, selecting useful information for storage in the temporary files of my mind.

I was good at this sort of thing, having spent twenty-five years speedreading weighty tomes that would quite possibly never make it out again from the deep, ghostly stacks of university libraries. I now filled my brain RAM swiftly with faces, names, dates, teams, transfer values, salaries . . .

Salaries.

Bloody hell!

16: Mortgage Repayment: 2/6

I had, of course, heard about footballers' absurd salaries. But it was the sort of unbearable fact that I was normally able to blank out. Tonight there was no escaping the truth. These brutish young men earned in six months of kicking a ball about more than I would earn in my entire career. Or, not to beat about the bush, my life.

Yes, I knew pretty well exactly how much I would make in the remainder of my time. Enough to pay off our brand-new twenty-year mortgage by the time I retired, that was how much. By the time I finished working I would own outright a small terraced house in SE11, hoobloodyray, and be unable to afford to go on nice holidays or to help my sons or my little daughter to buy houses.

It could not be right. It was simply *not possible* that thick little head-butting bastards who had never even heard of Schumann could throw their money about on multiple Ferraris, hideous so-called mansions in Cheshire and ludicrous houses on artificial islands in Bahrain while I myself would quite probably never be able even to own a house with four proper bedrooms, enough space to walk past the pram in the hall and a nearby school that vaguely approached the national average.

It was plainly and simply *wrong*.

Their stupid kids, named after American bloody states, for God's sake, would swan about buoyed up by unearned income, whilst my children, my hard-working, lovely, clever children, were drowning in impossible mortgage repayments, with me powerless to save them.

My eyes glazed over, screening out reality. Of course, they would say, —*The market decides, tough.* Twenty years before, I might have had a counter-argument. I might well have argued, twenty years before, that the government should intervene to limit such ludicrous incomes, reapportion such blatantly unfair wages, block tax-evasive trusts or redistribute a little of such clearly undeserved wealth by inescapable taxation on luxury goods. Twenty years ago, I might well have pointed out the fact that in the GDR there was no unemployment. I would almost certainly have pointed, as everyone else did twenty years ago, to the striking progress of literacy in Cuba.

I had not suggested these particular alternatives for some years. Even Cuba was looking rather dodgy these days. But alternatives there still had to be, surely? To prevent thick young footballers from earning in a month what normal, decent people earned in ten years. Or people buying football clubs with the billions they had made trading shares acquired cunningly from economically illiterate, indigent pensioners in Siberia. Or a thousand number-crunching arseholes in the City getting million-quid bonuses and thereby inflating alleged national wages and property prices so much so that the rest of us poor sods had to suffer another hike in interest rates rather than tax those few bastards a teeny little bit more?

How had it happened?

Why?

Who asked for a winner-takes-all world?

What makes us think there is nothing that can be done about it?

Q: Which major Western nation state one hundred and twenty years ago forced, repeat *forced*, all the big landowners in approximately one-third of its sovereign territory to sell all but a few hundred acres of their land to their small tenant farmers at a government-set fair price, and even gave those small farmers one-hundred-year, negligible-interest, state-backed mortgages to buy the land with?

CLUE: In 1989, an elderly farmer I knew laughingly showed me the receipt for his family's last-ever payment of 2/6.

Q: 2/6?

A: Indeed. Half a crown. The country was Britain. The elected British Government in then-British Ireland did it. Because they had to. Because people were so furious about blatant unfairness that they had started making British Ireland ungovernable. Did they want Revolution? No. Communism? God forbid, they were decent Catholics. They just wanted the chance to buy, repeat *buy*, the little bit of land they worked. They just wanted fairness. And they demanded it with boycotts, then riots, then guns. So they got it.

Things *do* change. Things *can* change. Things *must* change. It is *not* enough to say that things are the way they are, full stop. That is simply the idiotic voice that says, —*Whatever is, is right*, the crass metaphysics of pure contingency. No, no: *the way things are means things cannot stay the way things are.* Discuss.

But change which way?

How done?

By whom?

Decides who?

—There you are, Prof John. Where the hell you been? I been fighting every cunt off this seat for you. You missed the warm-up, mate. Only just in time. Two pints behind already.

—I, um, sorry, Phil. My mum called.

—Oh, well then. Mums is mums. Boys, this is Prof John, our new neighbour. I also calls him Einstein. On account of his brain. Doctor of fucking German. Bit posh for us, eh? But he likes a scrap too. Going to come out on patrol. Tell you anything about Hitler and the Nazis, he will. Try him.

—Hi, er, boys. Lager, Phil?

—Yeah. Get two in for yourself, you're behind.

—Sure. Good idea, Phil.

Now I had been seen talking to tough men I was better able to engage in the Darwinian struggle for bar space, and was soon inserting myself crabwise into a fine space directly before the beer pumps. Suddenly it occurred to me.

What if I finished the VIP, emailed it to a colleague and then called the police on the evening just before the Oxford conference. Imagine: *Plenary national peer-group paper given in absentia at Oxford as* Newsnight *East Germany expert questioned by police over machine gun in garden.* Enough to make *The Paper*, surely? Maybe even the TV news. God, if I just got the chance, just one chance, to make that one vital, memorable sound bite on the box! *Someone* has to get the next BBC series, after all. *Someone* has to be catapulted out of all this crap and into . . .

—Yes please, I can get you?

I looked up and found myself staring into a pair of cool blue female eyes.

17: A Goal for England

I blinked, and in a flash, with the edge-of-vision skills common to my profession, I had also taken in a fine pair of breasts without in the slightest appearing to look at them. The Polish barmaid Phil had spoken of, presumably. Pretty? Yes. But there was something else about her that made me stare.

—Hi, what I can get you? she asked impatiently. I held up a finger as a sign for her to be quiet. Suddenly I was back on home territory and filled with magisterial confidence.

—What? she mouthed, scowling lightly. But she was so taken aback that she obeyed.

—Say that again please?

—What I can get you?

—No, yes, hold on. Wait. Don't tell me. Yes. I've got it. *Cottbus*, said I firmly.

The barmaid blanched. She came immediately close.

—Don't-speak-German-to-me.

—But you're from Saxony.

—I am from Poland.

—You sound Saxon.

—Look, if you were German would you tell the English people in a shithole like this that you were German?

—Perhaps not.

—So here I am Polish, yes? How many nice cold lagers, sir?

—Um, what? Oh, yes, sorry. Three, please.

Well, an East German girl, here! That was a bit of luck.

I, that is, we, Sarah and I, could invite her round. For dinner. She could come into the university perhaps. It might be interesting for my students to hear it from her mouth rather than mine. Nice mouth too. She would be able to tell them about the aspects of life in the GDR that had been worth saving but had all been swept away by untrammelled capitalism. Sexual liberty, for example, sanctioned by Marxist theory and backed up by abortion virtually on demand or generous state childcare provision. Women's rights, yes indeed. She was youngish and yes, pretty. It would be quite fun, knowing her secret. A bit like in the old days of those bold, semi-legal poetry clubs in Dresden and Leipzig. Sharing. Comradely.

—Don't worry, I said softly, as she squirted nitrogen-packed lager into the last of the three glasses, —I'll keep your secret.

—I hope, she bit her lip. —Three pints.

—Call it ten pounds.

—Is ten pounds fifty.

—Christ. Well, um, call it twelve then.

—Thank you.

I winked at the girl, grabbed my pints, balanced them carefully together (*Ha! Now who's a nancified pen-pusher?*) and peeled manfully away from the bar, suggesting boldly that people should watch their backs while feeling her eyes fixed on my own.

Yes, it might be fun to pop in here, now and again over the next week. After all, the Very Important Paper was on a radical poet from Saxony. Perhaps if I talked to her it would help my paper get some new perspective, some little up-to-date snippet of information or social context that might make the bastards in the media sit up and take notice.

—There you are, Prof John, squeeze in here, mate. Nice, isn't she? Polish.

—Ah, said I, hoisting my beers over my new companions' heads and craning them down on to the table
with good skills, gloating warmly in the possession of
my secret information.

—We're looking in fucking good shape, I got to say,
Prof John. Fuck off! That was no foul, you lying, diving,
queer French cunt! You blind Spanish twat, who's side
you on? You can't give Laggsy a yellow fucking card
for that!

Now was the time to swiftly regurgitate a pointless
and just-collected fact that I would have completely
forgotten by tomorrow. Rather like in my finals at
Oxford.

—Fuck! I cried swiftly. —That's Laggsy out of the
next game, isn't it?

—Tha's Laggsy oot the next game, said a Scottish
commentator, as the teenage English multi-millionaire
in question spat gobfuls of obscenity at the referee, at
the French team, at God.

—Fuck, you're right, Prof John. Course. Fucking blind
Spanish cunt.

—Diving French cunt!

—What chance we got if the fucking ref's foreign
too?

—Shoot the cunt!

I nodded sadly, and noted the small but unmistakable motion of heads and eyes in my direction from
around the table. Done it. *Normality Established: Now
Reducing Head-Butting Preparedness to Level Green.* With
my place at the table now assured by my evidently
profound knowledge of soccer, I raised my glass
happily and found that when I set it down again with
a cocky thud it was already almost empty.

—Oi, Prof John, nice to meet you. What you fancy?
asked one of the men round the table.

Soon, I was quaffing a brand-new pint, and, before I knew it, another.

It was OK. My mother would call any minute and then I would go. I was just making contact with the neighbours, for the benefit of the whole family. God, I had forgotten the fine, fizzing feel of beer in your head. And the even finer rush of oneness around a pub table, pals that give you back-up for once. In the gang, of the people, among . . .

18: A Shit-Hole Run by the Red Army

Hoorah! A goal! For England! Cheers, why not? More drinks? Of course!

This was pretty damn good fun, actually, and what the hell was wrong with it? After all, the England team was almost as satisfyingly multiracial as the French and it was true: we *had* won the war against Nazism. And soccer was such a *European*, indeed *non-aligned*, thing to be good at. Thoroughly un-American! Yes, when you thought about it, England's passion for soccer showed that we did, after all, have cultural links which might yet resist the McCorporations and Hollywood!

The whole evening was clearing my head wonderfully, to be honest. Forget about the gun, it could just stay there for now, so what? A good decision, to come to the pub. Got me out of the bubble, blown away the cobwebs, set me up perfectly for my week of work.

More beer.

Why not? Who knows? Who cares?

What was I worrying about, anyway? The Very Important Paper was all but finished. So nearly finished that they had given it a *plenary* session. Exactly. More or less there. God, if only bloody Panke had agreed to come over in person, the selfish sod. *That* would get the media along. Maybe if I told him about the barmaid? Panke being like he is. Anyway, so what? Christ, I was going to show them all just who exactly had shot his bolt. Not John Goode, that was certain!

—Hey, Prof John, how long your missus away?

—Whole week, I grinned.

—Here, Prof John, after the match you fancy my place to see the new Abiyak DVD? Fucking funny! Fucking balls on that little fucker, eh?

—Aha! I grinned, to cover the fact that I was still trying to work out who the hell Abiyak was. After several seconds, during which I was forced to take refuge in my pint, I realised that I did not recognise the name of *Abiyak* because the last time I had heard him referred to had been in a pub in Sheffield, where they had called him *Oobyook*. In normal English, his name was Hubby Huck. He was a comedian whose work I had only ever seen once, at a meeting in a tough miners' club during the Strike. His act, called *Hubby Gets His Oats*, had consisted of him walking about with a child's hobby horse and wearing a guardsman's busby, props which he used as the excuse for endless crassly mimed double entendres about helmets, beavers and riding. He had begun his act by asking if there were any Pakis in the audience, and upon hearing silence, had yelled, —*Thank fuck for that!* to huge applause. I would absolutely have pointed out his blatant misogyny and racism to the stout striking Yorkshire miners around me in the club if they had not all been laughing so loudly.

—You coming along after then, Prof John?

—Well, look, that's really kind of you, but I've got this piece of work to finish, a job, it's pretty important really, might be a promotion in it, you never know. So I'd better not. But, thanks, lads!

—No worries. If you can't you can't. Your round, innit, Prof John?

—What? Sorry? Oh yeah, of course. Lagers, all?

I strode tall to the bar, a man taking his turn buying a large round for many tough men. My phone went off in my pocket. I decided not to answer my mother. Obviously, I had to buy this round in any case. I had accepted drinks, so I was obliged, *socially obligated* indeed, to buy them back. It was simply a matter of English working-class cultural etiquette. Which surely deserves as much respect as any other cultural etiquette? Absolutely. I could hardly start my new life, my life and my whole family's life, here, with my new neighbours, by failing to respect the dominant local cultural norms, could I? Certainly not. Yes, of course, I might have my own personal reservations about certain behavioural phenomena within this culture, such as sexism and racism and mindless violence, but, then again, I had reservations about many things. *I personally* would of course never pressurise a woman to wear a veil, nor accept *The Protocols of the Elders of Zion* as a guide to foreign policy, but did that mean that I went about trying to impose my 'First World' (!) version of what *civilisation* meant on to members of the Muslim *ummah*? Certainly not! Liberalism cannot be imposed. Unlike certain so-called world statesmen, I don't pretend to see myself as the world's policeman. Everyone has a valid point of view, after all.

So that was all right.

Anyway, I fancied another drink and the barmaid was right in front of me already, pouring my lagers unasked, as if I were quite one of her regulars. I smiled, warm in my possession of her secret.

—You know my country, so? she asked, at last.

—I used to live there. I live up the road now. I teach German, at university.

—You are university professor? Of German? Wow.

—Ha, I laughed, and for a dizzy second I was hit by a perfectly solid vison of a life with a woman who wanted absolutely nothing more than I could offer without effort.

I loved Sarah, of course. But I was haunted more and more by the thought, no, by the certainty, that I had not really delivered the life which I had at least implicitly promised her. On the other hand, think: *Frau Universitätsprofessor Doktor*? Ha ha, yes, a little barmaid like this, from a crap place like Cottbus, would be happy for life with that title! She would never seem tired or reproachful, she would never make me feel I had not really delivered, she would think a pathetic little terraced house in SE11 was a palace, she would treat me like . . .

Christ, to slip and slide inside, a simply wanted man again!

—Yep. Society and culture in the former East Germany. My speciality. John Goode. Doctor John Goode, actually, but hey: John. Great to meet you, er . . . ?

—Gretchen.

—Hi, Gretchen. I mean, the thing is, you know, people over here just know nothing. It's important for them to not just swallow the idea that *the West is always best*, isn't it? Of course, no one's saying the East was anything like the socialist paradise it claimed to be, but the regime was tied by its own ideology, right? Unemployment simply couldn't happen, could it? And think about it: if the East hadn't been there, as an ideological challenge, would the West ever have had social security and things like that? I don't think so. I really don't. And with the East *not* there, well, what's happening to the West, eh? You tell me. *Bush and globalisation*, right! You know what, I was thinking, maybe you could come in to the university one day, we'd pay you, of course, and talk to my students about it. We pay quite well, actually.

—I could use some more money. But what would I say to them? They are clever young people.

I looked into her blue eyes.

—Exactly. You could, for example, I mean, just as an idea, it's something I've been writing about recently, you could explain about culture in the GDR, anything you wanted to say, really. Women and sexual liberation, maybe? Yeah, that could be fun. We could have a chat about it sometime, one evening this week, maybe, when there's no Big Match on.

—Perhaps, she said.

—Don't worry, it would just be something to help them realise that there *are* alternatives and that there *were* things worth saving in the old East, right?

—Worth saving? Things that was worth saving from East Germany?

I refocused hastily on the front of her eyes rather than their blue depths.

—Hmm? Well, I mean, you know, apart from culture, and security, and women's rights, there was a sense of togetherness, of community, of people helping each other, of actually caring about each other, of, you know, well, of . . .

—Of course people help each other out. They have to because they are stuck all in a shithole run by the Red Army and they all have nothing.

—Sorry?

—The most people does what they are told. Except the ones that work for the Stasi. If you inform on your neighbours you get a week by the Black Sea, very fine. If you are clever at licking arsch you get a little summer-house they rob from some poor old farmer. Maybe a plastic car with three cylinders, very fine! And if liberals in the West really like your books or songs or films, the high communists might let you have a bank account

85

in Switzerland, like they all have one, like Mr Big Shot Brecht had one. You might even be allow go to the West and say things is not *quite* perfect socialism in the GDR yet. But, of course, you must left your family behind and kept on saying on all interviews that America is racist imperialist warmongering hell. If you try to leave without they allow, like they mostly do not allow, they shoot you down and you are hanging on the wire. They keep shooting people right till 1989. Then the Russians go bust. So nice Gorby tell that bunch of arsch-lickers that it is all over, they will not help them any more if they shot people down in the streets like this *Tiananmen Square Solution* they want to make. So goodbye, GDR. It all fall to pieces next day. Save? What hell is there to save about that?

—Um, well, I . . .

—If my great-grandfather had sense, he were gone to America when anyone could go there, the stupid arsch-hole. And what would my family missed out? The First World War, the inflation, Hitler, Auschwitz, Stalingrad, Dresden, forty-five years of the Red Army. Oh, very nice history. The GDR? You crazy? Why the hell you waste your life teaching young people about this heap of crap? Maybe you stop to drinking and think about what you do. The GDR? Just tell them it was only a shithole run by the Red Army and now it is gone, thanks be God.

—A what?

—A shithole run by the Red Army. What else you need say about it? You can manage those all, or you want a tray, Herr Professor Doktor?

19: Careers Advice

I turned away from the bar and aimed my tray back towards the table. She was only a stupid barmaid, for Christ's sake. What did she know? She had bought into the lie with the rest of them. She was just . . .

A shithole run by the Red Army?

Ridiculous. Uneducated tripe. Although in one very distant sense she did have a point: it was not quite so hot an academic topic as I had confidently believed back in the eighties. Or rather, had been led to believe.

Oh, that old bastard Professor White! I could still recall every word of his fateful speech to me in his gorgeous suite of college rooms, back in 1984. God, Oxford: I had loved the place. When first I came up from my parents' flat-fronted little house in the middle of nowhere, it had felt like being translated to a better, golden world. After three years there, I had become used to it, and wanted to stay on after my finals.

—Well, one must play to one's strengths if one really wants to do research, John. 'The Great War Roots of National Socialist Discourse'? Well, yes, of course, a fascinating subject. But, John, think. If you apply for a British Academy bursary, to study Nazism, here at Oxford, you will find yourself up against some clever people. Some very clever people indeed. The topic is always immensely popular. Do you really think that *you* can have something new to say about National Socialism? It may be that your best bet is to do something a little more, shall we say, current? And a little less, shall we say, congested? Now, for example, you have actually met some of these bold East German protest poets during your year abroad, you said? Who? Heiner Panke? Can't say I've heard of him. Then again, I've heard of very few people after Kafka, ha ha! But that's the whole point, eh, John? Far less trouble with methodology and theory when you can actually be the first to present the material. Now think about that! That's what I call a niche! You can make it your very own, do you see? Make yourself the sole expert! Thompson in London, he'd be the chap for you, for that sort of thing. Yes, something a bit different. More concrete. More *jobs* in that field too, John. GDR studies, oh yes, that's very much the coming thing, what with all this business about cruise missiles and evil empires and God knows what nonsense else. Very current. Very, what do they all say these days? *Cutting-edge*. Ridiculous Americanism. That awful woman can't last for ever. Things will soon get back to normal and then, why, John, in three or four years' time you'll be able to *write your own job description*, as they say! Even this old place, slow to change as she is, and perhaps wisely too, will no doubt eventually make a place for *that sort of thing* on the syllabus. Yes, yes, you could find yourself *very well placed indeed*, in five or six years' time, John. Do you know, I think we may indeed have found the door that is meant only for you, eh? Ha ha! Now, you must excuse me, we have rather an important meeting about a vineyard in Bordeaux which some of the Fellows want us to buy. Not the sort of thing one does lightly, but . . . Yes, anyway, excellent. Goodbye, John . . .

God, if only I had stuck to my guns.

Hitler and the Nazis! Every five minutes there's something on the box about Hitler. The swastika sells books that would normally be stuck for ever in the library stacks. If only I had acted straight away when the Wall came down! I was still young enough, back then, to reinvent myself. Too late now . . .

A shithole run by the Red Army?

Could she be right? Had I simply wasted my life? No, no, that wasn't possible. There had to be some way round this one, some way I could . . .

Of course! Father Eamon! He would set me right!

—Oi, come on, Prof John. What you doing? Get over here with those beers.

—Yes, sorry, Phil. I was just . . .

—Why-are-we-waiting?

I forced my feet to yield to my shrinking willpower and made it to the table, where a grateful crowd of orc-like hands clutched for the glasses before the tray even hit the table. I raised my own pint weakly in reply to the jolly mockery about my tardiness, then sank back as quickly and deeply into my seat as I could. The noise of the television and the cries of the massed drinkers now seemed to issue from some faraway planet. The pictures on the Big Screen looked like an ancient newsreel.

—Yeeeees! Goal! Fucking gorgeous!

—Ye-es! cried I weakly. The noise of the cheering pub passed over me like a big green wave. It surged into my ears and through my mind. Feverishly, I gulped icy lager. I needed to talk to Father Eamon and I needed to talk to him now.

—Inger-land! Inger-land!

—Tra-fal-gar! Wa-ter-loo!

—Ha ha ha!

—Collaborating cunts!

—Ha ha ha!

I had to leave. I made myself suddenly look round, as if in bleary response to a vibrating alert. I patted my pockets, as if searching for my phone, and looked at the dead screen as if at a text. I was pretty sure I had done it all convincingly.

—Oh shit, I groaned loudly, and got quickly to my feet.

—What's up, Prof John?

—Text from my mum. I've got to go and call her.

—Got to look after your mum, Prof John!

—Yeah. Sorry, er, boys. Excuse me, ta . . .

I shoved my way apologetically from the table. I aimed for the door. I turned for no reason and saw that the barmaid was watching me while she poured drinks for another man. I walked swiftly out from the pub and into the rain, trying not to let myself run until I was clear, already reaching for my phone, as if there, in my pocket, some wonderful salvation was waiting.

20: Antarctica Breaks Away

The pub doors swung shut, sealing off the warm, beery heaven behind them, and I ran up the bleak street through the cold rain, scrolling through my address book.

Christ. London? This?

I mean, who decided to arrange this country so that you had, absolutely *had*, to call the bloody property market right once every ten years? So that the *only* thing that actually mattered these days, the sole factor that decided your life and your children's chances, for anyone on a remotely normal income, was whether or not you bought a house in London ten years ago (—*I know, John! It's terrible! I really don't know what we'd do if we were looking now. It really isn't right!'*). Ha bloody ha. So nice of you to sympathise.

And what can I do about it now? Nothing. Economise, like Mum and Dad said? Well, yes, that would be really useful, if a colour telly still cost 5 per cent of a middle-class home and Majorca was only for the jet set and Edward the bloody Confessor was on the throne. If it could help get us a semi with sash windows in some place near a park where we could dare let the boys go out on their bikes alone on an early summer's evening, of course I'd tighten my belt for a few years. Tighten it? I'd pull it in until it crushed my liver against my backbone! But what can I do that is ever going to even scratch the top layer of paint off a one hundred and seventy-five bloody grand mortgage? Nothing! All I can do is pay up and pay up and pay up, every month, for ever and ever and ever and, and . . . and, oh God, Dad, why oh why didn't you just take out the biggest bloody mortgage you could get in the seventies and grab the biggest place you could lay your hands on before that cow Maggie went and encouraged every . . .

I found Father Eamon's number.

And what if, what if the most dreadful of all *what ifs* came true? What if (please God, no!) I'd paid through the nose at the top of the market for somewhere that was actually only just at the very high-tide mark of quasi-gentrification? If the social waters of London receded those vital few hundred yards for another ten years?

I rang.

Antarctica was once joined with South America and Australia.

The animals who happened to be standing in what is now Antarctica were all doomed on the very day in some rainy season all those aeons ago when the straits finally grew too wide to swim. No evolutionary leap could save them now. They continued to change and struggle for forty million years or more, but they might as well all have lain down and died that very day. Nothing of them remains.

And what about us? What about people socio-genetically engineered to succeed under Crafty Harold and Darling Teddy? Is there no place laid aside as a reserve for us? No quiet, backwoods peninsula where students are respectful, big houses are cheap and essays are done by hand? Where hard-working state-school boys are taking over the Georgian rectories while the gin-sodden posh sell up as they melt away in the face of history's inevitable march and punitive taxation? Where soccer players end up running pubs, if they're lucky? Where accountants are glad to be socially noticed by grammar-school teachers and where the rough people live jolly lives of full employment and weak beer, in lifelong work at sixteen, married off in a rented council house by twenty and safely waked shortly after sixty-five, all as planned for by Nye Bevan's experts?

God rot the blasted woman! If only the bloody useless IRA *had* got her!

—Come on, Eamon, answer the bloody phone!

No one could say that I had actually *promised* Sarah anything when courting her.

We never talked like that, obviously. Absurd, no way. We were young, it was love. I was a part-time tutor at the University of London; she was one of my students. God, I fancied her. I never dared even to try to kiss her, because what could a broke, four-eyed postgrad offer a beautiful girl like her? But the term before her finals, I landed my first real lecturing job. Being no longer her teacher, I was free to kiss her if I dared. And being now a proper lecturer, I dared. Soon afterwards I visited the house in Exeter to tell her parents I wanted to marry her. And when I looked back now, I was pretty sure that around that time I had hinted, or suggested, or at least acted and talked in such way that she could clearly infer, in a perfectly modern way, yes, true, but still, that by agreeing to marry me she would be choosing a life that, in the perfectly normal, natural, unspoken way of things, was going to involve a place like her parents' place, at the absolute very least, before very long at all, almost certainly in some nice (though vaguely defined) part of north London. Not a life that would drag her from one northern city to another, culminating triumphantly in this flat-fronted little terraced house in SE11 with not even enough space for an upright bloody piano . . .

—Well, John Goode, by God!

—Eamon! Thank Christ! I need to talk postmodernism and I need to talk it now!

21: Sucking Diesel

Eamon Sheehan was a gay historian I knew from the Irish pub in Kentish Town in the eighties. He had been a young man in Ireland at the time of the Pope's hysteria-inducing visit, days when a military coup was rumoured, holy statues were regularly seen to move and the ambitious all fled to London or America. Young Eamon, who hailed, said he, from a boghole somewhere beyond nowhere, mistook the gaseous cramps of the dying old cloth for the twitchings of renewed life and hitched himself, as did several hundred other likely young Gaelic lads in unlikely jumpers that heady year, to what turned out to be the fast-disappearing coat-tails of the Church: he found a vocation.

Another life washed up at one of history's tidemarks.

A lesson, no doubt, for all of us who tremble at the sight of massed young Muslim males chanting the name of their God: this, too, will pass as soon as they all get steady jobs in the financial-services sector. Unless they don't.

Eamon saw the darkness following certain unsavoury revelations concerning the priests of his own childhood. This was in the summer of 1989, just before my own job prospects were mortally threatened by the collapse of communism. He swiftly reinvented himself as a post-modern historian of Irish Catholic imagery, wrote a book full of photographs called *Kitsch Kerry Christ*, which you can find on practically every gay couple's shelves, and got a job teaching art history in Dublin; I speedily married Sarah and went off to Manchester and post-Germanunification studies. Having such differing lifestyles, we had met only rarely since, but the bond of those frightening months, our time spent cowering under fire in the trenches of utter career ruin with thirty bearing down upon us and our CVs blown to tatters, kept us in desultory e-contact: we had seen the Horror together.

—Are you busy, Eamon?

—Are you drunk, Johnnyboy?

—God no. Well, maybe a very little tipsy. So, hey, Eamon, have you got a minute or two?

—Hold on, let me just fire off a sexy reason for my handsome avatar leaving the virtual bar. Shall I claim that a gang of my postgrads just knocked on my door, wanting pre-club liveners in Stephen's Green? Why not? In cyberspace, no one can hear you lie. We live in the last brief golden age of the written word, an Eden where ugly fuckers with good keyspeed and ready wit can still arouse that vital first erotic spark. Universal webcams will spell the final victory of Body over Spirit and the death knell of European dentistry. Till then, I lie as fast and brightly as I can. There. Virtual persona off for cocktails. Now, what gives in the sad bad world of so-called reality?

—Eamon, I need your help.

—Then you must be in a fine old pickle, begob.

—I'm writing a big paper for the peer-group conference, a plenary paper, actually.

—You? A plenary paper? Well fuck me sideways. Not on that shite KGB-funded poet you pushed for years, I assume?

—Yes, actually, but that's the trouble: I've sort of, I don't know why, I've just started to, well, *think* about things. I mean, what if I've wasted my life, Eamon? What if the place I dedicated my life to studying was only ever a shithole run by the Red Army?

—Sounds like a reasonable description.

—So what if all my work just doesn't *mean* a bloody thing?

—Oho! Got you in one.

—You have?

—I see, my man, that you are suffering from an acute attack of losing trust in meaninglessness. You, hopeless fool, have backslid into wanting it all to *mean* something.

—My God, Eamon, you're right!

—Johnnyboy, I can see that we need to look at this again from first base. Allow me to demonstrate it by a concrete example, you hopeless Brit. I shall read to you from my blurb accompanying an exhibition hereabouts. This will, I think, make the importance of postmodern theory clear. Let's see . . . blah blah blah . . . oh yes, this is where I start to hit the sweet spot:

O'Leary's almost undetectable interventions in her (re)found objects, her Mother's/Madonna's fetishes of unquestioned adoration, undercut the whole project of 'Western' forays into so-called subjectivism and primitivism. Here the primitive is the known and the subjective gaze the conviction of Truth itself. With this subterranean dynamic, O'Leary structurally insists that the viewer question her engagement as viewer with the act of viewership, constructing an implicitly infinite (and hence perhaps by definition heavenly) range of meta-/physical subjects.

—Bloody hell, Eamon.

—Talk about heavy slice, eh? Now, tell me what that means, Johnnyboy?

—What? Well, um, I suppose it sort of means that . . .

97

—It means that if the right member of the curatocracy comes along to the gallery and I lay it on them with a trowel and they go away feeling that this could be a handy subject on which to base some of their own priceless spouting, a cokehead neurotic by the name of O'Leary makes a mint for strewing white rooms at random with her dead mother's yellowed collection of sixties parish newspapers from the ol' County Clare. And I, as her discoverer, the man who made her fit for theorising about, get on to the panel of the Dublin Modern Art Biennial next year, hence able to make young people's careers at will by the imprimatur of my bullshit, hence getting laid wherever I go despite being almost fifty and having European teeth, as happy as a cardinal in a home for orphaned boys, is what it fucking well means.

—Right. So, you mean, I should just think about how . . .

—Weaken not, Johnnyboy! Last millennium we had things called Right and Wrong. Guidebooks for life. You yours, I mine. The Pope and Charlie Marx. Until we were forced to realise that the Virgin Mary only works for illiterate farmers, that Lenin was a disaster for the twentieth century and that the Labour Theory of Value is right up there on the sanity chart next to the Holy Trinity.

—I suppose so.

—So if *we* were wrong, does that mean the *others* were right? The boring, hard-working, election-voting, shop-keeping, job-holding, tax-paying, child-rearing, mortgage-servicing, acceptable-level-of-violence-maintaining middle-of-the-road fuckers? *Right all along? Them? Admit that?*

—But, Eamon, if we admitted that, we'd be saying, well, we'd be saying that . . .

—Indeed. We would be saying that spoiled priests and defrocked Marxists should by rights be grateful to get work stacking shelves. Are we going to say that? Like fuckery we are! Instead, we shall say (wait for it!) that if *our* right was not right after all, there is, in fact, *obviously no such thing as Right and Wrong!*

—Christ yes, I'm starting to remember the theory. Phew!

—Phew indeed. So prepare to play and stop whingeing about *meaning!*

—OK. I will. I promise.

—Then let us see. How the fuck have you managed to get your peers remotely interested in this arsehole poet of yours?

—Well, he's been on the TV a lot in Germany recently. Gone on to politics in Saxony. Won a seat in Dresden. Anti-Iraq War, anti-globalisation, you know the sort of thing. Doing very well. And the German government's just collapsed, so I suppose that *may* have made a difference.

—And you are, as I understand it, the only UK bozo who has been insightful enough or desperate enough to have kept the faith with him all these years?

—It's only thanks to me that he's still on any bloody reading lists at all.

—Grand so. You are thus sole gatekeeper to a man on the box. A hearty dose of the ould pomo schtick and you are home and dry, surely?

—Yes, but I've forgotten how to *do* pomo, Eamon!

—Johnny, all you do is ensure that your discourse remains non-judgmental, anti-patriarchal and free of the implicitly crypto-fascistic desire for an absolutist closure modelled on the psycho-cultural blueprint of the essentially aggressive and always potentially rapist male orgasm.

—Coo.

—Coo indeed. You deny the *very notion of truth*. Which you have to admit comes in kinda handy if the truth is that you dedicated your life to studying a shithole run by the Red Army that no longer even exists and the man you strung your whole career on was a lying KGB-funded whore.

—Well, yes.

—The lesson continueth. Surely to God, now, post-Iraq, faced with the New World Order, we know only too clearly that history (*HisStory/HerStory/OurStory/TheirStory*) is just that, a story, someone's wholly fucking owned story, a myth propagated as propaganda by the current sole world hegemon and its consciously hired or unconsciously enlisted scribes and phallogical collaborators.

—God, that was good. *Phallogical*.

—You like it? Yes, I got a fair bit of topspin on that one, I fancy. Heh heh. So now, where was I? Ah yes. In 1961 the East Germans claimed that the wall which they had no intention of building was to protect society against capitalism, correct?

—Yes.

—And having indeed built this wall after all, they then shot anyone who was insane enough to try to escape to capitalism?

—Well, yes.

—Shite, these dictators make it tough, don't they? I mean, if Pyongyang and Tehran only realised *how* easily they could get us Western liberals onside, eh? But let's see. OK then. Now, in 1989, at the so-called 'End of History' everyone was ready to call the East German position a lie. One story of history had apparently triumphed. But is this really so clear now? From where we have now come to, does it not seem possible that it is precisely walls that we need (and perhaps always needed) to protect viable and historically grounded societies –

—Such as French society?

—Such as French society. Good example. Everyone loves the French. Well, everyone except a few fucking irradiated Polynesians, but hey. Walls, yes, walls to protect functioning societies, such as French society, against the, the, let's see now, against the . . .

—How about *against the global locusts of the free market*?

—*Global locusts*? Holy God, now I like that one. That's never yours, is it? No offence, but it's just too good to be John Goode.

—No, the second most powerful German politician said it a couple of years ago.

—Well, fair play to him, we'll buy that for a dollar, I think. Yes, we need something to function as a protective wall between us and the *global locusts*, and until (in Monbiot's apt phrase) we organise the *counter-globalisation*, the nation state may in fact, may it not, be our one bulwark against *Coca-Cola-acculturation*, our only salvation from the subordination of all nations (and national faiths, national cultures) to the dictates of the WASP überpower?

—Wow, Eamon, that's great! I think I've got it! It's all coming back! Can I have a go?

—Take it away, Johnny, and be good!

—So, I mean, well, if we accept the above, as surely we must, is it *really* going too far to suggest, er, that East Germany was in some very real ways the more authentically *German* Germany, compared with the mere NATO colony and US missile base of the West?

—Go, Johnny, go go go. You are sucking diesel now, my man!

—Great! Um, OK. So, so . . . what, ultimately, was the

guarantee of the GDR's continuing ability to insulate its citizens from the terrible ravages of neo-conservative free-market ideology, if not the robust defensive military and cultural structures of the Warsaw Pact? So by observing events for the KGB, exactly *who* was Heiner Panke, *in the end*, *really* 'betraying'? Germany? Or America? How's that sort of *sneery* voice for meaning quotation marks, Eamon?

—It works for me.

—Thanks! And well, um, is *the good of America* really to be our litmus test of all personal and political action? If so, what *exactly* is the difference between this position and the *with me or against me* of George W. Bush?

—Jaysus, Johnny, you got it! Always suggest that anyone against you is really just a supporter of good ol' W, then you start the game serving for the match with the sun right in their eyes. What a gift the man is!

—Thanks, Eamon! I really think I've got it this time.

—I doubt it, Johnny. But I am always here for you. And just make sure you give it with style, Johnnyboy, inasmuch as your lamentable physical equipment allows for style at all. Remember the secret of modern academic life: it doesn't matter what you're on the box for, so long as you're on the box.

—Great! Thanks, Eamon.

—My pleasure. May I get back to my other and better life now? I very much want to arrange an actual assignation tonight. Man cannot live by cybersex alone. At least, this one can't.

—I haven't arranged anything with anyone all week. I haven't been single since before the Berlin Wall fell.

—Ah, happy days of certainty and missions! But we have eaten of the apple, John the Good, and there is no way back. It would be very fab indeed to know nothing once again, wouldn't it just? To trust the smiling priest who just happens to like ruffling boyish hair. To march along with the bold comrades, convinced that the Warsaw Pact wants only peace and the IRA are a bunch of romantic rebels. Pity. Farewell, Johnnyboy.

I listened to the dead phone line for quite a long moment. Then I blinked myself back to earth. Yes, the past was a happier place, but it was gone.

Quickly, before I could begin to doubt my newly recharged postmodernism, I fired up the laptop. The Very Important Paper jumped out of its sleep again, wide awake. And yes, how plodding and serious it sounded, compared to the free-flowing playfulness of Father Eamon! That was what I needed. Right. Simple. Less boring stuff about *meaning*, and more pomo *topsp*in . . .

God, I had been so right to wait. The gun was perfectly safe where it was for now. All was still possible: the VIP would be a triumph and then, well, who knew?

Just to make absolutely sure that nothing impossible had happened in our garden while I was out, I opened the French windows and peered from the kitchen into the darkness.

Newton was still right, as usual.

There was the filled pit, just as I had left it, sitting quietly out in the cold and the dark and the rain. Of course. It could stay there safe and sound until I came back from Oxford transfigured by the VIP. As I stood there gloating at my own rationality, I found that my long-planned bottle of Olde English ale had somehow poured itself into a glass in my hand. As I savoured the hoppy slugs of beer, I suckled luxuriously on the cigarette that had produced and lit itself. Who cared?

All was well. Imagine! I could be out there now, digging the gun up like an idiot, getting soaked by that pouring rain, about to ruin my week, and hence my career, by calling the police, ha ha!

That pouring rain.

Which had been pouring for a good half hour now.

Into the pit.

Into the soil.

No, surely?

Oh Christ.

22: Archaeology

After a few seconds of panicked stillness, I recovered the use of my limbs and mind. Hastily, I dialled a number from my phone's address book. It was a former acquaintance in the Department of Archaeology at Sheffield called Brian. I had helped him, shortly before I left, with a German excavation report, so I knew him well enough to call. Just about.

—Hello?

—Brian, hi, hello! It's John. John Goode.

—Sorry?

—John Goode, who just left the German department up there. I helped you with that German thing, remember? That excavation report from Bavaria?

—Oh yes, yes. John. Of course. Right. Well. Hello. I thought you were in London now.

—Yeah.

—So, London, eh?

—Yes, London.

—I suppose you've had to cram the poor family into a two-room flat now, eh, John? Ha ha!

—No, we've got, it's a rather nice little house, you know, original sash windows and all that sort of thing.

—Oh. But *little*, eh?

—Well, obviously, Brian, London houses have always been rather smaller.

—Not sure I could get used to that, John. And I don't envy you taking on a mortgage this late. Mine's almost gone, of course. I suppose you had to get a bloody great big one?

—Mmm? A mortgage? Oh, a reasonable one, yes, but then, well, of course, London's London, Brian, and you naturally accept there's a premium for living in a good area. Well, pretty good.

—*Pretty* good? Crime bad there, is it, John?

—The Neighbourhood Watch are very active, actually.

—I suppose they have to be! Are the schools terrible?

—Oh, very multicultural, diverse, stimulating.

—I bet they bloody are, ha ha!

—Ha ha. So, hey, how are you, Brian?

—Me? Oh, great. But then I love it in Sheffield, John, as you know.

—Yes, I know. You always said so.

—Mmm, so, John, yeah, no, look, um, what's up? It's just, I'm cooking dinner right now, actually, and . . .

—The thing is, Brian, you see, I'm writing something about a book, it's an, a German thriller actually, and I was just wondering if I could check something technical about archaeology.

—Oh. Um, well, I suppose. If it doesn't take too long, because as I said, I'm . . .

—Great! Well, the book's a thriller, and it all hangs on this business about a man who accidentally digs up this suitcase.

—A suitcase?

—Yes. A suitcase full of . . . secret papers. And then he reburies it, you see. But then he changes his mind and digs it up again a week or so later, and he tells the police after all.

—He digs it up *again*?

—Yes. And he pretends to the police that he only just found it, you see.

—Sorry, John, will you run that by me again?

—It's quite simple, Brian. He digs the suitcase up at night. Then he buries it again. Then he digs it up *again* a week later and tells the police that he's only just found it. He tells them he called them straight away, like any decent honest citizen would.

—Well, why didn't he?

—Sorry?

—Why *didn't* this man just call the police?

—What? Why? Oh. Well, um, because, he, I suppose, I mean, as far as I can see from the book it was because he didn't want to get involved with the police.

—So, he's some kind of criminal?

—God no, he's just an ordinary man. It's just that he's too busy. With work.

—Doesn't sound like much of a hero to me.

—I found his motivation quite understandable, actually. Anyway, look, Brian, that all doesn't really matter. It's only a story. The point, the *purely technical* point, is, if someone really did that, would the police be able to *tell* that he'd actually *already* dug up the machine gun once.

—What machine gun?

—What?

—What machine gun?

—The secret papers, I mean. Sorry, God, oh yes, I forgot, there *is* a machine gun in the story, yes, it's, yeah, it was buried along with the secret papers, you see. But the machine gun's not important. Forget the machine gun, Brian.

—A machine gun would be pretty important to the police, surely?

—Well, yes, yes, I'm sure it would, in the real world, Brian, but this is a story and it's all about these secret papers, you see, not the machine gun at all. I don't know why I even mentioned the machine gun.

—Right. John, look here, I don't mean to be rude, but I'm just cooking dinner, as I said, and I was just enjoying a quiet glass of wine, just while cooking, you know, and to be honest this is all sounding a bit complicated. Of course, one's always happy to help out a colleague, or an ex-colleague rather. Even one who was in a completely different department. A different faculty, actually. But perhaps you could call another time, at work, when I'm a little bit less . . .

—I need to know this tonight.

—Well, look, John, I'm very sorry, but . . .

—Brian, this is for *The Paper*!

—For *The Paper*?

—Yes. It's a review, for *The Paper*. This German thriller has just been translated, you see. And so they've asked me to review it. For *The Paper*. I'd mention your name, naturally.

—A review in *The Paper*? When did you start doing that?

—This is my first one. Which is why I want to get it right, you see. And as I said, I'd mention your name. Fulsomely.

—Christ, John, how the hell did you get your first gig, you lucky bastard? I mean, that's the one that matters, isn't it? God, I've been offering to review archaeological books for *The Paper* for bloody years. Just a chance to show what I can do, that's all I ask. Of course I can bloody do it, if they'll just give me a shot. Standing on my head! But they never even reply to my emails, the snotty-nosed metropolitan bastards.

—Oh well, you know, Brian.

—Aha! Ah! Ha! Yes, of course. I do know. Ha!

—Sorry, Brian?

—It's just because you're *in bloody London* now, right? Aha! See? Christ, I always knew the media were like that! Well sorry, John, but I have to say that it's bloody ridiculous. This country is so bloody London-centric.

Which, considering that London is completely bloody un-English these days is a bit bloody ironic. Ha! Shit, damn, I think I've burnt this bloody fennel. Hang on. Oh bugger! Sod and damnation. Ow! Well sod the fennel then! Bloody stupid stuff anyway. Hang on, just get a refill. Right. So, come on then, John, how did it happen? What, did you meet the literary editor of *The Paper* at some poncy cocktail do in Islington? Or did you buttonhole him at some reading in the British bloody Library? Or sidle up to him at the drinks reception after some British sodding Academy lecture?

—How? Well, um, how it happened was, let me try to remember, oh yes, I had an hour between tutorials so I just popped over to the BM, the British Museum, you know . . .

—I know what the bloody BM is, John!

—Of course you do. I have lunch there quite a lot, in the courtyard. Very relaxing. And well, yes, this woman was at the next table as I sat down, very, you know, Brian, *London*-looking. She was reading a German novel and I recognised the author's name, you see, so I smiled at her and said, —*Is the translation up to scratch?* and she looked up and said, —*God, how would anyone know?* and laughed. You know, that sort of tinkly, posh laugh. So I said, —*Well actually, I'd know, you see*, and she said, —*Golly, would you really?* and it turned out she was one of the people on the books page of *The Paper*, and then one thing led to another and . . .

I now realised that while telling this innocent little pack of white lies, I had actually slid my hand half-into my trousers. Hastily, baffled, I withdrew it.

—Bloody London, I knew it! Christ, John, that's so unfair. That just could never happen up here. It's structural bloody apartheid, that's what it is! You'll be on the bloody telly next, I suppose?

—Oh, I don't worry about that sort of thing, Brian. If it comes along, it comes, of course.

—Shit, I *knew* I should have applied for that sodding job at Goldsmiths! And I would have, if it wasn't for the bloody kids. Ungrateful little teenage sods, I immure myself in bloody Sheffield for their sakes and now they think I'm just a boring old nobody. Hold on, just another splash. Well maybe I *will* go for the next London job. Not that anyone'll give me a new job now, ever again.

—Mmm? Why not?

—Well, I was desperate last term, you see. I needed to get another article out before the next research-grants deadline, or I knew the bloody head of department wouldn't back me for a sabbatical, and I've *got* to get away from this awful bloody place for a bit or I'll hang myself. So one night when I'd had a few I dug out some old stuff from my PhD excavations in America. Stuff I'd never used. I polished it up for half an hour then emailed it just on the off chance and forgot about it. Next thing I bloody know it's there in the bloody *Archeological Review of America*, and I'm buggered.

—But that sounds like a premier refereed journal, Brian?

—It is. So everyone'll read it. So I'm finished.

—What, was your paper wrong?

—Wrong? Excuse me, John, my findings were rock-solid. My technique was downright classic. I presented incontrovertible archaeological evidence that the Apaches regularly massacred entire villages of Pueblo Indians, women and children and all, during the late twelfth and early thirteenth centuries.

—Ri-ght. So . . . ?

—Are you deaf, John? I said *the late twelfth and early thirteenth centuries.*

—Yes, I did hear, but I don't really get why . . .

—Centuries before Columbus!

—Well, yes, obviously, but . . .

—John, the Native Americans were all peaceful, wonderful guardians of nature, living in harmony with their environment and with one another in a highly sustainable fashion, before they were ruined by their first contact with nasty vicious capitalist imperialist white men.

—Were they?

—They bloody well were if you want a job in any proper archaeology department in Britain or America. The only place that would take me now would be some foul hole in Texas funded by the First Church of Aryan Creationists. God knows how I'm going to get back into everyone's good books. If only I could do a few reviews for *The Paper*, that would help so much!

—I could put a word in for you, if you'd like.

—Could you? Would you? Put a word in for me? At *The Paper*? Would you really?

—Well, I mean, Brian, now I'm here in London I can just pop along to *The Paper* any time, to have a chat, can't I?

—God, yes, of course. Well, John, hey, that'd be *so* good. Well, hey, *that* deserves a decent top-up! Just a sec. Oh, damn, better open another bottle. Don't stop, John, go on while I just . . .

—No worries, Brian. So, do you think that you *can* help me with this review?

—What? Oh, that, yes, of course, hey, no problem! Fire away, John!

—Thanks. So, Brian. Now, in this book, as I said, um, our hero finds this, this *cache of secrets*. The question is simply this: if he reburied it and the next week he dug it up again and *then* called the police, would they be able to tell that he'd already dug it up once and reburied it?

—Yes.

—Sorry?

—Yes.

—They'd be able to tell?

—Yes.

—Oh. Oh, right. I thought, I mean, right. I see. Um, so, what, if it was only buried again for a few hours?

—I thought you said he buried it for a week?

—Well, yes, that's right. He does. I just, I was just wanting to, get my argument right. For the review. So, I mean, if the author *had* made his hero rebury it for just a couple of hours and then call the police that very same night . . . ?

—No difference at all.

—What? They'd *still* be able to tell?

—John, I can tell you if a Neolithic grave was broken into and then refilled on the same day three thousand years ago. I must say, I'm surprised at your lack of cross-faculty knowledge, John. Layers and levels. Strata and soil types. Basic to the whole of archaeology.

—Yes, yes of course. But look, I forgot to mention, though. This is really important. Actually, it's the central point. It's been, I mean, in the book, it's supposed to have been raining heavily while the suitcase was reburied. I was wondering, wouldn't that make it more difficult for the police to tell? Sort of, wash away the, the strata and the layers?

—John, just think about it, will you? The backfill within the pit has just been thoroughly disturbed and aerated. Well? Is it going to absorb the water the same rate as the soil in the surrounding undisturbed matrix of the strata? Will the walls of the pit be unchanged by having their surfaces exposed to air and water? Will the backfill simply remesh with the undisturbed dug surfaces?

—Well, I suppose . . . , I said, and pulled the curtain aside so that I could look out into the dark garden. Was I hallucinating, or could I really see, even in the dark, even with my untrained eye, that the filled-in pit was a blacker black than the rest of the black? Was it not indeed holding the rain, growing waterlogged, like a fresh-dug grave?—Well, I suppose . . . , I repeated stupidly.

—Well, of course not, John.

—And, um, I mean, how long will it stay that obvious?

—To the trained eye? For, well, basically, for ever.

—Oh God. Ah, right but only to the *trained* eye, you say, Brian? I thought, I mean, the, um, the author appears to think, that the police might not notice. Being, you know, untrained.

—What, don't they bring in any forensic scientists? John? I thought you said there was a machine gun involved as well?

—Ah yes. That. Yes, there is.

Here is the news. An Armalite discovered in SE11. Pictures from the scene. SWAT teams, men in haunting white coveralls, road blocks, vans, armed cops.

—In the real world they'd certainly bring in forensic scientists, John. I think your German writer is being pretty sloppy.

—No, no, they do bring in forensic scientists. Of course they do. In the book.

—Well then. Simple, John. Any half-decent forensic scientist would know straight away that this box of secrets or whatever it is had been very recently dug up and put back.

—Right. So, Brian, in other words, let me just get

this straight. If I, I mean he, the hero of this book, dug it up, then buried it again, then dug it up again, it wouldn't make, I mean, have made, any difference if it was that night, next day or in, say, a week. Whatever he did, the police *wouldn't* believe he'd only just found it?

—Not unless they were utterly incompetent.

—So basically, he was buggered the moment he dug it up and then reburied it?

—I'd have thought so. Does he get away with it, in this book of yours? Surely not?

—What? Well, yes, as matter of fact, Brian. He, yes, actually, he gets away with it. They believe him. They just take the machine gun away. The secret papers and the machine gun that isn't really important, I mean, after the ordinary sort of questions, obviously. And, well, then everything gets back to normal. It's quite a happy ending, really.

—Hmm. Well, literature's not my thing, John, never saw the point of it much, there are enough real mysteries out there without drama queens making up bloody silly stories, but I must say that this sounds like a particularly pointless one.

—Well, yes, the story's arc is perhaps a little weak. And I shall say so in my review. I just needed to find out if it's, you know, *technically* wrong as well. Which I gather it is.

—Absolutely. A load of rubbish! Your author simply hasn't done his research. And you can quote me on that. In fact, you bloody better had, John, ha ha!

—Ha ha. Well, thanks, Brian.

—You will mention me to your contact as well, won't you, when you have lunch with her again?

—Sorry? Oh yes, yes of course.

—I could review archaeology, history, anthropology,

anything like that really. I mean, I'm obviously fully qualified to do it, for God's sake, I just need the break. I can talk to a camera as I walk about without falling over things. I've been practising in the departmental technicians' lab, after work. I can even do it *with* a glass of wine in my hand, just like that cook off the telly, oh you know who I mean, John. Surprisingly difficult, actually, but I've cracked it now. And I've got this really wonderful idea for a telly series on archaeology. I mean just because I wasn't the supporting actor on some stupid comedy series twenty years ago doesn't mean I can't talk about archaeology on TV, does it? Just because I haven't got some kind of *trademark hair* or a bloody silly *regional accent*? I could *do* it, John. I could knock them dead. I just need to meet the right person, just to get that break! If I could only get about a bit more, see the right people, you know. Well, you *do* know, obviously. Look, I'm coming to a conference in London early next year, perhaps I could give you a call, we could have a drink, try to arrange a meeting with someone down there?

—Yes. Right. Bye, Brian.

I killed my phone.

Oh well then.

23: Liberal Blather

I sat there, dumb, unthinking. Obviously, I had to call the police eventually; but now I could obviously never call the police. It was already too late.

> Mr Goode, as you know, our forensic teams tell us that according to the evidence of the soil matrix, there is no doubt, I repeat no doubt, that 'a substantial period of time' must have elapsed between you finding the Armalite and you calling the police. Now, can you take us through your actions, and indeed your thoughts, during this substantial period of time, please?
>
> You found the gun. When, exactly? You did not immediately call the police. Why, exactly? You partially reburied the gun. For what purpose, exactly? You had a visitor. Who, exactly? You went to the pub. To do what, exactly? It seems that you normally hardly ever go to pubs, do you, Mr Goode? But tonight you did. You claim that you watched half an England match. But it seems that you normally care very little for the fortunes of the England football team, do you, Mr Goode? Yet tonight you claim that you went to cheer them on. Except that then you left the pub, halfway through the game, with England winning against France. Hardly

the behaviour of a real England fan, ladies and gentlemen of the jury!

You then made a call to a number in Dublin. The number of an Irishman whom we know to have been an active member of the Troops Out Movement. After which there was a further delay and a further phone call to an archaeologist, an expert on burial and concealment, before you finally informed the police that you had found a highly dangerous weapon which, I put it to you, you had immediately known to be such.

Or should I say, before you decided to inform the police? Because, clearly, that's what it was, a conscious decision, and one which took you some time, wasn't it, Mr Goode? Not the simple, instinctive reaction of a normal, law-abiding man. A dec-is-ion. And it wasn't an easy one, was it? Well, it took you almost three hours! Which clearly implies that during these three hours there was another, alternative course in your mind as well, doesn't it, Mr Goode?

An alternative to calling the police, when you have just found an Armalite in your garden? Now, what on earth might that alternative have been, Mr Goode? Or should I say Dr Goode? Ah yes, of course, a university lecturer. East German studies. Ah, and you were actually resident there, I see. Twice, in fact. You threw stones at the police during the Miners' Strike, didn't you, Dr

Goode? Sorry? It was only a very small stone? I see. How fortunate for the officer concerned! Now then, Dr Goode, I have some photographs from a recent anti-Iraq-War demonstration that I'd like you to look at with us . . .

Would they take my laptop away to search through it? Of course they would. They always do, these days. And my PC at work, naturally. Oh dear God, what had I said, and to whom, in chatty emails about Iraq and suchlike? About Bush and Blair? About capitalism in general? About the G8 riots in Germany? About the police themselves! I mean, I was not some maniac, just a perfectly normal humanities lecturer who blipped off, most days, the sort of clever, merry emails that humanities lecturers do blip off to one another, sure of mutual approval from fellow readers of *The Paper*.

Christ, it's just liberal blather, none of it actually *means* anything.

But would the police see it all that way?

Potentially not.

This was all so unfair.

So what was I going to do? Tell them or not?

Couldn't not. Couldn't.

Think properly. Think straight. Newton, not Einstein

Ring-ring!

—Sarah darling! How are you all?

24: How Hard Can It Be?

—Sarah darling! How are you all? Did you get there safely? Well, obviously you did. How are the boys and Mariana? Oh, I'm sorry. What? All over the taxi seat? Oh, darling, poor you. And how are your parents? Right. R-ight. Oh God. Well, perhaps the hotel would give them a less noisy room if you asked. Oh. Well, you could try asking again. Of course you have, sorry. Do you want me to try? I do speak quite good Spanish, after all. Well, yes, I'm sure they do, but it still some-times makes a difference if you can speak to them in . . . OK, OK, no, I'm sure you explained very well. What do you mean, they *just looked* at you? That's ridiculous. It's supposed to be a four-bloody-star place! I'm not shouting at you, darling, I'm just . . . Well, yes, it *was* a special last-minute website rate. I did tell you. I told you I'd got a great deal. And it was. Sorry, yes, I mean, it was in theory, it . . . Did I look on Tripadvisor.com? Well, I couldn't, could I, because they wouldn't actu-ally specify the hotel until after I'd booked, but they guaranteed four stars in the centre of . . . What, you mean deliberately, so that people *can't* look on Tripadvisor? Come on, darling, I think that's a bit far-fetched, I mean, surely . . . ? Who told you? Well, what would the night porter know about things like that? Yes, I'm sure he was very nice, but . . . Right. Yes, I agree. Absolutely. No, no, definitely. Leave. Walk. I'm sure that you can find somewhere good for that price. Or more, quite right. If you need to. Well, yes, of course I know you wouldn't pay more if you didn't need to,

I just meant . . . What? Oh, we've got, um, about two thousand pounds before our credit limit on that one, I think, although, I mean, obviously, we did plan this on the basis that . . . No, no, we didn't plan this on the basis that your parents wouldn't be able to sleep a wink, no. Certainly. I agree. Yes, wherever you can. If they *really* can't do anything about it, I mean. Me? Oh, God, yes, of course everything's fine here, there's no reason to worry about me, you go and sort out . . . Where was I earlier? Well, um, I must have popped out. Just for some air. Drunk? Of course not. I just, drank that bottle of beer quite quickly, that's all, to relax from work. Fine, absolutely, great, yes, the VIP's really coming along! Worth it? Oh, clearly, darling. No question. Yes, yes. I'll call tomorrow. No, I won't be popping out again tonight. Goodnight, darling!

I put down the phone.

Suddenly, I could feel every sea and mountain of the two thousand miles between Sarah and me. I was cold. I wanted to go back to the pub, and noise, and light.

Stop. Clear my head. No more pub, for Christ's sake. I'm supposed to be sobering up now.

What to do about the gun in the garden?

Concentrate.

What if I just dump it?

Jesus Christ, of course!

How obvious. I must have been mad not to have thought about it.

No gun, no police, job done.

Very well. The logic holds.

Just dig the bloody thing up, dump it anywhere, and good riddance.

Done and dusted this very night, then start afresh on the VIP tomorrow, as if nothing had happened.

I mean, how hard could that be for a man with a PhD?

PART TWO

Into the Forest

25: Power

Some ten minutes later, I squatted damply in the garden shed and surveyed the open suitcase, my unwanted treasure, by the light of the powerful lantern torch which my parents had given us as a house-warming present. They had chosen this not because it might be a handy thing to have about the place when a fuse blew, but because you never knew when far more than just fuses might blow. After all, they had lived through the blackout; they had trudged through the hopeless snows of 1947; they had nursed me, their precious only infant son, through the winter of 1962–3; they had seen out the energy strikes of the early seventies. They knew about power cuts all right.

I had strung their lamp from the roof of the shed, where it now gently swayed.

Light and shadow played over the wide-open suitcase.

The gun had no connection to me at this moment, did it? Of course not. None at all. It was not mine. It never had been. Provided it was not found actually *in* my garden or house (or shed). Or in my red hands. The danger to me now, the only danger, was being caught in the *actus reus* of trying to get rid of it. That instant would indeed smack strongly of guilt.

The logic was inescapable: having concluded (as I had) that I must get rid of the blasted thing myself, making the *act of the dumping* as smooth and swift as possible had to now be my prime and indeed only concern.

You see? Most criminals get caught simply because they are stupid: but I have a PhD!

But how to do it, exactly?

Dragging the suitcase out of its grave and across the lawn to my little shed, just for closer examination prior to disposal, had thoroughly convinced me that to lug the entire thing, as it was, out into the London night was in fact quite out of the question. Manhandling it across the garden, through the house, on to the street and (now in full view of everyone) up into the boot of the car, when I could hardly even lift it? Struggling to heave it out of the boot again and chuck it off a bridge without being noticed by anyone or picked up for parking on a red line? Impossible.

You see, I had decided, and so quickly that it had felt more like instinct than decision, that the river was the only place for it to go.

Consider: if I simply drove to some alleyway or indeed quiet roadside and left it there, who knew who would find it first? An innocent child or a horrible villain. Might the gun not go off in a waste crusher, say, potentially endangering the lives of low-paid workers? Indeed. What if a would-be murderer, who might otherwise never actually have murdered anyone, found it and now became a monster? Horrible. If it fell into the hands of racist thugs? Incalculable. Or say an overheated young madrasa scholar was the first to happen upon it and took this as a sign, at last, for him alone, from Allah? Disastrous, for community relations as well as for his victims! A resentful teen stalks the unlit alleyways, his acne boiling beneath his hood at a supposed lack of respect; he kicks viciously at an old suitcase in passing, stubs his toe, ponders, opens the box and finds within it his ticket to vengeance on the world? All too believable.

No, no, anything was possible here in London, this lair of countless darknesses. Into the river with it it was.

Total submersion in water for a long period had another advantage. This would (I gathered from a recent high-profile homicide case) radically reduce the chance of my DNA being identifiable if by some accident the gun was found. Not that there was much chance of this anyway, and as far as I knew I had never given a DNA sample in the first place, but you never know with police technology. Dr Crippen, after all, had been certain that he would get to America before the news of his crime broke.

Yes, one way or another, my course was clear: into the river, like some Celtic sacrificial helmet, safely put beyond all possible use. Let the archaeologists find it in two thousand years, and wonder! But it had to be quick and simple and mishap-proof. As things stood, the suitcase was just too bloody heavy.

Clearly, the vast weight was due not to the gun itself but to the gallons and gallons of foul old grease in which it was entombed. I could pour or shovel the stuff out. But then what of disposal? Even if the horrid filth did eventually slide down through the grate at the bottom of the drainpipe and so into the sewers (which was by no means certain), could I in all conscience visit such damage on the environment? Surely not.

And anyway, the suitcase itself was too large to fit through the windows of my Mercedes, so even if I did poison the local biosphere and thereby lighten the case enough to hoick it easily about with the gun still inside, I would nonetheless have to actually pull over, stop, get out, go round, open the door, get it out, lift it over the side and chuck it into the river, then get back in and drive away. All without awakening suspicion.

But! Now let us suppose that I simply did it the other way around. What, that is, if I took the gun from the grease rather than vice versa?

What a difference this would make!

Think: how big and heavy could an Armalite be? Presumably the 'lite' means lightweight. The gun was evidently in pieces, so the obvious answer was to take the bits out as they were and get them all to my car in an innocent-looking bin bag, or bags if need be, then drive off (having sobered up, of course).

You see? That way, I could just sling the bin bag(s) easily from the window of my car over the parapet of some bridge or other, quite probably without even having to fully stop. The suitcase itself, the mere guilt-less shell, I could just drop at the local dump anytime I chose.

There was, in short, no rational doubt.

Unpacking the Armalite was indeed the only logical option.

A distasteful job of work for a pacific and liberal man, to be sure, and one that I had certainly not asked for, but there you were.

With these firm and clear thoughts lighting my way and the torch swinging gently from the rafters of the shed, I swiftly laid out that morning's dismembered edition of *The Paper* carefully on the floor of the shed around the suitcase, to a depth of several sheets. It was the day of the weekly social-work jobs supplement so I had newsprint aplenty to work with.

I now shoved my fingers, with some difficulty, into the small rubber gloves Sarah uses when washing up, to save her hands (her lovely hands! One day we *would* get a cleaning lady!). Then I knelt on the newspaper, took a deep breath in case another bubble of rancid gas should belch forth, and boldly kneaded my sheathed hands deep into the cold stew of nineteen-eighties axle grease.

26: A Thick Bed of Liberal Broadsheet

Roughly I handswiped the cloying grease from each item as it came out and soon I was sure that I had fished out all that lurked within.

Arrayed on the thick bed of liberal broadsheet there now lay a small selection of heavy packages which had clearly been made with extreme care. They consisted of double or treble plastic bags, burned lightly so as to lock the openings, with bubble wrap between the layers, containing shapes entombed in some kind of putty-like substance.

I held a couple of these lumpish forms up to the gently yawing torchlight. Aha. Of course. Even I knew that. Those identical, cigarette-packet-sized things (there were six of them, all told) must clearly be the, well, you know, the reloading things, the *magazines* or whatever you call them. Boxes, in short, of bullets. *Bullets?* That sounded curiously dated and childlike. I had been given *bullets*, small silver plastic ones, with the belt of my cowboy gun-and-holster set, at five years old. *Ordnance?* Too technical. *Ammunition?* Yes, but possibly too formal still. *Ammo?* Too blatantly American. *Rounds?* Perhaps. *Clips* had I heard used somewhere? Whatever. Sheer deadly potential, waiting. Well sealed and packed, yes. Still live? How could you tell? Who knew? Who cared? Into the bag, very carefully. Ugh. You see! How right I had been to make sure that my disposing of the gun would cause no danger to any of my fellow men! Perhaps I should just lance each little package, to make sure the water got in? Hmm. Tough plastic, this. Thumb-proof.

Need a tool. Oh well, forget it then. The cold old Thames would defuse these bullets, in no time, surely, despite all their wrappings?

Now, what next? This fat, long, trapezoidal shape could only be the what, you know, the bit that you actually press on to your shoulder. The *handle*? No, no, no. The *stock*? But was that just with shotguns? Perhaps *butt*. Surely that was what the comics used to say? *The Jap fell with a grunt as Sergeant Malone's rifle butt crashed into his buck-toothed yellow face?* Yes. At any rate, there it is. Into the bag, and good riddance! Soon it would all be gone for ever, and everything would be OK again.

Just one minute, hold on.

Feel it again, the bag. Swing it, with those weighty lumps inside.

Well?

Do you seriously think that when there are another two or three similar objects in the bag, each obeying its very own orbits and epicycles of momentum, that you are, as you imagined, going to be able to simply swing the whole lot smoothly out of your car and over the ledge of some bridge without even opening the door? Go on then, try it. Well? More like a bolas than a bag! Absolutely perfect for catching, careering out of control, splitting.

OK then, several different bin bags it is.

Oh, very clever. You must be drunk.

We have just established, have we not, that the actual *act of the dumping* is the only risk? And now you intend to multiply the span of that vital instant? That seven-year risk? Idiocy! A blatantly gratuitous upping of the odds! It must be a single clean act of dumping.

And that, it was now clear, could only mean one thing.

It was quite obvious that, whether I wanted to or not, I had to put the gun together.

27: Thinking Clearly

I was relieved to find myself thinking so clearly despite the drink.

If the gun was assembled, in one piece, I would be able simply to fling the whole damn thing out of my car in a single swoop. Like a spear. I could javelin it out without even stopping, or whip it over the railings of some innocently sleeping mosque, for example. Now *that* would make sure no one ever bothered thinking about whether it had come from anywhere else, ha ha!

One throw, one single brief, discrete moment of danger, and I would be free.

Right then.

Surely it couldn't be that hard to put it together? After all, I had plenty of time, because I obviously had to sober up properly before driving out into the night with an Armalite, whether it was in bin bags or not. So I might as well assemble it, if that would make things at all easier, as it undoubtedly would.

Very well.

Let's see now.

Just as I had explained to my boys about their Flying Fortress gun turrets, the trick was to lay all the pieces out properly and take a good, relaxed look, with the end product in mind, not just charge wildly ahead with the first thing that seemed to fit.

Set out the packages then, without opening them as yet.

First clean this bloody grease from the bags. Rags? Here, Dad's old rags. Horrible goo. But there, it wipes off quite well. So: now to open the bags! Hmm, tough stuff. Need a knife. Has to be sharp. The Stanley knife, of course. Always knew it would come in handy. God, the fumes from this filth.

Open the door of the shed, that's better. Moonlight. Air. Very private and non-overlooked, yes, ha ha! Which is no doubt why *they* chose this house in the first place. Christ, would my head never clear? What idiot had decided that all beer had to be 5 per cent these days? In my Devon youth 3.6 per cent had been considered strong. Stupid bloody barmaid. Nothing, nothing compared to my Sarah. What, does she think just because she's young and firm-breasted she can dare tell me that my life has been . . .

Anyway, even 5 per cent beer would clear in a couple of hours. By about three or four a.m., I would be under the limit again. Not a bad time, really. It would still be dark and London would be dead. Just the time to lose an unwanted Armalite . . .

Here we are, at the back door. Shoes off, this time! Sit down. Wet arse still. So what? Who knows what nice Dr John Goode is up to tonight? A long time since I had such a secret! Carefully through the house, touch no wall or handle, creeping as if it's Christmas Eve, setting out presents. Good presents too, this year, special presents if the VIP goes well. Perhaps a Wii for the boys after all? Yes, yes, it's Jap-Yank crap but do we want them to be the only boys in the school without one? Mustn't train *them* up for life under Heath and Wilson!

But then, for life under what? Under ten feet of melted ice-cap water? Poor little sods. Must sort things out for them.

Here: the Flying Fortress kit.

Locate and cement assembly #1 (child's psyche) to assembly #2 (society), ensuring that all cogs turn smoothly.

The knife. Thanks, Dad.

So. And now back out.

Shoes back on, idiot.

Wet socks too now. Oh well.

The dark garden again. The big night. The little shed.
The wallowing torchlight.

Kneel again, select a package and slowly, slowly in
with Daddy's blade . . .

28: An Icy Male Paradise

My infant school.

As I slit open the first package, the smell of my infant school blossomed out at me again across the years. The effect was so strong that I rocked back on my heels and actually got halfway to shielding my face with my hands, as though this sudden leak in time must be the pre-echo, or perhaps the after-effect, of the booby-trap explosion that was going to kill me or had already done so.

But the world still spun, and I still breathed. Whatever the smell meant, it was real.

I now examined things rationally, and found that within their layers of plastic wrapping, the various pieces of the gun were encased in perfectly ordinary children's modelling clay. Hence, I realised, the curious squashiness.

Of course, the stuff must have absolutely no water content at all, so it never goes off. Just flour and oil. That would be it. Perfect protection. And see how easily it peeled away. Yes, each part of the gun had evidently been carefully oiled before being mummified in play dough. With WD-40 perhaps? My father had always used WD-40 on everything . . .

Slice, rip, peel.

Soon I had removed all the putty and was laying the gleaming components of the gun out in a fine and orderly fashion. That was the way. Order. Not for nothing had I spent my entire twenties filling box after box with colour-coded filing cards about soon-to-be-forgotten personages, soon-to-be-meaningless events and soon-to-be-remaindered books from a shithole run by the Red Army. I knew the value of thoroughness!

I stood up, my knees creaking lightly, and surveyed the puzzle below me from a godlike height. Right, now, boys. The *butt* and *magazines* we already have. And obviously there's no question about the bit I just opened. That's the *barrel*, everyone knows that! Interesting word, boys, when you think about it, suggesting clearly that the very first wrought-iron guns had looked, to their late-medieval makers and users, rather like *barrels*. As indeed they did. Now, the barrel must obviously fit on to the *body* or *chassis* or whatever you call it. Which must be this, the big part with that distinctive carry-handle thing I had recognised immediately (—*How did you recognise it, Dad? —Oh, never mind that just now, boys!*). Never realised the carry-handle was actually metal, part of the same casting. So, in that case, this packet must contain the actual main bit of the gun, the, well, yes, exactly, the *main bit of the gun.*

I now had the bullet things, the barrel, the what-everyoucallit that goes against your shoulder and the main bit of the gun. The form of the whole was clear. But what, then, was in the final parcel? Better see. A quick slash with the Staney knife and . . .

What? Damn!

This was unexpected. Lots of little squishy balls of clay wrapped together in a big plastic envelope. Shit, they must be vital little bits and pieces, like the screws and keys in some blasted IKEA flatpack. Quite a few of them. Oh God, perhaps I should never have started this. Well, it was too late now. Anyway, this was better fun than sudoku. Not to mention work on the VIbloodyP.

However, I was not going to be able to work it out by sheer meditation on the object before me. Technology had progressed too far for an all-round man: I was going to need detailed instructions, *locate and cement part #156* and suchlike.

A problem? No.

The web, of course. That icy male paradise where nothing is so obscure, so banal or so vile that you cannot find another man, somewhere, who has thought it worth setting down. An entire silicon cosmos generated by vast banks of servers stacked up in desolate, air-cooled warehouses on the edges of dead-end towns. A world without touch or feel, filled with the desperate yet drearily monotonous voices of lonely males, yearning for the only communication they can imagine, to share facts and lists and pictures. Somewhere deep in this clamouring void there were sure to be American gun-nut survivalists talking to fellow males who had happened to fixate not on cars, model boats or porn, but on Armalites.

Of course, I might have to pretend to be a White Supremacist to get what I needed out of them, but that would be easy: I could model my fascist-bastard chat room persona on Phil.

I strode happily back to the house, looking forward to some e-action and wiping my hands on one of my father's manly rags as if cleaning up from one piece of honest work simply to prepare for another.

Let's see now. Google. Ah yes, this is where experience and education pays off. *Advanced Search; Exact Phrase: Armalite Reassembly*. Now, let's see if we can find some real Yank nutters out there . . .

29: The Home of the Black Rifle

Within thirty seconds I found myself facing the gleaming homepage interface of **AR-15.COM: Home of the Black Gun. NRA#1 recommended clubhouse and armory for all things ARMALITE.**

—Of course. Trust the Yanks. Incredible! I puffed out loud to myself as I stared at this wide-open portal to a grotesque yet utterly public and perfectly unashamed realm. A legal world where machine guns were normal.

Unbelievable.

There were 1, 035 members currently online and a quick scan of the various forums revealed most of them to be blatantly insane. Chat was dominated by discussion of how to get round anti-assault gun legislation, what excuses could be concocted to own Teflon-coated bullets (which only evil lying Beltway scum referred to as *cop killers*, apparently) or how best decent folks should prepare for an imminent catastrophe which evidently loomed very large in the minds of many AR-15 owners and which they called simply *shtf*.

I had no idea what *shtf* was, but it seemed to involve one, several or in some cases all of a Katrina-style natural disaster, a vast al-Qaeda strike (probably with the collaboration of the FBI and/or the CIA), global warming, anti-global-warming campaigners, Cuba, sub-prime home loans, anti-Christian local governors, Hispanic birth rates, Black Power, Big Oil, Jewish Money, felons and liberals. The plot was of such labyrinthine deviousness that no one had any idea exactly what it might be, except that it was coming.

Jesus H! What is wrong with the bloody Yanks? I mean, look at this ad for a shooting range outside Las Vegas. Anyone can just turn up and blaze away! If I actually lived in Nevada, I could, however mad I was, just go there and buy an Armalite together with as many bullets as I wanted from their *armory* (stupid bastards, why do they spell things that ridiculous way?) and, then, well, then I could . . .

Oh well. What did I expect? America. Should make it easy enough to find some diagrams, though. Let's see. **AR-15 TECHNICAL INTRODUCTION**. Well, why not?

Click.

Ah, right. O-K. Hmm.

A-ha. Curiouser and curiouser.

Actually, you know, that really *is* pretty fascinating.

The AR-15 Armalite is technically known as an 'assault rifle', not a machine gun, is it? 'Assault rifle'? Well? Think about it. A splendid example of where an appreciation of history and language can help us. Who said teaching German history was useless? That term 'assault rifle' is clearly a direct translation of the German word *Sturmgewehr*. Now, this fanatically upbeat-sounding, offensively minded name was one of Hitler's personal favourites. No doubt the term 'machine gun' (*Maschinengewehr*) had, in the crazed and trench-locked mind of this former WWI Private first class (he was never a 'corporal' in the Allied sense), too many connotations of fixed and unbreakable defences. Hitler had personally insisted on the use of the word *Sturmgewehr* instead, just as he had made his engineers call a cannon on a tank chassis not a mere 'self-propelled gun' (how boring!) but a *Sturmgeschütz*, i.e. an 'assault gun'. Even though in both cases the weapons in question were actually desperate and defensive responses to growing Soviet power. Yes, the Nazis pretty well invented spin, and much good did it do them! So then, let us ask: how did this quintessentially Nazi name come to be used by the American army, replacing such time-honoured names as 'carbine' and 'sub-machine gun'? More expatriated 'good' German weapons engineers in the US after 1945, presumably (cf. Werner von Braun)? A giveaway sign of the excessive respect among 'Western' (i.e. American-led) militarists, booted or armchair, for the 'tactical excellence' of the *Wehrmacht* (each of whose defensive 'successes' not only killed poor conscripted farmboys from Ohio, Devon or Minsk, but kept Auschwitz open for another day)? Or simply the American military's addiction to euphemistic abstraction (cf. 'collateral damage'), which may well itself derive from the Prussian/German military tradition? Hmm. Perhaps there might be a nice little paper in this snippet? You see, you never know where you will come across inspiration! Yes, yes certainly, that might be interesting: 'The National Socialist Roots of US Military Jargon' by Dr John Goode (London)? Shit, the *New Left Critical Review* would take that one at the drop of a hat! They take anything anti-American, especially if the writer has just given a plenary paper at the national peer-group conference and . . .

And there it was.

I had been meandering about the site as I pondered my ideas, and had got as far as **FIELD STRIPPING**. Suddenly, unbelievably, there now stood as clear as day an entire technical drawing of an AR-15.

30: Special Relationship

I see. So *that* was what that bit was called. Not the *body of the gun*. The *main receiver assembly*. O-K. And that part I had recognised straight away, the part with that trademark handle, that was the *upper receiver*.

Who knew?

Tools required: ⅛" punch, 5/32" spanner. Thank God that Dad's tools aren't metric, then. Perhaps there really is something to the Special Relationship, after all!

Always work in a well-lit area and on a hard flat surface. There are many small pins and rings and they have a tendency to roll or fly away. Yes, yes, obviously, the same as with a plastic Flying bloody Fortress model, you idiot Yank. *This is by no means the only correct method, but unless you are experienced, follow the color-coded sequence presented and you will be successful.* Oh really? Will I? I should bloody think so you arrogant colonial shit who can't even spell English! *Color!* Well, yes, OK, I know that Nelson's officers were as likely to write home about the *honor of their colors* as about the *honour of their colours,* but that doesn't change the main point, which is that if some brainless bloody Bush-voting yee-hahing piece of Duff-sodden inbred Ku Klux trash can do it, I venture to suggest that I, *Dr* John Goode (Old England, Europe), who conquered the working rigging of a scale model of Lord Nelson's *Victory* at fourteen years of age and perceived in five seconds flat, earlier this very evening, how the retracting ball turret of a Flying Fortress should be linked to its undercarriage (*parts #165–181*), might *just* about be able to work it out!

If you are constructing your own AR-15 from new cast-ings, some of the small holes can have debris in them from the forging process. A small drill bit, turned by hand, will clean these nicely. You don't say?

Laughably easy.

But hold on.

No!

Yes.

Bill bloody Gates!

Even if the gun nuts at AR-15.com, or the people watching the gun nuts at AR-15.com, had not put cookies into my system, as they surely had, there was still the entire panoply of unseen demons that work away in the bottomless deeps of Windows: hard-disk traces, swap files, Internet trails, registry entries. There was no escape. Somewhere on my computer there would now be God knew how many ghostly references to AR-15s and Armalites.

Think about it and tremble.

If anything *did* go wrong, if I *was* caught dumping the gun and the police took a look (as they certainly would) at my laptop? Now they would find, as well as unguarded liberal chit-chat, the digital shadows left by my downloading technical drawings of assault rifles.

Shit.

There was no escape.

Now I would have to dump or destroy the bloody laptop as well as the gun. More bloody expense. More lies to Sarah. And who knows how to truly annihilate a hard disk? I would have to make sure it never got found by anyone, just in case. Into the Thames with it too, then. Surely, it would never be dredged up, and surely even if it ever were, a few weeks of total submersion in filthy polluted water would wreck the bloody thing?

I had no choice, sod it.

Impatiently, I waited while all my recent work was blipped across to the university and backed up on my memory stick. Oh come on, you heap of Japanese crap. For God's sake, this is supposed to be *broadband*! Einstein was right, time is relative and PC down-time is the longest kind of time in the universe.

But at last the interminable three and a half minutes had finished. Huffing with annoyance, I snatched up the printed-out AR-15 plans and rose swiftly from my chair.

—Aaaah! Shitting fucking stupid little . . .

Having recovered from the brain-shaking impact on the underside of the stairs, I got to my feet again and stalked angrily to my shed.

31: The Irrational Fear of Physical Violence

I was in no hurry to build the gun.

I had several hours until I was sober enough to drive, and my plan was in any case the sort best carried out during the coldest, darkest hours of the night, when the living give up and the dying die, and good, normal people are all asleep. So I took it slowly and methodically.

With my perfectly legal plans printed and spread out before me on the floor of my shed and a pint of double-strength coffee inside me, I had, rather to my own surprise, no great difficulty in reconstructing the Armalite using my father's Imperial-gauge toolbox.

The greatest problem was that I had firmly decided, just in case, to take great care that no possible trace of my bodily contact should remain on the gun.

After all, you never know who, public or privatised, might have access to your innocent bio-data in New Labour's quasi-police state! So I kept Sarah's kitchen gloves on throughout the entire process, though it made things very fiddly. But however long it took, nothing deterred me. No bruises and pinches set me back. This was striking, because I had often given up completely on a piece of IKEA furniture for much less. I was delighted to find myself working away at the sort of problems which would normally have stopped me dead.

—Here I am, Dad, look at me!

Yes, well, now, what next? *Install hammer in receiver with feet pointing rearward away from hammer.* Feet? Whose? Mine? Oh, I see. Yes, that seems right. *Use 5/32" punch to retain hammer in place as you insert hammer retaining pin.*

Fine, OK, got that. *When installing the bolt catch, first drive the roll pin about halfway into the rear hump from the rear of the receiver.* Rear hump? Rear hump? So, does that mean . . . Aha! Yes, yes, perfectly clear. *Install spring on to hammer, ends of spring to rear and shoulder on back of hammer.* Eh? Oh, I see. Yikes! Ouch!

I whipped my fingers out just in time to avoid them being seriously caught and checked that the rubber gloves had not been perforated.

As I worked away, I pondered this new ability to accept pain and endure fiddliness. I had often wished to feel like this. My father, who was by trade an electrical engineer, was so inured to volts and amps that he could hold a wired-up spark plug with his bare hands whilst the engine was running and happily show off the leaping blue sparks. I once saw him send an incautious friend flying across a garage by smilingly inviting him to do likewise. Perhaps it was just a question of becoming accustomed to anything? For example, if I had been systematically head-butted every day for some weeks, back in the early seventies, rather than repeatedly being surprised by spontaneous and unexpected nuttings every now and then over a period of dismal years, would I have become head-butt-proof? Perhaps Dad should have beaten me when I did wrong or acted spinelessly, not simply sighed and gone back to his shed?

Insert spring and detent into receiver. Compress detent in recess using 3/32" punch and rotate tool. Shit, this is a bit tricky . . .

My God, imagine it! Walking into a rough pub with absolute confidence that if any little drunk decided to have a go at me, I could simply take his first shot smack on the nose or cheekbone, then say, in good Devon:

—Right, mate, now we know you can dish it out, so let's see if you can take it . . .

Yes, perhaps after the Very Important Paper was done, I would sort out this irrational fear of physical violence once and for all. *Push out tool with pivot pin and rotate until detent is in groove of pivot pin.* Gotcha! Hey, why not? I could find a local gym where they taught boxing. Phil was bound to know of one. I could pay someone to hit me in the face, very gently at first, of course, until I simply grew to accept pain and became unafraid of it, and then of punching back.

How different my life would be. I could teach my new skill to Jack and William so that I need never worry about them being bullied again. Perhaps I should start tomorrow? It wouldn't take me long, surely? It wasn't as if I was that unfit. I could still swim a length underwater. By the time I came to give the Very Important Paper, I could've learned enough so that if any pebble-lensed, stoop-shouldered, bearded little shit dared to bring up Panke's membership of the KGB again, I could just step down from the lectern, walk through the rows of chairs with a bare-toothed smile on my face and deck the four-eyed little pen-pushing bastard with a single right hook to his flabby, chinless . . .

I pushed my spectacles back up on to my nose, and yawned. The drink had ebbed away, leaving a sour tidemark somewhere behind my eyes. My skin felt like thin old newspaper and I realised that I had, bit by bit, become thoroughly chilled out, here in the shed. I was grey. Perhaps I should just call it a night right now and crawl to bed and . . .

I finished the bit of gunsmithing I was doing and looked blearily down.

I blinked.

There, on the shed floor before me, quite unexpectedly, was a gun. A whole and entire assault rifle.

32: A Lump of Metal from the World of Men

Kneeling, I looked down at the finished gun and felt life prickle back quickly into my cheeks. I stood quickly up and shifted my weight this way and that, to look at the gun from every possible angle, as if I might thereby suddenly understand it. I leaned and peered. No secrets were revealed. I knelt again, stretched out a hand, and speedily withdrew it, as if the gun were some sleeping but highly aggressive animal.

Ridiculous. It was not alive. It was just a passive thing. It would do exactly what I wanted it to do, no more, no less. As the AR-15.com site had said a hundred times, guns don't kill people, people kill people. This object would, *could*, no more attack someone without me explicitly ordering it to, by a complicated and conscious process of loading, readying, pointing and shooting, than, for example, my laptop would or could send a lascivious email to one of my female students unless I myself typed one in and clicked it away with full intent.

Exactly. If I walked away right now and left the gun, it would just lie here for ever until the dust of centuries covered it. It had no will and no desire. It was neither good nor evil. And after all, when you thought about it, to know something of the feel of a gun was, for many males, indeed quite probably for a majority of males now living on earth, simply par for the course. Just another part of life.

I lifted it cautiously, only to get the heft of it.

There, you see? Was that so hard? Just a power tool, really. And one I had myself just put together. Nothing scary or mythical whatever, once you got your hands on it and your brain round it. Lite indeed. My father's old metal-shelled electric drill had been heavier than this, surely? And smaller than I would have thought. Just a normal lump of metal from the world of men who bowl tyres, flip manholes, hump crates. A thing cleanly made in a perfectly proud and legal factory somewhere, like anything else you care to name.

Now, why not try it? Just fit on the *buttstock* (ha, I knew it was *something* to do with butts and stocks). Simple. And see how my hands, which I normally assumed were just much too small for manliness, curled perfectly well around what I would until that evening have called *the handle thingy* but which I now knew was properly known as the *pistol grip*. We live and learn. No trouble at all for my index finger to slide into the trigger guard and on to the trigger itself.

Meanwhile, the left hand presumably goes here, under that fat waffly bit around the barrel, in fact aka, to we in the know, the *handguard assembly*. Like so. Yes, no doubt at all about that. Lift the barrel to horizontal, nothing to it really. Now, if I recall, you pull back that slide thing to *cock* it (really, does it all have to be *quite* so Freudian, tee hee?). It's perfectly safe, I know the thing is empty because I just *built it myself*, ha ha! Now, draw the buttstock into my shoulder. See how well it fits! And now close one eye, lower my head, squint along the sights and . . .

Clack!

Quite fun, actually.

I lowered it slightly and turned it in my hands. It shone darkly. There really was something about it. Like a fine camera, an expensive watch, a Mercedes engine. Chunky, sort of, yet light and exact. Purely functional and, perhaps for that very reason in a way, yes, in a

146

very real way, beautiful. You had to laugh, really, at the ridiculous English fear of this inert and guiltless piece of precision machine tooling. Really, we are just *so* tight-arsed. Or indeed, *assed*, ha ha!

Yes well, but that was enough laughing.

Now it was time to go and get rid of it.

With playful reluctance, I lowered the gun. I taped the magazines to the sides of the handguard. I snapped two links from a roll of stout bin bags and soon had the entire thing swaddled in black plastic. Jauntily, I slung it under my arm like an umbrella. How easy it all was. How ridiculously scared I had earlier been. A gun, so what? Into the river it was going. Yes: so easy to throw, now.

I stepped outside the shed and tested it, spear-like. Absolutely. If I wanted to, I would from here be able to guarantee clearing the garden wall without the slightest difficulty. I could do it, right now, were it not for my responsible fears as to who might discover it. Much, much better than trying to control a whirling bolas of metal weights flying about loose inside a bin bag.

You see? The practical application of pure reason. Excellent.

Away with it, then, and tomorrow back to normal. Back to work!

In fact, it had been an interesting evening, one way or another. Quite refreshing, really. Not often something unexpected happens, these days. God, how I was going to work tomorrow!

I yawned, left the shed and marched across our stupid little garden, my secret gun casually held in my arms. Little did anyone know, ha ha.

Through the house, grab the laptop and so briskly out, for the second time that evening, into the darkly luminous bowl of the London night.

33: The Genetic Make-up of London

I set happily off for Tower Bridge.

Geography, hydrography and psychology agreed on my destination: Tower Bridge was easy for me to reach and the water must be pretty deep that far down the river. I had visited it with the boys only two weeks before and I recalled the low railings beside the narrow pavements. An easy throw. And anyway, we all like the big moments of our lives to have good backdrops: it makes us feel as if nature gave a damn. Suicides choose beauty spots. Once the gun and laptop were safely drowned, I could stop and walk around in the quiet of the night, have a cigarette as I sat on the old cannons, where I had sat as a boy, and watch the wintry dawn.

I would make it memorable. From tonight, whenever I got bored or annoyed with life, I would recall this moment of picturesque liberation and be content.

That was the plan.

But as I drove northwards I found myself vainly trying to work out what the hell was going on in London tonight.

In my mind's eye, I had clearly seen myself cruising towards the big river along streets as deserted as in some sixties TV programme about an alien invasion. So why were there so many people about? It was an ordinary weekday night, for God's sake, and four-thirty a.m. Could Londoners really so deeply hate the Congestion Charge? What else could possibly send so many of them setting off for work so early in the late-November darkness?

Had flexitime gone totally mad under the merciless assault of the global free market, forcing all these poor sods out of bed so early? Had I missed a general-election night or a moonshot?

At length, of course, I had to admit that the roads and pavements were alive not with determined or exploited workers fighting their way to their jobs, but with drugged-up, drunken little arseholes who were still out partying. Our vile neighbours, who evidently considered it perfectly normal to start after midnight, were in fact merely like everyone else.

I drove onwards, stunned, now merely trying to avoid a crash, but my cheeks and stomach grew cold with the knowledge that I had set out, with an assault rifle under my passenger seat, into a world whose most basic coordinates were completely unknown to me.

The last time I had been out anywhere near this time of night in London had been on my twenty-seventh birthday. Which was not that long ago, for God's sake! We pub-crawled down Holborn to hit the late-night Fleet Street pubs (which had an *extension*, oh, holy word!), then wandered Smithfield, looking vainly for this amazing pub someone swore he had been to, where we could get a drink *even at 3 a.m.*! We never found it, and had headed back to Soho, where there was allegedly a Greek restaurant that would serve you wine all night if you kept buying food. We did not find that either, and ended up drinking coffee in Bar Italia, with Soho stone-dead around us, before walking back home to that rough, cheap place, Notting Hill.

Was it possible that during the span of my full-blown adult lifetime someone had fundamentally altered the genetic make-up of London's humanity, erasing all biological need for rest? How could people cope with this? Did nobody work any more? Or sleep? For a hundred thousand years, *Homo sapiens* had, unless excessive heat demanded a siesta or excessive latitude made everything nuts, gone to bed roughly when it got dark and risen roughly when it got light. Night had always been for thieves and troubled minds. I had been pissed many, many nights as a student but could count on one hand the times I had actually stayed up all night. No one stayed up all night. There was nothing to do if you did, and nowhere to do it, and no cheap substances to make it physically possible anyway. You couldn't even watch telly.

But now here everyone was.

I was still trying to adjust to this new reality as I arrived at the final approach to Tower Bridge. From the high Victorian iron walkways, lasers flashed and music blared. There was some kind of bloody night-club up there for God's sake, in full swing, at this time in the morning. On a weekday! And the pavements down here at ground level were thronged with drunken idiots photographing each other with telephones.

A billow of human seaweed suddenly washed out right in front of me: part of a large scrum of pissed gits had overflowed from the pavement and on to the roadway. I had to brake hard. The gun slid forward. I bent sideways in order to reach down, to shove its bag-shrouded butt back under the passenger seat. The bloody black plastic had snagged on something. I leaned further, feeling with my hand for what the hell was going on under the seat. I looked down too long, veered the car slightly, scuffed a kerb. Wild-eyed pedestrians shouted and spat. A horn sounded long and hard behind me. Headlights flashed angrily in my mirrors.

I looked hastily up from the gun and found myself staring right into the lens of a CCTV camera mounted high on the ironwork.

34: Cameras

I froze. Somewhere a monitor must be showing, and a hard disk must be recording, a pale monochrome image (or did they have colour, these days?) of my amazed face looking up through my windscreen.

Of course, I knew theoretically about CCTV now being everywhere. Indeed, *The Paper* had expressed outrage many times over the last few months, (a) at the fact that Big Brother Britain apparently had more CCTV than anywhere else in the world and (b) that Britons themselves seemed perfectly happy with this state of affairs and, rather than taking to the streets in defence of their liberties, as demanded by the stout burghers of N1 and NW3, usually demanded only to know how come *their* street had not got cameras yet.

So yes, I knew about the cameras all right: I had simply not factored them into my plans. CCTV belonged to the realm of MyFace, SecondLife and YouTube. I knew about things like that, and here and there I might even name-drop them into the odd lecture just to keep up the fiction that I was a relatively young lecturer, but I had no real conception of them, having grown to full adulthood in a world without them. They were not on my working maps of the world. They existed and I knew that they did, but they concerned me no more than online multi-player gaming.

Except now one of the bloody proto-Fascist things must have just recorded me weaving slightly but definitely as I leaned over to do something under the passenger seat while driving through a mass of partying drunks on Tower Bridge.

Hastily, I thrust the gun back out of sight, snags and all.

Christ, what kind of country had this become? A place where everyone was under surveillance all day every day (or 24/7 as the idiots would no doubt say now)? Where we were all assumed to be vaguely guilty until proven innocent?

But calm down.

Surely to God, the cameras would not be sharp enough to actually have seen the gun winking out from under the seat? Unless they really could see number plates from orbit. Could they? Could the police really say *enhance, enhance, enhance* and zoom for ever into the picture, the way they do in all spy films these days? Surely not? But what did I know about CCTV technology? Nothing. And now that my eye was in, I could already see the next bloody camera rearing up before me.

Fear gripped me. Not fear of the cameras as such, but fear of my own horrific ignorance, of my insane stupidity. My intelligence about this world was hopelessly out of date. I simply had no chance out here. I had to get back to safety, that was all.

I forced myself to drive slowly and carefully over the bridge. It was OK. The little shimmy had been nothing, really, had it? Surely, even if the CCTV were connected to some actual screen being watched by real live people, my tiny loss of direction would not be thought enough to send out a car to look for me, let alone make it worth checking up on me tomorrow? Of course not. And yet, I had an Armalite under my passenger seat. In central London, where there must be more cameras and cops per inch than anywhere else in the country. There was no question of dumping the gun here now. Flight and concealment were now paramount.

I U-turned as soon as possible and cruised carefully southwards back across the bridge. Figures flitted and loomed out of the bright-lit darkness, scanning me with reddened, dullard eyes to see if I was indeed an un-licensed minicab. I ignored them, other than to avoid crushing them.

It was OK. I already had another plan.

I would drive, very carefully indeed, to the M25. I would simply beetle slowly along in the leftmost lane amidst the massed traffic of a dark winter's morning rush hour. I would make quite sure that there was no one close enough behind to read my number plate and no cameras about. It did not matter how long this took or where I saw my chance. If I had to go right around the blasted thing twice, who cared? When the time came, when I saw my chance, I would just let the gun slip from my window, on to the hard shoulder and away for ever. Even if anyone saw the bin-bagged lump falling, no one in their right mind would stop on the dark, wet M25 just to see what crap some git had chucked out of their car. I would be free. Surely? So long as I was not actually on film throwing out the gun, I would be all right, wouldn't I? The gun would in all probability not be found for days, maybe even weeks. By the time it was stum-bled upon by some trucker taking a leak, tens of thousands, hundreds of thousands, millions of cars would be on film passing by in the vicinity. The police would not, could not check every plate, could they? Anyway, how would they know which batch of film to choose? Surely, even today, there was no way they would be able to . . .

—Christ! I slammed on the brakes, my wheels juddered as the ABS kicked in and my body shot forward against the seat belts. A ghostly young woman with a thin-lipped face and staring eyes, dressed in little more than underwear, stood square in front of my bumper, drumming on my bonnet, having leapt bodily out to stop me.

—Ta-xi-i! she screeched. —Yee-haah! Claire, get in!

—Peckham! screamed a voice beside my head. I jumped and turned. At my window battered another girl. She had employed blonde hair dye, shades and lipstick to construct, on some instinct, a Freudian mask of such primal effectiveness that all I could register was: blonde, shades and lipstick.

I could not move. My windscreen was almost filled by the half-naked, bloodless girl, who was now actually clambering over the bonnet in front of me. To my right, the insanely exaggerated assembly of eyes, hair and lips banged on the window three inches from my head. In the corner of my vision (I did not dare to look down) I could clearly see the black-wrapped gun, which had decelerated its way almost completely out from under the seat and had, on the way, torn partially through the plastic. The end of the *buttstock* was now sticking clean out.

For a wild second I considered simply gunning the engine and speeding off, with the mad girl still on the bonnet, if necessary. And then I saw, beyond her pale, young-old face, the eye of the next CCTV camera, staring directly into mine.

This time I was in genuine trouble.

35: Good as Gold

No doubt it took something a bit special to grab the attention of the underpaid, half-trained, part-time para-police minions who were idly scanning the banks of night-time images piping endlessly down the wires from the myriad cameras of London. And no doubt a screen filled by the half-dressed arse of a skinny girl climbing over the bonnet of a car while her friend screams at the driver, a shifty-looking middle-aged man out alone in his Merc at this time of night, was just the thing to do it.

Christ, they must be zooming in and locking on already. I had to stop this, and in a friendly way, and fast.

—OK, OK. Peckham. Fine, whatever. Just get in. No, no, the back, the back! I'm not opening the front! Right, get in and shut the door.

—Just drive, mate, we got money, see?

—Never mind the money. I don't want your money.

—Well that's all you're getting, mate, so don't kid yourself!

—No, I mean, look, I'm not a bloody taxi, OK? Now, please, sit still and just let me get off the bridge before I kill someone.

—Claire, he's a fucking weirdo. Let us out! I'm outta here!

—Don't! We're moving, for God's sake. You'll hurt yourself.

—You fucking stupid, Jez? You want to go back and see Skaggsy? Stay in the fucking cab.

—He said he isn't a cab. I'm outta here.

—Stay in the fucking cab, Jez.

—He's a weirdo.

—*You* stopped *me*, for Christ's sake!

—Skaggsy'll fucking kill us, you stupid cow. Driver, Peckham. We got money, see? And you just shut the fuck up, Jez, right? Stay in the cab.

—Ha ha ha!

—Ha ha ha!

—Now, er, ladies. Where did you want to go exactly? I don't really know London very well yet and . . .

—Peckham.

—Well, you'll have to show me the . . . this is ridiculous. Look, I'm not a cab. I'll drop you by the nearest tube and . . .

—We'll scream.

—What?

—If you drop us in the middle of fucking nowhere, we'll scream.

—We'll tear your fucking face off, mate.

—We'll tell everyone about you kerb-crawling.

—I wasn't! I'm a married man, with kids.

—Your missus know you're out here then, mate?

—What? Well, no, not exactly, but that's because . . .

—You like young girls, do you? Bet you do. You all do.

—Shut the fuck up, Claire, ha ha ha!

—Look, I was just, well, I just decided to go out, I . . .

—Yeah yeah yeah.

—He ain't going to make a fuss, Claire, you can tell.

—Na, he don't want to make trouble. You can tell.

—He'll take us home, won't you, mate?

—He'll be good as gold, won't he?

—Well, yes, of course, I'll take you, but honestly, you'll have to direct me. I really don't know this area at all.

156

—There you go, Jez. Told you he was all right.

—Cheers, mate. Ta. Next left, second right.

I obeyed, thinking only of the gun lying almost openly beside me. Just do what they say, and get rid of them. Then straight to the M25. Or maybe not? God, I needed to be careful. I needed to think, quietly and logically. I needed to sit in an old library somewhere, my natural habitat, and . . .

—Second right you said, er, girls?

—Yeah. Then keep on for a bit.

I turned as ordered. There was absolutely nothing else I could do.

36: No Cameras

We couldn't have been more than half a mile from Tower Bridge, but now we were at the end of the world.

I turned again as ordered and entered a long, low street where hopeless-looking shops, all with graffiti-covered steel shutters, stood in the patchy sodium light as far as the eye could see. A single grey-white lighted takeaway joint buzzed with shadowy groups of young people in hoods, gathered about cars drawn up at self-consciously crazy angles. Over the scene loomed high-rise flats which seemed to rear up from directly behind the dead shops, their tops lost in the foggy darkness. Their few lit windows, high in the air, made me shiver.

Sniff!

—That's better. Oh, nice gear, Jez.

—Excuse me, um, what are you . . . ? Oh God, look, that stuff's illegal. Sorry, look, you can't just go and take cocaine in my car . . .

—You want a line, driver? Fair's fair, Jez, give the man a line.

They smiled up at me with whacked-out eyes. What if I did? What if I took their drugs and then had a laugh with them and took them home and showed them the gun? Then they would know I was no ordinary boring old bastard! Then they might, who knew, they might even *both* decide to . . .

BAAAARP!

Suddenly the cabin was flooded by headlights and filled with the outraged blast of a horn right behind us. My grip on the wheel locked tight, my foot instinctively lifted off the accelerator and covered the brake. The glaring lights veered out, the horn blared again and then the car was past us and in front, brake lights glowing angry red. Eyes shone back at me from the death-pale masks of furious male faces, black faces and white faces but all lit to a zombie pallor by my own headlights. I had no choice but to stop or ram them. I hit the brakes.

—Oh fuck! Fuck! screamed the girls.

—Who are they? I cried, and *cried* was pretty well the right word.

—I told you, you stupid cow! snapped one.

—Fuck them. Drive on! screamed the other one.

I put the car in gear again and tried to swing out past my enemies. This was a public street, for God's sake, there were cars passing now and then on the other side of the road, there were even cars behind me. Surely nothing much could happen here?

But it could: the other car simply reversed into my path and yawed round deliberately to block the entire road. I stopped, disbelief stronger even than fear for a brief second. This could not be happening. They could not simply block the whole street like this. People could not simply be mounting the pavement to get past us without stopping. Where the hell were the cameras? There must be cameras. The five young men in the car could not seriously mean to just leave their car like that, get out and come strutting towards us. This was London, this was England, this was . . .

I flipped my lock shut.

The police. How long would it take the police to get to us? Mobile, quick.

The police? How could *I* call the police?

With terrifying ease, the obvious leader of the young men snapped the Mercedes star off my bonnet and pocketed it. Then there were faces at the windows, hands going for the doors, fists and boots on roof and panels.

—Jez, get out the fucking car, you bitch, and give me my charlie back.

To my amazement, the blonde girl buzzed her window down.

—It-is-not-fucking-yours, Skaggsy.

—I bought it!

—I gave you the fucking money!

—You lent it me, Jez, you bitch!

—You never fucking pay me back anyway.

—I fucking do, every time.

—Open the fucking door, mate.

—Go on then, mate, open it. He's my fucking boyfriend. Let me fucking out or he'll kill you.

—Yes, yes, right, fine . . .

I pressed the switch that opened all the doors. The blonde girl got out and smashed the largest of the youths round the face. Unfortunately, I caught his eye as he recoiled.

—What you fucking looking at, you old cunt? What you fucking doing giving my bitch a lift? You some kind of fucking pervert?

—Look, I was just going home, I . . .

—Listen to him. Posh fucking pervert.

—Leave him alone, Skaggsy, he only give us a lift.

—Fucking posh kerb-crawler in a Merc!

—Get him out!

I flipped the switch and my own door locked, but I was too late: the passenger door was already open, and arms were reaching in for me.

37: Dad Pants

It was happening. My nightmare. After all these years of work and qualifications, I had stupidly forgotten who I was and had wandered unthinkingly into the part of the comprehensive playground where no teachers ever looked, to be hopelessly surrounded by tough boys from the council houses.

I squirmed round and braced my back against the still-locked driver's door, thinking instinctively of trying to kick the grasping hands away. But I stopped myself before I kicked. I knew this scenario all too well. This was not normal male pecking-order violence with some logic and limitation to it, however nasty. If I hit back, let alone kicked back, there was no grudging handshake coming my way. I would only make things worse. I was *them*, the *other*, the boy with the clean uniform and the posh voice in the tough school, the lone straggler from the rival band of Cro-Magnons, the effete wine-sipping Muslim shopkeeper in the town surrounded by hill-farming, vodka-tossing Serbs. This was open season, sheer class hatred, that first cousin of genocide, and I was going to be very lucky if I got home at all tonight.

—Ah, he didn't do nothing, Skaggsy, he just give us a lift.

—Fancy my girl, do you, you old pervert?

So I didn't kick. I let them pull.

—Ha ha, his trousers are coming down.

—Ha ha ha!

Laughter! There was hope then.

My old childhood senses felt hope. If the rough boys were laughing at me, I might yet escape hospital. If I just played the clownish, posh punchbag, the man with no shame and hence no value, I might yet get away with a mild kicking. I could not remember exactly which underpants I had fished blindly from the drawer in darkness and somehow managed to struggle into whilst juggling a whimpering Mariana at five this morning, but I prayed that it was a good, baggy, comical pair. It seemed likely.

—Ha ha ha, look at his big baggy Dad Pants!

Yes! Hope! Thank God for M&S!

—Oh God, I exaggerated my own accent, —My new pants!

—Ha ha ha! His new pants! Get them off!

I let go of the wheel, shielding my balls with one hand as I allowed them to drag me over the central console, out through the passenger door and into the rain. It felt cold and greasy on my naked thighs. I floundered entertainingly around in the supposedly vital effort to save my precious pants. With a bit of luck I would look so utterly wretched when stripped of my underwear that I would have more value as entertainment than as boot fodder. And there were girls here, however scary, which made my position far more hopeful. Girls brake men. I made my senses freeze over, the way I had done so many, many times on walks home from school in the wintry dark, and just made sure that I managed to turn over as they pulled me free, protecting my vulnerable face and presenting, instead, my comical arse.

As my bare knees landed in the gutter and the puddles, I shut my eyes, left my body and flew to that quiet arctic library far beyond the kicks, a place I had not needed to visit since my mid-teens, but whose key now leapt straight into my forty-five-year-old hand.

Here we were again, then, after all. This was my place and I would never escape it. Oh well, what did Nietzsche say? We are all only old barrel organs with one tune and eternity itself turning the handle. Yes indeed. Ah, interesting, so *that* was what it felt like to be kicked up the cold, wet, bare arse by one of those ridiculously shiny, plastic-coated trainers I had seen on these young men's feet. Surprisingly painful. But only the arse. Just try unobtrusively to protect the balls, that's all; if they don't hit the balls, nothing matters much when you are knees on the floor and arsewise to your attacker . . .

—Ow! Ouch! Ag!

—Ha ha ha!

—Get the old cunt all the way out then!

—Look at his fat fucking old arse, ha ha!

At this moment my hands fell upon the cool metal beneath the passenger seat.

38: Unencumbered by Trousers

As my fingers wrapped around the Armalite, Newton gave up and Einstein took over. Time hit the brakes hard.

The laughs still cackled in my ears, the nylon-tipped trainers still pummelled my thighs and arse, but the gun, and my hands on the gun, seemed to exist in an entirely different time stream.

I clearly watched it slide free from the ripped, snagged bags as my right hand, finger already groping for the trigger guard, pulled it forwards and outwards. I rolled back, down and to my left, as the gun came free, *buttstock* first. My back hit the tarmac, the barrel swung high and round, landing plumb in my waiting left palm.

Unencumbered by trousers, I managed to jerk my feet up towards my arse and so make a springing arch with my legs and spine. I screamed aloud and shot myself backwards and upwards a foot or so. I had time to register clearly every gramme of the impact, every millimetre of give in the metal panel when my back and shoulders impacted with the rear door of my car. As I hit, my right hand landed plumb on the ammunition clips. I was tearing one of them free from the handguard before my naked backside had even settled again on the wet roadway. The hideous, shameful feel of the cold water up my arsehole was all I needed now.

—Aaaaaah! I roared with all my teeth bared, and then the little magazine slotted into the gun as if drawn by magnetism to its appointed place. My hand slapped it home with a *chunk* that could only be studio-enhanced. And when I, quite without thinking, snapped back the bolt with my left finger and thumb, the *chonk* seemed to issue from some deep and metal-lined cellar.

Time synchronised itself again, and I blinked.

So did they.

—Fuck, said one of them.

39: Respect

They froze. I froze. The whole world froze.

—Shit, shit, shit. Now look what you've made me do, you stupid little bastards. It's loaded and cocked. What the hell am I going to do now?

—Fuck me, is it real, mate?

—Of course it's real, you bloody little idiot.

—Respect, man.

—I don't want your brainless bloody imitation-Yank respect, you walking argument against everything I believe in. Actually, yes I fucking well do, because I've worked hard all my life, unlike you. But the main thing is right now I just don't want this sodding thing to go off and I have no idea how to defuse it or disarm it or uncock it, or whatever you say, without actually shooting the bloody thing off.

—Hey, man, we just thought you was, you know, just some old git in a crap Merc.

—Crap? You calling my Merc crap?

—Hey, no, only jesting. Safe, man.

—Safe? Safe? No it is fucking not safe, or at least, I have no bloody idea whether it's safe or not because I am just a normal bloody Englishman so what the hell do I know about guns? Eh?

—I dunno. Fuck. What do you know about guns? Shit, no need to point it! Fuck!

—Know about guns? I know sod all about guns, of course, you wandering benefit sponge! And, since I'm an old git, I'll point my gun at whomsoever I bloody well like, OK?

166

—Point taken, man. Whomsoever. No worries.

—No worries? What kind of bloody Australian surfing bollocks is that? Since when were there no worries? This is England, and yes, actually, there are worries. I'm worried about my kids and my bloody mortgage and a million arseholes like you. You bullied anyone recently? Made life miserable for any shy, hard-working kids lately, have you? Eh?

—Easy, man. We just want to go home, OK?

—So give me my trousers back, you foul little fucking cokehead.

—Sure, man. Cool. Get the man's trousers, Biggsy.

—Trousers, Skaggsy.

—It's not me fucking wants them. Give them back to the man, you stupid cunt!

—Oh yeah. Trousers, man.

—Put the trousers in the back of the car. Very slowly.

—They're there, man. Trousers in.

—OK. Now, move away from the trousers. Easy. Thank you. Back off, and let me get in. I really don't know how easily this thing goes off. I really don't. And I don't know where the safety catch is, if there is one, and I have no idea whether it's set to fire just one bullet or the whole bloody lot. I wouldn't want to save the taxpayer several hundred thousand pounds over the next few decades by blowing one or more of you in half, would I?

—No way, man. That would be very bad stuff. Look, hey, you win, no need to keep your finger on the trigger like that.

—Ah, but I can't move it, you see. I think that if I move it at all, I might move it the wrong way.

—You just keep your finger right there, man.

—I'll try. Oh, and would you give me back my bonnet badge, please? Or do you really want a taste of my little Armalite?

—I got it, man. Hey, sorry, y'know.

—Toss it into the car. Thank you, gentlemen. A bit further back, please. Christ, look at my arms, they're shaking. Would you just back off and give me some fucking space!

They backed off so fast that one of them fell over. He scrambled up, arms shouting *I surrender*, clearly terrified that his accidental fall might shock me into loosing off at him. His fear was the best thing I had seen in months. I heeled the passenger door shut (ah yes, the reassuring Mercedes *clunk!*) and walked round the car very, very slowly. Keeping the gun pointing out and up, I slid into the driver's seat. Then I very carefully lowered the barrel downward and arced it over into the car, making damn sure it never pointed anywhere near my face, until it was aiming squarely at the passenger door. I was then able to swing it through ninety degrees in a horizontal plane and lower it on to the passenger seat. It was now pointing straight forward. At last I dared take my finger away from the trigger. Nothing happened. I slid it forward and allowed the snout to dip into the footwell. There was now room to let the *buttstock* down over the front lip of the seat, lay the whole thing on the floor of the car then start to slide it back underneath, into darkness.

I sat there for some time, then found that the key was in my hand. I started the car. She caught first time, as always. Yes, I had done well indeed, motor-wise! As I drove off, I did not even bother to check my enemies. I could see them in the corner of my eye, standing completely motionless. I looked back once in the mirror and there they still were, as if waiting for an Edwardian photographer to say it was all right for them to move once again. Would they stay frozen there for ever, victims of my modern gorgonry, one of the sights of south London for generations to come?

Trouserless still, I steered, accelerated and slowed the car for perhaps five minutes like a learner suddenly left to go solo, with enormous care in the actual business of driving but without being in the least aware of where I was heading. The car's bonnet seemed to cover acres, the dash looked a mile away, the steering wheel felt as if it was made entirely from soft rubber. I saw a quiet space on the side of the road. I punctiliously mirrored, then signalled, then manoeuvred, and so pulled up in text-book fashion.

I sat there awhile, succeeded at length in making my hands release their white death grip on the wheel, got out of the car with some difficulty, opened the back door, found my soaking trousers and pulled them on.

For some reason, that clammy wetness gripping my legs was the final straw, a truly dreadful feeling, a lost memory of shitty infanthood or a dark intimation of cold senility. It shrank my soul.

I considered, took a couple of steps away from the car, leaned down and was quite calmly but very profoundly sick.

40: My Little Armalite

After the chucking-up had stopped, a mountain-top clarity dawned on me. I stood there leaning on the bonnet of my Mercedes. Through the tears squeezed out by the vomiting and the rain running down from my hair, I could see all too well.

My little Armalite, I had said to the hoodied youths. Well, I knew where that came from, didn't I?

No, no.

Oh yes.

Alone and cold before the court of my own memory, I swallowed queasily. I now knew why I had immediately recognised the silhouette of the *upper receiver assembly* so clearly. It had been a voice from a past to which, unlike most of my pasts, I did not refer.

Most of my peers and friends enjoyed my tales of manly derring-do on the Miners' Strike. They laughed to hear how I had boldly outraged the young Tories at college by singing 'Malvinas Argentinas'. They smiled wistfully at my Schweyk-like stories of the bad yet somehow good old days in East Germany. After all, everyone had a soft spot for the long-gone miners, no one thought the Falklands War justified and pretty well anything was better, or at least no worse, than America's sole world hegemony, wasn't it?

But even at dinner parties filled with fellow readers of *The Paper*, I never boasted, however drunk I got, that I had been for some years a fellow traveller of the IRA.

Said it.

Oh God.

I writhed as Memory stirred itself yet again.

For years, it had been a one-sided battle. My brain, being human, is equipped with a filter no computer can emulate. I have a crack five-star pre-installed utility called Self-Respect, which can wipe Memory pure every time. However often Memory came back and tried again, Self-Respect had always won, hands down. It *simply could not* be true. I *could not* have succoured and glorified thugs who destroyed ordinary people's lives and killed children with bombs left at bus stops. It was just not possible.

But Memory was armed now, backed by the fire-power of the gun in my car, and this time it was not going to give in. At last, it rebelled.

On the merciless screen of my mind, grey pebble-dashed council estates in Derry (*how authentic, how tough, how earthy!*) faded back nastily into life, their walls covered in murals of men holding up machine guns with very recognisable silhouettes. Ah, those trademark carry-handles.

Yes indeed, that was how I had immediately recognised the gun this evening.

I was winched back into that shameful past. From deep in my gutless guts, the long-dreaded words were dredged up, flecked in vomit.

No, please! I can't! I can't sing that.

But I could.

I now leaned on my Mercedes bonnet and began softly to sing, ludicrous faux-Irish accent and all, a man keening for my lost leftie soul, all alone in the dark and the November rain:

It's down by the Bogside that I want to be,
Lying in a ditch with me Provo company,

With a comrade to me left and a comrade to me right,
And a clip of ammunition for my little Armalite.

No, no, no. It had to go and it had to go right now.
Into the river with it.

For a terrifying moment, I realised that I was
picturing myself too, weighted down by the clutched
gun, plunging gratefully into the black waters of the
Thames. If I made it look like an accident, perhaps
Sarah and the kids would still be OK, insurance-
wise . . . ?

I looked wildly around. Now for the first time, I saw
where I was: a roadside in the middle of nowhere, somewhere in the deepest armpit of south-east London. A
hole without CCTV. Now then, without further ado.
Just slip the bloody thing out of the car and drive.

I spat a rancid gobbet of after-sick from my mouth
and sauntered innocently round to the passenger door.
I paused to let a thudding carload of scum pass me by,
laughingly avoiding their scornful gazes (little did they
know!) and then bent low in order to slide the gun out,
muzzle-first, and just lay it in the gutter, naturally planning to be very, very careful not to point it at anything,
especially myself.

But as my hand went for the gun barrel, I simply
seized up.

I just could not touch the thing.

Before I could stop myself, I had leaped back and
slammed the door shut again with a helpless little yelp
of animal loathing, as if I had just discovered that my
car held a very large and very deadly insect. I tried to
force myself to have another try, but now I could not
even bring my hand up to the door before it jerked
itself back again. My breath jammed. Sweat rose
instantly through my cold skin and my hands shook

uncontrollably. My face locked in what I knew must be a grimace of pure terror.

I stood there for many seconds, staring helplessly at my own car, getting soaked.

Then the corners of my eyes were alight with colourful flashes as the police car pulled smoothly up behind me.

41: Vulnerability Assessment

Pleasure would be too strong a word, but as I let the lights of the police car flicker in the wet lenses of my specs, I listened to my own breathing and felt a wave of positively Eastern fatalism wash over me. Not pleasure, but not pain either.

After all the endlessly impossible choices of the evening and the night, it came as a relief. Perhaps this was how real criminals felt when, after long days and nights feverishly plotting creaky alibis and trying to work out whether their mates had in fact already shopped them, they decided to just confess all and be done with it?

No more decisions. Thank God for that.

I was ready now, and so I looked round. Behind their rain-spattered windscreen, the policemen slowly unhitched their seat belts and exchanged some kind of merry quip. They would check the car, of course. They would find the gun, assembled by me, cocked and loaded. I felt my shoulders relax and my eyes droop at last with the wonderful liberation of unfreedom. Actually, perhaps *pleasure* was not too far off the mark.

The driver's window of the car buzzed slowly down. The officer looked out at the rain and addressed me as one might an idiotic child.

—Just wait for us there, would you, sir?

—Right. Um, right.

As the cops prepared their paperwork and their equipment in a leisurely fashion while keeping out of the wet, letting me feel the full force of the weather

and of their stately presence, I let the cold wind freeze
me over once again and prepared myself for this radical
change in my life.

Perhaps it would not be so bad, really?

Surely, in some way or another, the system would
recognise that I was not just any old criminal? I mean,
this was England. Surely here of all places judges could
spot, you know, that sort of thing?

```
Standard Client Vulnerablity Assessment
Client 129/676/CO Dr J. Goode*


Age of Client:      45
Ethnic Background:  White British
General Appearance: 5' 11", 13.5 st, light
                    build, clean-shaven
Distinguishing      Middle-class liberal
   Marks:
Education:          100th percentile (BA,
                    MA, PhD)
Establishment:      HM Prison Wormwood
                    Scrubs
Sentence:           Seven years
```

DETAILED ASSESSMENT
Dr Goode* has a peculiar status in this
establishment, the result of his
presenting a suite of characteristics
which tend to make a Client, in the eyes
of other Clients, worthy of 'respect'.

1) The AR-15 Armalite assault rifle is
generally known, even to senior UK Clients
with a background in armed robbery, only
as an iconic weapon from US films. To

have personally brandished one about, cocked and loaded, is thus approximately the equivalent to our Clients (in terms of 'respect') of a young offender having been convicted of joyriding at 150 mph through central London in a Ford GT40.

2) In the UK (unlike in the US) the vast majority of gun crime is carried out by Repeat Male Clients of HM Prison Service who also exhibit a marked propensity to carry out less extreme acts of violence on a daily basis. Hence Dr Goode* is (no doubt erroneously) perceived by senior and opinion-forming Clients as a spiritual comrade in terms of a broad capacity for criminal actions. He thus suffers none of the harassment or abuse normally experienced by our (very rare) Clients from social/professional class B.

3) Physically non-challenging and carefully dressed, making no effort to drop his aitches or otherwise modify the complex circumlocutions and arcane cultural references of social/professional class B (he has, indeed, placed his several degree certificates in prominent positions on his cell walls), Dr Goode* agreeably fulfils, to our other Clients, the stereotype of the Oxbridge Professor, by which title, abbreviated in the usual manner, he is universally known (though he never in fact attained such a position). He is the regular

recipient of gifts such as cigarettes
and pornography, the unofficial hard
currency of this establishment.

How long would I really get? Seven years? Five? Minus a few for parole? I might miss the boys being teenagers, but then again, at fourteen wouldn't they rather have a famous absent father who had been jailed for toting an Armalite, rather than an ineffectual old git following them round the house trying vainly to arouse their interest in German history or to lay down the feeble law?

Famous, yes!

I mean, how many people with PhDs and full lecturing CVs in the liberal arts go to prison for carrying automatic weapons around London? My God, I would be truly special at last! *The Paper* would not be able to resist me now, surely? When I got out, the TV series would be mine! I would get rich on the insatiable appetite of law-abiding people to slum it with criminals. I would probably earn more that way than by seven years' lecturing. And it would come in a lump sum, that was the vital thing which was never going to happen otherwise: think how this would affect the mortgage! Yes, yes, when you thought about it without being blinded by prejudice or bourgeois morality, a few years in prison would almost certainly do me more good than the same few years spent lecturing!

4) Dr Goode* appears positively to enjoy
prison life. Given that he was, says he,
for some years a blatant glorifier of a
bunch of green, fascist, terrorist
bastards just because it made him feel
tough and dangerous when he was in fact

a specky geek, he cheerfully asks on what grounds he should consider his present imprisonment in any way a global miscarriage of justice? He points out that he freely chose to spend his youth and strength, while others were surfing and dancing, beavering away in university libraries and wretched student rooms, unregarded and unloved, reading and annotating the works of a deservedly obscure writer (and, as it turned out, a lying, spying arsehole) from a now thankfully non-existent shithole which survived on the maps of Europe only so long as it was run by the Red Army. How, then, he asks, should he be imagined to view with any dismay the prospect of spending his tired and declining years in a prison library and a homely cell, visited regularly by the wife whom he never expected to win and the children (now resident within the catchment area of a decent school in Exeter) whom he never deserved, the object of many profitable offers for his memoirs (*The Paper* has already run several pieces on him), quietly reading the immortal works of Franz Kafka and suchlike?

*We are aware that the Home Office has asked HM Prison Service not to refer to Dr Goode by his academic title, but our latest legal advice is that we are obliged to do so. He is, as you know, currently appealing against the decision of the

University of London to revoke his
doctorate due to his non-liberal behaviour. His lawyers argue that . . .

—Been out tonight, sir?

—Sorry? No, no. Well, I mean, yes, obviously, but not in that way, no.

—We pulled you up because you were behaving somewhat strangely, sir.

—Yes, officer. You're right. I was. And I can explain everything.

42: Superbug

Oh well.

OK, here goes. Days in the cells coming up. Just have to tell the whole truth. And point out that if they look at the hard drive of any humanities lecturer in the country they'll find similar anti-American, anti-New Labour stuff, and that it all really means nothing. They could hardly argue that *every humanities lecturer in the country* is implicitly dodgy, could they? Of course not.

And yet, I was as guilty as sin. As a privileged, state-funded student at Oxford I had once nicked a milk bottle from the doorstep of a quiet little house where hard-working people and children slept. Just because I had been drinking all night and felt like it. I had been part of the moral rot, in big things and in small. Should I confess to that too? Yes, to everything: God, it was about time.

—I know I was behaving somewhat strangely, officer. And with good reason.

—I hope so, Dr Goode, because you'll appreciate that this doesn't look very good.

—Well, you see . . . I beg your pardon? Through the gauze of drink, fear and guilt, my brain pricked up at the unexpected sound of my own title. —How do you know my name?

—Computers, laughed the policeman, delighted at my amazement. —Just tap in your registration and there we are. Registered keeper of vehicle: Dr John Goode. Former address: Sheffield; six weeks ago registered change of address to London SE11. So, you new to London, Dr Goode, eh?

—Um, well, yes, I, got a job at University College, you see, and, well, anyway, look, I swear I'm not drunk, I'm happy to blow into the bag, officers! You see, the reason I'm out here, now, is, oh God, it's a bit special, actually, it's because . . .

—Oh, University College Hospital? My mum was in there last year. Very happy with her treatment too. Coming along very well. Perhaps you know her consultant? Dr Bracewell?

—Sorry?

—Dr Bracewell, consultant, genito-urinary medicine? he intoned, with insider's pride. I looked at his respectful face. My mouth shut once more. Light flooded my mind as my Englishman's class radar glowed. It had, after all, been trained every day of my life. It now kicked in with all the incalculable speed of an inherited instinct. I immediately knew that if I got my front foot forward fast . . .

—Aha. GU, eh? I think you mean *Mr* Bracewell, officer, since he's a consultant, ha ha.

—Yeah, that's right! *Mr* it was. I could never work that one out. Is *Mr* posher than *Dr* then?

—Only in hospitals, officer. I raised a finger in mock warning, and laughed again. The policemen laughed too.

—Funny, that.

—It is, rather, isn't it?

—Yeah, well, so, Doc, you're happy to blow into the bag?

—Of course.

—Lost your bonnet badge, I see, Doc.

I turned. The other policeman was strolling around my Mercedes, kicking the tyres and checking the lights.

—Yes, some young thugs, no doubt. Is that a problem, officer?

—No, no. So, you said you had a good reason, a special reason for being out and, to be honest, acting a bit noticeable, did you, Doc?

—Yes, I did say that, didn't I? And, of course, I have. The thing is, as I said, I'm not only willing to blow into the bag, but I think perhaps I really should do so. After all, I don't want there to be any doubt about this. Because, you see, because the good and special reason I have for being out, and yes, I admit, acting a little strangely, is that, in fact, um, look, this is rather difficult, officer, officers, rather. We don't want this getting about, obviously, but, well, the reason I got lost and had to stop and be sick, as you saw, is that I'm not feeling terribly well. I'm due for an early check-up at work. Before I go anywhere near the patients. Just a precaution, but even so . . .

—A precaution, Doc?

—Between you and me, officer, and I must ask you to let this go no further for now, your mother was lucky to have gone in last year. Our press officer would deny it, of course he would, but the fact is, well, there's no getting round it: the superbug's about on the wards again.

—The superbug!

—'Fraid so, officers. No, it's not a pleasant thought. In here, should I blow? Obviously. I should say that this is only a precautionary check-up. It's very probably not what I've got at all. It's far more likely I've just picked up something else on my rounds. All sorts of nasties knocking about in hospital, eh? The, um, clinical probability of it actually being *the* superbug, the flesh-eating one, you know, er, *Superbugii morbidus necrosis*, is really very small, thank God, but obviously, officer, well, with something so contagious, and quite frankly incurable, I'm sure you understand that I don't want to be getting close to my patients, or indeed anyone else until we can be quite certain. There. Did I blow hard enough? I think that's me clear, then, isn't it? Oh, and I should wash my hands as soon as I reasonably can, officer, if I were you. Better safe than sorry, eh? So, was there anything else, or am I OK to go for my check-up? You're sure? Well, sorry to have given you any reason to stop, officers. Goodnight!

43: Prague, Of Course!

The first hints of dawn were creeping into the winter's night. The world was no longer just a blanket of darkness in which the odd floodlit patch stood gratefully out, but was composed once more of blocks and forms in shades of grey and black. Houses, streets and buildings took shape again, and as they did so, their various illuminations seemed to glow with unnatural force. Now that the cars were growing almost visible as cars, their brake lights seemed to roar red; the green of the traffic lights was suddenly blinding.

Was it just that my tired eyes were reviving a little with the day, obeying some primordial, tidal call to awakening? Was it some plain scientific phenomenon to do with contrast and suchlike? Or might it be a deep wash of hormones flooding my mind now that I had got away with it, ha ha, and was rejoicing in the firm knowledge that the sun was coming back, the night was over and my path was clear at last?

Calling the police was now quite out of the question, of course; I would never again dare to touch the gun until I knew what I was doing; I could hardly leave it lying around in the passenger footwell of the family Merc until Sarah and the children got back. The facts were plain.

Conclusion?

That I had one week in which to (a) learn how to safely handle a weapon the mere possession of which could land me in prison for many years, (b) defuse the bloody thing and (c) dump it secretly. And then get back to bloody normal and get down to work on the VIP and try to save my life.

It was clear that there was only one place in the world I could go to learn about my Armalite.

Nevada, America.

Just about the last place in the world I would have chosen to go, the very heartland of Blue America, the Chapel of the Lost Souls of Capitalism, but logic is logic: where else could I just turn up and shoot?

Of course, I would have to work out some story to explain why I had suddenly flown to Las Vegas, in case anything went wrong and I did indeed get caught dumping the gun, because if that happened, the cops would certainly check up on where I had recently been.

What could I say? It would be hard to claim that as a lecturer in German I had suddenly discovered a vital professional reason for flying to Las Vegas just when (as it turned out) I had discovered, and failed to report discovering, an Armalite.

I could say that I was addicted to gambling. But that might be hard to back up, in terms of cash moved in or out of accounts and suchlike. Or prostitutes. Why shouldn't I be addicted to them? Men were. Especially when their wives were suddenly away for a week! Yes, that would work. I could claim that rather than sleep with my students, and thus abuse my position, I had elected to use prostitutes, who are, I recalled having once read in a *HIM* magazine article in my dentist's waiting room, apparently better-looking in Las Vegas than anywhere else on earth. In fact, when you thought about it, if I decided it was necessary to support my story, I could, in fact, really hire a prostitute in Las Vegas. I would, of course, not actually sleep with her at all, just talk to her and take her card to prove that I had been with her. Once this was all over and an alibi no longer required, I could have a laugh with Sarah about it all.

But what if, on the other hand, it did all go wrong and I needed her? Would my prostitute remember that I had been there, yes, but had not actually wanted sex with her? Well, if she did, I could always say that, actually, I was addicted to prostitutes *not* for sex but because with prostitutes I could just drink and talk, just be with a pretty woman and let it all out without feeling that I had let them down and ruined their lives by pretending to be something I could never live up to. And rest on their breasts and ... Hmm. Perhaps it would just be easier to do it and be done with it. I mean, when you thought about it, every known society has had whores. For most men at most times and places in history, Kafka for example, going to whores has simply been part of the landscape, so, really, my story would be more believable if I really did find a girl and ...

—Fuck you! I yelled, as two red spots slid in front of me, glowing carnivorously from out of the fat arse of a spanking-new BMW, forcing me to step hard on the brakes.

I hit my horn, blinked, and found that I had, without realising it, got on to some stretch of urban dual carriageway which was already running bumper-to-bumper slowly in both lanes. This time it was the Congestion Charge, no doubt. These were no careless partygoers, but men crawling damply to work, mortgages clanking on chains from their bumpers. I caught the driver of the BMW clearly tapping his head at me in his mirror. Without thinking for a moment, I mouthed, —'Yeah yeah yeah', snapped my fingers at him as if making a shadow puppet of a crocodile, slapped on my right indicator, twisted the wheel and put my foot down. Unfortunately, the Teutonic bloody brain in my horsepower-eating autobox simply refused to kick down.

—Come on, you heap of Stuttgart crap, I muttered aloud, but nothing much at all actually happened. The power was simply not there. Then the gap was gone and I had to pull hastily back in behind the big BMW amidst outraged horns and lights. My rival driver saw my discomfiture, and looked into his mirror.

Being a primate, I have, like all of us, an amazing ability to catch the meaning of facial expressions. I was left in no doubt at all that the bastard was laughing at me and looking pityingly at my seven-year-old car. And who could blame him, the shit? I had openly tried to get by him and had openly failed. I was the public idiot, the failed would-be lane-hopping git in the powerless old Merc. And I knew he knew I knew he knew and so on to the crack of doom.

—Big deal, I shrugged back at him. But his radar was as good as mine, and it did not play at all. He grinned smugly. —Fuck you, I sneered. At which he actually zapped down his window, extending his hand out from his cocooned cabin and into the real, rainy world in order to give me a slow and thoroughly authentic two fingers. As he did so, the incomparably crap strains of Queen drifted from his car.

I stared for a moment.

He was as old as me, four-eyed like me and even rounder in the face, his ridiculous haircut frantically gain-saying baldness. A rumpled suit jacket of no great cut or cloth hung from a hook behind his fat-padded right shoulder. An ordinary middle-aged bore with a spiritual life of zero. Almost certainly, he worked as some kind of glorified bookkeeper in some firm of which he owned not a bit. He was, in short, most definitely in my league.

And he was such an utterly cultureless arsehole that the best thing he could think of to listen to on his no doubt many speakers as he drove to his crap job on a wet November morning was Freddie fucking Mercury, for Christ's sake.

And yet he, this image of banality, was driving a car worth ten of mine, and laughing at me.

This was not the deal.

44: The Enemy

Never mind chucking stones (well, a stone) at cops and singing songs about the evil British Army and shouting along with chants against capitalism in general and America in particular, I now, for the first time in my life, felt that I had The Enemy clearly in my sights.

It was all his fault.

His and his countless ilk's.

We were all doomed to global warming because this godless idiot and all the millions who thought and dreamed and shat just like him could not live for a single weekend without watching Sky and buying electronic crap they had never even heard of till last week, air-freighted in from factories stuffed with slave workers on the far side of the world. Our planet was dying just because morons like this thought it was their inalienable human right to fly to fucking Florida for two hundred quid and have iPods to play Queen for hell's sake and vast great watt-guzzling plasma screens just so they could watch Manchester sodding United and *Big* bloody *Brother*.

And drive big new BMWs that made my Mercedes look like shit.

Well, I was not letting this one get away with it.

At the next opportunity, I swung myself niftily outwards again, but he had seen me coming and was there before me. I cut back. So did he. Open and declared warfare. We both knew it: he who chooses the least slow lane wins.

At slightly over normal human walking pace, the

BMW and I tangoed desperately across the crawling lanes. We crossed and crissed a dozen times in our slow-motion dogfight, often almost causing entirely harmless low-speed shunts, both aware only of each other and of every nuance in the lines of traffic ahead, neither able to gain a definite edge. Sometimes the squab of my seat drew almost level with his. At these moments, the two feet of cold morning air between our cars crackled with our point-blank refusal to make eye contact. Once my nose was actually in front of his and I could feel the sweat breaking out under his armpits. But then he pulled away again, gaining several yards. Each time a lane seemed to be loosening up, he, being in front, saw the gap first. You had to hand it to him, he was a worthy opponent. At one stage, some complete idiot in my lane actually *slowed to let someone out in front of them*, for God's sake, thereby losing me an entire car's length just when the BMW was, in any case, gaining maybe a foot per second. I thought for a horrible moment that I had been blown away, that my enemy might have some kind of decisive local knowledge. I foolishly looked straight at him. He flicked a scornful glance at me and shook out his shoulders.

Shit, what had gone wrong with the world? How could nobodies in nothing jobs drive cars that made mine look like a fourth-hand heap of crap from the free ads (as indeed it was)? This was not the deal. I, a full university lecturer, for Christ's sake, could not afford a half-decent place to bring up my family because Maggie bloody Thatcher and her successors, blue or red, had fixed things so that shallow, stupid twats like this, the objects of seventies comedy, could call themselves executives and buy houses and price everyone else out of the bloody market. Christ, what had been so wrong with the seventies anyway, when the workers were workers and proud of it, and book-keepers were just bean-counters, and university lecturers could live in big houses with sash windows and . . . ?

I kept my eyes peeled for another attack, and found myself saying aloud, in a Devon accent I had swiftly lost at Oxford and never used again:

—The Merc 1.8: a *bit of a plodder*? Let's see about that, shall we, my lover? It's not the car, it's the driver, my dear. It's not the dog in the fight that matters, it's the fight in the dog!

Both lanes had speeded up now. We were travelling at very nearly fifteen miles per hour. At such speeds, every action is decisive. I pulled swiftly out once more and got a volley of noise and halogen from a ridiculously young arsehole in a spanking new Range Rover. I replied with the 'L for loser' sign (which my sons had taught me a week before). He was evidently young enough to get this, for he moved to within inches of my rear bumper, filling my mirrors with sound and light. I hit the brakes for a second and made him lurch down nosewards to avoid shunting into me before closing in again, mouthing fury.

I laughed. Another man drawn into the fight. The war spreads. The more the merrier. I leaned on my own horn when a Volvo blocked me, and got a vicious silent snarl for my troubles. Excellent!

Suddenly my head was filled with voices.

I pricked up my ears. What was this? Was my tiredness getting the better of my mind? As I hunted for a gap, the words grew clearer.

I seemed to have been patched in to the heads of every other man in every other car I could see. I *was* every other man on the road. I knew their hearts. And I knew they knew mine. For us all, this was no mere journey to the office. It was our primordial breakfast before the reasonable day's work, a dawn enactment of the lunatic zero-sum psychodrama called maledom.

—Oh yes, the Mondeo's showing just why it was car of the year all those years ago.
—Ha! Who says diesels are sluggish?
—Does he really think that heap of French crap can mix it with an Audi?
—And just *slides* in there ahead of the Toyota! Oh, nice move.
—He may not have a turbo but, boy, has he got guts!
—'Fraid not, mate.
—Baby on board? No you fucking haven't.
—Oh, did I cut you up? Soooo sorry, you little cunt.
—Already gained at least three places by that neat little manoeuvre!
—What you fucking doing *braking on amber*, you stupid fucking . . .
—You want to have a fucking go, do you, my lover? Fancy your chances, do you, you fat fucking cunt? This time tomorrow I'll be blasting away with a fucking Armalite in Vegas, so you just watch your fucking . . .

I lapped up the voices and smiled. For the first time this millennium, I lit a cigarette in a car. I buzzed down my window so that I could drive with my right elbow leaning out, trailing smoke signals of twentieth-century hardness. It was a tad chilly and damp, to be sure, but what did I care? I was a man again, no geeky neurotic, but the tough sports commentator of my own life-as-a-game:

—Yes! He makes it through just before red! Talk about nerve! And that was vital! The BMW thought he'd really lost him then, but think again, mateyboy! A *bit of a plodder*? I don't fucking *think* so!

Some of us soundtracked our attacks with rap, some of us went to war to Wagner, some did battle under the cheesy banner of Queen, but all of us were men with their own eagles and trumpets. I flicked my CD player on and selected disc three. Ah yes, Beethoven 5/ Kurt Masur/ Leipzig Gewandhaus/ DG, 1988, splendid, and that's D for Deutsche and G for Grammophon, not for Dolce & fucking Gabbana, arse-holes! Only the best is good enough for the workers! Knuckle under? Eat sand? Better death, whether by a Trojan spear, a rival gang member's bullet or a BMW on a wet November morning. Give in? Not yet, not yet!

On perhaps the fifteenth lane-swap, fate intervened in dramatic fashion. An Alfa in the BMW's lane stopped dead and the driver raced frantically round to his boot, phone jammed to ear and face twisting away from the the rain, to check for something whilst simultaneously trying by desperate shouts and smiles to pacify what was clearly a screaming baby in the rear seat. What an arsehole, ha ha! The queue behind him was thus held up by at least thirty seconds, which even at our once again lower speed represented at least ten yards. They all went ape, of course. I cruised triumphantly past the BMW at last, my stream of traffic doing a good half a mile per hour better than his, all his extra horsepower completely in vain. I smiled at him and saw his feeble hatred: oh joy!

But I, Dr John Goode, PhD, being an expert in deferred gratification, also thought ahead, beyond my immediate moment of triumph. We were approaching a set of traffic lights. After them, I could see that the road narrowed quickly back down to one lane. Who knew what would happen as the lanes merged? I might find that one of the people in front of me was too polite or too slow away from the lights. A woman, maybe, or even, God forbid, a learner. The BMW might yet be able to draw ahead before the lanes merged and muscle back in, ahead of me for ever. Imagine his face as he slid past! No way could I let that happen. No, if I could cash in my lead right now, and get in front of him but *in the same lane*, while he was not expecting it because my lane was still moving faster, he would have almost no chance to get back at me. I would have won.

Of course, the actual moment of vacating my lane was fraught with danger, but my plan was based on absolute surprise. As we neared the lights, I took a calculated risk and simply bullied my way, without indicating, in front of the car which lay ahead of the BMW. This car was a Toyota driven by a woman and so obviously it did not count: she was a mere collateral sufferer of our manly engagement. She braked an inch from my passenger door. I apologised profusely with gestures to her, but my eyes were all on the BMW.

He reacted, as I knew he would have to, but ha! He was too slow, as I had guessed he would be, the boring fat bastard! Too scared of a shunt, he thought twice about moving out and actually looked round backwards to check before he made his move. Pathetic. By the time he jumped, he was too late. Stuck halfway, he made a complete and undeniable arse of himself. As we stood at the lights I gloated and laughed.

I could not resist it. I turned Beethoven up to the limit, clicked off my seat belt and got halfway out of the car, continuing to make Mediterranean signals of guilt and remorse to the woman in the Toyota until she waved me away with a faked and weary smile. But of course,

I had not really opened my door and got the right half of my body wet just to say sorry to a *woman driver*. No, this was man stuff.

I was armed.

Yes, I had in my hand the bonnet badge of my Mercedes. When my defeated enemy could bear it no longer and caught my eye at last, as he had to, I kissed the chrome star and held it mockingly up to him, making big *wanker* signs with my free hand amidst the crushing blasts of Beethoven.

Ha!

Interviewer: So, what is the cure for stress, Herr Nietzsche?

Nietzsche (cackling insanely): Ze cure for stress? Victory!

45: Of Course!

My unloved home loomed up before me, and I parked very, very carefully. With my finger and thumb, as if shrouding an unspeakable corpse, I shrinkingly tweaked the black bin bag back over the snout of the Armalite so that nothing could be seen from the street. I locked the car and went inside.

The house ticked with silence, impossible mosquitoes hummed at the edges of my hearing. I shook my head, ducked it to avoid hitting the stairs, and settled myself before my laptop, to book the inescapable trip to Las Vegas.

I took a savage delight in my unsafe surfing. I needed no precautions because the laptop was already doomed. Bill Gates could do his worst, I was a free man now and could look at whatever I fancied.

I advance-googled *Armalite shooting Vegas* and immediately hit the jackpot. There, to the right of the results (the *Leaving Las Vegas Bar Experience*, the *Erotic Las Vegas Experience* and suchlike), was a paid ad for *RimShot Tours to Las Vegas and Prague from the UK*.

I leaped to my feet, poleaxing myself once again on the woodwork.

Prague, of course!

Still unable to stand and blinded with the pain, I nevertheless rejoiced.

Prague was perfect. Prague was once an Austrian-owned, German-speaking city. I could later make up a million reasons for why a German lecturer would go there, without having to invent (and then back up!)

wild tales of prostitutes or gambling. Though that would, in its way, have been quite fun. Prague was so much easier. There is Kafka, obviously. History of the World Wars, easily. Fall of Communism, naturally. And Panke!

Prague is only two hours from Dresden, and Dresden, after all, was where Panke lived and worked. It would be so easy to claim that I had gone to try to see the man who was the centre of my life's work. —*Having decided to go to Dresden, officer, I realised that I should perhaps visit the . . . museum in Prague.* Yes, that would be utterly watertight!

I crawled, groaning but triumphant, back on to my beloved chair and summoned up the Prague website.

Shoot in Prague! Short, cheap flights! Better beer and cheaper clubs than Vegas! Advance booking not always needed! Ideal for stag nights! Try out the world's most awesome weapons! Rambo's Kalashnikov, Clint's Magnum, Arnie's Terminator 2 *pump-action shotgun, US Army's Armalite, we got the lot!!! Sandwich and beer free with every booking! Free places for group leaders!*

Christ, Kafka's bloody city, where I had stood almost alone in the famous square at night, back in 1987, now a mere haven for stag nights, pole-dancers and gun freaks! The unacceptable face of freedom!

However, what had to be done had to be done. I found the sites for the Prague City Museum and Kafka's Library. I made minimalist enquiries about opening times to both *info@* addresses. I then booked a single flight to Prague, returning from Dresden, and a train ticket from Prague to Dresden. Finally, I prepared a cunning email to Panke. What fun to actually employ one's cleverness for once! My note stated clearly that I wanted to just discuss some points face-to-face before finalising my Very Important Paper on his life and work; that I would be flying to Prague this very morning because I wanted to check a reference for a possible future article on Kafka, and that I would be catching the 17.56 from Prague, arriving Dresden at 20.15, and staying in the hotel opposite the restored Frauenkirche. I hoped he would be able to meet at such short notice, I concluded.

I blipped the email off and cc-ed it both to my university address and to our departmental secretary. Who cared what the reply (if any) was? I now had an utterly believable itinerary for a lecturer in German who was going to see Heiner Panke but who had just wanted to check something in Prague while he was over.

By tomorrow evening I would be home, confident in my ability to safely handle, defuse, disassemble and dump an Armalite.

Genius.

But there was something else.

What if Panke actually *did* agree to meet me?

Suddenly, I knew: *that* was what had been missing from the Very Important Paper. The tone of Panke's voice again, that rumbling fighter's voice that always said *we*. Never *me*, always *we*, always enfolding you in a wonderful joint adventure. —*The West needs to listen to us, little doctor. To our voice*, Panke had said, when we were arranging the details of grants and fees for Panke's trip to England in 1989. How grand it had been to be the trusted friend and publicly acknowledged intimate of a man who could say *we* like that. The tour of England, May 1989. Just before I finally dared to ask Sarah out. Just before I got my first job. From university to university, in Panke's company, introducing

Panke, driving Panke, drinking with Panke. Virtually booking my first job in advance while visiting the University of Birmingham German Department with Panke! Sleeping with the second-prettiest girls (at last!) in every department we went to because I was sat at the right-hand side of the wild, laughing Panke and they could all see that Panke treated me virtually as a near-equal! That great summer of 1989, crowned by my wooing and amazing conquest of Sarah, all thanks to the brimming confidence radiated into me by life with Panke!

—Gatwick, I ordered the cab. —No no, I don't need a quote, I know roughly how much it is. What? *How* much? Well, for . . . yes, yes, fine, whatever. Yes, as soon as you can.

46: Legroom

I don't know when psychologists say that our formative years are supposed to be.

Are they those shadowy pre-school days of big places and looming faces, voices kindly or stressed? Or our first real experience of the world, when we are six? Or perhaps those long, dreamlike afternoons of bikes and reading, before sex rams its hormones into our unready little bodies? To be popular and courted at sixteen: perhaps this is all that matters? When is fate set fast? Twenty-four? Twenty-eight? Who knows? But as I entered the departures hall at Gatwick I knew one thing for certain: that whenever they may have been, my formative years had been spent in the now-prehistoric age before cheap bloody flying ate the world.

I mean, look at the bastards! I had travelled Europe by thumb and by train, when crossing borders always meant showing passports, often meant booking visas and sometimes meant interviews in cold little rooms at unearthly times of the morning with armed men standing near; when changing money could be compulsory, changing it back could be illegal and carrying Kafka could stop you getting into Czechoslovakia; when going to Prague, say, meant really, really wanting to *go to Prague*, not just clicking a bloody mouse on the next cheap weekend break that happened to take your fancy @escapeyourcraplife.com. And now all these unthinking cretins were in the check-in queue before me!

I had been quite certain that the flight would be almost empty and that I would be able to get a window seat, maybe even one with more legroom. I mean, who would want to go to Prague on a wet Tuesday morning in November? As an experienced traveller from the lost age of interrailing, I was equipped with the vital lightweight minimum: I had my favourite, plumpest goose-down pillow with me, crushed neatly into an oversized Marks & Spencer carrier bag. Nothing more important than a good pillow on a long journey. I was planning to check in and get my window seat with plenty of time to spare, and then, gloating in the certainty of a good kip before I got there, call the Prague shooting people from a call-box right here in Gatwick. Clever, see? No records. All worked out. No wonder I had got a first-class degree!

But now I checked the desk number again, and stared. A grey coldness ran down my spine and into my knees as I saw the length of the queue. I mean, yes, of course, I had heard that Prague was a popular destination these days, and I could well recall the atmospheric place. I had stood in the deserted Wenceslas Square at midnight in 1987 and watched that strange procession on the famous clock, and yes, it had felt very special.

But I was me, I had read Kafka and knew the history of this place built on fault lines. What could Prague possibly mean to all these idiots?

Dear God, what right did these morons have to think they should be able to take days off work just because they felt like it and fly anywhere they wanted for peanuts while children slaved away in the Third World to make their foul trainers and logoed jumpers? Was the ozone layer going to die, were the ice caps doomed to melt for this? So that these slack-mouthed, uncomprehending louts could wander around like hideous modern caricatures of eighteenth-century aristocrats, off to yet another city they did not understand in the least, just to alleviate the crushing boredom of their meaningless lives? Was I, who had studied European culture for years, going to be stuck here for ever in this queue just because so many of these ridiculous little gits had decided on some whim that they fancied a couple of nights pissed in Prague this week?

I mean, why can't there just be, for example, well, say, an exam, a little test you have to pass before you are allowed out of the country? To prove you know at least something, anything about where you are going. Nothing too hard, just a few simple multiple-choice questions would be enough. Which great European war was started by an incident in Prague in 1618? What was the official language of government in Prague in 1890? When was the Prague Spring? If you can't answer those, excuse me, what the hell right do you have to think you can just jump on a plane and blast the upper atmosphere to hell with untaxed kerosene so that you can blunder unknowingly around a place that could have been thrown up last year by Disney for all you know? If people don't even know that, why should I have to queue behind them? Why should my children have to compete with theirs for college places and jobs and houses?

—Sorry? Row twenty-eight? But, I mean, that's right at the back, isn't it?

—Yes, Dr Goode. The flight is very full today, as you've no doubt noticed.

—Um, I was wondering, you see, I know that those seats are pretty cramped and my legs are quite long and . . .

—Yes, sir, that's why we only allocate those seats to our last passengers.

—Oh God. Well, OK, can I at least have the window seat? I'm very tired.

—The window seats have all been allocated, sir. Row two may be available for a cash upgrade on-board, at the discretion of cabin crew, sir.

—May be?

—That's right, sir. On a first-come-first-served basis.

—What, you mean, if I fight to get on early and pay extra I might get one of those front seats with room for normal human legs?

—At the cabin crew's on-board discretion, sir.

—How much are they?

—Twenty-five pounds one way, sir, on-board, if available.

—That's more than the flight!

—That's right, sir. Funny, isn't it?

—So, OK, who do I see, on-board?

—Me, sir.

—Oh. Well, I don't suppose I could, you know, book one now?

—You're welcome to contact me on-board, sir. I'm check-in staff just now, not on-board crew.

—Right. I see. Oh well then, see you on board! I mean, *on-board*, ha!

—Excuse me, sir.

—Sorry?

—Are you quite sure that carrier bag will fit within the on-board-baggage guide rack, sir?

—Hmm? God, yes, don't worry about that.

—Have you actually checked, sir?

—Well, no.

—We do ask people to check, sir. That's why the guide rack's there, you see.

—It's OK, it's only a pillow, actually. I'm an experienced traveller.

—I'm sure you are, sir, but will it fit in the on-board guide rack?

—Well, yes, of course. It's only a pillow, for God's . . .

I tried to keep the anger from my voice, and to stop myself actually clutching the soft, fat pillow to my chest. For hours I had been allowing myself to look forward to the moment I nestled down into its familiar cocoon, earplugs in ears, safe from the world. And now they wanted to take even this little salvation away from me on some absurd pretext.

—Can I *see* it fit please, sir?

—Um, well, Christ, OK, OK. Um, I might have to squash it down a bit, of course.

—Would you mind squashing it down for me, sir?

—Yes, yes, of course. There, you see. Hold on. There. Oh, for God's sake, I'm sure it'll fit in. It must. This is ridiculous. Oh, come on, you stupid bloody bag of Norwegian . . . There. OK? In.

—That's fine, sir.

—Thank you so much.

—But will it still fit when you stop holding it down?

—Sorry?

—If you let go of it, sir, will it still fit?

—Well, yes, I mean, virtually. Of course, it's bound to, sort of, puff up a bit.

—On-board baggage has to fit into the guide rack *without* being pinned down, sir.

—Oh come on, this isn't baggage, it's a pillow.

—If it's on-board, it's baggage, sir.

—Look, it's going to be squashed under my head, isn't it?

—Not in an emergency, sir.

—What?

—If there's an emergency evacuation you won't be asleep, sir, will you? You'll have assumed the impact position. Where will your oversize on-board baggage be then, sir? It might be blocking an emergency exit.

—A pillow, block an exit?

—Someone might fall over it. That's why we have size regulations, sir.

—No it isn't, it's so you can charge people for extra baggage!

—Passengers abusing staff will not be permitted on-board, sir. As it says there right in front of you.

—Yes. Sorry. Sorry, look, it's just, I mean . . .

—If you'll just stop holding your on-board baggage down, sir, we'll see, won't we?

—Right. Fine. Whatever.

—Oh dear. That *has* puffed up quite a bit really, hasn't it, sir? I'm afraid that's going to have to be checked in. Checked-in baggage is five pounds per item, sir.

—But what good's a pillow to me if it's in the hold?

—I wouldn't know, sir. It's your baggage, not mine.

—Look, OK, you win, how much extra do I have to pay to take it *on-board*?

—We're not permitted to offer an additional on-board baggage allowance, sir.

—Oh for God's sake, I'm desperate to sleep on the plane, I've offered to pay, can't you just bend the rules a little bit?

—Sir, we are a budget airline, we don't offer on-board sleeping facilities on a two-hour flight. Relax, why don't you, sir? You're only going for the cheap beer and a good time, after all.

—No! No I am not! Not me. I'm going on important business.

—With just a pillow, sir?

—Look, it's all very complicated, but the point is I need to get there in good form, so can't you, for God's sake, just bend the rules a tiny little bit for once? I'd write a letter of thanks to your boss. I am a doctor, as you see from my passport.

—Now, let me ask you a few things, sir. One: what good would a letter to my boss do me if it said I had broken the rules? Two: where would the rules be if I bent them for everyone when the flight's rammed full? Three: why do you think I'd bend them just for you? Four: if you've got such an important meeting, why don't you go with a premium carrier, club class, so you can arrive nice and fresh for business? Five: I'm closing here now, *Doctor*, so did you want to check your pillow in or leave it behind?

47: An Anglo-Saxon Name

Like a cheap coffin in a crematorium, my pillow was carried away from me up the squeaking belt. I only just managed not to cry with the unfairness of it all. But then I dug deep into my reserves of strength. I was a man. I had arrangements to make. I hurried to the nearest payphone and, having fished for their number in my pocket, called Prague RimShot Tours.

—He-llo, RimShot! answered a voice with a positively Dickensian north-Kent whine.

—Oh, hi, er, I'm coming to Prague just to, anyway, I saw on your website that you do shooting.

—Tell you what, what did you think of the website?

—Sorry? Oh, well, very good.

—Nice, isn't it? Classy? Just invested heavily in that. Shooting, yes, no problemo. Our speciality, in fact. Not to be confused with the cheap and cheerful pistol ranges. When did you want to come, sir?

—Today, actually.

—Ri-ght. Short notice. Might be possible. How many in your stag party?

—One. Me. And it's not a stag party.

—Well, no, a stag party for one would be a bit unusual. Though tell you what, if you *was* going to do a solo stag, Prague would be the place! Now, thing is, our minimum is usually four shooters.

—Then I'll pay for four.

—You see? Always a solution to these little problems. Was it shotguns, pistols, rifles? Rambo, Clint or Arnie, ha ha? Or all of them?

—I want to shoot an Armalite, that's all.

—Oh yes, very tasty weapon. Nice. I can see you know your stuff. Yeah, we can do that. Ammo's more expensive, though, I should warn you.

—That's fine. But I want to be shown the gun properly.

—Individual tuition, eh?

—Exactly. This afternoon.

—Well, it'll be a pleasure. Make a nice change from the stag-parties. I'll be honest with you, we've been trying to position ourselves more upmarket. Lot of cheapo competition on the stag-night trade these days, Riga and Tallinn, you know, so we'd be delighted to accommodate the wishes of, how shall I put it, a premium customer who is obviously a serious enthusiast. Tell you what, I'll only charge you for three shooters, and we'll forget the extra cost of the ammo, how's that? And I'll get you our best man. What time this afternoon?

—I want you to meet me off the plane as well. I get in at one and I need to be back at the railway station to get the 17.45 to Berlin.

—Ri-ight. I'll have to charge for the pick-up. Tell you what, we'll go back to the four-shooters price but I'll pick you up at the airport and take you back to Holesovice Station my very self. How's that for executive service?

—Perfect.

—Now the bad news is that's going to have to be about, oh, well, hmm, got to be knocking on four hundred euros all in. Now, at a push I could maybe . . .

—That's fine.

—Oh. Right then. Great.

—So, look, what, do I just bring my passport? Do I need any special, I don't know, shoes, gloves, glasses?

—Passport? No, God, we don't bother with that sort

of thing. Not out here. Just turn up and bring the dosh and get ready for some fun, eh? Ha ha! All the gear's ready and waiting. See you at the airport. Oh, tell you what. We don't take cards, not set up for it yet, as such. Cash only, sorry. You OK with that?

—Oh yes. Cash is fine.

—Perfect! Better have your name, eh?

—My name? Yes, of course . . .

Hold on. Think. No passport? Cash? Incredible. But then, shit, that meant . . .

—Hello, mate?

A name, any name! Every little extra layer of disguise might help if anything did go wrong when I came to dump the unloaded gun. Not that it would, but I might as well, given the chance. Any name, any name at all! My God, and if I shaved off my beard as soon as I got back? It would be strange to not have a beard, of course. I had had it since beginning my PhD in 1984, it had served me well throughout the Miners' Strike and my years in the Irish pub in Kentish Town. I had courted Sarah behind it. But it had to go. If I could go and shoot not only under a false name but also bearded, no one would ever be able to link the new and beardless me to some shooting range, whatever happened, even if it all went wrong and I was caught dumping the gun, even if some clever bloody copper decided, despite my Dresden alibi, to check my every possible move in Prague and see if . . .

—Hello, mate, you still there?

—Sorry, sorry, line went for a second. Yes, of course, my name is, it's . . .

My mind had locked off. What name would I use? Shit, come on, just any good old English name would do. Anything believable, anything I'd be able to remember easily for the rest of today, that was all.

Nothing got through the mesh, except one. It was a ridiculous name, but it was English, or at any rate Anglo-Saxon. I would have no trouble remembering it, and it was the only one I could hear in my head right now. So I gave it, helplessly, trying not to giggle as I did so.

—Gotcha. Flight number? . . . Lovely. I'll be there myself with the old sign round my neck. See you in Prague at one then, Mr Bush!

—Oh, call me Tony, I replied.

48: Tons of Flab Wobbling About in a Big Net

Americans, hard-working pioneers, are happy to pay the going rate for what they want so long as they get it. Englishmen, the dispossessed heirs of Empire, cannot give up on the thought that they deserve a little upgrade in life for free.

Many of the people crammed on to the wretched flight to Prague, notably the few linen-clad folk who obviously considered themselves a cut above, tried various entertaining ruses to try to get the vacant front-row seats without paying. The stewardesses, who I guessed were on some form of bonus scheme for selling these seats, blanked them all smilingly. No one was prepared to cough up the actual money.

Normally, I would have quite agreed with these stoutly English sentiments, but today I was so tired that I simply bit the bullet and handed over twenty-five quid (though I counted the notes out with the huffing bad grace demanded by my national heritage). I thus managed to get a seat where I could almost stretch my legs out straight, allowing me to lean my head on the fibreboard cladding and close my burning eyes at last.

Perhaps it is because I never flew anywhere until my twenties, but I can never sleep on planes, even with my pillow, until we have passed the point at which the newsmen would say *on take-off* or *shortly after take-off*. And when a flight is as full as this one was, I find it impossible to rid myself of the horrible awareness that as we leave the earth every rivet in the airframe and engines is straining at the absolute limit of tolerances decided upon by the accountants who work out exactly how long this plane has to last, flying backwards and forwards to Prague three times a day every day (and to Glasgow once a day in between) like some winged bus, in order to turn a penny for the owners.

At such times, the thought of human body fat is my one consolation. You see, there must be a small, unintentional, built-in safety margin on European flights. After all, the accountants and engineers at Boeing and Airbus presumably have to do all their load-to-propulsion-to-lift calculations based on the bodyweight of the average American flyer, which must be significantly higher (say a stone per person, at least) than that of the average Old Worlder. If this is indeed the case, as it must be, unless American versions of all planes actually have fewer but larger seats put in, which seems unlikely, a European flight, even one packed to the gunwales, is in fact taking off with several tons of human blubber less than the designers have been forced to allow for.

I always imagine these tons of flab wobbling about in a big net, tied to the back of the plane, being gratefully released just as the wheels heave to escape the ground . . .

Fat or not, the accountants had got it right, as usual: fully laden with human cattle, we nevertheless made it to the happy cruising level at which the engine-whine drops and there is now really nothing very much to go wrong. I considered for a moment the absurd miracle of flight. I tried to rediscover a fitting sense of wonder at this dream of millennia. At least someone on this plane had the spiritual resources to still feel it!

Soon I was yawning.

Pillowless, my face slid and slipped on the plasti-cated wall of the plane; my neck lolled, my head fell this way and that, snapping me out again and again of deeply unpleasant dreams. In one of them, I had left little Mariana in a shed that had caught fire and was desperately trying to call help on my phone, but could only hear distant angelic singing on the line. In another, I found myself in court facing a benchful of tearful thirty-somethings, the little kids whose doorstep I had robbed of their breakfast milk in 1983, thus (it tran-spired) providing the final catalyst for their widowed dad to throw himself into the river that day and condemn them all to lives of abuse in unregulated chil-dren's homes. A dozen times I blearily reset my head and dropped away once more into such unnerving scenarios, but I was finally awoken beyond hope by the tinny ravings of the PA as the cabin crew desper-ately hawked sandwiches, perfumes, drink. I checked my watch and found to my disbelief that we were only half an hour into the flight.

I spent the next feature-length stretch of time staring greyly at clouds, trying not to let the sour resentment at my wasted twenty-five quid bloat into complete disproportion. Twenty-five quid, for nothing! Think what that could buy in, well, in Prague.

But this was no time for petty whinges. It was OK. Everything was perfectly planned: Prague airport, go to shoot Armalite without showing passport/credit card, train station, two hours odd of wonderful sleep (*with* my pillow!) on the train, get to Dresden, cab to posh hotel, clean up, get in touch with Panke (just for the record), have a quick drink to relax, early night in a big bed (thank you, God!), then tomorrow meet Panke if he was about, if not a bit of reading in the university library, then back to London and so home, confidently de-cock the gun, shave my beard off, dump the gun and my laptop into the Thames way downriver (somewhere without CCTV), then get back to normal, start growing my beard again and polish off the VIP.

A remarkable feat of line management, under the circumstances.

Shit, I should have gone into business or PR in nineteen eighty-bloody-four. Why did no one tell me the age of the academic was ending? I would be *how* rich by now? What insanity of nurturing had made me think I was too good to go into trade? Stupid bloody leftie parents . . .

49: Waste the Pig

Just as the accountants had predicted, the plane landed safely at Prague, and we disgorged even as gangs of no doubt underpaid and undertrained local youths scurried to pump the flying bus full of super-flammable liquids yet again.

In the arrivals hall a small figure stood waiting with a badly handwritten sign, made from a hastily torn cardboard box, for TONY BUSH. I saw him before he saw me and just had time to dive behind a tall fellow passenger in order to cram on the brand-new stupid yoof cap I had bought for this purpose at Gatwick. Even with my beard soon to go, I wanted to make absolutely sure of nonentity, and I had read somewhere that Caucasians (unlike most other people) always remember hair colour first and best when asked to recall a person. With this vital identification now hidden, I turned back and walked up to my meeter/greeter.

—Ah, hello.

I suppose he had expected something better. A City-cum-military bearing, perhaps. Not a shambling fool wearing dozed-in middle-aged M&S clothes under an Oxfam tweed jacket, topped off with a sort of ski-cap thing designed for an idiot teenager.

—Oh. He-llo! Tony Bush? he asked, all too clearly hoping that he might yet be wrong.

—Yes. Gerry Beaks?

—Yeah. Well. Great. Good flight, Tony?

—Yes, thanks.

—Welcome to Prague then. No luggage, Tony?

—Just my pillow.

—Travelling light, eh? Why not? Right you are. This way. Your carriage awaits.

We went out on to an airport concourse that could have been anywhere in the world. We crossed into a car park where the brands of the vehicles narrowed it down to anywhere in Europe.

—This your first time in Prague, Tony?

—First for a long time, Gerry.

—Real kicking city now. Tell you what, you got a hotel? I can fix you up with a great room for forty quid. Four star, nice big beds, near all the action.

—I'm going to Berlin tonight. You said you'd get me to the station, remember?

—And I will. The 17.45. But if you change your mind . . .

—Thanks, but I've got to go to Dresden. I mean, Berlin.

—And I'll get you there. Here we are then, Tony.

We stopped beside a deeply unprepossessing Toyota saloon that must have been older even than my Merc. There was a mildly awkward pause.

—So, right, that'll be just four hundred euros, Tony. Cash, as we agreed, yeah?

—This *is* going to be a proper personal tutorial, right, Gerry? I want to actually learn how to, you know, make it safe, and things.

—Nah, nah, absolutely. Got you our best tutor. Trained with our lads and the US Marines. One, two, three, four hundred. Lovely, ta. Perfect. Sign there, it's just a disclaimer, in case you shoot your own foot off. Not that it's ever happened to us, but tell you what, some of the less shall we say exclusive outfits, well, bunch of blokes from Hull pissed on a stag night, you can imagine. Great, ta, Tony. Now, normally speaking we can't do full auto here, but I have got you, being as you are obviously a rather different kind of customer, on to a range that has military-grade clearance. Which means that for a modest extra fee we could in fact do full auto, because let's face it, Tony, full auto is what we all really want, isn't it?

—No thanks, I don't want full auto.

—You don't? Oh. OK. Front or back, Tony?

—Back, please. I need to sleep. Got my pillow, you see. Had a bad night, last night. With the baby.

—Your baby drink you under the table did he?

—Sorry?

—Ha ha, come on, no offence, Tony.

—OK, OK, my family's away, I got a bit drunk.

He turned round from the driver's seat and looked me full in the eye with a pimping smile.

—And why not, eh? When the cat's away, eh? Look, I'm here for you, Tony. You've paid me good money and I'm going to make sure you get what you want. Tell you what, think of me as your very own architect of pleasure here in Prague. No need for a man to go lonely in Prague, Tony. Just don't touch the toms on the streets, they're all Ukrainians and White Russians. Rob you blind. The girls in the clubs are mostly Czech, or at least Slovak, much classier. I can get you a VIP pass to any of the best clubs for a tenner, first two drinks on the house.

—Gerry, I don't want anything like that. I'm just here for the shooting.

—Each to his own, Tony. So, what *exactly* did you want in your special tutorial? Not trying to pry, that's not my job, my job is to deliver what you want, Tony, I just need to know, so I can deliver, right?

—Well, like I said, I have, I just want to . . .

—Look, Tony, I better tell you straight right now. We don't do pigs here. Nor cows. Nor deer. Not even chickens.

—Sorry? What?

—Now, there was nothing on the site about animals, was there? You may have assumed, but assumptions is rash, Tony. I know, I know, you've heard about them doing cows and pigs in Tallinn and Riga. But this ain't Tallinn or Riga, Tony. This is Prague. We're part of Western Europe these days. More or less. Whereas Tallinn and Riga, well, that's practically bloody Russia, isn't it? So they do things Russian-like. I just want you to know straight away. Sorry, but it's no-can-do on wasting the pig.

—Fine, fine.

—Now, having said that, Tony, tell you what, there is just a chance that if I make the right call we could get you a goat on the quiet, but it is going to cost, I got to tell you that.

I felt a sudden air pocket in my soul rather like the time when I was twenty-one and a gay friend of mine first told me about fisting and rimming. Disbelief, then vertigo. I would never have guessed such things existed. But now I did. And now I could quite clearly see the tethered, unknowing creature, the bestial faces of the drunken Englishmen. I didn't *want* to know such things existed. I didn't want to know about gay fisting and Ukrainian hookers and people machine-gunning animals for fun. Jesus Christ, why do we have to know so bloody much these days? Why had I ever had to find the sodding gun?

—I don't want to shoot animals, thanks, Gerry.

—Oh. Well, that's easy enough then. So, like, what is your interest, Tony, if you don't mind me asking? Just so that I can deliver the correct experience for you?

—Research, Gerry.

—Research? Ri-ght.

—Well, I really must get some sleep, so if you don't mind . . .

I closed my eyes tight and took thankful refuge in my cold, deep pillow.

50: Into the Forest

I did not sleep, of course. I could no longer imagine how I had ever gone to sleep, or ever would again. I merely lay with my head on the fridgy linen and watched a gloomy world go blankly by as we skirted the fabled city.

The outskirts of Prague had the desolate, building-site atmosphere you find at the edges of any Mediterranean city, except here everything was mud rather than desert. The oases in this desolation were formed by vast, new, low industrial units emblazoned with the logos of well-known Western brands. Once beyond this, the satellite towns slumped into pure Stalinist grey, though with a surprisingly large number of old houses, churches, castles.

At one point we were wallowing along a straight road between vast, hedgeless fields when we suddenly stopped so sharply that I braced myself and turned my head to look our fate in the face.

A great dense cloud of big black crows had got up from the ploughed earth and was crossing the road low, right in front of us. I had never seen so many in one place: we simply had to wait until they had passed on. What had drawn them all to this field? I couldn't get a picture out of my mind: a cow tethered to a stake in a field while a grinning, bestial gang of English scum prepare to shoot it to pieces for a stag-party laugh.

I'd never been interested in darkness. Darkness was for the hopeless. I just wanted a house with tall bays and sash windows, in a normal place full of normal people. Christ, it had to be possible. But how? When you thought about it, my future, and hence my children's best interests, would be best served by an almighty bloody great economic (and especially housing) crash, and the sooner the better, if only I could use my intelligence and cultural-historical expertise to call it right for once and sell up first!

Yes, as I watched the muddy Czech fields go by, I could see the headlines clearly:

Readers of *The Paper* rejoice as economy collapses

They may be nice, liberal people, they may care about the Third World and lose sleep over seals, but our readers (as opposed to our editors, who are all loaded and living in N1 or NW3, of course, the bastards, but still have to pretend, now and then, that they share the hopes and fears of teachers and nurses in Leeds) are jumping for joy as bad news follows worse on the economic front.

With house prices down by over 50 per cent in the last year, sea levels rising palpably, oil at $120 a barrel following the Israeli strikes on Iran's nuclear plants, tankers full of African refugees hammering at the gates of Europe, Romanians taking every job in Germany, China in hyperinflationary chaos, India at war with Pakistan, the High Street deserted and City redundancies turning into a flood that is quite literally visible in the newly locked-out, trauma-tised, tear-stained figures shambling each new afternoon into Liverpool Street Station, it no longer seems quite so stupid, so pathetic, so spine-less and laughable, so utterly lacking in ambition, nous or any sense of the way of the brave new free-market world, to have chosen two decades ago to take a steady but poorly paid career with a modest but government-backed pension in a field where, even today, very few people are ever really and truly sacked. Yes, suddenly it's the teachers and lecturers and civil servants who are strolling happily into north-London estate agents' offices (the ones that are still open!), where they would not have dared to even slow down in passing just twelve months ago for fear of being laughed at by some spotty little esturine-English-gabbling, Hugo Boss-shirted, degreeless little shit who now goes in daily terror of his Porsche being repossessed, ha ha ha ha ha!

—Nearly there, Tony, wakey-wakey!
—What?
I awoke just in time to feel the car swing off the metalled road and lurch into a forest. My heart sank. I'd vaguely imagined that the shooting range would be something like an old airbase, but I now realised that it was going to be a forest. Why does it always have to be a forest? Forests are where big bad wolves and murderous rapists lurk. Where people who hate people live. Where people go when they want to shoot guns and skin things. I would cut them all down, the forests: I would make parks with knee-high hedges of box and avenues of roses and light. I did not want to go into a forest.

But go in we did. The wheels spun in mud, bit again, took us deeper into green darkness. On the trees I began to notice small red-and-white metal signs saying STŘELNICE. All of them had rusting bullet holes in them. Then we arrived at a compound of low wooden buildings. I got out, and straight away plunged my foot lace-deep into a sucking puddle of oily mud. All around me was the sound of guns.

I'd never heard guns before. Why would I? I'm English. It was nothing like the noise on films. Not deep roars. High, thin cracks that whipped into your abdomen, followed by long, rolling, hissing echoes.

I did not like the place at all. I did not like the noise which made me jump and the mud which had me sliding. I did not like the cold that bit and the damp that clung. I did not like the dank wooden lavatory block that you could nose at fifty yards. I did not like the shaven-headed man who was sitting on the steps of the main shack, earphones pushed on to the back of his head like grotesquely menacing Mickey Mouse ears, drinking a bottle of beer and looking steadily at me with watery-blue abuser's eyes. I pulled my inadequate tweed lighter and tugged my ludicrous hat down over the tops of my ears. I must have been mad to come out here.

Ghosts seemed to nibble at the edge of this gloomily wet and woody world, the ghosts of so many Europeans driven out into forests at gunpoint to dig their own graves. I wanted to go to bed. I wanted to go home. This was not my world.

A platoon of the Russian Army crossed the compound in front of us.

—Christ, do the Russians use this place?

—No, that's just a local club.

—A club?

—Yeah. Local Slavonians. Not Czechs. The Czechs think of them like we think of the Irish. You know, thick and drunk and dodgy, ha ha! They dress up in Russian uniforms, they come here, they shoot Russian guns and drink vodka. It's some kind of Slavic Brothers thing. Don't ask me. Don't worry, they're harmless enough. At least it isn't a Red Army club, eh? Ha ha!

—Gerry, look, I think perhaps I'm just too tired, I think perhaps . . .

—Here we are. Your teacher. George, this is Tony Bush.

I looked down at my mud-caked lecturer's shoes, trying to think what excuse I could use to wave the man away but still have a chance of getting some of my euros back. I just wanted to flee, to run from this nasty forest world that was so palpably not mine. I was a normal Englishman, for Christ's sake, what was I doing here? We don't do dark forests of dripping pine in England, thank God.

—No, look, Gerry, I'm really sorry but the thing is . . .

—Hello, I am very pleased to meet you, Mr Bush. My name is George. Is good joke, yes? Ha ha. I look forward very much to our special afternoon.

A delicate olive-skinned hand was stretched out to mine, and I looked slowly up from the ground. I saw light-coloured camouflaged combats with very neat sand-coloured boots, a US Navy Seals baseball cap and a big, loose, black-and-white chequered scarf of the sort made famous by the first generation of Palestinian terrorists (I had worn one myself for several years in the early eighties as a badge denoting general-purpose radicalism). Earphones nestled around a lightly bearded chin, high up in the folds of this scarf, looking not in the least absurd or unpleasant, for they framed the enchanting smile and dark, friendly eyes of quite the most beautiful man I had ever seen.

PART THREE

Firestorm

51: Singing for the Dying

When George handed me the gun for the first time, he must have known that I was scared of it. I don't know if he actually saw my hand shaking as I tried to load the bullets into the magazine, making an awful hash of it (I tried to sort of slide them in, of course, not simply press slowly but firmly down). But if he saw my fear, he gave no sign of it.

—Sorry, I stammered. —It's just, I'm, it's a little bit cold out here, isn't it?

—You will grow warm. This jacket I like. Is very good, the English, how you call it, *tweedy*, yes? Is very tactical.

—Tactical? It is?

—Yes, yes. No noise when you move. This is very important, Toni. Most people do not remember this, I often have to tell these idiots, no Gore-tex! Think, Toni, you are in forest. You are hunting bad guy, but he is hunting you too, oh yes. What you do? You watch? No, no. You listen. You hear him long time before you see him, in forest. These ears, these are your early warning system, Toni. When a man dies, these are the last thing that go. Why do people sing around the bed when a man is dying, Toni?

—What? Oh, well, actually, you see, in England, we don't actually sing when people are dying.

—No? This is very foolish, Toni. The man who dying, he cannot move, he cannot feel, he cannot talk, but yes he can hear singing. So now you know. Next time you are with a dying man, your friend, you sing for him. You sing nice song for him to hear, goodbye, my old friend.

—Right. Right.

—So, now, you are in forest, Toni, you listen for your enemy, with all your ears. And he is listen for you, of course, oh yes, this bad man who wants to kill you, kill your sons. And now you are understand, yes, Toni? Yes, if he is wear black Gore-tex thing from Austria and you are wear this good green brown English tweed, I tell you, Toni, aha, you win. You hear him very good, then you see him, then you get him first.

—Well, I had no idea.

—But now you have idea, yes? Good. This is why I am here, Toni. To give you idea.

And he did.

Like a patient piano tutor, he massaged my grip into place, his fingers upon and over mine; like a kindly but strict ballet master correcting a girl doing bar exercises, he gently pressed behind my knee to angle my weight a fraction forward and downward; like a painter, he stood back to observe me and then, like a hairdresser, he moved in and laid the flat of his hand on my left cheek, so as to carefully set my right cheek against the plastic buttstock. Most of all, his soft voice was that of a man communicating undoubted expert knowledge of a thing he truly loved.

I was grateful to give myself over, body and soul, to his complete certainty. It was better than any holiday. At last, someone else was in charge of my life. It felt like the best four hundred euros I had ever spent.

—I see now you are a tall man, Toni. This is the shorter version of this gun. It is my favourite. For close work in urban environment is quicker, I show you afterwards. But perhaps if Gerry tell me before, the longer version would be better for you. Let me see. But no, I think will be all right. Yes, is fine. So. This is the safety switch.

—Ah, that one.

—You see, with your thumb, is very easy. Like this, safe. Like that, live.

—Is that all you have to do, to make it safe? Just that?

—Is all, yes. Now you can drop it, kick it, nothing happen.

—Right. Oh well then. Ha. God, that's so easy.

—Oh yes, is very good design. So, yes, this is *safe* and now you click this and now you are *fire*. Do not worry. What can happen? Still nothing. Your finger on the trigger now please. Not with the hook of the finger, this will spoil your aim. Just the first part. No, no. There. Yes. Very good. Now, listen and look like I do. You breathe in, you breathe out and then just when you finish to breathe out, before you breathe in again, you press, softly, smoothly, yes? But wait, my friend, first you put on your ear-protectors, yes? Or else you never hear a girl sigh again in your ear, poor Toni!

—Right, yes, sorry!

—Now you go.

—Right, um, I suppose it will, you know, kick back at me?

—This gun kick? No, no, Toni. Not she. Not if you hold her close.

—Right. Sorry. OK. Breathe, right.

—Good, Toni. And now you shoot.

—Right. Now I shoot. OK.

BANG!

52: A Mere Liberal Englishman

I blinked with disbelief. Then I remembered that I needed to breathe in again, and did so.

It was impossible.

I, a mere liberal Englishman, had just fired an assault rifle with live ammunition and nothing spectacular had happened. I had not dropped the gun shamefully from the kick-back. There had been, indeed, hardly any kick-back at all. I was not deafened. My finger had not been taken off. No burns had seared my face. The world turned as normal beneath my feet. Normal, that is, considering that I was in a shooting range and had just fired an assault rifle.

—Perfect. Again. No, too fast. Again. Very good. Again. Again. Now we check the gun. Always, this is very important.

As George came to stand beside me once again, I forced myself to stop smiling like an idiot. I bit my lip, furrowed my brow and made myself listen and watched with all my concentration.

—First release magazine, here, with your finger. Yes, here.

—Oops, sorry, dropped it!

—Yes, it drop fast. You see, for speed of change this is very good. If you are in moving firefight, maybe you let it fall and leave it. But be careful how many you have left! If you drop all clips, what you do then when you need to reload?

—Yes, gosh, I see.

—Good. Now, you look in here, yes? This is very

good with AR-15, at end of clip the chamber stay open, you can see. So now you look. Is there thing inside the chamber?

—Um, no. Nothing.

—So, is clear. Very Good. Now roll the gun this way. You see this? Now you just, how you say, you hit this button with this flat part of your hand. Not hit.

—Slap?

—Yes, very good, slap. Not too hard, but hard enough. Just like you slap your girl on the ass when you show how you like her. Slap! There. Very good. You see? You hear this click? Exactly. Now you must make the safety shot to be sure one hundred per cent. You point at safe place or at ground if ground soft. You make the shot, yes. Nothing, you see. So now you are all safe.

—Safe, right.

Yes, safe I was. Totally safe now. And God it felt good.

—So now we try again, from start. You see? Already you know the gun, now you are not so nervous. Is much better. Now the gun she is your friend.

—Um, George, sorry, I was just wondering, if, I mean, if there was actually a bullet left in the gun, sort of stuck, or if you were halfway through a clip?

—Oh, this is very good question, Toni. Stupid me, I do not tell you. From start I know you are special pupil. It is very easy. First you make sure is on safe, yes, here? Then you just do like you cock it again. You see? Now the chamber is open again. If there is round in, now you can just turn the gun, she fall out so easy, you catch. Or you can pull her out with these fingers if she stuck bad. But I do not think this happen to you ever with good ammo like I give you from United States. Maybe with Belgian ammo or Czech ammo. Sorry, my new country, but this is true. So sad. So, now we shoot again, yes?

Bang. Bang. Bang. Bang. Bang.

—How that is feeling, Toni?

—Ha ha, it feels, I mean, well, it felt better that time, I think.

—I also think. So now we check the gun like I show you. Good. Very good. And slap, yes. And safety shot. Very good. Now we see how good you have shoot, yes? Come, Toni.

—Right.

I pulled the earphones down around my neck. The plastic conches made a strangely comforting collar around my jugular veins.

So now I knew. I could make my Armalite safe in a few seconds. How easy it all was! How absurd that I had not known. But now I did, so all was well.

I could leave now, really.

But then again, I had paid, I was here, they were getting me to the station and, well, consider: if I went away now it would seem extremely weird. Certainly it would. Who knew if Gerry might decide to tip the police off about this curious last-minute student with the (surely the idiot had seen?) blatantly false name and ridiculous hat, who suddenly upped and left right at the start of an expensive class? I'd stick out as clearly as an Arab in Florida asking to learn just how to *steer* a Boeing. And George was so warm and enthusiastic. I was, it seems a strange thing to say, but it was true, I was actually moved by his simple desire to tell me what he knew. And every bit of knowledge is a good thing, surely? So why go now? Why insult him?

We walked slowly up the range, to where fresh paper shapes of symbolic human forms had been taped over the targets. But there was no sign of damage to them. I felt deep shame, compounded by the vague feeling that I was treading on cursed ground, and wished once again that I was somewhere warmer, drier and safer, far from all guns. But George chatted companionably away.

—You see how there is no kick-back at all, Toni, hardly any at all, like I tell you? Exactly. You think it will kick, it does not. That is why I like this gun, I think she best in the world. They say she jam too much, always we hear this, but I say, here is not Vietnam, if you treat her right she will be good for you. I think you like too, yes? The AK-47 jump much more. Too much I think. There. This is good. You see?

Good God. I hit it!

—Yes, nearly all times. This is not so good grouping, I tell you true. We fix this. But for begin is fine.

I stared. The holes in the paper were smaller than you would make with a stabbing biro. But holes they were. I could already shoot! I felt a ludicrous grin tugging at the edges of my mouth. Suddenly, I wanted very much to giggle and slap my leg.

—You think this hole is small, yes? This is the small bore for you. But remember high velocity. So there is no kick and the hole is small here, but the high speed will destroy, how you say, when it go in it will kill all the, in here, I do not know the word, I am sorry.

—Internal organs?

—Yes, yes, exactly. The internal organs. And, of course, the round she will tumble when she hit, so exit wound is much greater, Toni.

—Ah, of course.

—If you get shot close with Armalite, is better than get shot at two hundred yards, because the bullet she is not yet tumbling. She go in straight, out straight, pow.

—Yes, I can see that would be true.

I watched, trying not to smile with pride, as George

placed small black stickers over my ten bullet holes. Six were clearly within the angular outline of the humanoid form; two were high and to the left, one low and to the right. I had only missed completely once. How could it be so easy? I did not trust myself to wire plugs safely enough for use in my kids' bedrooms, but I could already hit a man-shaped target with an assault rifle six times out of ten at fifty yards. And come close enough to scare the shit out of the bastard another three times out of ten, ha ha!

But of course it was easy, I reminded myself.

I was a cultural historian, I should know that. The medieval longbow had a far quicker rate of fire and as great an effective range as the musket right up to the Napoleonic Wars. So why bother using muskets? Because it takes years to train up a longbowman, but any idiot farm labourer can be rounded up, taught to fire a gun reasonably straight in half a day and then sent out to charge cannons or shoot demonstrators. Extraordinary, nonetheless, to have it demonstrated so concretely. No wonder governments keep these things out of people's hands . . .

—I think you miss these two because you use the hook of your finger, like I tell you not. This pull the gun, like this, you see? Give me your hand, I show you again now.

—Oh yes, I see. Sorry, George.

—No, no, this day is for you to learn. Toni, I see you are wise man, serious about gun. I like this. Most days is just drunks from Germany, England, Holland. This is not why I make career as instructor. You understand me?

—Yes. Actually, George, you know, my career didn't really turn out as I expected either.

—So you understand. I am Muslim from Sarajevo. You know this city? Of course. My father has shop, one day it will be for me. What do I know about guns? Nothing. But then the Serbs come, the Chetniks. So now we fight, or we die. We have some good guys with us, mujahidin, paid for by CIA. They train me, they teach me Arabic for jihad. All paid for by CIA, yes, ha ha, crazy! But we have no guns, why? Because nice England and nice France say no sell no guns to anyone. Oh, poor us, the Serbs already have the tanks and the artillery! But at last the Americans bomb the Serbs and we are so happy. The airstrikes come, bang! We see a big ammo dump go up, in the mountains, where those Chetnik bastards been shooting us for a year, killing our children, our mothers. Boom! We know this time it is they die. We cheer. Bill Clinton very good guy, Americans very good people. I go to train with US Marines. Never again I am the one who do not know to use gun, I say. Very good. So I am trained. I think maybe I get career in executive protection. But now Americans make this war in Iraq. They cannot win, they will lose. Now everybody think they are stupid, everybody hate them. You think I show my nice certificates from US Marines now? I am so stupid I want my head cut off? I want to go to America. But guess what? I am Muslim. Muslims were good guys in 1994. Now we are bad guys. Not so good to get visa now, oh no! Maybe I go to England. But I think is not much gun work in England?

—We don't really do guns, in England.

—Still, maybe I think I try. I like British Army. I train with them also a little in Germany. I meet very funny guys. So, enough, I waste your money talk of me and my life. Not professional. So sorry. Perhaps we have nice coffee later, then we talk.

—Yes, that would be nice. And really, George, it isn't a problem. It's, well, actually, it's nice to talk.

—Yes, very nice. But now it is time for tuck-tuck.

—Tuck? Well, yes, a sandwich would be nice. I'm pretty hungry, actually. Missed breakfast. And dinner, come to think of it. Amazing, that you use that word. *Tuck*. Did you learn it when you were talking to our army men? I mean, obviously, yes, don't get me wrong, George, it's a perfectly good word for *food*, well, *snacks*, you know. But pretty old-fashioned. Sorry, George, did I say something wrong?

—I do not understand, Toni. You want to stop and eat food?

—Um, well, sorry, I thought you said it was time for *tuck*?

—Tuck-tuck, Toni. I teach you tuck-tuck next. Two quick shots.

—Oh. Oh, I see. God, sorry, yes, of course.

—You are happy we go on? I can stop. Karel can make you sandwich.

—No, Christ, George, please. This is what I came for. And I'm very glad I did. Tuck-tuck, eh? Two quick shots?

—Yes. This is very important, Toni. Think, Toni. If you need to shoot them once, you need to shoot them twice.

—Well, yes, I suppose you would.

—The Israelis are very *haa haa! aah*! Always they go full auto, but with full auto most times the third shot go where you think? Yes, no one knows. Also, is hard to count your shots with full auto. I can do this counting now, full auto, but many times when I start I get it wrong. This is very important. You must know always how many shells you have left, or maybe you see two bad guys, you think, aha, now they are mine, but you have only one shell left. You do not know this. You get one but then, ah! Poor you! This is why with US special forces always we use just two quick shots, you see, not full auto, just tuck-tuck.

—Right. Tuck-tuck.

—So, this time you load the magazine all yourself, yes? Good, that is better. Always tap on the table. If you wearing helmet you can tap on this too, like that, make sure the bullets all right inside. No jams. You try. Yes. That is good! So. Now you put clip in. You are on safety, no problems, you see? And now cock. And now you stand like so. I show you. Sorry, leg like this, like I show you. Good. This arm a little lower. I tell you. You watch I do, you copy me. You take all weight of gun only in right hand, to see. I always think this is best. Good. You see? Balance like this. The left hand now, just to steady her. Good. This is low ready position. You can walk like this all day, you see? You can look around, you do what I do, Toni. You can look around, maybe you see something, easy to bring her up, yes, like this. Oh, nothing. Back down. Very good, Toni! But now, aha! You damn sure you see something, some bad guys there, there, and there maybe. So now you go high ready. Still you can look around and easy cover your ass, but now when you see the bad guys, is very simple just swing up this little bit, then tuck-tuck.

—I see, yes. Yes, ha.

—So, now we try with live. You are cocked, is good, so now switch to fire. Do what I do. Low ready. Ah, over there, I think bad guys. High ready. Yes, I see bad guys, that target there, three o'clock, Toni.

BANG-BANG.

—You get him, Toni! Just tuck-tuck, you see. Exactly! Very good. And again we do it. Low ready. We walk, we watch. Oh, look out, Toni, bad guys five o'clock. No no, five o'clock is over here, Toni.

—Oh, sorry . . .

53: Outside the Liberal Box

Cold? Not any more.

We stood and we knelt and we lay prone. We shifted from target to target mid-clip, at his calmly shouted command. We let the magazines drop where they fell and slapped in new ones with scarcely a break, taking care to stagger our changeovers and thus be able to cover each other from our virtual foes as we did so. I began to see what George meant about my tweed. It made no noise at all. From somewhere beyond the big sandbanks, the Russian Army fetishists were firing off incredible, teeth-juddering blasts from a World War II heavy machine gun. I could hear my heart thudding fast inside my earphones.

Swiftly our notional enemies fell before our fire. I don't know who George was shooting at in his head (I imagined that it was nineties Serbian mortar groups), but my own targets were very well-defined, my own mission clear.

Margaret Thatcher I got with ten out of ten shots, five bursts of tuck-tuck right into her chest, the bitch. I turned round to grin at George so quickly that my ear-protectors fell off, then forgot about them in my excitement and nearly deafened myself when I moved swiftly on to waste Blair, for whom I decided a few in the face would be more fitting, as the reward of treachery. George rolled over a wall and landed cat-like on the ground beside me.

—This is good, Toni, your enemies fall. You slot them good.

—Slot?

—Is what British special forces say. Always they slot people. Is not good English?

—Slot? Oh yes, it's a perfectly good word. I just never heard it in this context. I'm not sure what it must be derived from. Presumably from some notion of fate, of us all having a *slot* allotted to us? Or perhaps from slot as in a *slot in the earth*, a grave?

—Toni, you are clever man. You know much, I see this. But still you must learn. When you kneel to shoot, no bone on bone. Your elbow here, not there on your knee bone.

—No bone on bone, gotcha, George.

—Yes, you learn good with me, Toni. Now, this time I cover you, you go first, yes?

—Rightyho!

How refreshing to be the beginner pupil for once. A very fertile experience for any university teacher, when you thought about it, to learn absolutely from scratch a subject which they had never expected to encounter. Enlightening. Especially with regard to teaching students from underprivileged and unconventional entrance streams. Absolutely. Should be part of every colleague's Best Practice. Must mention this place to those pathetic cretins in the Staff Development and Quality Delivery Unit, ha ha!

And how enlivening, how useful for the cultural historian indeed, to feel that one is acquiring an age-old though of course essentially undesirable human skill. Guns, after all, are merely the latest development in missile weapons (as opposed to shock weapons), no fundamentally different in philosophical principle or tactical use to a Stone Age bow and arrow (as opposed to a club). Get them at distance, enemy or prey. And fascinating to discover this whole new vocabulary.

Mentally stimulating, rather. A long time since I had seriously learned something entirely new. Bit rut-stuck, had I become? Good for the synapses, this? Undoubtedly.

Tuck-tuck.

And indeed as our guns jerked and banged, I found myself thinking with a whole new clarity, as if my mind itself had been switched firmly on to 'safe' for far too many years.

I mean, when you thought about it (*tuck-tuck*), my allegedly English fear of guns was perfectly stupid. I (*tuck-tuck*), as a sophisticated intellectual and cultural analyst, really should know better than to merely accept such alleged normality at face value! Why, in fact, had Englishmen (*tuck-tuck*) for many centuries rarely been encouraged, let alone obliged, to train with guns? Simple: because having (*tuck-tuck*) led the way in deposing and/or decapitating their rightful kings by force of arms, they had then given up killing each other and had taken to attacking foreigners with a bloody great navy (*tuck-tuck, tuck-tuck*), to which over time they so devoted themselves that from Trafalgar onwards no one could threaten them, whilst they could intervene at will in the politico-military settlements of others. For the next century the Royal Navy was to the world what the USAF became after World War II: a force which, if it could not actually occupy and control territories, could damn well bugger them up (*tuck-tuck*). Having been overtaken by technology and America during the Second World War, this navy found itself briefly eclipsed by the RAF before being gratefully re-equipped with the biggest gun (*tuck-tuck*) ever devised by man, one that could level cities Bible-style and which only a few other countries on earth were allowed to possess.

No wonder Englishmen don't need to know about guns.

Tuck-tuck. Tuck-tuck. Tuck-tuck.

And think: *Bleak House,* you could pop into a shooting gallery just off Leicester Square and blaze away any time you fancied. *Five dozen rifle and a dozen pistol.* Dr Watson casually packing his revolver in his stout Edwardian luggage without Conan (*tuck-tuck*) Doyle making any great fuss about the telling. Elementary. Always go armed east of Aldgate! You could hardly call Dr Watson un-English!

Tuck-tuck. Tuck-tuck.

Now *that* felt right. Yes, unless I was much mistaken, that would turn out to be *bloody* good grouping. So much for Ronald bloody Reagan. Press with finger, let it drop, in with the new clip, *chonk!* Already cocked, you see! Yes, I have to say, George is quite right about the AR-15, it really is rather . . .

Over there, George? Right. Mine. *Tuck-tuck.* John Major. Well, perhaps he didn't really deserve that. *Collateral damage.* Sorry, John.

Morover, consider: what, when you thought outside the liberal box for just a moment, could be more convenient for capitalism than an entire country full of people who have been nurtured to fear and loathe the very instruments without which they can, if and when the need comes, be cowed easily into submission by a few battalions of the armed lackeys of big business and the corporate state, eh? Oh yes! Whereas compare and contrast the capacity of the small wee Bogside to resist, simply because armed with a few dozen Armalites. Precisely! Ever since the Normans built castles no Saxon peasants could ever hope to storm, there has been an arms race between the ruling class and the rest of us. And look who's won it. Well, quite. I mean, imagine for a minute how differently the Miners' Strike might have panned out if we'd had a few of these babies!

Ah, yes, and there he is, whatshisname, you know, that American or was it Canadian bastard Thatcher hired to come in to break the miners, the first of the new breed of million-quid-bonus fat bloody union-busting cats, got him in the sights easy as pie: *tuck-tuck*, goodnight! Slotted the bastard, ha ha!

54: A Black, Bloody Insurrection

I had fired off many, many rounds without noticing, through the sights, any smoke from my own shots. When watching George, I had now and then caught a very slight and incredibly brief whiff of shadow in front of his gun when he fired. But now we reached some mysterious tipping-point of light.

The wet, brown-green afternoon slid over quite suddenly into a real November country nightfall and everything changed. The next time I looked over at George to receive his waved instructions (he was as totally serious as an eight-year-old boy at play), the darkness had fallen and I was amazed to see six-inch licks of flame dancing sideways out from the chamber of his gun with every ejected shell, and his muzzle spurting great comic-book blooms of red and orange fire. The blasts showed every bone in his face and lit off reflections inside my specs.

My God, I must look like that as well!

Pretty damn cool, in other words.

Hard and *bloody* scary.

If my colleagues could only see me now.

If only my boys could see me now.

God, what if I just kept the gun for a couple of years? Ha! Oh yes, in a couple of years Jack and Will could be as teenaged as they wanted, but there would not be much danger of them thinking me an old pointless git on the evening I cajoled them out to my shed on some blithe pretext (—*Have we got to, Dad? Why? What's the point? Bor-ing!*) and there, in the soft lamplight, showed

243

them how to strip and load a real live AR-15 Armalite assault rifle!

Ridiculous, of course.

Back to reality.

Reload.

Cthunk!

Now, who was there left to slot?

Capitalism itself, why not?

There it is: capitalism personified, a slick-haired shit of about forty sat in his bloody spit-new Porsche braying hands-free into his Bluetoothed BlackBerry, a man of zero spiritual or intellectual distinction who is about to pocket another million quid, on which he will in one way or another make certain he pays virtually no tax, for his part in crunching the numbers or clauses of some bloody private-equity hedge-fund, asset-stripping deal made by people no one has ever heard of who will now be allowed to sack hundreds of hard-working people before selling niftily on.

Tuck-tuck! The Porsche, that piece of sheer rub-their-noses-in-it consumption, veers, its windscreen suddenly a web of cracks, the smug grin on the driver's face now a mask of idiotic surprise as he looks down at the stain rapidly totalling his Armani suit.

Watch, I say, watch: for ye know not when the tuck-tuck cometh!

And who is this next up? Ah yes, a north-London estate agent. Of course. Who better? Revenge is black pudding, as the Germans somewhat curiously put it.

Hello again, Mr Young Estate Agent. Yes, that's right. I said up to four hundred thousand pounds. I said nothing special. Yes, I said *anywhere at all* in north London with three human-sized bedrooms. I said all I want is a normal house in a normal area where my eleven-year-old boys can ride their bikes in the park alone now and then. Yes, I said I'd expect the schools to be reasonably OK. No, I don't mind if a bit of work needs doing. Go a bit higher, you say? Quite a bit higher? How much is quite a bit? Oh, I see. Another hundred and fifty? And that, you say, might just about *shade* us, wasn't that what you said? Into the what did you call it? The ballpark? What a lovely word. American, right? Sorry, let me explain. I, who have never been unemployed and who got on the property ladder as soon as I could, what with having studied religiously for my current profession throughout my twenties, have just offered to nail myself to the ground until the year I retire just to get a normal little house for my family. And you say I'll have to *go quite a bit higher*. I see. Now, how precisely shall I do that, Mr Slick? What's that? Oh, your own in-house mortgage advisor can probably help me *work it up* to five or six times our joint income? If we're economical with the truth, ha ha? So, hold on, correct me if I'm wrong, what you actually mean is: if I lie about what I earn, your colleague will be able to pocket the fat commission on a mortgage deal that will enable you to pocket the fat commission on a sale that will end up with me signing for a mortgage I cannot possibly afford and which, therefore, unless property prices continue to rise at over 10 per cent per year for ever, will inevitably leave me bankrupt and homeless? Well, that's very kind of you both. What nice men you are. But I'll tell you what, how about you tell this bullshit to my little friend, fuck face? Not such a figure of comedy now? You know what the linguistic root of the word *mortgage* is, O deeply qualified professional young man? You want to find out? Yes, try to scrabble away to safety behind your desk, but you will not escape vengeance.

Tuck-tuck.

Blood over the flat-screen workstations, the carousels packed with flats at half a million quid tumble as dying fingers grasp at them. The earth, a very slightly cleaner place. He shoots, he scores!

Talking of which, hark! Who is this nineteen-year-old with no GCSEs, a reading age of twelve and several Bentleys?

Why, who but Sean Scally, one-time plaguer of teachers, long-time bully of his fellow children and now world-renowned screamer-at of referees, a ruinous example of sudden and undeserved wealth to thick teenagers everywhere. Nothing personal, Scallo, but no society can function with examples like you held up every day. Why the hell shouldn't you pay 80 per cent tax? You and Liam bloody Gallagher. Meet Mr Tuck-Tuck, Scallo.

Tuck-tuck.

He drops his ridiculous cocktail and crashes face-first into his Cheshire swimming pool.

And now?

Ah yes, you, you Bluewater-cruising godforsaken arseholes, because of you the planet is going to die and my kids are going to have a shit life. I believed in betterment, but all you care about is how quickly you can *get your hands on the brands*. Jesus fucking Christ, was it for this that the Tolpuddle Martyrs did, well, you know, whatever it was they did? And you have the same vote as me! Insanity! Well this is where the craziness stops, right here:

Tuck-tuck.

As for you all, you hoodied and hoodless suckers-up of so-called 'benefits', you ruiners of the social democratic settlement, you serial abusers of a wonderful system designed to save decent workers from hunger between jobs, you two million who thought you were too good to do the jobs that six hundred thousand hard-working Poles have found in England! Hanging round robbing and dealing and spawning the so-called street culture that is going to make my poor boys' schooldays a Calvary. What's that? Oh, really? Only *just over a quarter* of all government spending, and hence of my tax, goes on what they call *Social Protection*? How modest. Only just over a quarter? Well well. That's OK then, what am I being so small-minded about, comfortable homeowning citizen that I am? I'll tell you bloody what! I am not a human, my unprivileged little mate, never mind a comfy one, I am a mere machine for paying bills, and I just about make my quota every month on month, year on financial year, and if I'm lucky I'll make it to retirement without falling behind, so that I can start being *really* poor.

Very nice.

Very bloody nice.

So hear me, the lot of you, up and down, in your Porsches and your estate agencies and your TV studios and your malls and your dole queues and . . . you know what this country needs?

A real bourgeois armed uprising at last!

A black, bloody insurrection of the hard-working, over-taxed and unbenefited. A dictatorship of the normal suckers, merciless with revolutionary discipline against all who utilise tax shelters or vandalise bus shelters. Down with all the dealers, in drugs or securities. Let fairness prevail on pain of summary execution. Welcome to the Day of Judgment, roll up and get your low-number party cards, all ye who never lied to social security or sat down with a tax barrister, and let our battle-cry be: *righteousness*!

Tuck-tuck! Tuck-fucking-tuck. Tuck-tuck-fucking-tuck.

Oh fuck this fucking tuck-tuck for a game of soldiers, I want full auto and I want it now, I want to really cut loose and . . .

—Hey, Tony!

—Aah! Oh, Gerry, um, hi, sorry, what?

55: A Deep and Very Middle-European Ditch

—Tell you what, Tony, we better wind up if you want to catch that train to Berlin! Here, you look like you're loving it!

—What? Oh, yes, of course. Um, very, interesting. Christ, really, is it that late?

—Time flies in the zone, eh, Tony?

—God yes. Right. Right. So, well, er, George . . .

—Toni, I hope you think this was good day.

—Oh, yes, very. Very, George. I just wish . . .

—I told you George was good! Just time to down a quick beer if you fancy, sandwich too, all included just as per, why not, eh? Everyone likes a beer afterwards, Tony. Funny, but true.

—A beer? God, yes, actually. I could murder one. Um, Gerry, hey, I really enjoyed today and, well, I was wondering, actually, you see, I'm pretty flexible time-wise the next few days and, um, well, I mean, I could come here again, very soon, maybe tomorrow, or the next day. But only if George is available.

—Toni, I am there for you when you want.

—Great! Well then, Gerry, look, how about I book up right now? Here, look, I've got the money. Four hundred, right?

Gerry immediately stepped, or rather bounced, close to me and took me round the shoulder.

—Tell you what, put your money away, Tony. We can talk prices in the car. Now, let's be going. I'll sort it for you. That's me, eh? There's my car. Let's get on our way, shall we? Don't want to miss your train. We can get that beer at the station. Cheers, George, thanks for . . .

—Gerry, you wait.

—What's that, George?

—Toni, you tell me how much you pay him for today?

—Tell you what, we'll sort this out later, George.

—Toni. I am your friend, you tell me.

—We're getting pretty tight for time, Tony.

—Toni?

—I paid him four hundred euros.

—Now look, George . . .

—Four hundred, Toni?

—I was going to tell you, George.

—Toni, you watch. Gerry, you fucking bastard, you give me more one hundred fifty euros right now or you not get off this fucking shooting range. I kick your ass good. I shoot your fucking tyres out. Then we talk, you, me, Karel. Toni, I sorry, so sorry, this fucking bastard say you pay him two hundred fifty euros; is seventy-five for me, seventy-five for Karel for range, hundred for him. This is normal price for two English. Four hundred? Very nice for Gerry. So now I take his wallet. I am no thief, Toni. I do only what is make thing right. I take this fifty, you see? Fifty. Food for my kids, you see? Now you get one hundred back, I think that fair. You think that fair, Toni?

—George, no, you keep it.

—Toni, no.

—Yes, yes, please, George. For your kids.

—Toni, you are good man. I keep fifty of this, I give Karel fifty. You come back here tomorrow, next day, we do very good shoot, nothing for me, seventy-five for Karel range. I give you ammo what it cost me, maybe thirty, forty, nothing more to pay for you. We do really good course. I show you all US Marine tactics, very important. You want to do night-sight shoot? Yes, of course. So we can do night-sight shoot, at six o'clock is dark enough. You will like this, I promise. Karel has very good night-sights. For you and me nothing extra; a hundred extra for anyone other. You see, I am your friend, not Gerry. Now you know me, fuck Gerry. You call me, here is my card, my number also here my mobile, you see? I pick you up, thirty euros here and back to Prague. This is very fair price. We shoot, we talk like friends. You see? Fuck Gerry.

George gave Gerry what looked like quite a harmless little shove but which sent him tumbling backwards into a deep and very middle-European ditch.

—Um, look, George, the thing is, I need to get to the train station. Sort of now.

—Yes, of course, I know this. I take you. No problem. Plenty time. We go?

—Right, yes, George. We go.

56: God Knows

I feel that for the avoidance of doubt I should stress one thing: I did not want to have sex with George.

Not in the least. If he had proposed sex (George? Impossible!) I would have been horribly disappointed. I wanted things which are far more important than sex to us men. I wanted to drink with him. I wanted to drive with him. I wanted to talk with him, and agree with him and him to agree with me. I wanted to swap stories with him and find that, despite all the obviously vast differences in our lives, there was a strange undertow of fated congruity. I wanted to go looking for girls with him and wake up in the morning and go and have a big breakfast with him and talk about the girls before arranging to meet and drink with him again in a couple of days. I wanted his son (who was ten) to be friends with Jack and William for life. I wanted his daughter (who was nine) to marry one of them. I wanted to be as near as possible to him. No: I wanted to be as near as possible him. Not to his cock. To him. I wanted to be his blood brother. I wanted a formal alliance with him, for ever.

Anyone who has a fully grown personality won't understand this.

Most men will.

As George's old Passat circled the could-be-anyplace outskirts of Prague, I found myself no longer caring where we were going. Just being with him made me feel safe. It was like riding at night in my parents' car, a tired child. The reassuring voice, the soft illumination of the dashboard, the washes of meaningless lamplight passing in the dark outside, the cool glass of the window on my cheek and . . .

—Ow! Sorry. Sorry, George, what was that you were saying? Sorry, I just, I'm so sleepy! Sorry, that was so rude.

—No no, Toni, I see you are tired. I know combat fatigue, this is like this. I think you are too tired for train. You stay in my house, I have bed for you.

—George, that's so kind of you, but I can't. I have to go to Berlin. There's a man there who is very important for my life. If I don't go, I'll be in big trouble.

—Toni, please, now I ask you tell truth to me, your friend. I see you shoot. I see you watch. I think you are man in big trouble now.

—Yes, you're right, George. I'm sorry I lied to you. I'm not going to Berlin, I'm going to Dresden. Look, I'm not even called Tony, but I'm not going to tell you my real name. Not now, anyway. But . . .

I took off my absurd cap and felt my hair fall down again at last. Before I could stop myself, I was telling the truth, at long last. It felt so good that I wanted to cry with happiness. And, somehow, the fact that I had to tell it all in simple English made it even more of a liberation.

—This is me, George. I have an Armalite at home in England. That's why I needed to learn about it.

—I think Armalite is not legal in England, Toni?

—No, very illegal. Exactly. George, I found it, in my garden. I was planting plum trees, that's all.

—Yes, plum trees, very nice.

—And it was just, there. I wasn't sure what to do. I did nothing, then it got too late. I thought if I told the police I might get into trouble. I tried to dump it, but I ran into these bad people and I had to cock it, and so now it's loaded and I was too scared to touch it again so I came to you. Now I can make it safe again, and then throw it away. Thank you.

—This is all very foolish, Toni.

—I know, I know, obviously, I should have just called the police right away, but, you see, well, England's changed and . . .

—You throw your Armalite away? You give it to the police? Why?

—Sorry?

—No, Toni! I come to England, I get it, if you do not wish have it. Your Armalite is very valuable thing. In my little car is very easy. Maybe they check me when I drive in. Oho, Muslim from Bosnia, quick check him: I understand this, is not their fault. But aha! No big checks for a little car coming out from England! No, of course not. Why? Who takes an Armalite out of England into France? Ha ha!

—Look, um, Toni, I really don't think that . . .

—Oh, of course, I am joking, Toni.

—Oh good. Ha. God, sorry, George, I'm so tired, I really thought for a minute there that you actually meant, you know, that you were going to come over and . . .

—I would not take it from you, Toni. I am your friend. It is yours.

—What?

—God has given you this thing. Lucky man, you must keep it. Tomorrow or next day we do night shoot and I teach you all maintenance you need. I give you genuine US Army kit for cleaning and such.

—George, I mean, look, thanks, wow, that's really kind of you, but you see, like I said, it's illegal just to have it at all, in England. Very, very illegal. And, you know, what would I ever do with it?

—Nothing, if God wants.

—Well, right then. Exactly.

—But maybe God wants other things, who knows, Toni?

—Um . . .

—Toni, we are friends. I tell you story. I am born, you know, in a country Yugoslavia. Yugoslavia government, army, money, flag, police, school, passport, all things. Not such bad police like Russia, Czechoslovakia, East Germany. No Red Army. Nice beaches. German girls in summer! Yes, of course, police. Yes, of course, government. Yes, of course, picture of Tito on all walls. Oh so nice. We salute if we like or if we not like, hello Tito we love you so much, all this shit, yes? But anyway. People know what they do, what happens. You do this, this happen, you do that, that happen. So you know. You say yes this, yes that, when you know is bullshit, you must do thing some asshole tell you because he got big friends, but you live. You make things little, little better, every year. You can maybe build new house, like my father build. And you do not need Armalite in this house, what for you need? Then one day all change. No country, no police except bad police, no army except bad army, tanks, guns, your new house shot down, your friends killed, no chance in safe haven, thank you, United Nations. Oh yes, very nice. Thank you, Germany and France and Britain. So then you wish God you had Armalite in your house, then you kill the bastards before they kill you.

—George. I'm so sorry for all that. Yes, we should have stopped it. I understand. But you know, that isn't going to happen in England.

—Toni, I know you are clever man, I think maybe you are too tired for think, poor you. If you never touch this Armalite again, you are never be in trouble, I am right? You keep it safe, it does nothing, yes?

—I suppose.

—Of course. Not suppose. So this is very good, this mean you have a good life. You win, happy man. England is England, nothing has changed, your house is safe, you leave your Armalite to your boys for if they need it, you never need to shoot anyone, you die happy and people sing round your bed. God give us peace in our days. But if you need it, Toni, aha! Then you are damn glad it is bloody there. And you are not scared make trouble with police and such, because there is fucking bloody great big trouble already, this is why you need to get your Armalite, yes?

—Well, that's logical, yes.

—Yes, very logical. Now you think better, Toni. When this day come, if it come, God knows, if you need to get your Armalite but it is not there because you threw it away. For what? For nothing. On that day you curse yourself, you tear your face, stupid Toni, you say stupid me, I throw away my Armalite for nothing and so now my house will be taken, or my daughter will be robbed or my sons will die like rabbits. No, Toni. Think good. You keep your Armalite, you win or you win. You throw it away, maybe you win, maybe you lose. So you keep it, or you are silly man.

—Yes, I suppose you're right, I . . . No, George, sorry, look, this is crazy. England is England. We've got the English Channel. No one's invaded us for a thousand years, well, apart from the Scots, and that doesn't really count. No one's had their money stolen by the government since the seventeenth century. That's why Russian billionaires put their money into London. Nothing like that is ever going to happen in England. It couldn't.

—Toni, I am sad you speak like a fool. I have told you my life. Does man know what things will come? No. God knows.

57: What Things Will Come

I looked into his dark eyes. He was speaking the pure truth as he knew it, as he had learned it. And as I looked at his truth, all of sudden I seemed to see other truths.

My parents' truth, for example. They had been right to bring me up as they had done, as right as anyone can be. In the world they knew as normal, the world they had come of age in, accountants were book-keepers, professional footballers ended up running pubs if they were lucky and university lecturers lived in big houses and wore tweed. Those had been hard, provable facts. All around them, as the fifties turned into the sixties, they had seen grammar-school people who had gone to university making hay in fat state or quasi-governmental jobs while country houses were being sold off for peanuts to pay taxes. They had not been stupid. They had been observant and wise and had seen what worked. They had done the right and rational thing. They had loved me and done the best for me and they had, in consequence, readied me perfectly for life in the world of JFK and Harold Wilson.

Everything had changed, that was all. The hard facts had turned out to be as soft and floppy as Dali's watches. Like some Ice Age cave family faced with the melting of the glaciers, they had found that all their precious survival lore was suddenly quite worthless. They had equipped me, their only son, with all the tricks they knew: but they were all just tools for a vanished world.

And what would clever I do, in my turn?

My sons and my daughter, assuming no dirty terrorist bomb or melting ice caps or Sino-American nuke-fest got them first, would do jobs, assuming there were any left, which did not yet even exist, assuming the world continued to do so. Who knew? How would they, as grown people, see my world? Would they look back at this world, our world, now, as a paradise wilfully thrown away or as a fool's paradise waiting to get it? What great event would finally bring down the curtain on the longest post-war boom and the Pax Americana? Whatever, it was a safe bet my sons and daughter would not be coming respectfully to me for advice on life when they were twenty-five.

Money, yes.

Except that I would have none.

On the other hand, if all went well with the world, my boys and my sweet daughter might pre-order the genders of my grandchildren in advance, straight or gay, in twenty or thirty years' time, engineering them free of faults. By 2050, or whatever it would be by then, they, my own children, might be able to download their entire minds and conquer death itself at last.

I might be part of the lucky, spoiled post-war boom-time West that had never had it so good and never would again, or I might belong to the tragicomic last generation that would ever have to die. *In the tortured decades between approximately 1870 and 2050, men had lost their belief in God but still had to die. The result was Auschwitz and Wal-Mart, discuss . . .*

—I think you understand, Toni?

I looked deeper into George's war-zone eyes and saw the skies of London darkened by the Luftwaffe, the roads of Europe crammed with refugees. I saw the unspeakable cattle trucks heading for the unthinkable, packed with people who still found it all unbelievable. I saw my own mother at ten years old, throwing herself to the ground in a little street in Cricklewood as an unseen V-1 choked off above the low clouds. My father, a teenage conscript, pouring heavy machine-gun fire into masses of Chinese infantry at point-blank range on a hillside in Korea until his machine-gun barrel jammed, expecting to die by bayonet until the last-ditch US air strikes incinerated a thousand more Chinese teenagers in clouds of napalm. Myself newly born, asleep in a West Country garden in a high old pram as the vapour trails of the V-bombers and B-52s embroidered the skies, ready in the air lest the Russian ships did not turn back from Cuba that day. The huge lorries, as rectangular and lumpish as cheap green plastic toys, hauling cruise missiles through English lanes. The mechanic rushing out of the country garage in Ireland where I had just pulled in to fill up, shouting to everyone that Kiev had been nuked, that Reagan had actually gone and fucking done it, and everyone on that little forecourt looking immediately skywards, triggered by a lifetime's drip-fed fear, to watch powerlessly for the MIRVs. The Berlin Wall falling and my career going up in smoke along with a generation of certainties. The hellfires of 9/11, of 7/7, of rush-hour Madrid. The face of a teenage boy gunned down last week not half a mile from our front door for dissing someone by text. The mortgage rate hitting 15 per cent again as whole continents of ice toppled booming into fish-stripped seas and entire nations went marching for food and oil and even water . . .

What happens next, in our time? Our children's time? George was right: God knows.

58: Erbyerk Again

—Perhaps you're right, I said at last.

—Yes. Toni, you have ammo too?

—What? Um, yes, actually. Yes. Half a dozen, um, clips.

—It is still OK?

—I don't know. How should I know?

—You should try it.

—That might be rather difficult, in England.

—Toni, you can go to the forests or the mountains.

—Well, the thing is, we don't have forests and mountains, in England. We hardly even have proper countryside, these days.

—A country without forests and mountains? I did not know. Well, is possible to know pretty good if ammo is OK without you shoot it. Tomorrow I show how you know.

—Right. So, I mean, look, George, you seriously think I should just keep it safe and, and . . .

—Safe and oiled. I think serious. We are men, Toni. Men must think serious. You keep it safe and oiled, Toni, you win or you win. Is very good situation for you. This is my opinion. So, here is Holesovice Station. You have not much time, sorry I talk so much but I think it important. I hope you come back, tomorrow, next day.

—Yes, George. I will.

—So, we hug, you go Germany.

—Right. Oof! Yes. I go Germany.

—You call me tomorrow, Toni. We are friends.

Oh, the balm of that word. Someone who would stand by me even in gunfire. A friend in the cold playground of life. I wanted to get George to England, find him work, place his children in good schools, help him buy a house in our street. Perhaps there were places we could go, in Wales or Scotland, to hike like boys again and fire off our little Armalites in innocent safety before cooking sausages and beans on fires of twigs and settling smiling down to sleep right under the stars, with no one to want a thing from us, far from all mortgages. Perhaps if the VIP went really, really well, if I got the TV series, or maybe if I won the lottery this weekend, I could make all this happen, this simple life? How much would I need to pay George to have him just come over and live in the little cottage in my big garden and just, well, look after things for me?

—George, if anything goes wrong, I mean, if I can't actually get back from Dresden in time tomorrow . . .

—Nothing is certain, Toni. Hope is all we have.

—Well yes, I suppose. So if I can't make it tomorrow, I'll get over again soon. Really, I will.

—Yes, you must. I am here. Toni, please I have one favour ask you. If we do not meet tomorrow, if you go back to England now, when you come back again soon, you can bring me some little things from England?

—Of course, George!

—You can bring me Manchester United shirt for my little Jan? Number eleven, with 'Jan' on it?

—Absolutely no problem. Jan, number eleven.

—And if you can, please, some DVDs of Erbyerk?

—Sorry?

—You do not know him, Toni? Oh, you must learn. Is very funny English man, many times when we with British Army boys from Gloucestershire we watch DVDs and laugh so much, ha ha ha, yes, I remember! 'Erby say: do not watch if easily offended!' Yes, this warning was true, ha ha!

59: The Shock Outrunning All Pain

The wide, high train had come all the way from Budapest and was now threading along the banks of a mighty river through mountain gorges. It had a splendid old buffet car and signs in five languages everywhere you looked. This was travel as it should be, and I had somehow managed to find a real old-fashioned compartment all to myself, thus avoiding the many young tourists whose world-English chatter offended me (oh, really, was Prague *cool*? How profound!) and whose general attractiveness, or rather sheer, cleanly hopefulness (but isn't that the same thing, really?), made me uncomfortably aware that I was a troubled man of forty-five who had not slept, washed or had sex for too long.

But it all gave me no joy. Even the fact that I had a cold bottle of beer in my hand, another two by my side and my trusty pillow plumped-up ready for sleep at last could not make me feel any better. Led astray again. Thought I had found someone who could guide me. Like with Panke, all over again. Hubby fucking Huck. Christ, when would I learn? Men can't deliver because there's nothing there to give. It's all just show, just status games and playground strutting . . .

Hungry, lonely and grey with exhaustion, I drained my beer and buried my face as deeply as I could in my pillow's downy embrace. Thank God I had brought it, this little piece of M&S so far from home. As the train jogged timelessly along, my exhaustion took over and a warm, snug fantasy began to envelope me.

Imagine, if only it *had* been a wartime bomb under my lawn last night, not a gun!

When better, discuss?

The spade blade nudges the decades-old alloy once again. Once too often, once too hard

The family were safely away. The vast mortgage we had just taken out, just to move to bloody London, all because of my so-called career, would have been instantly paid off. My pension would have been topped up as if I had died on the last day of my full-length work life. The tragedy would have left them pretty well sorted out. What more can any man do?

True, deprived of my earning capacity, the family would probably have had to move back from London. But in all honesty that would probably do William and Jack no harm. Frankly the school they had got into was not terribly good and the secondary schools were . . . Balls. *Not terribly good?* Who was I kidding? The primary school was shit. The secondary schools were all war zones. With me safely dead, and with the insurance payout, they could flee. They could go to Exeter. My children would see Sarah's parents every day and my parents every other weekend. Jack and William's secondary school would be at least passable. A fair bit of white trash, no doubt, in an Exeter state school, but a couple of rat-like louts per form, whose dads are hardly ever there and may in any case also be their uncles, is not the same thing as half the class being aspiring gang members who wouldn't know what a dad was. Sarah could work part-time and have Mariana looked after by her parents, her own old storytelling relatives, not by strangers paid to pretend they cared. Yes, my children would be socially and financially provided for. What father can do better than that, these days? *The best time to die is when your death will most help your children. Discuss.* Indeed, from a certain point of view my bit part, or rather my blink-and-you-miss-me-oh-you-just-did crowd scene, in *Life on Earth* would have been performed as perfectly by sticking my fork into a rusting old Nazi bomb last night as it would be by forcing everyone to endure life in SE11 just so I could work my balls off teaching crap about an extinct shit-hole run by the Red Army for another twenty years.

Beneath the cold earth, the aged Nazi plates give and shift. Enough, at last, for contact.

I hugged tight the warm thought of instantaneous oblivion. It was even snugger than my pillow.

Boom.

What would it feel like? Wouldn't it be so fast that *feel* was probably not even the right word? How fast do human nerves react? The gap between burning your finger on a pan and pulling the finger away is almost measurable. If a ton of high explosive goes off between your balls, would the mind, blithely thinking that it was merely digging a safe little garden, not cease completely to exist before the pain ever hit home? Examples, legion, from military history, of men hit by death decisively and by surprise and found with unmarked bodies and calm features. No agonies of despair. No long wait in a bright room for a nasty chat with an overworked young oncologist. No slow decay in a savings-draining rest home that smells of old piss. Surely it would be rather like that time a couple of months ago when, lost in gold-tinted daydreams of the London job, I had walked at a fast aerobic stride right into a Sheffield lamp post. *Thump.* The shock outrunning all pain for a good second. Which would be enough, in this case, to get me to for ever. Instantaneously ended.

Snuggle snuggle.

60: In *The Paper*, At Last

The train trundled on and I closed my eyes.

And imagine. If I really had set off a wartime bomb, I might, after all, have got my obituary in *The Paper*.

The tabloids would certainly have seen the funny side of a lecturer in modern German history and politics (who had been on national TV) being killed by an old German bomb. They would scarcely have been able to resist the headline, not on page one, naturally, but perhaps only a few pages in from the front: *Achtung! For you ze lecture is over!*

And then, surely, someone on *The Paper*, high up in an airy, gold-windowed office in Docklands, might idly have taken notice of me at last? Yes, the mighty search engines of *The Paper* would have been fired up. They would swiftly have shown that I was a lifelong subscriber to themselves, that I had a flawlessly left-liberal publications record (several of my articles were quite easily available, on request, in the stacks of some of the better university libraries) and that I had been just about to give a soundly anti-imperialist paper at the major national peer-group conference in Oxford, and a *plenary* one at that. The editors of *The Paper* (I could scarcely imagine their soft-suited power and rumpled elegance) might well have judged that I would have done great things in my field had I not had this ironic encounter with a piece of Britain's wartime heritage (I had already contributed to *Newsnight*, after all). They might have decided that the unexpected loss of such a man indeed merited *The Paper*'s notice, if only for a hundred words or so in that little round-up of minor obituaries.

Minor, perhaps, relatively speaking: but in *The Paper*! Sarah would cry, of course.

Sarah.

God, I wanted to talk to her. I grabbed for my phone and dialled.

—John? I've been trying to call for ages.

—Oh, sorry darling, I've been, um, in the British Library. You have to turn your phone off in there, you see. So, did they give your parents a better room, darling?

—No, we've moved hotels.

—Oh good.

—The new one's fine. And it's not that much more expensive, so don't worry.

—I'm not. That doesn't matter.

—Well it sounded as if it mattered yesterday.

—No, it doesn't. And it didn't. Sarah, look, I just wanted to say that I really . . .

At this moment the tannoy once again began to announce in Czech that the buffet car was out of food until Dresden. I knew that it would now repeat the message in German, Hungarian and English. I had no alternative but to hastily kill my phone. Having just told Sarah that I'd been working until very recently in the British Library, it might be a little hard explaining that I was now on a train heading from Prague to Dresden. And I didn't want to have to explain anything at all. I simply wanted to tell her, well . . .

When I was sure that the message had finished, I called again, my hand this time cupped close around the microphone.

—John?

—Hi again, just lost you on the train, sorry, darling. Look, I just . . .

—That sounded like some foreign language.

—What? Foreign? No, darling. Well, no more foreign than usual on London bloody Transport, eh, ha ha! Sorry, darling, was that a bit too like one of Hubby Huck's jokes?

—What? A bit too like who?

—Oh, nothing.

—John, are you all right?

—Me? God yes. Just a bit tired. From hammering away under the stairs all day, you know, trying to get the VIP finished. For us all. Tuck-tuck, tuck-tuck, ha ha.

—Tuck-tuck?

—The keyboard.

—Under the stairs? But you've been in the British Library?

—What? Oh, yes, just the last few hours. Well, you know, something came up, I needed to, check a rather obscure point. Even more obscure than most of my points, I mean, ha.

—You don't sound very well, John.

—Oh, it's just, you know, working a bit hard, all on my own here, probably not quite *depressurised* yet.

—Well, it's what you wanted.

—Oh, yes. It is. And everything's going to be fine. Everything. I promise.

—Perhaps you should go for a walk.

—Yes. That would be good. God, if we only had forests and mountains like this, eh?

—Like what?

—Hmm? Oh, I was just, I was reading a, a holiday brochure. That I found lying about on the train.

—John, we've already decided that we can't take Mariana on a big walking holiday. Even if we could afford one.

—Perhaps we'll be able to soon, eh? After I give the VIP!

—Yes, well, let's wait and see, shall we? John, I'm serious, I don't want to come back and find you've wasted hours on the web *again* looking for amazing bargain holidays we're never actually going to go on, because even if they're amazing bargains they're still never quite cheap enough for us. Not this week, John. In fact, never again, please.

—Absolutely, darling. Sorry about that. It's just, right, well . . .

—You were about to say something, just then.

—Was I? When?

—When we were cut off. It sounded important.

—Hmm? Oh, must have been, just, I'm, I'm glad your new hotel's better.

—Right.

—And, well . . .

—Yes, John?

I heard a noise and looked round. A youngish couple had stopped at the sliding door to my compartment and were now blatantly surveying its vacant acres.

I had managed so far to deter interlopers by using well-remembered tactics from my interrailing days: I had taken off my mud-caked shoes, plonked my visibly damp-socked feet on the seat opposite and made a little display of my beers. Whenever anyone had seemed tempted by the empty seats I had spread my arms, yawned without covering my mouth, scratched my unshaven neck and generally tried to radiate as farm-yard-like an aura as possible. I quickly went through this routine again, but saw immediately that I was in trouble. Scrub-cheeked young Germans and hard-working, respectable Czechs might think twice at the sight of me, mid-American teenagers might grimace

268

and pass hastily on, but these two were stocky types with distinctly Accession State clothes and luggage. They had clearly seen far worse things in their hard lives beyond the Danube than a somewhat rumpled, middle-aged Englishman drinking from a bottle of beer with his shoes off. Any minute now they were going to slide the door open and challenge me to deny that there was room for them, in whatever language they spoke. My cover might be blown. Time to hang up.

—Hello, darling? Can you hear me?

—Yes, perfectly. What's wrong, John? John?

—Darling, I-can't-hear-you.

I killed the phone again just as the door slid open.

My unwanted new travelling companions, a pregnant young woman and her partner, did not, in fact, even bother to ask for form's sake whether they could come in. They bustled in without wasting their hard-earned smiles on me, sure of their equal rights to my compartment. With the efficiency inherited from generations of transnational rail travel, these New Europeans began to stow their baggage and to lay out a home-made picnic that looked as if it could keep a large family content until Vladivostok. A sudden ravenous jealousy now added to my pique: jealousy of their copious snacks, for I could not in fact recall the last time I had eaten a thing and was painfully aware that I had now missed the buffet car, but also jealousy of them being a young couple journeying together somewhere, laying out a big picnic which had clearly been prepared by them or by some other family member.

I drained my beer and laid my bristly cheek back into my pillow, contenting myself with a rather fine daydream in which I had the Armalite with me, on the luggage rack above my head, and could, if I so wished, at any time produce it, handle it with

George-like aplomb and smilingly demand a tasty, paprika-laced treat as the price of my contribution as an Englishman to EU structural subsidies . . .

I sank further into my pillow.

As the train jogged timelessly along, my exhaustion took over and . . .

What?

My eyes were snapped incredulously awake by an unmistakable smell that had crept into my throat.

Cigarette smoke.

Impossible.

The Slavic bastards were smoking in the bloody compartment!

61: Gunsmoke

I flipped around in my seat to glare full-on at them. I spread my arms wide and frowned, but this universal or at least pan-Caucasian gesture of disbelief met only with bafflement. They looked back at me, then at each other, as if to ask each other whether either of them had any idea what was making this madman so indignant. Then a left-field guess dawned slowly on the man's face and he looked at his cigarette before scanning the compartment just to confirm what he already knew: that it could not be the cigarettes that were making me so outraged, since this was clearly not marked as a non-smoking compartment and the default setting of the world was, as everyone knew, *smoking*.

I sank back in disbelief, like some hero trapped in a Kafkaesque nightmare. It was impossible that these people could be within their rights as they did this to me, yet clearly they were. Never had the gap between justice and the law, between *what should be* and *what is legally allowed*, been so blindingly plain.

I tried to breathe only through my nostrils, but as the blue clouds of smoke slowly filled the entire place it became clear to me that I had no alternative but to yield to injustice and move. I was not sitting with bloody *smokers*. So I was going to have to give up my beloved, sleep-necessary window seat. No more could I use the cushions opposite on which to stretch my legs luxuriously out. I was going to have to pick up my pillow and walk away, with no certainty that I would find so comfy a place on the whole long train. Quite probably I would now have to muscle in on half a dozen happy young people and sit there feeling old, uncool and unclean. But there was no alternative.

Except that there was.

—*Bon dia, scushe, exishte la poxibilitate de prendare una xigaret?* I asked, smiling, for I had by now established that my companions were Romanians and thus spoke the handiest language on earth, the only one which you can actually make up as you go along and be more or less understood provided you stick to everyday needs.

—Si, exishte, they replied, with satisfying amazement. They did not quite smile but were clearly relieved that there was now a logical explanation for my scowling behaviour: I was not mad, I was simply a foreigner dying for a smoke, the way you do. The begged cigarette appeared, along with a light. I smiled, nodded thanks, mimed delight and relief, sucked deeply, opened my second beer and sat happily back.

As I did so, the collar of my old tweed jacket shoved itself higher, and I caught, amidst the horsey fibres, a smell I had never found on my clothes before. A strange and slightly sickly mix of talcum powder, WD-40 and bonfire night. And something else. Yes, that was it. Burning metal. My first day at my secondary school.

I would, had I been born a year before, have been safely bussed twelve miles to the grammar school, to take my place amongst the at least partially bookish and studious. But it had all gone comprehensive by the time my turn came along, so I walked to what had been the local secondary modern. This place had for some decades equipped for life stout Devon youths who had sex by thirteen, drove tractors and played darts in pubs by fourteen and delightedly left education soon thereafter. And so it fell out that our very first lesson of our very first day was to take up a piece of steel so that we might each forge and rivet our very own coat hook, to serve us for all our schooldays, using a bloody great red-hot coke-fired miniature blast furnace, anvils and hammers and all. I stared in disbelief as my turn approached, and was simply too scared to pull my red-hot lump of metal out with the yard-long tongs, despite the teacher's shouts and the laughter of my new classmates. By the time I had been ordered, stung and ear-clipped into grasping it with the metal jaws, the steel had gone beyond whitehot, had caught fire and was burning, crackling like a giant, hellish sparkler, sending out foot-long lightning bolts that bounded across the floor and made my fellow pupils dance joyously for cover. The teacher was forced to rescue me and the classroom. He snapped that I was a bloody useless nancy boy, and shoved me aside so hard that I fell on to the bare cement, thus setting the seal on my playground fate that morning and for years to come.

That smell it was. Burning metal.

I sniffed tweed again, inhaled tobacco again, sucked beer again, sat back and smiled: gunsmoke!

62: A Little Speed Hump for Real-Estate Speculators

By the time we reached Dresden the tall, wide buffet car had provided me with three further beers and a packet of American cigarettes (provided by a Hungarian waiter in a small act of private enterprise). What with the drink and the fact that it was years since I had been on a German railway, I forgot how high the trains are and stepped from the door into unexpected nothingness, falling with a small yelp of shock on to the platform.

I lay there for a moment, flat on my back, almost laughing with delight at this proof that I was indeed back in good old Europe, and that I could still roll instinctively from a fall without hurting myself like some old git.

From this surprisingly comfortable position, I surveyed the grandeur of the renovated Hauptbahnhof. State spending? We have no idea what it really means, in Britain. Or at any rate, since we pay the bastards enough in taxes, they must be spending it in some mysteriously invisible way. On wars and preparations for wars, perhaps? Well, you could see what they did with the stuff here. The place so dripped with public money that the nineteenth-century building seemed like a proud showcase for some extraordinary new form of high-tech transport. And this was supposed to be a deprived region!

I climbed to my feet, dusted down my pillow, winced slightly at a new pain in my back, and looked around for the exit. Yes, I was a bit drunk, but so what? I deserved it. I had learned to fire an assault rifle today and could now look global warming in the eye with less wretched, rabbit-like terror.

After all, what would really happen, when The Day came, when the Thames Barrier finally gave, for example? Society would not disappear overnight. Emergency laws would be enacted, citizens enlisted, state-supporting elements co-opted in the fight to preserve some form of civilisation. A well-spoken and indubitably English man titled Doctor, able to swiftly show his mastery of an assault rifle, provide one himself and make it clear that he was quite prepared to use it if ordered to, against carloads of hooded looters, for example, would be sure to find a welcome for himself and special treatment for his family. Yes, in a very real way, I had today made an important investment in providing for my loved ones' futures. Life for the family man is about more than just work. Well done, John Goode.

Well, I mean, obviously that was all rubbish, just my little joke.

What I had done was simply learn how to make the bloody gun safe so that I could dump it when I got home. Object achieved, well and truly. Lost my fear of guns entirely. Piece of piss, to disarm it, now. So if I wanted another drink or two, and I did, I could bloody well have one. Or, indeed, two. Nice pure German beer, mmm, yes, what harm could that do anyone? I would simply call Panke and tell him I was too tired to do anything that night. Assuming he had even got my message, that was. I could meet him tomorrow or go home without even seeing him. I could go back to Prague and do that night-shoot with George. A night-fighting capability, after all, might well be decisive for my family's survival when *shtf*, whatever that was . . .

—Nonsense, I laughed aloud. It was all just a jolly daydream. In the real world, my plan was watertight, caulked with hard logic. Whether I actually saw Panke or not was immaterial. I reminded myself firmly: all I had ever wanted from my trip to Dresden was a firm cover story about why I had gone to Prague. That story would be complete and cast-iron the moment I had checked into the hotel and called Panke from my room.

Clever, you see. Not a PhD for nothing!

I almost chuckled aloud at my own cunning and walked out of the station, past the easily missable bronze-and-stone memorial to the people who had been seriously beaten up by the police on this very spot not twenty years ago for asking to be allowed to travel outside their country.

I knew the way of old. Straight down the Berliner Strasse, through the state socialist architecture to cobblestones and glories restored without thought of expense. I would wander around them and have a quick nightcap, why not? Bound to be some little old magical pub, always is in Germany, maybe have a chat with someone or other, a woman maybe, just to practise my German, then back to wonderful five-star hotel linen (oh God!) and a splendid night of baby-free sleep far from the Armalite and Phil and noisy little hooded gits in cars and the sodding mortgage and . . .

What mortgage rate was that poster offering?

Was that all Germans paid? Bastards. Hmm, yes, that made you think . . .

I did not mean to stop before the poster outside a closed bakery-cum-cooked-meat-takeaway and start thinking earnestly (though a little drunkenly) about the East German housing market. But my poor deformed little British subconscious locked on. It had been battered by decades of radio and TV programmes in which *successful businessmen* were introduced like modern-day saints and people's frantic scrabbles up *the property ladder* were illuminated as though this represented their souls' hard-fought ascent towards Nirvana. We may not be a nation of shopkeepers any more (shop-keeping hours are too much like hard work), but by God we have become a grand gang of would-be little landlords. My innermost being had been hounded every weekend of the millennium by *Your Property* supplements whose legions of hacks were obliged to find endless new financial terrors or opportunities to justify their employment. The very core of my mind had been mutated by incessant jabbering articles about how Bulgaria (or was it Albania? Or Latvia?) was the next no-lose property hot spot for monetaristically sophisticated British investors.

Helplessly, my conditioned mind spiralled off into bold entrepreneurial leaps of imagination about remortgaging cunningly in London so as to extend my property portfolio Eurozone-wise and thus let other poor suckers who needed a place to bring up their families (but could not afford to buy) fund my fat little workless existence in happy years to come . . .

Such heaven!

The small matter of whether I could actually even afford my own mortgage at the moment anyway could soon be fixed, surely, with some sophisticated modern financial uptooling? And where better to uptool than London? I mean, shit, what if I geared myself to the limit and bought a place in the most run-down shit-heap rustbelt brown-coal part of the old East Germany? After all, I had some unusual local knowledge. Berlin was obviously chucking euros at the region.

For the love of God, why oh why hadn't I bought a

high-ceilinged old flat here back in 198bloody7? I could have got it for nothing, almost.

Then I remembered that there was actually a very good reason why I had not bought a place back here in nineteen eighty-seven. There had been, back in nineteen eighty-seven, a certain tricky little speed hump here for would-be real-estate speculators. They called it Communism and its principal backer was the Red Army.

I arrived in the floodlit square around Our Lady's church and smugly located my splendid hotel. A band of musicians was playing squeezeboxes and balalaikas to dinner-jacketed, long-gowned punters spilling out from the launch party of a Russian jewellery shop next to the hotel. So much for the Red Army. But perhaps I would pop in once I had fixed up my room. If I strolled in, blithely twirling my hotel key, surely I could blag a glass or two of free champagne? Just a merry nightcap before sliding into my doubtless gorgeous bed for sleep, sleep at last.

Then I noticed the two men in the hotel's big doorway, looking at me.

They did not seem to fit together in any way of normal social logic, yet were clearly here as a team. One was a tall young man with a long, pale face and somewhat glittering glasses, wearing a shirt and tie under a dark blue suit of slightly too sharp a cut to be daily wear. The neat turn-ups on his trouser legs lay just high enough to show that he was wearing boots, not shoes. His companion was far shorter, considerably older, with long, greying hair that hung down well over the shoulders of a leather waistcoat that was never going to button again over a large beer gut that stretched the black T-shirt underneath. His trousers were also of leather, brown, not black. Had it not been for the fact that his locks were floatingly clean and that he too wore slim-rimmed gold glasses, he would have looked like a refugee from an American bikers' convention.

The young, suited man caught my gaze and looked me swiftly over once more. He turned to elbow his companion.

The police, of course!

I stopped dead in the empty square, and looked down at my feet. I could see my own multiple shadows on the floodlit cobblestones. The cornered Harry Lime in *The Third Man*. Even now, I could perhaps still run. But for how long? Where? For what? Even in my somewhat tiddly and careworn state, I could see that my only hope now lay in giving myself up with a good grace, insisting on extradition and relying on British justice to deploy its well-known prejudice in favour of the educated classes.

And God, I was tired of being on the run. Once more, I felt the deep rush of relief as I thought of telling all. Surely, they would have beds in German police stations? Yes, somehow it would be easier to confess everything in German. Absolutely everything. About how I had publicly sung bold songs in Lottie's bar (with, as it turned out, the happy agreement of the local Stasi), accusing the evil West German state (that mere American satrap) of being viciously fascistic in its treatment of essentially good-hearted and Che-like Baader-Meinhof murderers . . .

Me?

Oh yes, me. Guilty, my Lord, both as charged and not.

Knowing that the German police are all armed, and not wanting my internal organs destroyed, I stuffed my pillow under my arm (I simply could not bear to let it go) and set my course towards the two men with my hands well away from my sides, my fingers spread and pointing upwards, my palms out towards them like some plaster Jesus showing his holes for doubters. As I neared them, I smiled and spoke firmly in German, relishing the strange freedom that comes with speaking fluently in a foreign language. It seemed fitting that my reckoning should come in another tongue. Fitting, and for some reason far less fearful. As if, like a holiday romance, it didn't really count.

—I'm Dr John Goode, I said. —And I surrender.

63: Leader, Lead: We Demand to Obey!

—You are Herr Doktor Goode? asked the tall, creepy one.

—Yes. And I surrender. Of my own free will. Please note that and take it down in evidence against me. Or rather, for me. For me the war is over, ha ha. Sorry, just a stupid English joke. God, I don't know why I said that. Now, about the gun . . .

They looked at me and laughed. The short fat man clapped me on the shoulder.

—Herr Panke told us to look out for a little man with a beard. He did not warn us about your English humour, ha ha!

—Herr Panke?

—Of course. Who else?

—Oh. Ah. Well, um, wow, that's so kind of him. Of course, we're good friends, and . . . well. Great!

Well, that was more like it. Good old Heiner. How pleasant to be greeted with respect like this. Herr Doktor Goode. Well, and why not? That was who I was. Thank God for a country where academics are still treated with a bit of awe.

—Herr Panke is glad that you are here, said the young man, stressing the surname and title.

—I look forward greatly to seeing Heiner again, I replied, stressing the Christian name.

—So. This way, Herr Doktor, he yielded. —You have only your pillow?

—The serious man travels lightly, I said.

—Nietzsche? asked the fat man.

—Panke, I said. —*The Ballad of the Dancer's Thighs*. I used to sing it with him. A most interesting poetic structure.

—Ah yes, nodded the young man, —You are true devotee, Herr Doktor. But the delay in your train, no doubt due to Czech incompetence, means that we must rush if you are to arrive in time for your speech.

—Sorry? I asked, certain that my German must be getting rusty.

—Herr Panke did not tell you? asked the young man

—No. He didn't say anything. Speech?

—Ah, sighed the fat man happily, —that is Herr Panke! A man who knows that people will say *yes* to him has no need to ask in advance, Herr Doktor, does he? We happily serve, when the leader of the pack calls. What were we doing before, but only waiting for his call? That is man, yes? That is our place. The Herr Doktor is too wise to feel absurd notions of individual pride. He knows that the leader is merely fulfilling our own wishes: *Leader, lead: we demand to obey!* That is true freedom.

—Right. So, what, Heiner wants me to give the VIP, I mean my paper, on him? Tonight? Where? The university? But it's not really quite ready yet, and actually I'm a bit, you know, tired, and . . .

—Not at the university, said the young man.

—Not?

—Herr Panke, he continued, and his specs lit with battle, —has, thanks to the latest opinion polls, attracted much attention, Herr Doktor.

—Yes, I know. He's even becoming known in England, and we don't usually care about any politicians except our own and the Americans'.

—Excellent, Herr Doktor! Tell them this. We expect many new potential supporters at tonight's meeting.

—A political meeting?

—You are an Englishman, dear Doktor, said the fat man, folding his plump hands together across his belly. —A foreigner, in the strict sense, though of course the English are not truly foreigners. Not Americans, at least, not yet, ha ha! You still have some culture of your own. And yet one who has dedicated his life to spreading the word of Herr Panke.

—Well, I wouldn't exactly put it like that.

—Dear Doktor, Herr Panke asks merely that before his speech you introduce yourself to the audience with a few words and tell them how highly regarded he is in England.

—Me?

—You know our movement's programme, Herr Doktor? demanded the tall man.

—Naturally. I've just completed, virtually completed, a rather important paper on it. I know you stand against the evils of American-led globalisation and for the rights of the European working class. For greater European unity. For the preservation of European forests and wildlife. For affordable social housing for all Europeans. For state loans to help businesses that employ local people, and . . .

—Exactly, Herr Doktor! You understand us perfectly. Will you say so?

Would I? I felt a little somersault in my heart. Heiner wanted my support. He wanted me to stand shoulder to shoulder with him. And I would. I would stand there on whatever podium they put me on, and I would proudly talk of *my friend Heiner*. I would stoutly pronounce that lovely word: *we*. My God, and I might even be able to get him to come over in person to help me give the VIP next week. What a double act we would be, and how much better is every double act than a mere solo performance! The Oxford conference would be a triumph. And that meant that all was well and would be better . . .

—You see, Marcus, Herr Panke said his good little Doktor would not let us down. I heard him saying so to his women.

—His women, grumbled the young man.

—Herr Panke has always had his women, has he not, dear Doktor?

—Good old Heiner! I laughed. —Women, eh? Well, of course, I shall be delighted to offer him whatever covering fire I can give, ha ha! So? Shall we go?

64: Women, Indeed!

Within minutes, I was sat in the back of a big Mercedes taxi, ignoring the passing cityscape of Dresden and my two companions, gloating quietly in a pleasant and private world.

From within, I was lit by the small but potent furnace ignited by a double espresso and the large schnapps on which I had insisted before leaving the hotel and had flung down with rather superb abandon. Outwardly, I sniffed my tweed lapel and smelled again the memory of gunplay that lurked within that rough wool. I smiled. I felt somehow more real than I had for years.

Suddenly, I wanted to call Sarah.

But good sense prevailed.

I knew that I was, if I were honest with myself, now very slightly but nonetheless undoubtedly drunk. This might be rather hard to explain to Sarah, given that she had taken the kids away to let me work. Also, because I was very slightly but nonetheless undoubtedly drunk, if she indeed realised that I was very slightly but nonetheless undoubtedly drunk, as she certainly would, and I tried to explain myself, which I would then have to, I might well, being very slightly but nonetheless undoubtedly drunk, let slip accidentally that I was not only very slightly but nonetheless undoubtedly drunk but was also very slightly but nonetheless undoubtedly drunk in Dresden, Germany.

—Ridiculous, I snapped at myself.

There was no need to bother Sarah. I was merely going to see Heiner Panke, in whose work and doings

I, as his sole UK expert and gatekeeper, had a perfectly legitimate interest. Women, indeed!

—So, Herr Doktor.

—Sorry?

—We are here, dear Doktor!

—Ah, yes, of course. Um, excellent.

I looked out and for the first time in some minutes registered a world beyond my own mind and body.

We had stopped outside an eighties public sports complex, as squat and square and glassy as they are the world over. As far as I could tell from the posters on the doors, we had come to see the regional table-tennis championships. But then I saw that these were being hastily covered over by new posters showing the letters DEBB (meaning 'German-European Citizens' Movement') and a symbolic fist smashing a dollar sign. The blocky shape of the fist itself seemed to be lifted straight from a Black Power poster of the sixties, or one of those stencilled efforts so common in the days of Troops Out and suchlike, but its colours (creamy skin outlined in darkish red) were very like those from Soviet-era propaganda. It was announced that the topic of the evening was *Freedom from the Market*, and that it would be led by *the famous poet, singer and member of the regional parliament, Heiner Panke.*

The mere sight of the last two words made my breath come shorter. They were in the title of my PhD, they occurred in almost all my (quite numerous) publications, they sat at the very heart of the VIP. Those two words had formed the keystone of my life for so long, had, coupled with the letters KGB, almost brought down my career and now, in six days' time, might save it. *Heiner Panke*. It seemed less the name of a person than the mysterious password to my fate.

More busy helpers, wearing DEBB WILKOMMEN!

sashes over Sunday-best leather blouson jackets and somewhat Heidi-like dresses, were waving into the darkness or conversing encouragingly with the drivers of cars and small, aged minibuses. There was a lot of frenetic, hard-smiling, low-church sort of effort going into things, and more white male socks than I had seen in many years. My younger escort surveyed this all with glittery-spectacled satisfaction. He exchanged vaguely salute-like waves with several of the helpers, who were clearly glad to have been noticed by him and redoubled their happy efforts. The fat man opened the door for me.

—Remember, dear Doktor, say nothing that the left-wing press could misinterpret, ha ha!

—Well, of course not, I replied. —I am a thoroughly liberal man myself.

—The left will do anything to discredit our movement. Because they know that it is we who speak for the workers now, while the so-called left-wingers today are merely the hired thugs of worldwide capitalism. Half of George Bush's advisors are ex-Trotskyists, of course, and they still want what Trotsky wanted: to impose their revolution, their so-called 'freedom', their 'next stage of history', upon the entire world, irrespective of any culture or nation, at gunpoint.

—Mmmm, I said, —at gunpoint, indeed. For a second I saw again the muzzle-flashes in the darkness of the Czech forest.

And then, in front of me, the crowds of milling people parted like a shoal of fish, and, preceded by his own bow-wave, up strode the man himself, Heiner Panke, right up to me and crushed me in his well-known but long-lost bear hug.

—Well, my little Doktor, there you are at last! Come to my arms!

65: Like any Good Teutonic Politician

It was still there, that quality that had always made Panke the bringer of fresh air into the bar, the appointer of places at the table, the chooser of what was going to happen next. The man who had made the drunken evenings mean something twenty-five years ago, who had been so undoubtedly the alpha male of the place that merely being acknowledged as a favoured acolyte could get you a shag. And even though I now knew that part of his mysterious ability, back then in the old days, to make things happen, open doors and so on had been due to his secret rank in the KGB, he still had it.

I saw and, even more clearly, felt the smiles of the people all around me as he almost spun me off my feet. A mighty feeling came over me, as it always had done in his powerful embrace. Here, there were no more decisions and duties, no choices and alternatives, no worry and guilt: all I had to do now was stick close to Panke, and nod, and bask in his sun.

In German the same word means 'his' and 'to be': I was his, and I was glad to be.

And yet, there was something different now.

As he bear-hugged me, I found myself thumping him manfully in the ribs. I saw, and was strangely delighted to see, that he was taken aback by this physical reply. So much so that for a fleeting moment he looked almost comically like an elderly aunt affronted by someone's lack of manners. But he was already halfway through introducing me to a circle of very well-turned-out women, and I clearly felt him repress the shock as his arm glided off from my shoulders.

—How wonderful to meet you, Herr Universitäts-professor Doktor!

—Heiner has told us all about you!

—All the way from England!

—His oldest supporter!

—You used to sing with Herr Panke?

—The Herr Doktor has never wavered in his devotion!

—His great friend!

—A glass of beer before your speech, Herr Doktor?

A girl in a dirndl-like dress appeared between me and my little circle of smiling women, happily offering half-litre glasses of beer emblazoned with an eagle logo soaring over the outline of the former East Germany. Her jolly sash said 'Brewed to the German Purity Laws among *us!*'

—Well, why not? I laughed, grabbed one, studied it for a moment and sipped it thoughtfully, as if beer were a rare treat to me. Then I pronounced —Ah, *real Saxon* beer!, downed it in one like any good Teutonic politician, and replaced the glass on the barmaid's tray with a tiny but definite formal bow of thanks.

The top-up hit me with grateful speed. I had reached that stage of drunkness that I had not felt for many years, not since the old days in the Irish pub, in fact: that level where the beer goes down like water so long as the music continues, when every serious conversation bores and befuddles you, but when you can still hold your harmonies (or at least firmly believe that you are doing so) as long as the drinks keep flowing.

And as long as the women keep smiling.

God, it was nice to be among women again. Not university women, but women made up and dressed for the night, women who wanted men to fancy them and be men and drink beer and be strong. Perfumed women who hung on the words of men and smiled and nodded with carefully eye-lined eyes! Panke's women!

—You flew especially to support Herr Panke, Herr Doktor? How wonderful.

—I am delighted to support Heiner, I replied airily. Again I caught a tiny flicker of discomfort in his eye. A dark and inexplicable joy welled up in my heart, as I felt, for the first time ever, that I was no longer his safe little doctor but a man with an agenda of his own. A man worthy of negotiation. A man to sit down and cut a deal with.

—And the time is upon us, dear Doktor, said the fat man in my ear.

—Perhaps the Herr Doktor is not really prepared, said the tall young man, who seemed to have a supernatural ability to guess Panke's thoughts.

—This is no audience of students, little Doktor, nodded Panke, thoughtfully.

—Leave them to me, Heiner, I laughed. —My safety catch is off and I am live to fire!

—What?

—Excellent, said the fat man, utterly unaware of the tectonic shifts in male ego that were rumbling before his eyes. Panke was too off-balance to react decisively. By God, and I *was* ready. I had kept this man in grants and royalties for a decade. Now I would show him who it was exactly who needed whom, tonight!

—Then let us go, I drawled. —Until later, merciful ladies, I nodded to them all at once, barely suppressing the insane desire to click my heels. Then I turned smoothly away from them all, leaving the quite unmistakable eddy of social triumph in my wake, and strode into the waiting hall.

66: I Have a Dream

The tall young man introduced me as the highly distin-
guished academic scholar and old friend of Herr
Panke, *Herr Universitätsprofessor Dr John Goode, London,
En-gel-lant!* I stepped up to the podium, smiling.

I let them wait. What did I fear? I who could hit a
target with ten out of ten rounds from an Armalite!

I looked slowly around. Ranks of plastic seating had
been pulled out from the walls along both sides of the
hall and across one end. My platform was slightly thrust
away from the remaining end wall, so that the last three
or four seats of every row on each side were actually
behind me. The hall was packed, and smelled like all
modern sports halls: concrete dust, disinfectant and tired
air, but this time mixed with cheap perfume and warm
leather.

I had, of course, been intending to say merely a few
words about Panke. But it felt so damn *good* up there
on the platform. And there was something deep and
mysterious in the air, something that tickled my
antennae. A strong, subterranean current. Insufficiently
washed almost-central Europeans, yes, and that cheap
perfume and that leather, but more even than that.
What was it? I sniffed mentally, and caught it.

The sour radiation of resentment.

The lurking wish to be told what you want to hear:
that it is all *not fair*. That you have been cheated.

And, by God, you know, they *had* been cheated, these
good people! Just as I had been! They had been led to
expect so much, only to be cheated by reunification

and globalisation. They had made a deal in 1989, just as I had made a deal in 1984. They had been openly promised the good life by the West, just as I been implicitly promised the life of a seventies don. And what had I got? SEbloody11! And what had they got? Thirty per cent unemployment, second-class status, total insecurity!

Oh, I knew exactly what they wanted, these modest and good Germans who believed in honest work and quiet lives. I never even had to wonder how I should start my speech. I simply opened my mouth and out it came ready-made, in a quiet, fireside tone that made all the shuffling stop as the audience were forced to strain and listen.

—A decent normal house, a good school, a safe park, quiet nights, a proper free kindergarten and a real job that will be there next year. All anyone sane wants. That and a bit of respect and just enough well-earned money to not be worried about money every day of our lives. Well? Was that so much to ask from the twenty-first century?

I looked up, questioning with my eyes. A ripple of attention was spreading through the audience, a subtle mass movement of people shifting their bodyweight and their expectations slightly upwards. I spoke the same words over again, softly still, still softly enough so that they would have to listen to catch every word, but this time with hints of power coming on. Yes, this was better than lecturing!

—Was that so much to ask? I demanded again.
—Well? Was that so much to ask?
—No! cried a few voices, as if positively forced to call out by the silence I had left hanging. Murmurs of support, sighs of expectation rustled around the hall. I thought I saw Panke's face in the corner of my eye, peering through

the wired glass of the big double doors through which he was waiting to make his late, grand entrance. Annoyed? But I had no time for any individual now. Not even Panke. I was here in the hall and I was them.

And I liked it.

Dear God, what a relief to be *us* again, not just me! This was the feeling I had loved on demonstrations and marches and in the Irish pub, the heady joy of oneness, of unity, of circulation sweetly rolling through veins conjoined beyond the lonely little world of I!

I looked at them. At *us*. My heart filled. I smiled sadly at *our* troubles. I nodded solemnly, making my gaze float slowly around the room, as though looking each person in the eye while in fact avoiding any eye contact at all. An old lecturer's trick, of course, but this time, for once, it felt genuine. Why look at any one meaningless person when we were, all of us, *us*? Finally, I looked behind me to my left and then to my right, and opened my arms a little, as though these were not the latecomers who had got the crap seats, but particular comrades of mine, people who did not require much more in the way of enlightenment.

—Do you hear me? I asked quietly, in a flawless Dresden accent. I felt again that breezy rush of unreality that comes from speaking easily in a language that is not your own. It could hardly fail. —Do you hear me? I asked again, more loudly.

Talk about theatre, this was giving it to them all right! They nodded happily, hearing themselves enacted in the mouth of this important foreign visitor, this intimate of their leader. Then I surprised them, made them sit up, made their heart rates rise suddenly with a snappy, almost snarling, hint of what might come later.

—Because it is time we were heard! Yes!

Then I immediately held up my palms to halt any

applause. To dam back the tension. God, I was good at this. But where on earth had I got this shtick from? Oh yes, of course. Who says German studies is a waste of time nowadays, eh? This was the reward for my having sat through *Triumph of the* bloody *Will* every term for twenty years (it's always a good standby if you need to kill two hours of contact time and get student bums on seats). How ironic! To be using that fascist bastard's very weaponry against him!

—I met Heiner Panke here in this city twenty years ago. Twenty years. The bad old days. So our decent liberal politicians say. The bad old days when you had to listen to Party bullshit. When you had to nod to Party slogans. When you had to smile when the Party said smile. And of course they are right, our decent liberal politicians. Oh yes. You did have to listen to Party bullshit. You did have to nod to Party slogans. You did have to smile when the Party said smile. Yes, yes. That was the price. The price we paid for jobs that lasted, for colleges that taught everyone and hospitals that treated everyone, for streets that were safe, for rents we could afford, for neighbourhoods where good, ordinary, normal people lived. Terrible, say our decent liberal politicians. What a price to pay. Imagine! To have to listen to the odd bit of Party bullshit. To have to nod to Party slogans now and then. To smile a couple of times a year when the Party said smile. Unbearable. Horrible. Look at yourselves now and be thankful, say our decent liberal politicians: you lucky, free people! Yes. We are free now, my friends. All we have to do now is listen to bullshit, nod to slogans, smile when we are told to smile. Oh yes, my friends. We have to listen to bullshit about *free trade*. We have to nod to slogans about *competing in the world market*. We have to smile when they tell us that our jobs are being *restructured*, that we must be more *flexible*, that we must *be realistic* in this lucky new world. Well, that is the new price, my friends. The price we pay for all this *joy*. For living in permanent fear of the sack. For colleges and hospitals that take only the rich. For streets we hardly dare walk after dark, for rents and mortgages that suck the life from our veins, for neighbourhoods where no decent normal person would choose to live. Oh lucky people. Oh free people, say our good, decent liberal politicians.

And who asked for *this* kind of freedom? Well? Who here in this hall asked for so-called *free trade*? Who asked to *compete* with countries where children slave for a dollar a day? Who asked to be restructured, to be flexible, to be realistic? You, sir? No, sir. You, madam? No, madam. And not I, my friends. Not I! And you?

—*Nein!*

—*Nein,* my friends, *nein*! But please, my friends, hear me, thank you. Thank you. There may be those who ask: what is this Englishman doing, speaking like this of German troubles? A fair question, my friends. For these are indeed the troubles of Germany, as anyone except our decent liberal politicians can see. But they are also the troubles of England, for they are the troubles of Europe! Ask any decent Englishman, any decent Dutchman, any decent Frenchman: did you ask to 'compete' with countries where children slave for a dollar a day? You know the answer, my friends. What is the answer?

—*Nein!*

—*Nein!* We did not ask for this. We did not ask for this so-called 'freedom'. And what *do* we ask for, my friends?

I looked around my people. I had them right in my sights. For twenty-five years I had been dealing in academic crap, buttressing every suggestion with foot-notes and references, framing every argument as careful debate, not because that was honest and true, but because that is how you win the day there. Cunning sap, not hearty storm. Here, I was pure at last. Letting it bloody well rip at last, laying into the globalising bastards and exploiters and ruiners of ordinary, decent lives like mine. The bastards who had broken the deal and robbed me of my nice normal north-London semi with the sash windows; and had broken countless other families as well, raped whole countries, impoverished entire continents in the name of profit! Well, I was our spokesman now and my heart opened wide. From my earliest childhood memories half-remembered words arose and united with stuff I had been reading only a few days ago. The timeless chants of righteousness united and entwined within me. My voice dropped deep even as my chest swelled.

Speak? No. Now was the time to sing!

—When the architects of Europe wrote the confident words of the Union and the Declaration of Human Rights, they were signing a promissory note to which every European was to fall heir. This note was a promise that all Europeans would be guaranteed a decent and secure future. Now is the time to cash that cheque. Now is the time for what is ours by rights. It would be fatal for the rulers of Europe to overlook the urgency of the moment and to underestimate the determination of the European people. This winter of discontent will not pass until there is an invigorating spring of hope. Those who hope that we the people needed only to blow off steam and will now be content will have a rude awakening if Europe returns to business as usual. There will be neither rest nor tranquillity in Europe until the people of Europe are granted their rights. The whirlwinds of revolt will continue to shake the foundations of this continent until the bright day of justice emerges!

I paused. I looked at them all.

Chthonk! The magazine slammed home.

Ca-chunk! I cocked her. The French Revolution did not happen because the poor were starving. The poor had always been starving. The French Revolution happened when someone told the poor that they *shouldn't be* starving. Discuss.

—Sixty years ago, the nations of Europe joined hands together. Their union came as a great beacon of hope to millions who had been seared in the flames of war. It promised a better future to end the long night. But sixty years later, we must face the tragic fact that the future is not growing better. Sixty years later, we find ourselves crippled by the struggle to survive. Sixty years later, we find ourselves a mere island in the midst of a vast ocean of capital. Sixty years later, we find ourselves exiles in our own land. Everything has been globalised except our consent. A handful of the richest men in the richest nations – Who are they? Where are they? Why should they rule our lives? – use the global powers they have assumed to tell the rest of the world how to live. And when these new rulers of the world cloister themselves behind the fences of Seattle or Genoa or Berlin, or ascend into some other inaccessible eyrie, they leave the rest of the word shut out of their deliberations. When, like the cardinals who have elected a new pope, they emerge, clothed in the serenity of power, to announce that it is done, our howls of execration serve only to enhance the graciousness of their detachment. They are the actors, we are the audience, and for all our catcalls we can no more change the script to which they play than the patrons of a cinema can change the course of the film they watch. They are the tiniest of the world's minorities, and their rule, unauthorised and untested, is sovereign.

Who are they? The global locusts!

These global locusts, without homeland or people, dare to tell us that modernisation is necessary. Well, we do not find it necessary! They dare to tell us that globalisation is inevitable. Well, we do not find it inevitable! They dare to tell us that the future is mapped out for us. Well, we do not want their road maps! They dare to tell us that nothing and nobody can resist their idol, the Market. Well, my friends, I say unto them: we had a deal.

We had a deal that Europe was to be the oasis of freedom and justice. We had a deal where our children would all be happy, prosperous Europeans.

We had a deal.

I say to you, my friends, we have come here today to demand that our deal be honoured.

So let freedom ring from the prodigious hilltops of Bavaria, from the mighty mountains of the Alps. Let freedom ring from the warm shores of the Mediterranean to the bracing coasts of the North Sea and the Atlantic's wild cliffs!

Let freedom ring from the curvaceous hills of France!

Let freedom ring from the mythic banks of the Rhine and the Elbe!

Let freedom ring from every molehill of Holland, and from every mountainside of Austria, let freedom ring.

Because we had a deal. And when this deal is honoured all of Europe's children will be able to join hands and sing in the words of the old song, 'Free at last! Free at last! Thank God Almighty, we are free at last!'

67: Tutus for Party Bosses

I stepped blindly from the stage on wings of applause, plucking and draining another glass of beer from another delighted Heidi without so much as pausing, strode manfully up to the double doors and walked straight through them and into the corridor, where I knew Panke was waiting.

Well, I tried to. But God had other plans. He had made the doors open the other way.

—Agh! God . . .

I came to my senses on the floor, my specless eyes struggling to focus, and found myself looking up at many unknown, worried faces and one well-known one. I watched the decision form in his eyes.

—Doktor, come to my arms, cried Panke. In a second I was indeed in them, and, for the first time ever, as an equal. —What a team we make, is it not true, my friends? How shall I follow him? he laughed. —I think I shall come to help you give your paper in Oxford after all, my little Doktor. It will be fun, no?

—God, yes, Heiner, I mean . . .

Panke suddenly leaned back slighty from his hug and his nostrils twitched.

—What is that perfume you are wearing, little Doktor?

For a second I was about to tell him, but I held the floodgates shut. Perhaps later, when we were alone, we would drink and I would talk.

—Oh, it's just, it's called Gunsmoke, I think. Um, Hugo Boss Gunsmoke.

—Not bad, he nodded, then clapped me powerfully and publicly on the back before proceeding into the wall of cheers beyond the door to the big hall.

The fat man beamed at me and bowed his head slightly. The tall young man was obviously having great difficulty not springing to attention at my every glance. The women smiled their lip-glossed smiles. And in my head, that noise of applause simply continued as I was passed now from smile to smile, handed from womanly clasp to manly shake to comradely clap on the shoulder, as if on a production line of respect and admiration.

Beer appeared on demand. After so many years spent steadfastly but hopelessly defending the encircled trenches of my self-regard against the ceaseless attacks of age, failure and social decline, it felt wonderful. Better than wonderful. It felt like life itself.

It felt like love.

Christ, I was living in the wrong country! Being a university lecturer still meant something here! And in Germany you were judged by what you did and stood for, not by the accent you said it all in and whether or not you had sash bloody windows.

I mean, why not just up sticks and come here and make Sarah and the boys come too? For the price of our foul little terrace in SE11 we could come here to Dresden, where I would see Heiner all the time and have this amazing status and all these smiling friends, and buy a vast flat with . . .

My God, Panke was coming to Oxford in person! I swung on my heel fairly successfully and, freshly glowing as I was with the hieratic nimbus of my body-hug from Panke, addressed the tall young man with a certain curtness.

—Heiner is coming to my meeting at Oxford. I need to announce this great event to the English media. Your

BlackBerry please? He obeyed with the speed of a man who had a simple, innocent love for orders, whether giving or taking them. I had so often emailed the European editor of *The Paper* in vain that the hallowed address was by now imprinted on my mind. It was one of the few possible conduits of my salvation and I would know it by heart even on my deathbed. Within two minutes, no more, I had blipped off my tidings in appropriate fashion:

> Heiner Panke, founder and leader of Germany's anti-capitalist pro-European DEBB (17 per cent last time in Dresden + tipped to beat 25 per cent regionally in upcoming emergency elections) has just confirmed that he will be in person @ my plenary address on his work @ the major Oxford peer-group conference (8–9 Dec, St John's Coll). You are heartily invited to interview him (and indeed me). (Dr) John Goode.

I then copied the body of the message (no cc-ing for such vital stuff!) and inserted it into a fresh email to *Newsnight*. Well, one hardly forgets the address of a national news programme to which one did, after all, contribute substantially not that long ago! To this version I simply added, after my name, the words *Major Contributor, 'Checkpoint Charlie Checks Out', broadcast* 5 *May* 1990, just in case the editorial team had changed over the past few years and were no longer quite sure who I was.

—A most useful device, I nodded, as I handed back the BlackBerry to the grateful young man and plunged into another beer. My mind was spinning with a new world of real possibilities. My name might get into *The Paper* at last. Maybe on to *Newsnight* again. Would having been twice on *Newsnight* allow me to describe myself as a *regular contributor* to it on my CV? My God, if I played my cards right, according to Eamon's instructions . . .

—Herr Doktor, you were magnificent!

I refocused my eyes to make them look outwards at the world, rather than inwards at my sunlit future, and found myself in front of a particularly attractive woman of about forty who was looking at me in a particularly attracted way.

—Merciful lady. I bowed ever so slightly.

—You spoke for us all. You know what we all thought when the Wall came down? We thought it would be the same, only better. The things that were bad about this place were so simple and so obvious: the Stasi, the border guards, the Party. And they were finished! For years we had heard nice people from the West saying that there were good things about the East: education, culture, no unemployment. We thought it was so easy, so clear. We would get your freedom to travel where we wanted to go and say what we wanted to say, but we would obviously keep the good things we had. My friends in the theatre and I would be able to do all the amazing and experimental work the DDR hadn't let us do. No more dancing ballet in tutus for Party bosses!

—Ah, you are a ballet artiste? I smiled, as if culturally impressed. Visions of leg warmers and physiologically unlikely sexual positions zipped for a second behind my eyes. Well, for God's sake, what do you expect? Also, I tried not to giggle, because I found myself thinking treacherously: *I know, Frau glorified dancing girl, you thought they'd keep up all your grants and maintain five huge state-funded theatres in Berlin with a hundred full-time technicians in each of them, except that now you'd be subsidised for doing* Romeo and Juliet *naked and walking about on stilts in nappies for no apparent reason with people playing the saxophone badly.*

—I am indeed a ballet artiste, she intoned graciously. —But now I stage shows to celebrate the launch of a new Mercedes or the opening of a new conference centre. And I think I am lucky to get the work, and everyone I used to know is desperate for me to take them on – dancers, musicians, actors, designers. And I always tell the pretty young ones to make sure they smile at the board members.

—Terrible, I nodded, looking secretly at her high-heeled shoes and fabulous ankles. I could see us now, clinging together, her legs wrapped right around me, like two survivors in the rubble of some vast war. She would understand.

—Sorry? I said, rematerialising from this happy vision to discover that I had completely failed to hear her last question. I smilingly signalled that it was simply the noise in the foyer that had made me miss her words of wisdom, and leaned a little closer still. From here, once again using my lecturer's skills, I could look right down the front of her dress while maintaining eye contact.

—You did not bring your wife with you? Heiner said he has seen her photograph. He says she is very pretty.

Now, fluency in a foreign language can easily get you into trouble. So it really wasn't my fault. I intended to tell my ballet dancer simply: *This time (i.e. for once) I've left (i.e. not brought) the (i.e. my) wife in England.* However, perhaps through excessive long-term and short-term tiredness, or rather too much drink, or a slight natural rustiness in my German due to having not been able to get away for ages because of my beloved kids, or maybe all of the above plus the facts, for example, that I had just experienced a moment of triumph and that it was a very long time since an alpha woman looked at me like that, I somehow made a tiny little slip of grammar and intonation so that it actually came out as: This *time (i.e. at last) I've left (i.e. dumped)* that *woman in England*.

I would have immediately corrected myself, no doubt, except that a small and intense man of my own age now plucked daringly at my sleeve. I turned and frowned, but he spoke before I could object to his intrusion, and he obviously knew that his words would do the trick.

—Grundmann. Herr Panke's press secretary. Responsible also for his tour diary.

—Of course, I said graciously. This little creep might well be the one planning Panke's trip to Oxford next week, so I had better keep in with him. —You will excuse me a moment, merciful lady?

—Naturally. Until later.

—Until later. So, Herr Grundmann?

68: The Global Locusts

While I let this pathetic but perhaps important functionary have his ration of face time, I grabbed yet another beer from yet another Heidi and kept a careful side-eye on the dancer, to make sure she did not escape or give up on me.

—Herr Doktor?

—Mmm? Oh, yes, sorry?

—Or rather, Herr Colleague. I may call you that, for I too am doctor of German history.

—Splendid, splendid.

—Herr Panke tells me that you are speaking on his works to the Conference of British and Irish University Teachers of German next week.

—Yes, actually. And Heiner has just told me that he'll be there too.

—I am currently finalising arrangements.

—Of course. The English press will all be there.

—I did not know. That is good. Now, Herr Colleague, I ask you to use your influence, substantial as it must be, to get my own paper a hearing at the conference.

—Your paper? Well, you'd have to write to Professor Bill Adams at Midlands University to see if he can slot you in at the last minute. Slot, as in *get you in*, I mean, not as in *shoot you*, ha ha!

—Sorry, Herr Colleague?

—Nothing, nothing.

—As you wish. But you would support my application, Herr Colleague?

—In principle, of course, as a friend of Heiner's, I mean, not that I have much influence.

—My paper is important.

—I'm sure it is. This beer is excellent, isn't it?

—As you know, Herr Colleague, so-called historical truth is always just myth, the story written by the victors.

—Of course, of course.

I was looking at the dancer and hardly listening to him. I felt that very soon I was just going to be drawn across the floor without any intention on my part, as if on sexually magnetic roller skates, towards her. I looked down openly at her strong, tanned legs. She saw me looking, and did not mind that she had done so. I plucked another foaming beer from the tray of a passing, pigtailed cowgirl and raised it privately to her. Christ, I could almost feel my hand stroking up her stocking already. And slowly the knickers slide aside and . . .

—I particularly admired the way you brought up the *global locusts* of financial capital.

—Mmm? Ah yes, yes, them.

Yes. There was no doubt. She wanted me to go over to her. From inside the hall I heard a roar of outraged agreement at something Panke had said. God, this was more like it! Excitement, drink, political radicalism and knowing that at the end of the evening you were, as Heiner's sidekick, odds-on for a fast, uncomplicated and indeed quite romantic . . .

—Why do we allow our lives to be run by these face-less players of the markets, who dwell amongst us, yet with no loyalty to any country or community?

—Why indeed? Well, I'm glad you liked my speech, do please send me your paper right away, I'm looking forward very much to *taking out our enemies*, ha ha, with Heiner next week, perhaps you'll be there too? Now, if you'd just excuse me a moment, I promised to join the lady in order to discuss the lamentable situation regarding state support for serious art and culture in our brave new free-market world, and . . .

—And of course we know who the *global locusts* really are, is it not so, Herr Colleague?

—Sorry?

As he said *global locusts* again, he raised his fore-finger to form a hook which he stroked, as subtly and secretly and unmistakably as a mason's handshake, over the entire length of his nose.

I could not move. I could no longer see the dancer. All I could fix on were the bubbles slowly rising to the surface of my beer.

For a greasy second I was back in the working men's club, during the Strike, with Hubby Huck the Racist Bastard on the television and roars of laughter all around me, drinking up and not objecting; or in a crowded bar in working-class Madrid on the night a gang of terror-ists almost killed the elected British Prime Minister, raising a glass and cheering along; or in the Irish pub on the night some twisted fantasist suggested, whilst tuning his guitar for another ballad to which I planned to harmonise, that the IRA's Remembrance Day massacre was probably the work of British Intelligence, nodding away and ordering another Guinness.

Once again, I felt the icy certainty that if I had any guts I would just walk out right now, away from my comrades and the beer and the music and warmth and the life and the ever-present chance of unthinking sex. That I must change my life and be alone.

Probably, I had been mistaken.

Surely?

Look, the man might well just have had an itchy nose.

People can have itchy noses, for God's sake.

Or it was some complex and ironic joke which I had imperfectly understood due to my German being good but not perfect.

Yes, that would be it.

Ridiculous to even think of leaving.

What? Offend Heiner? Desert my beer and my triumph and my new friend with the great legs? For what? For the cold lonely night?

And all just because I thought, *thought* mind you, that I might have detected some little unpleasantness in *one* of Heiner's many supporters? Absurd.

I was tired and I hadn't really been paying him my full attention, and he had an itchy nose or had been making a joke and I'd had a few drinks and perhaps I was a bit guilty about having lied to Sarah about where I was, not that anything was going to happen, and anyway, yes, I had almost certainly just imagined the whole thing.

Fine.

I smiled vaguely at the little man, raised my glass to him and turned to go back to my dancer. But he held openly on to my arm. I looked down at his hand.

—Herr Colleague, you will understand why I need your help. We must stand for the truth!

—Of course. Now, I really must . . .

—Our opponents will stoop to any lie, just as Bush and Blair invented the lie, which we now all know to have been a lie, of their so-called weapons of mass destruction in order to justify their imperialist war.

—Certainly, I said impatiently, and tried to free my arm. But his little hand was strong.

—Just as their forefathers, Churchill, Roosevelt and Stalin, invented a far greater lie to justify the perverted, the impossible, the insane alliance of British imperialism, Stalinist Bolshevism and American free-market capitalism. What possible common interest could these forces have? Only one, Herr Colleague! Then, as now, it was this: the prevention of a strong and united Europe under the natural and inevitable leadership of Germany! Then, as now, they needed a story, a grand lie, to justify to the world their criminal and genocidal actions, to ensure that Europe would stay helpless and that Russia's millions of Jews could at last, as they had planned for years, pour forth from Russia under the disguise of *discrimination*, with the sympathy of the whole world.

—Sorry?

—Exactly! The whole world was made to feel *sorry* for the poor Jews. So that they could occupy the Arab lands, as required by the plan of the Jewish oil millionaires of Jew York! The final masterstroke of that most cunning and tenacious of races! Oh yes, one cannot refuse them admiration, Herr Colleague. To have tricked the entire world! For, of course, only *one* lie was great enough to do their work, the greatest lie in world history, the only lie which could enable them to destroy Germany and hence enslave Europe whilst *at the same time* providing the excuse for the founding of the criminal state of Israel! The grand lie of the Holocaust! Herr Colleague? Where are you going? Herr Colleague?

—You must excuse me, Herr Grundmann, I've just remembered, I've got to, um, call my wife, I'll just, I'm afraid we Englishmen aren't used to such good German beer. Please tell Heiner that I am very tired from my journey and, and, that I'll of course see him next week, but that I'm, ah, yes, merciful lady, my apologies, I . . .

69: Straight Down the Line

I stumbled on watery knees from the sports complex and into the grey tower blocks of outer Dresden. Out of the rain and the dark, there was a glow in the black sky that could only be the halo of floodlights from the restored glories of the city centre. I headed for this beacon of hope, but no sooner had I set out towards it than the glow seemed to darken, to grow red, and for a terrifying moment I thought I was heading not into light but into the firestorm.

There was no doubt.

I was going to have to withdraw from the Oxford conference.

No more VIP.

Which meant no more late and unexpected career break.

Which meant forget ever, repeat ever, reviewing for *The Paper*, or being on the box, or any of the other dreams that even now, at forty-five, allowed me to kid myself that this life, this salary, this house was not actually *the* life yet, my *only* life, the rest of it.

I had no choice. My brain might be steaming with beer, but on this point there was only a merciless clarity. As I staggered through the night, scarcely seeing cars, trams, pedestrians, I was already mentally composing the email that I intended to send from my hotel (assuming I could find my hotel):

To: ProfAdamsW@midlands.ac.uk.
Subject: Oxford Conference Plenary Paper Withdrawal

Dear Bill,

I am extremely sorry, but I am going to have to withdraw my paper from the Oxford conference. I fully appreciate the unexpected honour of being invited to address a plenary session, but I have no choice in the matter.

I am in Dresden (having also done a little research in Prague, just for the record) visiting Heiner Panke. As you know (this being frankly the only reason you invited me to speak at all!), his DEBB party seems likely to make a considerable electoral impact in the upcoming emergency German general election. To many liberal observers, who will of course swallow almost anything provided it is laced with anti-Americanism (how impotently and uncleanly we loathe the Yanks!), Panke's party has seemed to be a radical pro-European attempt to re-enfranchise a neglected and underprivileged sector of the former East Germany, whose communities have suffered greatly from reunification and globalisation. It fact, I can now reveal that it is a bunch of neo-Stalinist, and indeed neo-Nazi, bastards.

Of course, Bill, many colleagues (I name no names) seem to find no difficulty whatever in performing the most extraordinary mental gymnastics to avoid making admissions of this kind. I know it's insane for me to even hope that these people (they will know who they are) would for a moment show me any respect for my decision. OK, then. You, for example. Yes, *you*. Christ, come on, Bill, can we have a *little* bit of honesty in an academic forum, for once? You made your career peddling Jacques le Coque's so-called *déconstructualisme* to wide-eyed British campuses in the eighties, but when it was revealed that le Coque got his first university job by collaborating with the Germans in 1943 and that *just maybe* this was why he said that 'history is an illusion' did you confess he'd fooled you? Did you hell. You'd made it on to various panels and committees by then, and you made *bloody* sure you stayed on them, didn't you, Billyboy? And now you jump through the post-Thatcher hoops and push the New Labour buttons as neatly as any of Brezhnev's functionaries toeing the party line. So no doubt you think I'm just a plain old sucker for turning down a slot that could easily have made my career. That could maybe even have got me into *The Paper* and maybe even on the box. Meaning that unless a dozen or so of you smug bloody so-called colleagues all happen to suddenly drop dead some time soon, I am now for ever doomed to being no one and will never make Professor and . . .

It was all so bloody unfair.

Did I *really* have to back out?

I walked round a corner and was suddenly out in the vast, cobbled square of the Frauenkirche.

Of course, I must call Father Eamon again!

Surely he would know of some clever postmodern sidestep I could yet make. Some sprightly play on words that would get around the small detail of that hooked finger.

I phoned from the cold old darkness of the haunted Dresden night, and the mere sound of his voice spread clean, green, guiltless, Irish light.

—Hoi. Johnnyboy! How's the man? So, did I cure you of your adolescent yearning for meaning? Is your paper now lit up with merry postmodern freeplay?

—Absolutely, Eamon! I mean, like you said, it's all just play, isn't it? There's just one little glitch left, nothing really, I'm sure it'll be easy for *you* to solve.

—You need a cute little drop shot to leave them flat-footed?

—Exactly, Eamon!

—Well, fire away and make sure you cite me.

I quickly outlined the situation to him (minus the gun, of course). When I had finished, there was only an ominous silence.

—Eamon?

—Jaysus, Johnnyboy, I pride myself on my court coverage but I don't think even *I* can get to that one.

—What?

—This German actually did the ould finger-down-the-nose thing? Shite and onions!

—Oh come on, Eamon. We lived in fantasy worlds about the Russians and the IRA for years.

—We did, we did. And you jumped through seriously tricky fucking mental hoops to justify marching alongside medieval theocrats. When it comes to evasion, no better men than us. All we need is a teeny-weeny crack of equivocation and there we are, lining up a clean passing shot. Someone else to blame. If the USofA would only stop being imperialist, the poor old USSR would embrace peace and love. If the evil Britz would only piss off, the IRA would just sing romantic ballads. If the Anglo-Saxons only stopped supporting

Israel, the Arabs would stop wanting to wipe it from the face of the earth. If only . . .

—Exactly, Eamon! So if we found ways round all that, surely, I mean . . . ?

—Holocaust denial? C'mon, JG, get real, no can do. That's a one-hundred-and-forty-mile-an-hour serve straight down the line. Can't even touch it. Auschwitz is game, set and match.

—But I've hung my whole career on Panke!

—Mmm, yeah. Bad call. Johnny, listen to me good. I, who am not famed for sticking overly to principles, tell you straight: dump those Nazi fuckers, and fast. In fact, for the avoidance of doubt, don't call me again until you've done it.

—What? Eamon!

—You heard correctly. Right now, you, my old comrade, are in grave danger of stinking by association, and I don't even want your name on my phone record again till you go public on this. Byeee!

—Eamon? Eamon?

I stood alone in the white-bright floodlights. Impossibly, I heard the distant sound of a vast, droning fleet of bombers nearing in the black Dresden sky. I staggered back and found myself clutching the flame-grilled stones of the Frauenkirche, holding on to those baroque rocks for dear life as vast squadrons of plastic Flying Fortresses rained vengeance.

From out of the firestorm arose the unleashed demons of a lifetime's self-delusion. And for the second time in twenty-four hours, I heaved up my guts in terror and despair, spraying the authentic German cobblestones with several quarts of authentic German beer.

70: Low Overheads

If I hadn't been so horribly ill the next day, I might well never have made it back.

My shattered body demanded my complete attention, leaving no space for the suicide-spawning horrors of self-loathing. Every step of my journey had to be completed according to conscious and precise instructions from my mind to my limbs. These orders often involved the swift enlisting of whatever rail, handle or wall I could find within reach. I was just an old, ill animal creeping back to its cold and lonely lair, to lie down, curl up and breathe its last in pain and peace. My sole high-order mental activity during the day was a permanent, fearful care for exactly where, and how far away, the nearest lavatory was to be found. At any given moment I would have welcomed the Gestapo man who, finding my papers to be out of order, marched me smartly off to be shot in the back of the head without further ado.

And, since I was done for, everything was simple now.

I was going to move my family after all.

But not to north London.

No, I would take them deeper, ever deeper into south London.

I was going to find us an ordinary brick-and-Artex-and-uPVC house on a normal suburban estate somewhere no one has ever heard of, full of regular hard-working folk near a reasonably good school.

We would be normal people, like everyone else.

I had wanted to bring my kids up with some insight, some culture, some alternative from all the crap, just so they didn't buy into it all without thinking. But exactly what timeless wisdom and culture was I planning to impart to them? I had been wrong about everything and it was time to make sure that *I* paid the price, not my kids. So that was that. I would no longer try to equip my children for a life they would never have. Playing the piano to at least grade five? Discussing Kafka and Marx round the dinner table? What help would that be to them when they were twenty-one and fighting for jobs against the whole of Eastern Europe and the Indian subcontinent with huge student debts that I wouldn't remotely be able to pay off for them?

Decision made. We were moving to nowhere. If any bloody estate agent talked about a house *packed with original features* I would just say, —*So what? Features are cheap on eBay. Now tell me about the catchment area.* If they mentioned *conservation area*, I'd say, —*Conservation shmonzervation, talk to me about catchment.* If they said *period property*, I'd say, —*Why should I pay more for old crap? What's the catchment?* If they said *high ceilings*, I'd ask about *high exam scores.*

And if the local good school was run by some church, so be it. Shit, that all used to be just a handy way of selecting without saying so, but that maniac Blair positively encouraged the bastards to actually bloody *mean* it. So now, if you want your kids not to get kicked, you have to smile inanely as you listen to some old queen in a nightie spouting metaphysical lunacy. Whatever. We can't afford to go private, so tough. My stupid bloody leftie parents didn't have me baptised or confirmed, because they thought things were actually *going to change*, ha ha! But I could set that right. I was clever. Within a month I could easily be talking theology with the vicar or the father or whoever it took. I would quote Martin bloody Luther at them if they wanted, for or against, depending – who cared? In German! Lying? Certainly not. I would merely be adjusting the modes of my discourse to correspond to the prevailing zeitgeist, and who could blame me for that?

No more Schumann, my darlings. No more little lectures on art history. No limits on watching crap TV. We'll have fine eazi-2-kleen uPVC windows and a small mortgage. Our ceilings and our overheads will both be low. You'll have Playstations and Sky coming out of your ears, boys! We'll bother your little heads no more with useless knowledge that was really only ever meant for the posh and just trickled down slightly for that brief period after the Second World War when there was a curious phenomenon called Social Mobility. Bring you up as weirdos with tastes too sophisticated for your place in life but too poor to ever indulge them? Not us.

How simple and lager-filled things were all going to be. How dreamless. And soon I would be just archaeology:

Ah yes, observe. A fine example, *Homo londonensis* from the *Early Chinese Plastic Crap Age.* An individual of no great rank, almost certainly, since he was unearthed in what was then to the south of the river, which (as we saw in last week's lecture) seems to have represented a clear and distinct watershed, possibly tribal in nature. A troubled culture, it is certain. The records are scanty because the socio-environmental disaster which overwhelmed their society was, once the unseen tipping-point had been reached, so sudden and so overwhelming. It appears, however, that they had access to virtually limitless amounts of plastic-electronic artefacts, many of which have no discernible function and must therefore be regarded as totemic objects. They seem to have worshipped a now entirely mysterious pantheon of demigods called *TV celebs*, whilst living in superstitious dread of an undescribed but evidently hostile entity known as *the mortgage rate* . . .

I stumbled at last out of the cab and into our street without even thinking seriously about the Armalite lying there in the Mercedes before our door.

So what? Let it stay there!

What difference did it make now? The VIP, and with it my career, was about to be cancelled in any case. The police could do nothing more to me. I might as well just leave the gun in the car, call them, as soon as I felt well enough to face them, and tell them absolutely everything.

Problem solved.

In fact, it would save me even having to confess to that bastard Bill Adams. Yes, indeed: now that would be an easier email to send altogether. The message leaped clear to my mind as I fumbled for the keys to the front door.

Dear Bill,

I'm afraid that having spent the last five days (!) under police interrogation for no other reason than that in New Labour's police state anyone who, perfectly innocently, as is of course the case with me, happens to find an assault rifle in their back garden, university lecturer or not, is immediately suspected of being a terrorist, I am in no position to deliver my paper on Heiner Panke at the conference. Please accept my bitterest regrets. If any senior committee members feel, as I hope they do, so outraged at this new evidence of the disastrous consequences for Britain that flow from our poodle-like support for Bush's so-called War on Terror that they wish to contact the media, and thus maybe even get me an interview in *The Paper* after all . . .

Yes, well, something like that.

I slid shivering through the door of our house and was greeted by the grey emptiness of a cold house at sunset in winter.

I am aweary, aweary.

The sight of my little Edwardian writing desk under our stairs and of my beloved Victorian captain's chair waiting before it felt like a sentence of death. They would never make it to north London now. No more of that. They were wholly inappropriate to our coming new life in SEgodknowswhat. Flog them off in the free ads or on eBay. IKEA for us from here on in.

Unable to bear the sheer silence of the house, I lowered my head very carefully under the staircase, sat at the laptop and logged on. At least in cyberspace there would be some evidence of my existence (*I have email, therefore I am*), even if it was only more demands from the Quality Delivery Unit.

There were indeed many new messages from them. Oh well. I was going to have another fifteen years or so of this, so better stop carping and get on with it. More whining students. For God's sake, yet another petition from that idiot against the ban on Israeli academics. What chance does he think he's got of getting *that* through the union AGM? Another automatic non-answer from *The Paper*, bunch of snooty bloody . . .

What?

Wait!
Oh my God. It was not automatic and it was not a *no*.

Dear Dr Goode,

Thanks for yours. If Panke's DEF going to be there himself (can you reconfirm this pls if poss from his own office, no offence!) the Asst Acting European Editor will send me along re: piece on New European Left/Anti-Globalisation. That wd be fun. I haven't been back to Oxon since I left last year! I see you were there too. What coll when? Maybe you left before I came up. Anyway it wd be fun, wouldn't it? Cd you email asap BRIEF notes on Heiner Panke/aims of the DEBB/recent electoral stats/yr CV? Sadly no cab funds here for me yet (boo!) so cd u meet me @ Oxon station?

kr
Alex
(Alexandra Hesmondhalgh)

I leapt to my feet with a cry of despair that was cut short as my head rammed into the underside of the stairs. The stunning crunch threw me to me knees and set off a new tsunami in my head and bowels, to match the one raging in my soul. After all these years those bastards on *The Paper* had finally recognised me, just when it was too late to do me any good!

Retching yet again, I now knew that the sheer injustice of the world was finally proven.

71: Saved

I sat on the bottom stair, my head sunk deep between my shoulders. If only I had never found the bloody gun! What had I done to deserve this?

I wanted to call Sarah, very badly.

I tried to rehearse how I would inform her of our new and somewhat more modestly conceived future. But as I began to construct my well-argued explanation to her, something happened.

I lost the power of mental speech.

The words would not come out, they would not even begin to form. I was trying to talk to her but I could not begin to see her face: my mind's eye simply failed to conjure her up. As soon as I even began to think about what I might say, the person I was addressing stopped existing.

Myself I could quite easily see, standing by the gas-fired barbecue on our little tarmac drive, stubby bottle in hand, swapping opinions about the relative merits of Chelsea and Manchester United, Ford and Toyota, *The X Factor* and *Big Brother*. No longer haunted by lonely dreams but happily sharing the bright, blatant wish-world of millions. After the odd night in the local pub (opened in 1990), my male neighbours and I would watch Hubby Huck. So much for me. I would adapt, not die. As for Will and Jack, I could, without too much trouble, almost joyously reimagine our boys as regular teenage lumps untortured by bullying or insecurity, headed seamlessly for banks or IT companies, and why the hell not? They would soon be out-earning me, and

I would be glad. Even my beautiful Mariana I found little difficulty seeing as an unthinking little princess of suburbia, utterly fitted for the modern world. I would happily greet her accountant husband-to-be.

But not Sarah.

When I tried to imagine Sarah in the little low-ceilinged lounge of our identikit home, or in our small and eazi-2-kleen kitchen, or going up the narrow, slow-rising stairs towards the flat-faced modern door of our uPVC-silenced little bedroom in the arse-end of nowhere, or talking about what happened last night on *BB* with our neighbours, there was just nothing there. Sarah plus *that* life was simply an equation that could never work out, the square root of minus one, matter and anti-matter occupying the same place.

I knew right then that whatever I said, however much I argued that it was all for the benefit of our children, Sarah would never agree to live like this, not because she *didn't want to*, but because she *couldn't*, because if she did, she would, in that instant, cease to be herself.

The woman I loved and had always loved and will always love could never, ever be that.

And so, you see, it was my love for her that pulled me through.

I had weakened, yes.

Lost in the mapless new world, I had been about to abandon everything I believed in.

I had been ready for re-education.

I was prepared for malls, muzak and Sky. To love even *Big Brother* and *The X Factor*.

But she, my angel, was my salvation.

The physical impossibility of Sarah and *BB/TXF* co-existing in the same space made her my eternal and indestructible truth, my mighty fortress, the rock on which my cowardice shipwrecked and my selfhood clung.

She gave me back all the hopes of the seventies.

Only the best is good enough for the workers.

She flung open the tall sash windows of my dreams again, taking me back to a lost age when uPVC and market discipline had not even been invented, let alone conquered the world.

Stop now? Give up? Accept the bosses' offer and get back to work?

Not I.

UPVC?

Oh, I don't think so.

Not for Sarah. She had always been my sash-window girl.

Sashes and Schumann, by fuck, she would have.

Yes, sashes and Schumann and all that go with them.

I was the clever boy from the rough comp, and fuck me if I wasn't going to make the deal stick.

It's down by the Bogside that I long to be.

I wasted not a moment more.

I carried my doomed laptop almost tenderly out to the garden shed. There I placed it on the oil-stained sheets of *The Paper*, which lay there still. I opened my father's toolbox, bent low, inhaled deeply from its manly depths, then levered the computer bodily apart with a large screwdriver and, wielding a two-pound lump hammer (MADE IN ENGLAND), speedily reduced its Far Eastern innards to small fragments of plastic and metal. It felt bizarrely like something I should have done many years before, and left me laughing with the ancient delight of sheer liberation.

The cow was right after all: freedom is freedom is freedom!

I gathered the resulting shards carefully up within

the newspaper and plunged the lot into the grease-filled suitcase. I lugged the suitcase across the garden, through the house and out into the street. I opened the boot of my car and heaved the suitcase in.

—What you up to, Prof John? Oh, nasty bump that. Awkward boots, these Mercs. Made you jump, eh?

—Yes, actually.

—Here, Prof John, you look like shit warmed up. I can smell the beer and puke off you from here. Well, leave a man alone, what do you expect, eh? Nothing good, that's for sure! What you got in there then? You chopped up some tart and taking her to the river to dump her? Ha ha!

I looked my neighbour in the eye properly. I realised that I had never done so before. For the first time I was not trying to please him, so for the first time I held his gaze. With ancient certainty, I saw his eyes, and with them his judgement of me, change for ever even as I stared back. Still I held the look. I wondered if I should show him the Armalite under the passenger seat. How he would look at me then! But I controlled myself.

—Sorry, Prof John, you OK?

—Just thinking, Phil. You said you can get new plates for a car, right?

—Oho! You on nine points, Prof John? Fucking cameras, eh?

—No. But I have got a little job.

—A little job, Prof John?

—Tell you what, just let me dump this old suitcase, then fancy a pint later on, Phil?

PART FOUR

Homecoming

72: *Et in North London Ego*

Darling, it's three a.m. and I'm sitting here in my rather large and lovely cedar-clad shed (how cleverly I got it to just scrape in beneath the height-limit of the planning regulations!) in the really almost substantial garden of our modest enough but very pleasant and these days ludicrously desirable Edwardian semi. But I'm not working on the script for the new show, I'm afraid. Instead, I'm standing on the small mezzanine platform above my writing table, looking out of my special little chapel-like window high in the eaves, making this supplementary recording exactly a year after what you've just heard.

I mean, it does seem rather as though I've got away with it, but you *never can tell*. Particularly as it now seems that I must, sadly, employ my little Armalite again. I have taken all the precautions a clever man can take, and my cover story will again be tailored to the prevailing mood of the country, but only God knows how it will pan out. So if you do, at some point, indeed still find yourself needing to sell my story, your potential buyers might want to know how it felt to have clawed my way back to the normality that was all I ever wanted for us.

So how *does* it feel, to be here now?

To have read *Pooh* to Mariana, to have helped Jack and Will do their interesting homework for their frankly rather posh (though theoretically comprehensive) school, then to have smoked my evening cigarette in the garden whilst secretly watching you playing

Schumann to yourself until the first guests arrive from all corners of north London to help celebrate my new commission from the BBC?

How the hell do you think it feels?

It feels bloody good, is how it feels.

Just right, in fact, is how it feels.

This is what Tiggers like best!

And all because my little Armalite gained me, in less than one minute of full-auto action, the sort of name-and-face recognition that one usually only gets by slaying a Beatle, throwing twenty billion dollars at the New Hampshire primary or grilling a bit of fish on the box.

The TV footage was actually very good. As you'll no doubt remember, if only because it was reused yet again in that prime-time advert I did recently for insurance to *protect your loved ones* in case of unforseen events . . .

73: *Sic Incipit Gloria Mundi*

We press PLAY.

I, John Goode himself, walk to the podium of the Oxford Conference with Panke beside me: I small, plump and shy; he large, loud and leader-like. The camera swings to take in the applauding lecturers, their faces fixed in the idiotic chimp-like smiles that tell you they are looking at a higher-status hominid.

Panke, little knowing what is in my notes, makes a joke in German that gets the hall guffawing, and the subtitles tell the world: *My little doctor feels a little tired. Indulge him. I never saw him drink so much beer, even when we sung together while the wall was still standing!* He claps me so hard on the back that I stagger and drop my notes. As I kneel to pick up the papers, Panke sighs and speaks again. The captions inform us that he is saying: *I had better help. He might get my life backwards! We might end up back in the bad old days. But in fact, you know why the Chinese are so happy? They still have their wall!* At this, the lecturers roar with delight.

And now the masked gunman walks into the room.

When you know what's coming this makes a fascinating few seconds of viewing, and I have often stopped the film myself here. Look: those on the spot, who don't have hindsight, are incredibly slow to take in what's happening. Like all decisive events, my would-be killer enters the frame of history well before his significance is realised, and even when he's been seen, the clearest reaction on all those unexpecting faces is simple disbelief. This cannot be happening. No doubt we will all look like that when the oil finally dries, the first vast tidal surge hits, or Iran nukes Tel Aviv.

Then he sprays bullets into the ceiling, bringing down plaster, screaming in Arabic, and they believe, fast.

Once again, the subtitles come to the world's aid: he is demanding that the cameras should keep running in order to show the world the fate of *the devil Goode, child of hellfire and servant of Zion*. (I suppose I really shouldn't have written to all the papers a week before, saying that if my union wanted to boycott Israeli academics, it should do the same to all scholars who took salaries from self-proclaimed Islamic states. Only the most right-wing of them printed it, of course, but that was apparently enough.) He grabs the podium microphone and adds, live, in shouted English: *No phone or all die! Where is John Goode?*

I am, at this point, less than six feet from him, but he looks around again and pauses in confusion.

This is the point at which, on that first *Newsnight*, the impossibly rugged ex-SAS novelist, brought in to explain the botched assassination, freezes the pictures.

He tells how, the night before, whilst I, all innocent of my impending doom, had been very openly pub-crawling Oxford with my colleagues, an email had been sent to several major newspapers from an Internet café near Finsbury Park. Coming from a group calling itself the Caliphate Committee, the message threatened *fire for the enemies of Mohammed (PBUH) who succour the devil Zionism*. The same terminal at the same Internet café had downloaded and printed, not two minutes before-hand, a copy of the Staff Contact Sheet from the Student Experience Assurance Unit, freely available on the UCL website, showing myself smiling plumply, hair around my shirt collar, tie loose, bearded and wearing large, heavy spectacles. This document had, as it happened, recently been updated (by myself) to stress the proud fact that I was giving a plenary address at the upcoming national conference in Oxford, even giving the precise time and place.

However, by the time of the planned shooting, I was clean-shaven, crop-haired, dressed in a black roll-neck jumper and sporting my new Dolce & Gabbana rimless glasses, the very model of a modern modern linguist.

The ex-SAS novelist now compares blown-up versions of these two images and explains that I have *recently modified my personal appearance* (a lesson to all in public life, he hints), meaning that *outdated intelligence* has *degraded* the gunman's ability to *acquire the target*. It is this unexpected complication, this minor but very good example of the *fog of war*, suggests the shagsome former warrior, which has led to my would-be killer's evident *combat stress*, leading to the second burst of fire over my peers' heads.

The one-time soldier hits PLAY again and the footage resumes.

That second blast of bullets sends the assembled scholars cowering even lower. *Show me Goode or all die!* screams the masked terrorist. This is a decisive error, says the voice of the ex-SAS man over the images, for in *combat stress* it is hard, terribly hard, it seems, to maintain an *accurate round-count* when firing automatically.

I count three! roars the gunman, jumping down to the front row of seats where the most senior Germanists of Britain and Ireland shrink in terror: *One!*

Behind him, I slowly rise to my feet.

Panke clings to the floor in a highly unleaderlike way. There is no *Spartacus* moment. On the contrary, a few of my colleagues actually point out to the gunman what is going on behind him. He swings. *I am John*

Goode, I say, steadily. And without the slightest hesitation he shoots me down.

The images freeze again.

The ex-SAS man explains once more: the gunman's unprofessional failure to *maintain an accurate round-count* has led to his having only one bullet left when he actually comes to *neutralise the target*. This means that he now has to *break off the action and reload* after having shot me once, which is apparently a very bad thing when *in contact*.

Things move once more. The world sees the faceless gunman wrenching furiously at his gun. It sees him slap and pull and push until at last a bit of the gun comes free. The bit that holds the bullets, you know, whatever you call *that*! He allows it to drop to the floor and starts trying to fit another one in. But it seems not to go. Pause again. Digital effects allow us to zoom in to the frozen image of the gun itself. Our expert points out the notorious flaw of the Armalite ever since Vietnam: its tendency to jam. This proves fatal, or rather (the militaristic scribe, having unconsciously fallen into the camaraderie that binds all trained psychopaths, hastily corrects himself) non-fatal.

Unpause. The gunman lets fly a final volley of Arabic oaths, kicking me and spitting at me. Pause again, so that a pixelated and voice-disguised expert from GCHQ can comment on my enemy's language, which, like the email from Finsbury Park, apparently betrays *the grammatically poor Arabic of a non-Arab Muslim, containing phraseology characteristic of the Afghani jihadist camps.*

And now run on to the memorable end. A car horn is heard to blare repeatedly outside, and the gunman, after some hesitation, turns and runs from the hall. After a ridiculously long while, women begin to sob and men pull themselves cautiously upright. No viewer can see this section of the film without inwardly screaming at them all to hurry up and help me. Eventually, some do. Panke is not among them. He remains prone. Phones appear in people's hands. Others run for the doors. I insist on being carried to the microphone, where, despite being evidently in great pain and visibly losing blood, I am able to declare that while I quite understand, and therefore forgive, my attackers, and indeed join with them in condemning Bush's imperialism, I will never be silenced by the enemies of truth and look forward keenly to a new Democratic administration in the White House that will forge closer links with Europe to peacefully resolve the situation in the Middle East in a way that will recognise Palestinian aspirations yet guarantee the security of Israel. I finally stress my full commitment to a multicultural Britain free of all religious bigotry, apologise for being unable to deliver my paper, movingly declare my love for my wife and children, faint, and am shortly afterwards taken to the Radcliffe Hospital, where I spend the night under armed guard in what the papers call *a serious but stable condition* and which, in my own memory, stands out as a timeless little holiday of beatific, opiate happiness.

74: The Avoidance of Tragedy

No one was ever arrested for my shooting.

There was briefly a public appeal to locate a particular car which had been CCTVed near the scene carrying what turned out to be false number plates, but the lead came to nothing.

Two days later, the Caliphate Committee staged a just-failed attempt (using, it was soon established, the very weapon which had been fired at me) to shoot what's his face as well. You know, what's his face, the lecturer who'd actually started the email campaign against the boycotting of Israeli academics. Two bullets missed his head by less than a foot. *Tuck-tuck.* What's his face did try, understandably, to make a bit of a fuss about it. But you see, you've quite forgotten about *him*, haven't you? Of course. Everyone has. *What's his face* is all *he* will ever be. We all know the name Bobby Sands, but who were the other saps who laid down their little long-haired lives so that Mr Adams could one day josh happily with Dr Paisley? No, I got my (near) martyrdom in first and I got it in *live on TV*. And so up I sucked it without even trying, every last drop of that sweet oxygen, publicity.

The TV images flew around the worlds real and virtual. My stoical acceptance of the fact that I would probably never be able to move my left shoulder much again was impressive. My absolute forgiveness for, and understanding of, those who had tried to kill me was saintly. My absolute refusal, once I had recovered consciousness, to accept any security precautions at all in hospital was heroic. And I had the required bomb-shell to drop whilst everyone was briefly looking my way.

Upon leaving hospital, I told my press conference that I had dark suspicions. I had been about to denounce the ex-KGB man Panke's DEBB as a neo-Nazi party (I waved my notes at them like a second Churchill). Few hacks could resist the idea of a conspiracy linking those three epochal foes, Muslim extremists, Russian agents and German Nazis. The resultant speculation ensured that having got into the media, I continued, for those vital follow-up few weeks, to be chatted about in ye olde saloon bar of the global village.

I had broken with Panke at last. I was no one's little doctor any more. I was in the media, therefore I was me.

Eamon was the first to see what this meant and to call with his congratulations:

—Jaysus, Johnnyboy, talk about putting away a smash! Advantage you, and championship point, my man! Just don't fucking choke now!

—Does that mean I'm back in your phone book, Eamon?

—Straight back in at speed-dial number one, Johnny the Goode. Now, go make hay!

The hay pretty well made itself, actually. There was no need to employ researchers to seek out further informa-tion about me. It provided itself, drawn by the irresistible magnet of airtime. Past and present colleagues queued up to confirm my unimpeachably left-liberal credentials by quoting our long-standing email exchanges on the evils of Bush, Blair and suchlike. Middle-aged veterans of the Miners' Strike dredged themselves up from the slag heap of history to describe how I had, in my youth, stood boldly up for the rights of the working man. Hairily Gaelic folk with fiddles popped out from pubs around the Holloway Road to relate, watery-eyed, my staunch championing, Englishman that I was, of Irish freedom. A stout, salt-of-the-earth type from my own street in SE11 was interviewed, describing how *We calls him Einstein down the pub, see, on account of his brain, but there's no side to Prof John, mate; he buys his wheels in the Free Ads, he knows his footie and he loves a few pints watching an England game, just like the rest of us. Doesn't mind a scrap either, and he looks after his old mum.* A poor-quality phone video, recorded in a sports hall in Dresden, showed me making unmistakable homage to the great Dr Martin Luther King and lambasting globalisation.

Some people feared that the hatred of the Caliphate Committee (a small breakaway group, it was thought) might be replaced by a full-on fatwa as my fame grew. Speculation about whether (or why, exactly) one might be pronounced kept the opinion columns bubbling away. I maintained, of course, a flawlessly liberal position on the whole business, absolutely deprecating violence of any kind but perfectly willing to cede the right of a minority community feeling itself under attack to defend itself on issues central to its cultural values. When *The Paper* (acting on an anonymous tip-off) obtained and published police photographs of me marching amidst young and serious Muslims two years before, on the vast anti-Iraq War demonstration, pregnant wife, sons, home-made NOT IN MY NAME banners and all, several of the more liberal radical imams in Britain went so far as to almost unreservedly condemn the notion of killing me.

The timing was happy.

Up was coming the twentieth anniversary of the Warsaw Pact's collapse, that sea change which had caused my career such inconvenience. Those mysterious, omnipotent *telly people* at the BBC needed a plug-worthy person to front the requisite HBO co-production on this weighty subject. They felt obliged to use someone who was actually qualified. Say what you will, poor old Auntie is the last bastion. Who else, then, but the liberal champion of truth who was undoubtedly an expert and now had a Unique Selling Point as *You Know, That History Bloke Who Got Shot by al-Qaeda or Was It the Nazis or the KGB?*

Nor do I let people forget it. In my first series, *Europe Chained* (a history of the Warsaw Pact countries 1945–89), I never failed to heft, load or mount whatever weapons were in question (a *Panzerfaust* from Berlin, 1945; a petrol bomb from Budapest, 1956; a Soviet tank from Prague, 1968; a border guard's AK-47 from the Berlin Wall, 1989) with manly yet sorrowful asides about my own personal encounter with ballistics.

Since I was now on the telly, I came under increasing pressure to at least allow my family to be placed under armed protection for a while. I agreed with great (and public) reluctance to put my children before my principle. During the *Newsnight* debate on the subject, I came up with the rather brilliant idea, though I say it myself, that on grounds of liberalism and multiculturalism my loved ones' weapons-trained police minder should himself be a practising Muslim.

This caused some problems, there being no such officer available in the UK. The Home Office, however, so liked the idea that when, coincidentally, *The Paper* picked up on and featured a Bosnian Muslim (agreeably European and highly photogenic) who had trained with the British Army as well as the American Marines, and who was now seeking to join the SAS under the new US-style Service for Citizenship scheme (introduced to stem the impossible haemorrhage of home-grown soldiers due to Iraq), it was very easy for me to have somebody else suggest that this might well be the ideal man for the job.

Rather fun, having George around the place. And what with him being so damn good-looking, so dangerously sexy and so often in contact, via me, with bored media folk, he has, of course, already landed his own TV documentary (and hence, book deal).

As for my shows, well, the viewers, besieged by interest rates and fear of crashes, seeing all Europe voting for policies that would have been thought virtually fascistic just ten years ago, love what I sell.

And what do I sell?

Reassurance, of course.

The avoidance of tragedy in a frightening world.

They see a plump man who has been *shot by terrorists* and is still perfectly happy, perfectly liberal. And they shall get more of the same. I have just completed my new series, *History's Walls*, in which I make the regulation *epic journey* in my trademark old-shape bonnet-badgeless C-Class Merc (for the continual on-screen use of which the grateful manufacturers have secretly promised me a spit-new E-Class whenever I choose to take it), wandering about in front of the Great Wall of China, Hadrian's Wall, Offa's Dyke, the Maginot Line, the Berlin Wall, once again, and the Arab–Israeli dividing wall. The final *ep* (I find it hard not to call it that, these days) ends with a cutesy dissolve from Checkpoint Charlie to Charlie Chaplin, with Arab and Israeli students laughing together at the warm-hearted tramp. I then sign off the series with the following blithe coda:

EXT. THE ARCTIC. DAY.

Dr John Goode smiles despite the evident pain in his left shoulder as he leans over the stern of a boat to watch a vast iceberg thunder into the sea.

GOODE

Yes, the sea may rise a few feet. I don't deny it. A few species may become extinct. So did the Roman Empire. A few maniacs may attack freedom. I should know! Ow. Sorry, just a little twinge. But our children won't have to dodge V-1s, like my parents did. And they won't have to lie awake wondering if tonight's the night some faulty computer unleashes the cruise missiles, like we did. Oh, some little things may get a little worse, and the line of human progress may suffer little blips, but it is a great, strong, ancient line, and in the big picture it is going only one way: up, and onwards. Goodnight, and sleep well. Because, you know, you really can.

So here I am, on all our tellies and therefore, by the natural osmosis of the water-cooler world, in all the windows of all the bookshops, right up there with people who kick balls about, cook vegetables or suggest home improvements on TV.

And, hence, in north London. Where else?

Oh, I know it won't last.

But it doesn't have to. The vital lump sums have put me back where I always should have been, and there I will stay, media career or not. You see, my academic salary is somewhat over double what it was last year. Many of our new universities offered me instant personal chairs in return for the recruiting-value of my name, so I was able to negotiate, with transatlantic heartiness, a thumping raise that cannot be reneged on.

In short, I have been able to buck the free market and win back what I never actually had but always *should* have had: approximately the comparative social, financial and domestic situation of a senior humanities academic from the early seventies.

Result? Happiness.

It was a rather nice house-warming party this evening, I thought.

Intelligent, well-educated people discussing the burning issues of the day as discussed in *The Paper* that morning (indeed, as discussed there by some of the very people present) over a little too much good red wine (and in the case of the assistant European editor and her Hungarian artist friend, a line or two of cocaine in the downstairs loo). All fine, liberal stuff.

My parents arrived dressed in a suit and twinset respectively, both of such fine cut and cloth that they had clearly been made to measure, though not in the last few decades and not for the present owners. Good old Oxfam!

—Well, it *looks* like a pretty solid house, John.

—I hope so, Dad!

—But I still can't believe you paid, what was it, *half a million quid* for *this*?

—*Half?* Um, oh, yes, *about that*, Dad. Anyway, it's ours now, eh?

—Education will always win through in the end, John! We always said so.

—You did, Mum, and you were right. Come on, come in. Will, Jack! Granny and Grandad are here. Come and get their coats, will you?

Eamon was on top form, quite a hit in his heavily

designed suit of sheeny black with many zips where no zips usually are.

—Jaysus, beaten on to the box by Johnny B. Goode, who'd've thought it! Talk about a high-kicking serve to the backhand court! I have to say, I never thought you'd be able to change your grip *that* fast. How the fuck much is Hollywood paying you for that consultancy gig?

—Eamon, Eamon, we don't talk money in north London. The word is *fun*, here.

—Sorry, the non-English fifty-acre farmer in my soul.

—But actually, yes, consulting on *Siegfried* is very, very good fun.

—As opposed to giving intellectual justification for a slaughterhouse of fascist shite?

—Really, Eamon, *Siegfried: The West Stands Firm* is a serious, high-end filmic recreation of the dawn of northern European literature which employs the latest CGI techniques to bring Dark Age reality back to life.

—A crisp return, my man! Excellent. But wasn't it a bit full-on to have *that* many kinda-ragheads get disembowelled by our big blonde hero?

—It's all in the original poem, Eamon. More or less. And I always prefer the word *slotted* myself, don't know why. Now, come with me and, ah, Daisy, there you are, I want you to meet my absolute best friend, Eamon.

—Hello, Eamon. What fun that suit is!

—It called, I bought, what could I do?

—Daisy, I was just thinking, don't we need a piece on socialist-realist art for the next series?

—Yes. Do you know anything about socialist-realist art, Eamon?

—That horrible shite? Not at all. Why the fuck would I? But by tomorrow I'll be able to rally from the baseline all day about it. *SoRe*, I think I'll christen it. Doesn't that sound like fun to you guys? *SoRe: the new PoMo*, I see it all as plain as day.

—I think Eamon would be fun on the show, don't you, Daisy?

—Yes. Oh well, that's OK then.

Poor old Brian from Sheffield was embarrassing, of course, and I know it seemed strange to have invited him. But I did have my reasons. I passed by him often, kept his glass full and tried to keep an ear cocked in his direction:

—Excuse me, sorry, I just wondered, do *you* know if the literary editor of *The Paper* is here? John said he would be.

—Actually, it's *she* and I am and those are my shoes you're pouring wine on.

—Oh. Oh God. Sorry. Well, perhaps I am a bit, I mean, has John mentioned me to you? I've been trying to find you all evening, you see, *I'm your man*. I could review absolutely anything archaeological, historical, biographical, anthropological. I mean, obviously, I'm fully qualified, and, well, I *am* a friend of John's! It's great, what's happened to good old John, eh?

—Wonderful.

—It's so funny. You see, I'm *sure* I remember, not long before he got shot, we had a chat on the phone, I admit I did get a bit drunk afterwards, thinking about London and, well, *The Paper* and my idea for a televison series and things like that. It's a fantastic idea. Perhaps we could work on it together? Well, yes, anyway, I'm *almost* sure, when I think back, that he said something about a machine gun. *Before* it happened, I mean. But obviously, he can't have, can he?

—Perhaps you were drunk.

—Do you know, I may have been. I did ask him once about it, I called him when I was a bit drunk, but he just laughed and said I must be drunk, which I *was*, actually, and . . .

—Eugenie, darling, *there* you are!

—John, darling, there you are! *(Who the hell is this?)*

—Brian, come out to the garden, will you? *(So sorry, Eugenie!)* There's someone else I want you to meet.

—Oh. Um, so, if you've got anything, absolutely anything on history, anthropology . . .

—This way, Brian. You know, Brian, you're a bit drunk.

—Yes, I suppose I am. Sorry, John. I mean, it is nearly Christmas, isn't it?

—It is, Brian.

—Do you think she'll give me anything to review?

—Oh, I think we can do better than that.

—Better than reviewing for *The Paper*?

—Jayne from the BBC was telling me she's got a new series about archaeological discoveries in the Middle East.

—I could do that! John, I could! Really! Will you tell her I could? Will you?

—Well, the thing is, it's a little bit of a hot potato, Brian. It's about events right after the Prophet himself, you see, and it does rather seem to contradict some of the stuff in the Qur'an. A couple of Iranian archaeologists have already been beheaded for working on the material. I know *you* wouldn't be afraid of the physical danger, Brian, but as a liberal man, obviously, you'd have to consider whether any Western infidel has the cultural right to even discuss issues of such importance to the *ummah*, and which –

—I could do it, John! You know I could! Please let me do it!

—Well, I'll have a word. Look, Jayne's over there, why not go and tell her yourself right now. Make sure everyone realises you know the dangers and *aren't afraid of them*. That'll impress her.

—God, John, right, thanks!

—See you later, Brian. Hello, Jago, hello, Caspian. Hello, darling. Enjoying the party?

—Mmm. Leticia's got two spare tickets for that lieder recital at Wigmore Hall tomorrow. Shall we go?

—Absolutely. Ah, there's George. Will you excuse me, darling? I just need to grab him for a sec. You do look lovely, you know. Ah, George.

—Yes, Jonni?

—I wonder if you could come with me just for a second. *So* sorry, Tamsin.

(—*My God, John, your friend George is so . . .*

—*Yes, isn't he?*)

—George, I think Brian may be a problem. I got him down here to see what he remembers. I'm afraid he remembers enough and gets drunk enough to say it.

—This can be very bad for us, Jonni. For our children too.

—I know. Brian's going to be in the papers soon because he's about to agree to do a programme that might offend some Muslims very much indeed.

—He has children, Jonni?

—Yes, but there's no mortgage on his house and his pension'll be paid out for ever. His sons will be all right, George.

—Poor man, if he offend Him with a hundred names!

—I'll call Phil tomorrow.

—You call only from phone box, Jonni. This is very important.

—Well of course, George.

—Tell him I bring new bootleg Erbyerk DVD for him, special live show Erby do for army and police only. My friends in SAS give me. Extra funny. *Erby's Big*

Bayonet and Truncheon Show, not for easily offended, ha ha!

—Oh yes, I must look at that one too.

—I do not think you like Erby so much, Jonni.

—Well, you see, I think I've just sold Channel 4 my idea for a postmodern reinterpretation of Hubby Huck's humour. I mean, the way Hubby *boldly foregrounds* racism and misogny witnesses a true fascination with *otherness*, don't you think?

—Ah! You are clever man, Jonni, too clever for me.

—Oh, it's a classic Freudian erotic transference, which clearly suggests that underlying Hubby's apparently offensive humour is a *genuinely liberational dynamic* that is systematically rejected by *the elitist media establishment* precisely because it's implicitly, um, implicitly, er, oh fuck, I've forgotten how it goes after that. Never mind, Eamon'll remind me. Well, see you later, George. Tamsin, here he is, you can have him back now, lucky you!

—John, *there* you are!

—Antonia, darling, *there* you are! How was the street music in Brixton?

—Just *vibrant*! And it all ended with the *most* impassioned plea for the end of stop-and-search powers for the police. We'll get *that* in tomorrow, just you wait! So much for that racist bloody cop on the radio the other day, eh?

—The black one, you mean?

—Yes, him. Claiming that the black community might *want* more police about. I ask you, who on earth is the ridiculous man listening to? Well, he should have been there tonight! The *youth on the street*'ll be partying till dawn. So *edgy*. I thought we'd never get home. They just don't *have* real taxis down there, it's quite extraordinary. We had to take the vilest minicab in the world and I'm quite certain the driver had never been north of the river in his whole life. *Such* fun. Now, John, have you signed the petition yet?

—No, actually.

—Hilary darling, John hasn't signed the petition yet!

—John *hasn't signed*?

—He *must* sign!

—*You* must sign, John. *Everyone* has.

You see, our local comprehensive school, Jack and Will's school, Mariana's future school, has a catchment area rather unusually deficient in pupils from poor and/or ethnic backgrounds. For some reason it always scores well over double in every respect what the average north-London state school can manage. The new head is threatening to take advantage of the government's proffered route to greater independence. *Selection through the Back Door!* is the cry of we stout defenders of the comprehensive ethos, who have paid a million quid and upwards to make bloody sure our children will go to a good school full of nice people, irrespective of whether or not they have any brains.

I signed, prominently.

—And we *must* try to get the story into *The Paper*, John.

—Well, it was in there last week, wasn't it?

—So it was. Then we must try to get it in again.

—I'll ask Deborah.

—Will you, John? This is *so* important for *the people of Muswell Hill.*

—And, by the holy God, your selfless intervention on their behalf will earn you all crowns in Heaven!

—I beg your pardon?

—Oh, don't worry, Antonia, this is my friend Eamon. He's from Ireland.

—Oh well then.

—But, Johnny, surely *this* is *East Finchley*?

—East Finchley?

—East Finchley? *Here?* Who told you that?

—Well it did kinda *suggest so* on the tube station, and I'd *almost swear* I saw N2 on the street sign outside and –

—Now, now, Eamon.

—Hey, people, I jest, I jest.

—Well, thank God for that!

—Dad?

—Hello, Jack, hello, Will. You still up?

—Dad, George said next time you go abroad on work he could take us paintballing.

—*Special* paintballing!

—Night-time paintballing!

—With like night-sights!

—Über-cool!

—He said we *really should* go.

—Just in case we ever need it.

—He said it's just like being a Scout, really.

—*Be prepared*, you know, Dad?

—Only much, much cooler.

—Can we, Dad?

—I'll talk to George. Now off to bed. You've got the school skiing trip tomorrow and you need to get some sleep.

—Ski-ing? Like, *nooo*, Dad.

—Dad, it's *snowboarding*. G'night.

—What charming young men. Now, John, there's *someone else* from the BBC who wants to talk to you . . .

Yes, a very nice party.

Having said all my goodbyes and filled the dishwasher, I was having my second and very last cigarette out in the garden, watching through the window as Sarah played the piano to herself, alone in her secret little world, just as I always loved to see her.

I had made everything all right and –

And then a voice spoke from the darkness behind me.

—Thou hast it now, King, Cawdor, Glamis, all.

75: Normality at any Cost

—Ah, Eamon. I thought you'd gone.

—Oh, I'm in no big rush. You happy-family folk have to score your sleep, of course, and where better than Nwhateverthefuckthisis, but the party starts late in the bad old parts of Zone 1, where degenerate wealth meets impatient youth. That's entertainment, begob! I just wanted to clock you by moonlight before I head off.

—What was that you just said about *Cawdor and Glamis*, Eamon?

—You wha'? I was merely complimenting you on the legwear.

—You were saying you like my trousers?

—*Fantastic-looking, corduroy, glamorous and all.* They go so well with the tweed. Not an original combo, but always effective.

—Oh. You see, I thought you said something else.

—About corduroy? What else *is* there to say?

—Eamon, I'm not going to even *try* to play word games with you.

—I wouldn't. I hit too deep and too hard for you, Johnnyboy. Though I suspect that when it comes to reality you have the odd shot in your locker that I just couldn't live with.

—Hmm. Shall we leave it at that, then?

—Absofuckinglutely. You can count me in for the long march, Johnny, and rely on me to help dish out the shtick.

—The shtick? What on earth do you mean, Eamon?

—Ah. C'mon, Johnny, this is me and the mics are off.

We all have to eat and some of us have to eat better than others, but I mean to say that guff on your shows about *human progress* and *walls between us falling* and everything getting better and better: gas stuff, my man!

—But Eamon, everything's OK now.

—For you, JG.

—For us, Eamon.

—I stand gratefully corrected. But human progress? That's all class-A bollocks and you know it.

—Do I?

—You really believe the Arabs and Israelis are going to sit down one day and make up? You really think that if the ice caps melt or Iran gets the bomb, *nothing much will really happen*?

—Well, not up here it won't, Eamon.

—You think? Maybe the Lord has made a hedge about you and blessed the work of your hands an' all that, but no man is an island, Johnny, even in the best of all possible worlds.

—No, that's Hampstead. But if you *do* cultivate your own garden, well, you never know what you'll find. You might even come across something that might come in handy if things *do* ever go *really* wrong.

—Ah, so you admit they just might?

—Of course I bloody do, Eamon. We know that. Look what happened to us in 1989. And it wasn't just us. Look at this street.

We did. From the garden, we looked up and down the back of this quite pleasant but entirely nondescript run of perfectly modest north-London semis.

—Twenty years ago the people who live in this street wouldn't have been seen dead here. They would have thought it was like a set for some comedy about accountants in suburbia. They would have laughed at us. And now we're all so bloody happy to be here. No.

Not even happy. Just *relieved*. And now come and look at something else.

I took him down to the back of the garden and into the shed. I guided him up the ladder on to the clever little mezzanine and invited him to look out through my special chapel-like window high in the eaves. The window that is, in a sense, the whole point of the shed. The window which, as I had calculated correctly, would, if placed at that height and faced that way, allow me to sit on my little platform and gaze between the houses behind us, right down southwards over the whole of London. I watched Eamon to see the effect. The moonlight fell full on his face, bleaching it of all colour and expression.

—Big bad beautiful place.

—Yes, and full of people working away on the edge of exhaustion, only ever a few months' bad luck away from repossession.

—Ah, Johnny, never fear, these're only wee Brits. They'll take whatever shite.

—I wouldn't be so sure, Eamon. People who never really wanted much can go very funny when they don't get it. Most Germans never voted for Hitler when they had any choice. Hardly any of them wanted another war. Not one in a million of them wanted anything remotely like Auschwitz. In twenty years they'd lost a war, then their savings and then their jobs, and Stalin was next door. They just wanted *normality* back. But enough of them wanted it back at any cost. Any cost at all.

—Maybe best not push the plain people too far, so?

—Best not. Lord, give us peace in our time.

—Amen to that, Johnnyboy. Well, I must away, the mere sight of the old place laid out like that beneath me has set off a Pavlovian cry in my country boy's guts. Black cabs and cocaine, the call of the W1 wild!

—Enjoy, Eamon. Talk to you tomorrow about socialist realism, yeah?

—I already see the topic sitting up nicely for a big forehand winner. G'night and act your name, comrade.

My old friend left for his life and I came down from my eyrie and went back to mine, to my wonderful children and to Sarah. She was still playing Schumann as I walked up behind her and ran my fingers through her hair, guiltless at last, able to love again, a man once more, for the first time since the Berlin Wall fell.

This was the deal.

So really I don't know why I am back here again now, in my perfect shed high on a hill, way above every kind of sea level, up at my special little window, recording these last words.

I have tucked up my children (*tuck-tuck-tuck*) and, for all I know, just sweetly conceived another. The love of my life sleeps in our high-ceilinged home, right where we should be at long long, last. But I find that when I gaze down over London I can see bright flowers of fire in the corners of my eyes. I feel again the unexpectedly gentle kick to my shoulder and sense the hairs on my neck begin to rise. When I sniff at my lapel I smell a scent I know cannot be there.

So much for Newton.

I swear I can see right down there through the night, across the black river and into the grave-cold south-London garage where my little Armalite lies waiting.

It has got me everything I always wanted. I can now remain the nice, liberal man who has never even fantasised (as far as I can remember) about seeing anyone getting physically hurt (apart from Maggie and George W. Bush, obviously). Poor Brian will have to be dealt with, sadly, but after that I should really just lose the bloody thing while the going is good, and never sit here again, talking at night about it to no one.

Of course I should.

But then again, what if there really is *fucking bloody great big trouble* one day? What if the ice really does melt and the waters rise and the border guards tear off their uniforms, throw down their guns and run?

After all, I mean, these days, God knows.

The author wishes to thank Academi and the Arts Council of Wales for the bursary given to help the writing of this book.